GW00363179

Praise for *The*

'A journey into the worst har...
... and yet throughout it
love' GILL PAUL

'Absorbing, heart-rending . . . superb storytelling'
TRACY REES

'I was utterly engaged . . . the characters brim with life, the
plot is elegantly handled and the writing is terrific'
LIZ TRENOW

'Totally absorbing, heartbreaking and heart-
stopping' CELIA REES

'Endearing characters, terrific plot, and a superb sense of
time and place made this riveting book unputdownable.
I loved it' PATRICIA SCANLAN

'Historical fiction at its best, *The Last Lifeboat* completely
swept me away, leaving me breathless with emotion. A must-
read' CARMEL HARRINGTON

'A devastatingly beautiful tale of survival and
courage' AMANDA GEARD

'Broke my heart and then mended it again'
KATE THOMPSON

'A heart-wrenching read' ANTONIA SENIOR,
THE TIMES

'This earth-shattering novel is both harrowing and
hopeful' *WOMAN'S OWN*

Readers love *The Last Lifeboat*

'I was gripped from start to finish'

★★★★★

'Beautifully written, incredibly moving'

★★★★★

'Thrilling and emotional and harrowing ... I couldn't put it down'

★★★★★

'Such a beautiful book!'

★★★★★

'An utterly compelling read I feel I will come back to again ... don't let this one pass you by'

★★★★★

'The characters in the book are wonderful. A story of bravery, endurance, heartache and joy'

★★★★★

'A masterpiece of emotional storytelling'

★★★★★

'A triumph of a book ... had me in tears of happiness and sorrow'

★★★★★

'A gripping, poignant, well-researched, beautifully written novel'

★★★★★

The Last Lifeboat

Hazel Gaynor is a *New York Times*, *USA Today* and *Irish Times* bestselling author known for her deeply moving historical novels which explore the defining events of the twentieth century. Her debut novel, *The Girl Who Came Home*, won the 2015 RNA Historical Novel Award as well as becoming a *New York Times* bestseller, and has sold nearly half a million copies to date. Her work has also been shortlisted for the Historical Writers' Association Gold Crown and the Irish Book Awards, and her novels are translated into 20 languages.

Originally from Yorkshire, she now lives in Ireland with her family.

To keep up to date with Hazel and her books, please visit hazelgaynor.com and connect with her on social media:

🐦 @HazelGaynor
📘 @HazelGaynorBooks
📷 @HazelGaynor

Also by Hazel Gaynor

The Girl Who Came Home
A Memory of Violets
The Girl from the Savoy
The Cottingley Secret
The Lighthouse Keeper's Daughter
The Bird in the Bamboo Cage

With Heather Webb
Fall of Poppies
Last Christmas in Paris
Meet Me in Monaco
Three Words for Goodbye

THE
LAST
LIFE
BOAT

HAZEL GAYNOR

HarperCollins*Publishers*

HarperCollins*Publishers* Ltd
1 London Bridge Street,
London SE1 9GF

www.harpercollins.co.uk

HarperCollins*Publishers*
Macken House, 39/40 Mayor Street Upper
Dublin 1, D01 C9W8

First published by HarperCollins*Publishers* 2023
This edition published 2024

2

Copyright © Hazel Gaynor 2023

Hazel Gaynor asserts the moral right to
be identified as the author of this work

A catalogue record for this book is available from the British Library

ISBN: 978-0-00-851870-7 (PB)

This novel is entirely a work of fiction.
The names, characters and incidents portrayed in it are
the work of the author's imagination. Any resemblance to
actual persons, living or dead, events or localities is
entirely coincidental.

Set in Sabon Lt Std by
Palimpsest Book Production Limited, Falkirk, Stirlingshire

Printed and bound in the UK using 100% Renewable Electricity
by CPI Group (UK) Ltd

All rights reserved. No part of this publication may be
reproduced, stored in a retrieval system, or transmitted,
in any form or by any means, electronic, mechanical,
photocopying, recording or otherwise, without the prior
permission of the publishers.

MIX
Paper | Supporting
responsible forestry
FSC
www.fsc.org
FSC™ C007454

This book is produced from independently certified FSC paper to ensure
responsible forest management.

For more information visit: www.harpercollins.co.uk/green

For Tanya,
in memory of your dear mum,
Joan Flanagan

War! Listened to Chamberlain's announcement over the wireless this morning. All very serious until the dog stood up during the national anthem, which made me laugh and then set everyone else off, too. Probably inappropriate to find humour at a time of national crisis, but it might be the last laugh we have for a while. Besides, it was a useful way to hide my tears. The children leave for the countryside today. I don't know what else to say about that.

Mass-Observation, Diarist #6672

Mid-Atlantic. 17 September 1940

Alice can't breathe. The wind snatches her breath away, leaving her gasping for air as she half-jumps, half-stumbles into the lifeboat and falls, face down, against the boards. She tries to pull herself up, but the lifeboat pitches violently as another monstrous wave smashes into them and throws Alice into a woman beside her. The woman loses her grip on the rain-slicked mast and tumbles, with extraordinary grace, into the dark ocean, her white nightdress unfurling around her as she spins and twirls like a ballerina in a pirouette. Too shocked to respond, Alice can't look away.

'Miss! *Miss!* Can you help the children?'

A tall man in plaid pyjamas emerges through the rain. He grabs the mast to steady himself as he points toward something at the other end of the lifeboat, but the storm steals his words and fear smothers Alice's ability to respond. She clings desperately to the bottom of the mast and tries not to think about the falling woman as she searches for something familiar to orient herself amid the chaos, but there is nothing. No stars, no moon, not even the bright hue of the flares they'd sent up to alert the other ships in the convoy to their distress. Every source of light Alice has known during her five days at sea has been extinguished, leaving a darkness so intense that there is no obvious point at which the ocean ends and the sky begins. Everything is upside down. Upended. Destroyed.

'Miss! The children!'

Through the roar of the wind, Alice hears a high-pitched mewling, but her attention is caught by an elderly man leaning dangerously out over the side of the lifeboat as he reaches for a hand in the water. Alice watches through the blinding spray from the waves as another man joins him, then a third, and then the man in the pyjamas stumbles forward to help, each of them reaching and grasping until one of them grabs the hand, but the heaving swell sends the lifeboat rearing up, and the pale fingers slip from his grasp. Again and again, they try. Twice, Alice thinks they have her – a woman in a white nightdress – but the ocean is in no mood for mercy. Another huge wave lashes the lifeboat and the woman is swept away. The men sink to their knees, their battle lost. The elderly man sobs like a child.

Amid the fury of the storm, and the chaos and noise of the two dozen or so terrified souls crowded into the narrow lifeboat around her, Alice tries desperately to remember her training. But the simple remedies for seasickness, the songs and games to keep the children entertained, the procedures to follow 'in the unlikely event' of an instruction to abandon ship are of no use to her now. There was no protocol to follow for when you found yourself in an open lifeboat in a furious storm, your ship torpedoed by a German U-boat and sinking fast, lifeboats all around you capsized, damaged and waterlogged, leaving desperate souls floundering in the raging water.

Alice crawls forward, infant-like, on hands and knees. Concealed iron rivets and hard wooden ridges dig painfully into her skin. The wind screams. Needle-sharp hailstones hammer against her forehead. She shuffles blindly on, bumping into huddled forms and clambering over bare feet and legs. All around her, male voices call out instructions she doesn't understand. 'Pull the Fleming gear.' 'Under the thwarts.' 'Lash him to the gunwale.' There is so much noise, she can't think straight. She lunges forward as the boat pitches sharply down and another wall of frigid seawater drenches her from head to toe, sluicing down the back of her thin cotton jacket and blouse, seeping into her torn stockings and forming lakes in her best leather shoes.

At last, her hands connect with a low bench-like seat. She hauls herself onto it, wraps her arms around her body and closes her eyes to the nightmare surrounding her, just as she had as a frightened child crouched at the back of her grandmother's wardrobe, willing the awful noises downstairs to stop.

'Miss! I need you to help them!' The man in the pyjamas has returned. His eyes are wild, his voice urgent. 'You're with the seavacs – the evacuees. One of them escorts.'

It is a statement, not a question.

Alice nods as her eyes settle on a tangle of reedy arms and bare feet huddled against the thwarts behind her. Barely able to distinguish one child from another, she counts five boys and one girl. They are each bunched up into a tight ball, hands wrapped around their knees, heads bent against the wind and rain. She doesn't recognize any of them.

'They're not from my group.' She shouts to make herself heard above the storm. 'I was assigned to lifeboat seven.' There must be another escort in this lifeboat. Someone responsible for these children. 'Are there any other children?'

5

The man grabs her shoulder. 'No. And I don't care which bloody lifeboat you were assigned to. They need you to help them, for Christ's sake!'

His words swirl and snap at her as the lifeboat plunges violently down again.

Alice's teeth chatter uncontrollably. Her entire body convulses with shock and fear and cold as the lifeboat rears and bucks wildly. She clings to the seat, too terrified to move. 'Please, just leave me alone! Help will be on the way.'

The man stumbles forward so that his face is right in front of Alice's, his eyes fixed on hers. There is an intensity to his stare, but there is also compassion. 'What's your name?'

'Alice. Alice King.' She can hardly speak she trembles so much.

'Listen, Alice. I know you're frightened. We're all bloody terrified.' He looks up as someone shouts for help from the other end of the lifeboat. 'They're crying for their mothers, and you're the only woman in the lifeboat now.' He stumbles away from her, responding to the panicked shouts and screams now coming from every direction.

She shuffles toward the bedraggled creatures. The five boys are dressed in their pyjamas. The girl wears a thin lace-trimmed nightie. Only one of them wears an overcoat. Only one is wearing shoes. 'It's all right, children,' she says as the lifeboat plunges down. 'Help is coming. Is anybody hurt?'

They all shake their heads. That is something, at least.

Alice peels off her jacket and drapes it around the girl's narrow shoulders. 'Does anyone have a coat, or jacket?' she shouts out into the dark. 'There are six children here. If you have anything, pass it down.' If they don't drown, they'll surely all die of hypothermia before the night is out.

The boy wearing the coat tugs on Alice's sleeve and grabs her hand. 'Where are the others?' He is barely able to get the words out, his teeth chatter so much. 'Where's everyone else?'

6

The wind screams and the lifeboat pitches wildly as Alice looks helplessly at the seething ocean and the dark that surrounds them before she turns to the boy. He is relying on her to have all the answers now.

'I don't know,' she says, her voice heavy with fear. 'I don't know where they are.'

Part One – Departure

I

Four months earlier

Kent. May 1940

As she often did in a time of crisis, Alice King turned to books. While others were determined to dance and knit their way through the war, Alice intended to read her way through it, especially over the next few days during the annual family trip to Dover. The prospect of spending time with her awful cousins was bad enough, but it was the reason for the visit, the anniversary it marked, that filled her with dread. She was debating whether a second Dickens would see her through the ordeal, or whether Jane Austen was the woman for the job, when Maud said she would be off then.

'Try to enjoy yourself, Alice. Even a little.'

Alice settled on Austen. She lifted the book from the shelf with a weary sigh. 'Thank you. I'll try. At least I'll see Kitty.' The thought of seeing her sister drew a smile from Alice's lips. Dear Kitty. Alice wondered (and dreaded) what her latest news would be.

'She's dragging herself away from her beloved London after all then?' Maud pulled on her coat, despite the warm day. 'I can't see the appeal. All that traffic and noise, and the possibility of air raids.'

Alice agreed. She much preferred the open spaces of Kent's rolling landscapes, the big starlit skies, the audible breaths of the sea. 'Kitty and London were made for each other. She only laughs when I worry about her being there, but you know what she's like. She's having a bit too much fun if you ask me, apparently oblivious to the fact that there's a war on! Hopefully a weekend by the sea will blow a bit of sense back into her.'

'And maybe Kitty will blow a bit of nonsense back into you.'

'What do you mean?'

Maud hesitated as she turned in the doorway. As the former headmistress of the local school she knew Alice well, first as a pupil, and, more recently, as one of her teachers. 'Don't take this the wrong way, dear, and I know it's a difficult occasion for you, but maybe a weekend with your sister is exactly what you need. I remember a time when it was you who was the adventurous one, always with a plan to go somewhere and do something. Everything doesn't always have to be so serious, even if Hitler *is* breathing down our necks.' She offered an encouraging smile and buttoned her coat. 'Anyway, I've said my bit. See you in a few days. And don't forget to leave the key under the geranium.'

As the bell above the library door settled, Maud's words niggled and nagged at Alice. She *was* the serious, sensible one, reluctant to step outside the familiar, while Kitty lived such a vibrant, almost fictional, life in comparison. And Maud was right. It hadn't always been that way, but Alice rarely thought about the girl who had been full of wild ideas and plans for great journeys – and wasn't even sure she'd recognize her if she met her now.

Alice took longer than was necessary to finish up, finding any number of ways to delay the journey to Dover. Her brother,

Walter, was driving, and their mother wanted to be away before three. She shelved the last of the day's returns and tidied the display of Ministry leaflets. Her hand stilled for a moment as she considered the grim progress of war. Their array of advice on all manner of things, from how to identify different types of poison gas to the unbearable business of how to humanely exterminate the family pet, was increasingly alarming. Alice remembered how appalled everyone had been when the first leaflets were issued after the announcement of war. Now, eight months on, and with the threat of Nazi invasion drawing ever closer, war had crept into every corner of life until Ministry leaflets were ten a penny, and the once unimaginable had somehow become the inevitable.

Before she left, she put up the blackout screens and took a moment to savour the musty silence. She loved this little library with all her heart, loved the brackish breeze that whispered through the gaps in the rotten old woodwork of the mullioned windows, loved that it was now home to a small collection of literary treasures sent secretly from London for safekeeping until the war was over. She wished she could put herself in safekeeping in the library until the war was over, burrow between shelves heavy with books whose endings were long imprinted on her. Yes, books were safe and certain. The world beyond the library walls was anything but.

Alice's stomach churned as Walter turned the car into the familiar driveway of their grandmother's house in St Margaret's Bay. She loved her grandmother dearly, but hated this forced occasion of sombre remembrance. She didn't need to come here to remember her father. She remembered him – thought about him – every day. The particular date and circumstances of his death were something she wished she could forget.

'We're going down to the beach,' Kitty announced, grabbing Alice's hand as they stepped out of the car. 'We'll be back in time for dinner.'

Before their mother could reply, and with Walter happy to leave his sisters to catch up on the latest gossip, the two of them ran off, just as they had as young girls, the sea breeze tying knots in their hair as they'd pulled off their shoes and socks and ran to the water. Alice was relieved to escape the stuffy formalities of the house and head toward the small beach a short walk away. Her heart felt instantly lighter at the sight of the sea ambered by the afternoon sun, at the sense of possibility and freedom she always felt when she was near the water. 'Imagine where we might go, Alice! Imagine where all the world's oceans might take us!' As she recalled her father's words, spoken over their last game of chess, she heard the echo of a life that wasn't hers anymore, and as she looked toward the coastline of France, clearly visible in the distance, she imagined Hitler looking back at Dover's majestic white cliffs, carefully working out the next move in his own sinister game. His recent invasion of France and the Low Countries had brought the war terrifyingly close to England's doorstep.

'Do you really think he'll invade?' Alice aimed a pebble across the unusually calm water of the English Channel, but her technique was terrible, and rather than skipping across the surface, it sank without trace. 'I know everyone's expecting it, but I still can't believe it will happen. Not here. Not to us.'

Kitty laughed at her sister's pitiful attempt. 'You need to get down lower and flick from the wrist as you throw. Look. Like this.' Kitty's pebble skipped elegantly, six times, across the water. 'See. It's easy.' Kitty made everything look easy. She was the swan of the family, effortless and graceful. Alice had always felt like a waddling mother duck beside her. 'And, yes. I suspect he will invade,' Kitty continued. 'The question is: When? Hopefully not tonight anyway. Invasion would be bad enough. Getting stuck here with Cousin Lucy would be truly horrifying.'

Alice soon tired of skimming pebbles and looked for shells instead as they started to walk along the shoreline together. 'I hate being in this constant state of almost-war, always wondering, always on high alert.' If Hitler did invade, the south coast counties of Kent and Sussex would be the first to see the Nazi flags. Her stomach heaved at the thought. 'It's so awful, isn't it, to think that just twenty miles of sea separates us now.'

Kitty linked her arm through her sister's. 'Your problem is you've had too much time to think about things since the children left.'

Alice had certainly missed her busy days in the classroom since the school had closed last September following the announcement of war. She missed the unpredictable exuberance of the children, their curious minds, their innocence. Teaching was a demanding job, but one she loved. She was good with children – they often made more sense to her than adults – and had quietly hoped to take her teaching experience further and apply for a position at the prestigious Benenden Girls' School. But the evacuation of children from coastal towns to the countryside had interrupted her plans. Still, Alice hoped the possibility might return along with the children, whenever this was all over.

'You must be bored silly, stuck at home with Mother,' Kitty said. 'I honestly don't know how you stand it.'

'I don't have much choice, do I? You know she doesn't manage well when she's on her own.'

Kitty shook her head. 'I know she's taken advantage of your good nature for far too long, more like. She can't expect you to stay with her in Whitstable forever.'

'I don't intend to stay there forever. And I'm not stuck at home. I'm volunteering at the library in case you'd forgotten.'

Kitty laughed lightly. 'Oh yes. "Read for Victory!" Isn't that your slogan? I sincerely doubt books are going to save us if Hitler does come marauding over the Channel. What will you do, fire Shakespeare at him from a cannon? Death by a Dickens and two Austens?'

'It doesn't sound like a bad way to go. And, actually, it's books we need to save from him. Anyway, you shouldn't scoff. There's a lot to be said for reading a good book and forgetting about the bloody war for a while. Entertainment is good for morale. People need a way to distract themselves. Talking of which, how did it go with Terry?'

'It's Terence, and he was a charming distraction until an air raid interrupted things. False alarm, as it happened, but it rather ruined the moment.'

Alice laughed. 'Yes, I suppose it would!'

'Anyway, it's you who needs a Terence, not me!'

'I had one, briefly. And we both know how that turned out. I'm perfectly happy without a man to complicate things.'

Kitty grabbed Alice's hands. 'Patrick Swift was a rotten swine. Not all men are like him – some are actually rather lovely – and time isn't exactly on your side. You'll be *thirty* soon, for goodness' sake!'

'Not for another two years. And thirty isn't that old.'

'It's *ancient*!' Kitty laughed and threw her arms skywards in exasperation. 'Don't you ever wonder, Alice? Where else? What else? *Who* else? You're such an odd thing, content in your narrow little life.'

'Ouch!' Kitty's words landed on Alice like nettle stings. She knew her life must seem small and dull compared to Kitty's vibrant existence in London, sharing a flat with other girls, dancing at weekends, working for a new government department in Mayfair. But life didn't always *feel* narrow to Alice. Mostly, it felt familiar. Comfortable. Safe. Or at least it had until Hitler had invaded France. 'Am I really that dull?'

'Yes!' Kitty pulled Alice affectionately into her side as they turned and made their way back toward the house. 'Well, not always. You're occasionally dull,' she concluded. 'Mostly, I think you're afraid.'

'Of what?'

'Of change. Of doing something different. Being someone different. I want you to *do* something, Alice. Something reckless and unexpected. Something brave. Run away and join the bloody circus if you must, just promise me you won't spend the rest of your life rotting away at Willow Cottage with Mother like a wizened old Bramley.'

'Goodness, Kitty. Narrow and dull, "a wizened old Bramley" – are there any other insults you'd like to throw at me?' Alice punched Kitty's arm fondly.

Kitty laughed. 'Plenty more insults where those came from, but I'll save them for our cousins.'

But deep down, Alice knew Kitty was right. Her work at the library, surrounded by books, filled her heart with joy, but part of her longed to do something reckless and unexpected and brave. She just didn't know what, or how.

A loud whistle caught their attention. Alice turned to see Walter waving from the path, indicating that they should come back now. He was so like their father that, for a moment, she could almost believe it was him, waving his daughters back up from the beach, a proud smile on his face.

'Come on. Race you back!' Kitty set off at a sprint. 'Last one there has to sit beside Cousin Lucy at dinner!'

Alice followed in futile pursuit. 'That's not fair! Katherine King, you're a terrible cheat!'

As they ran, a brisk sea breeze ballooned out their skirts and sent Kitty's hat tumbling wildly along the sand. They chased it and laughed until their sides hurt, and for a few carefree moments, the prospect of German invasion was forgotten. That was the exasperating thing about the war. It was everywhere and everything, and yet it was nowhere and nothing. It was an impossible riddle, a puzzle without a solution.

*   *   *

After dinner that evening, Alice excused herself with an imaginary migraine. She lay awake in the small guest bedroom beneath the eaves, listening to the rattle and creak of the rafters as a summer storm rolled in across the south coast. Her father had always loved a good storm. He'd taught her not to be afraid as they'd counted the seconds between the roll of thunder and the crack of lightning, calculating how close it was and then how far away as the seconds reassuringly increased, and the storm passed.

But some storms never left. The aftermath of his death still rumbled and roared, and grief still raged in Alice's heart as she counted the seconds and willed the winds to settle and the storm to blow itself out.

2

London. May 1940

Lily Nicholls hardly noticed the blossom that spring. It didn't last long anyway, scattered by unseasonal winds that easily blew such fragile things away and carried the ugly business of war, and Hitler, ever closer in return. Like most Londoners, Lily was jittery. The air-raid warnings in her South London terrace had, so far, been false alarms, but elsewhere, people weren't so lucky. Recent reports of civilian casualties in the Netherlands were truly awful. It was unimaginable, and yet the facts were unavoidable, printed in the newspaper alongside cheering advertisements for Bourneville cocoa and HP sauce, because life carried on, even when it didn't.

In the small back kitchen of 13 Elm Street, Lily absorbed the latest awful news with her heart in her mouth. She read out the occasional line or two from the newspaper. Mrs Hopkins, her neighbour, tutted and sighed and said war was a terrible, terrible thing. 'And they're talking about another wave of evacuation,' she added as she rolled out an unappealing grey circle of potato pastry for a Homity pie. 'Sending the kiddies overseas this time. They'll have us all shipped off to the moon next.'

Lily glanced up from the newspaper. 'They can talk all they want. I won't be sending Georgie and Arthur away again. Although Georgie has her heart set on going to Australia for some reason. Honestly, that girl will be the death of me with her plans and schemes!'

Mrs Hopkins put down her rolling pin and poured two cups of tea from the dribbly teapot. She treated Lily's kitchen as if it were her own, and Lily encouraged it. She enjoyed the company, even if she didn't always enjoy the resulting pies. Lily was terribly fond of Mrs H, as she called her. Like the Russian nesting dolls that stood on the sideboard in the front room, the woman had a seemingly endless supply of herself, always ready to cheer someone up, or lend them an ear, or make them a pie when they couldn't summon the energy to make it themselves. She'd been especially kind in the immediate aftermath of Peter's death. Mrs H hadn't gossiped and speculated behind Lily's back, or avoided her, like others had, as if Peter's death was something you could catch. Lily would be forever grateful to her for that.

Lily licked her thumb and turned the pages as she looked for the crossword puzzle, but her hands stalled as she read another awful headline.

'What's wrong?' Mrs Hopkins asked. 'Lil? You've gone ever so pale.'

'It says here that a civilian liner has sunk in the Atlantic with heavy loss of life after a torpedo strike from a U-boat.' The *unter-seeboots* frightened Lily even more than the thought of bombs falling from the sky. At least bombing raids came with a warning and gave you time to run for cover. U-boats lurked beneath the water. There was nowhere to shelter at sea. She folded the paper and tossed it into the pile for collection. She didn't want to read any more news. 'Bloody Germans. They're everywhere.'

'Who's everywhere?' Arthur ran into the kitchen and proceeded to hop on one foot around the table. Hopping was his latest fad, and a welcome relief from his previous fascination with walking backwards. 'Are the rotten Nazis here?' He fired an imaginary machine gun at Mrs Hopkins for good measure.

'Arthur! Don't do that.'

Lily's voice carried an edge that surprised her and brought her son to a sudden stop. She hated to see him play-act war so easily. She especially hated him mimicking gunfire. The war had made such staunch British patriots of those who were too young to fully understand what they were saying. 'Nazis'. 'The Bosch'. 'Jerry'. 'Fritz'. It sounded wrong coming from such inno- cent voices.

'Tickles, Arthur,' Lily said, brightening her tone as she pulled him onto her lap and squeezed his skinny knees until he wriggled and giggled. 'Tickles are everywhere. There's no escaping them!' He didn't shriek and writhe as much as he had when Peter had tickled him with his great hands, or when he'd hoisted Arthur up onto his shoulders in a dramatic swooping arc, but Lily did her best. She did her best to fill all the gaps Peter had left behind.

Georgie arrived at the back door a few minutes later, red in the face after playing skipping games in the heat. She was such a determined, athletic child. Lily really had no idea where she got it from, coming from such un-sporty parents. She loved the solid bones of her, loved every freckle on her flushed cheeks.

'Get a drink of water, Georgie, for goodness' sake. You look as if you're about to combust! I can feel the heat coming off you from the other side of the table.'

Georgie gulped a glass of water, burped (which rendered Arthur helpless with laughter), and pulled her latest treasures from her pinafore pockets. She proudly displayed them on the kitchen table. 'Three feathers, two nice stones and a piece of coloured glass.'

Lily said she would look at them properly after tea. 'You'll have enough feathers to make your own bird soon! And *please* take them off the table. You don't know where they've been. A rat could have been at them.'

'A filthy German rat.'

'Arthur!'

'The Nazis are everywhere, Georgie.' Arthur fired a pretend gun at his sister. 'They're sneaking around in their torpedoes, killing everyone.'

'Arthur! That's enough.' Lily hated to hear him going on like this, talking of Nazis and death so casually.

Georgie laughed at her brother's mistake. 'They're not sneaking around in *torpedoes*, silly! Their submarines are called U-boats. The torpedoes are what they fire out of them.'

Lily had heard enough. 'Children! Honestly. Go outside and find something useful to do. Play hopscotch. Or find a tree to climb.'

'I thought you said it was dangerous to climb trees.'

'It isn't half as dangerous as getting under my feet when I'm trying to make tea, Georgie Nicholls! Now off you both go.' Lily shooed them out with her apron and shooed Mrs H's cat out with them.

When they'd gone, Mrs Hopkins said she was happy to sit in with the children any time. 'If you want to go out dancing, or anything. Have a change of scenery.'

Lily smiled. 'You're very kind, Mrs H, but I'm happy to leave the dancing to other people for now.'

'It might do you good, you know. I understand life is very different for you now, dear, but you're far too young and pretty to be sitting around here waiting for the gas rattle.'

Lily scoffed at the notion. She didn't feel young, or pretty. She felt much older than her thirty years, even though people were always surprised to discover she had a ten-year-old daughter – 'You don't look old enough!' They wouldn't say it now. The last few months had aged her beyond her years.

Mrs Hopkins put the pie in the oven and gave Lily's hand a squeeze. 'Well, the offer stands if you change your mind. Why not pretend you're going out, at least? Put on a nice dress and pour a sherry. We might be thinking about bloody potatoes morning, noon and night, but we don't need to look like one, too!'

Lily promised to do her best not to look like a potato. In her heart, she knew Mrs H was right. Peter would want her to go dancing. He loved to dance, loved to take her out all dressed up and smelling of Yardley roses. She remembered how she used to give a little twirl when she'd finished getting ready. 'Will I do?' she would ask, and Peter would tilt his head to one side and smile and say, 'You'll do and a half! Who's the lucky man?'

That evening, not long after blackout, Lily made her way upstairs. The nights were long and lonely now. She was tired of the relentless cheer of the comedy shows on the wireless, tired of the news, tired of knitting and sewing. She'd taken to reading by candlelight until she eventually felt sleepy. Not that she slept well. It was almost impossible to relax. She flinched at every sound, and frequently got up to check on the children. Her nights now passed in a restless pattern of fear and worry as she watched the sky and longed for the reassuring hue of daylight.

As she looked in on the children, she found Georgie still awake.

'Can't sleep, love?'

'Arthur's talking in his sleep again.'

Arthur was fully out of his sheets and half-dangling over the side of the bed. Lily lifted him back in, turned his pillow and kissed his hot little cheek.

She sat on the edge of Georgie's bed then and smoothed the hair from her forehead, just as she had when she was a baby. She smiled at the memory of the tiny terrifying bundle the midwife had handed to her: velvet hair, seashell ears, peach melba cheeks. Peter had said she was the most perfect thing he'd ever seen.

'Are you frightened, Mummy?'

'Of what, love?'

'Of the Germans. Harry Gilbert said they'll make us say Heil Hitler and talk in German, and I don't know any German words apart from Luftwaffe and Nazi. What if I get into trouble?'

Lily tutted. 'Don't you mind Harry Gilbert. He's a horrid boy, saying such things. You won't have to speak in German. And no, I'm not frightened. The brave men won't let them invade.'

'Brave men like Daddy?'

Lily's breath caught in her throat as she bent to kiss Georgie's forehead. 'Yes, love. Brave men like Daddy.'

To Georgie and Arthur, their father was a hero. Lily had made absolutely sure of that.

When Georgie had finally settled, Lily went to her own bedroom and lay on top of the bed sheets in the dark. She imagined Peter beside her, imagined the soft rise and fall of his chest. She reached out her hand to his side of the bed and wrapped her fingers around the unbearable void. It wasn't just his absence, but the fact that he would never lie there again. Ever. It was impossible to comprehend, impossible to accept.

In the silence, she let her mind wander back to the bright February morning when delicate frost lacework had decorated the windowpanes and the biting cold had sent roses blooming in her cheeks as she'd watched him leave. She didn't know then that it was the last time she would see him, but she was glad now that she'd stood on the doorstep a moment longer, glad she'd noticed the dimples in his cheeks, the strands of gold in his hair, the pause as he'd turned to look over his shoulder. She still wondered what he was going to say, and why, in the end, he didn't say anything, but walked quietly away, without looking back.

3

Kent. May 1940

Alice endured the three days in Dover with the help of Kitty's good humour and Walter's calming dependability. She knew the closeness between the three of them irritated their mother and wasn't a bit surprised when she took the opportunity of the confined car journey back to Whitstable to share her frustration and disappointment with them all.

'There must be *something* useful you can do, Alice, besides sorting library books,' her mother pressed from the passenger seat. 'You should join the Red Cross. People will think you're trying to avoid doing your bit, and we've quite enough of *that* with your brother making a disgrace of us all by declaring himself a Conscientious Objector.'

From the driver's seat, Walter rolled his eyes at Alice through the mirror. Like their father, Walter was a gentle giant, but he was also stubborn and decisive. Alice respected his decision not to sign up, even if it hurt her to hear the cruel names and accusations of cowardice he endured. 'You have to back yourself, Alice,' he'd said when she'd asked him how he could stand it. 'Of course, it would be easier to sign up, but easy isn't always right, and life isn't always perfect. Real life is lived in all the messy difficult bits.' Walter was the glue that had held Alice together since their father died. In her eyes, he would never be a coward.

'Or why not do the civil defence training and become an ARP warden, like your cousin?' her mother continued. She'd been easily impressed by Cousin Lucy's tiresome monologues about what the role involved.

On and on it went. What about this? Why not that? As usual, Alice's mother saw her as a problem that needed to be fixed. Alice stared out at the sea and wished she could sail away to some distant land where she didn't have to *be* anything.

They continued the journey in frosty silence until Kitty tried to lighten the mood by talking about her new job.

'There's an awful girl in the typing pool, and you honestly wouldn't believe how often some of the men's hands stray. It's like working with a load of octopus. Or is it octopuses? Maybe it's octopi? If it isn't, it should be.'

It was such a ridiculous thing to say that the three siblings burst into laughter, which irritated their mother even more because she couldn't understand what on earth was so amusing.

'Are you enjoying anything about the job?' Alice asked, grateful for the break in the tense atmosphere as she wiped tears of laughter from her cheeks.

'The uniform's nice,' Kitty said. 'Navy skirt and cream blouse. I'm mostly typing up responses to letters of enquiry so far, but Tony has told us to prepare for a deluge of applications when we officially open next month. He'll be talking about it on the wireless next week.'

'Who's Tony?' Walter asked.

'Anthony Quinn, MP. The overseas evacuation programme was his idea. Churchill wasn't keen, apparently. Thinks it will send the wrong message to the enemy.' Kitty took a long inhale on her cigarette and blew smoke out of the open window.

'I thought you'd given them up, Kitty?'

'Don't be such a nag, Mother.' Kitty took another long deliberate drag and blew the smoke in the direction of her mother. 'You should all listen to Mr Quinn speak. Take an interest in my work, for once.'

Alice protested. 'I always take an interest in your work!' It wasn't strictly true. Kitty had a tendency to flit from hobby to hobby, job to job and romance to romance like a pollinating bee. Alice had learned not to become too invested in her sister's latest love affair or place of employment (apart from offering sensible advice and a shoulder to cry on when either thing didn't work out), and, as a result, she hadn't fully understood the nature of Kitty's new role, other than it being a clerical position that involved processing paperwork for evacuees. 'I promise I'll listen to Tony What's-his-name. Happy?'

Kitty nodded. 'Happy! And I want a full report afterwards!'

Alice saw Kitty onto the London train and wished she could keep her in Whitstable longer. For all that Kitty loved London, it made Alice nervous to think of her there.

'Please take care. And go straight to a shelter if there's a raid.'

Kitty brushed Alice's concerns aside and said she worried too much.

'It's my job to worry about you. That's what older sisters do.'

'Come up to London sometime, will you? I'll take you dancing. That's what younger sisters do.'

Alice kissed Kitty's cheek. 'Maybe.'

As she watched the train depart, she wondered when she would see Kitty again, and a more sombre part of her whispered the unspeakable *if* she would see Kitty again. Departures and goodbyes were so awful now, laced with doubt and worry. War had altered and removed so many things, but perhaps the greatest loss was certainty. Everything was a question, and – like many things – answers were in short supply.

By the end of a wet and windy week, Alice had almost recovered from the ordeal of the trip to Dover, although her mother hadn't stopped crowing about how wonderful Cousin Lucy was. Alice took the opportunity of a break in the weather to cycle to Mason's farm, where Walter worked. Following his tribunal, he'd been assigned to a Reserved Occupation. He was lucky. Some Conscientious Objectors were being sent to the front as stretcher-bearers, or in other non-combat roles. Another local CO had volunteered to work in bomb disposal. Alice hoped Walter would be spared the same fate.

It was a sunny, lavender-scented afternoon, when it felt impossible that the world was at war. With air force training flights now being conducted over Kent's fields and coastline, the Phoney War had become much more visible and real, but the skies above Alice as she cycled were quiet and clear, and her mood matched the bright day. She laughed as she freewheeled along the dry rutted tracks on her father's old bicycle, jostled about on her seat like a ragdoll, but her mood quickly changed as a sickening whine sliced through the warm air: the unmistakable sound of an aircraft in difficulty.

Alice pulled hard on the brakes and brought the bicycle to a juddering stop in a puff of dry earth. She looked up, shielding her eyes from the sun. High above, a trail of thick black smoke billowed from an aircraft as it dipped and rose in a chaotic motion, and then flipped forward and tumbled wildly toward the fields and apple orchards ahead. The fields and apple orchards where Walter was working.

Alice put her head down and pedalled furiously as the engine's whine reached the height of its pitch and then, after a brief chilling silence, a violent explosion ripped through the air, like a crack of thunder in a summer storm.

'Please not Walter. Please not Walter.' She raced on, as fast as she could pedal, the wheels shuddering over the rough dirt tracks.

As she turned the corner at the end of the lane, she looked up to see Walter flying towards her on his bicycle.

'Oh, thank God.' Alice flung her bicycle to the ground and ran to meet him. 'Did you see it? I thought it had hit the farm.'

'Came down a couple of fields over,' Walter gasped, catching his breath. 'Come on.'

'Come on what?'

'Let's go. I didn't see a parachute. Poor bugger might be trapped in the wreckage.'

Alice was horrified. 'We can't go! We should get help—'

'*We* can help, Alice. Come on.'

Before she could say anything else, she was back on her bicycle, pedalling hard to keep up with Walter.

The stench of smoke and aviation fuel hit her first. Eyes smarting, she covered her mouth with her headscarf as Walter threw his bicycle to the ground, clambered over a low fence and ran through the scorched crops toward the burning wreckage.

'Walter! Be careful! It might explode again.'

Walter stopped before he reached the mangled plane.

Alice hitched up her skirt and followed him over the fence. As she caught up with him, she hesitated. A few feet ahead, a burnt and broken form lay among the barley, the flattened stalks stained a deep crimson.

'Dear God.' Alice clung to Walter's arm. For a moment, she couldn't work out which part of the pilot she was looking at. She'd never seen a body so broken and injured. The smell of burning flesh made her retch. She stood, frozen, as Walter walked forward and crouched down beside the limp figure.

'He's still alive!' he called over his shoulder. 'He's still breathing.'

'He can't be.' He couldn't possibly be.

Alice stepped forward, heart racing, eyes blurred from her tears and the acrid sting of fuel in the humid summer air. As she approached, the pilot fixed his eyes on hers, not with a look of pain, despite his horrific injuries, but with a look of absolute fear. A low moan escaped from his lips as he mumbled an almost indecipherable word.

'Did he say "Mummy"?' Alice was sure she'd heard him say Mummy.

Walter talked to him, soothing him. 'That's all right, fella. Had a bit of a bang, that's all. Take it easy there.'

It wasn't possible to tell how old he was, only that he was far too young to be dying in a field in Kent. Alice felt bile rise in her throat. She turned away and vomited.

When she'd recovered, she forced herself to step forward, forced herself to lift the man's bloodied broken hand and hold it in hers as Walter continued to reassure and comfort him. She felt the fabric of the scorched jacket sleeve, air force blue, still warm to the touch; the sensation of something soft, then hard beneath her fingertips. Flesh and bone. The heat and the smell were overwhelming. And then she heard it, unmistakable this time.

'Mummy.' It was all he could say, over and over in a panicked whisper. 'Mummy. Mummy. Mummy.'

And then, silence.

His eyes were still open, still fixed on hers.

'Is he . . .?'

Walter nodded and gently closed the pilot's eyelids. 'Pass me your scarf.'

Alice untied the knot beneath her chin and passed the square of Liberty silk to Walter. He quietly recited the Lord's Prayer as he draped the headscarf carefully over the pilot's face. He was so calm in a crisis, always knew just what to do, but he was angry.

'So much for all Churchill's talk about our heroic fighter pilots. What bullshit.'

Whatever Alice had imagined war to be like, this was beyond all comprehension. It was the second time she'd seen death up close. She hoped she would never see it again.

4

London. May 1940

Lily left the children in with Mrs H and walked to the bus stop on Clapham High Street. It was a long journey to Richmond, but Mrs Carr had asked Lily to stay on as her daily when the family moved from their Chelsea townhouse to The Beeches, and Mrs Carr paid better than most. Lily could do without her employer's erratic temperament and her airs and graces, but she couldn't do without the money.

As the omnibus rumbled on, Lily picked up a discarded copy of *The Times* from the seat beside her and tore out the page with the cryptic crossword. It took her mind off things for a while, but not for long enough. Too soon, she was walking up Richmond Hill, hanging up her coat in the boot room, pulling on her apron, going through the familiar routines of her day.

'Clemmie and Charlotte are having such a terrific time in Canada. Did I tell you they're staying with a cousin of Tom's in Montreal?' Mrs Carr stood at the large bay window in the dining room and fussed with an extravagant arrangement of roses she'd picked from the garden that morning. 'You should send the children overseas, Lilian. Especially now that the government will cover the cost.'

Lily hadn't even heard the words evacuation or evacuee a year ago. Now it seemed she couldn't get away from them. Evacuation was all anyone seemed to talk about, and it nagged at Lily like a splinter in her mind.

'You did mention that the girls were staying in Canada, yes.' Lily knocked cobwebs from the wall sconces, dusted the picture rail, and responded in all the right places. She was used to Mrs Carr's ramblings, well aware that the woman lived on her nerves and sweet sherry. Although temporarily suspended by the fact that he'd gone off to war, Tom Carr's longstanding affair with their daughters' ballet teacher was common knowledge among those who knew the family. Lily would feel sorry for the woman if she weren't such an insufferable snob.

'They're both absolutely charmed by the place,' Mrs Carr continued. 'They torment poor Molly, writing to tell her about everything she's missing. She's furious to have had to stay behind, but it's her own fault for riding a horse that was too big for her when she was expressly told not to. That girl never does as she's told! Anyway, she'll follow her sisters as soon as her leg is better. It has turned into the most wonderful experience. I'm so pleased we sent them.'

Lily ran her feather duster over the silver tea set on the sideboard, and while she wanted to say that she thought children were better off at home with their mothers, she kept her thoughts to herself.

Mrs Carr held a bloom to her nose and remarked on the scent. 'Smell this. It's divine.'

Lily inhaled the delicate sweet scent, but it was the bloom itself she admired the most, the intricate repeating design formed

34

by the petals. It reminded her of the mathematical problems she'd loved at school, the quiet working out of sequences and patterns. Part of her still craved that mental challenge. Sometimes – especially when she was with Isobel Carr – she felt as if her brain was turning to jelly.

Mrs Carr finished tweaking the roses and stood back to admire her display. 'You really should consider evacuation for Georgina and Arthur,' she pressed. 'Tom says that now the French have surrendered, Hitler will invade the Channel Islands next, and then they'll strike for the mainland. Nazis, on *British* soil. I simply can't comprehend it. Can you?'

Lily said no, she couldn't comprehend it. 'I don't think anyone can. Not really.'

'I might ship off to Canada myself if things continue to deteriorate here,' Mrs Carr continued. 'Tom wrote last week to suggest I give over the rose garden to grow potatoes and other vegetables. Can you *imagine*?' She sighed dramatically.

Oh yes, what a sacrifice, can you just imagine? For a moment, Lily pictured herself telling Peter the story over tea later as they spoke about their days – though he'd met the woman only once, his impression of Mrs Carr was uncanny – only to be hit, as she often was, by the fresh wave of loss at remembering that he was gone.

'Molly is sulking upstairs, by the way. I'm afraid you'll have to dust around her.'

Lily quietly got on with her work, but the conversation left her irritable. Many of England's Big Houses had already been given over to the military as hospitals and convalescent homes, and yet life at The Beeches stubbornly continued as if there wasn't a war on at all. God forbid the rose garden would have to be given over for potatoes.

As Lily had been warned, Molly Carr refused to move from her bedroom, so Lily worked around the child as she griped and complained that it wasn't fair that she couldn't go to Canada with her sisters.

'I'll have to go with the unfortunates when my leg is better,' she said.

'The unfortunates?'

'Evacuees whose parents can't afford a ticket. The government will pay for them. But I'll be travelling first class, so at least I won't have to mix with them.'

Lily bristled as she swept around a pile of trunks beside the wardrobe, waiting to be packed with Molly's many dresses and coats as soon as she was given the all clear to travel. She hoped Molly Carr and her misplaced sense of privilege had a terrible journey to Canada whenever she did go, and that she would be horribly seasick all the way.

Later that afternoon, while a stew bubbled away in the oven, Lily sat down with the crossword. She was stuck on thirteen across *Coming apart (11 letters)*, when her attention was caught by a discussion on the wireless.

She turned the volume up as Anthony Quinn, MP, a rather pompous-sounding man, set out the details of the new Children's Overseas Reception Board. '*We call it CORB, for short,*' he said. '*Under the scheme, children from areas most at risk from enemy bombing raids will be evacuated to Australia, New Zealand, Canada and Jamaica, where host families are eagerly awaiting the arrival of their young British guests. The children will be accompanied by carefully selected volunteer escorts who'll be with them throughout the journey. We anticipate some twenty thousand children will be evacuated overseas through the new scheme.*'

He made it sound so straightforward. Pleasant, even.

'What's that man saying?' Arthur raced into the room, hurled himself onto the settee and proceeded to drive his toy car along the imaginary roads he saw in the faded jacquard upholstery. 'Are we going to be seavacuees? *Are* we, Mummy? Can we?'

'Hmm?' Lily turned the wireless up a notch as she jotted down the address of the CORB offices in Mayfair. 'In a minute, love.'

As the programme reached its conclusion, a question was asked about the safety of the evacuee ships. Mr Quinn cleared his throat and stumbled a little over his words. '*A full naval escort will be provided, and while the threat of U-boats cannot be ignored, all necessary precautions will be taken. The risks of the voyage are clear*,' he added. '*The decision to evacuate is one for which any parents listening must take sole responsibility.*'

Lily turned the wireless off, scrunched up the piece of paper she'd written on and stuffed it into the pocket of her apron. He made it sound as simple as choosing between chops or mince for tea, but there was no easy solution here. Keep the children in England and accept the threat of German bombs and invasion, or send them overseas and accept the risk of them being torpedoed on the way. It was an impossible choice. Unbearable.

'Are you sending me and Georgie away on a big ship?' Arthur jumped down from the settee and did an impromptu sailor's jig.

Dear Arthur. He'd been hopping and skipping and whirling about as long as Lily could remember, as if life was far too exciting to simply walk through. *Arthur is an energetic boy with a tendency to fidget in class* was a familiar remark on his school report.

Lily scooped him into her arms. 'No, love. I'm not sending you away on a big ship, or on a little ship, or in a hot-air balloon! You're both staying in London, with me.' She pressed her nose to the crown of his head and breathed in the sweet nutty scent of him. Her funny little boy. The much-longed-for second child who'd made their family complete. Since Peter's death, Georgie and Arthur had become Lily's entire world, all the unused love and affection she had for her husband now shared out among her children. Love was one of the only things there wasn't a shortage of during a war, and Lily gave hers generously.

She closed her eyes for a moment and thought about the broadcast she'd just listened to. She couldn't bear the thought of sending the children away again, especially not so far, even if the government *were* covering the cost. It had been bad enough sending them to the Cotswolds during the first wave of evacuation last September. They'd been given a warm and loving home with a retired nurse and her husband, but the ache of separation was too awful. It was Peter who'd first suggested bringing them home, the threatened invasion and gas attacks having never materialized. 'I know it's only been three months, Lil, but it feels like three years, and Christmas won't be the same without them.' She knew neighbours and friends considered it reckless to bring the children back to London, but she didn't care what other people thought. The only thing that mattered was what she and Peter thought. They'd always made the big decisions together, which was why it was so hard to make this decision alone.

At teatime, Georgie announced that Beth Ingram's cousin was being evacuated to stay with relatives in Australia. 'Can *we* go to Australia, too, Mummy? Beth's cousin says it's very hot and nice there.'

'What on earth is this obsession with Australia, Georgie? And don't speak with your mouth full. And elbows off the table.'

Georgie sat up straight, her brow creased in concentration as she ate the rest of her tea in great hurried mouthfuls. She looked so like her father sometimes it was almost as if he was sitting there with them. 'Well? *Can* we go?' She put down her knife and fork, her plate empty. 'Imagine if we saw a real kangaroo, Arthur! Or a koala bear!'

At this, Arthur jumped down from the table and hopped around the kitchen like a kangaroo until he made his sister laugh.

Lily loved his exuberance, but she was tired, and his antics that evening tugged at the frayed edges of her patience.

She cleared the dinner plates with a determined clatter. 'You can see kangaroos at the zoo. Anyway, even if we did have relatives in Australia – which we don't – we think you'll be better off staying at home.' She still spoke about 'we' and 'our', unable to make the adjustment to 'I' and 'my'. 'We'll make the best of things here, together, like we always have. And that's the end of it.' She put her teacup down a little too firmly on the draining board, knocking another onto the floor.

Her terse response and the noise of the breaking cup made Georgie cry, which made Arthur cry, and that made Lily cry because although she put on a brave face in front of the children, sometimes everything felt like a broken teacup and it was all too much. She sent the children out to play and took a quiet moment in the pantry. She didn't like them to see her cry.

As she dabbed her eyes and steadied her breathing, her gaze strayed to Peter's old pullover hanging on the back of the pantry door. She pressed a sleeve to her cheek. It still carried the familiar scent of his trade as a signwriter: mint and lanolin from his artist soap, turpentine, linseed. She'd never got round to darning the hole in the elbow, the worn strands of wool forever frayed now, the neat stitches eternally unravelling.

Unravelling.

Of course.

She fetched the incomplete crossword from earlier. Thirteen across. *Coming apart (11 letters)*. Unravelling. She completed the puzzle, but it didn't give her the usual sense of satisfaction. Like Peter's old pullover, she, too, was coming apart.

Later, when the children were in bed, she took the crumpled piece of paper from the pocket of her apron. She smoothed it out and looked at the information she'd scribbled down. *CORB, 45 Berkeley Street, W1*. She thought about the way the man on the radio had stumbled over his words; the uncertainty in his voice. '*The risks of the voyage are clear. The decision to evacuate is one for which any parents listening must take sole responsibility.*'

She folded the page carefully, slipped it back into her pocket and picked up a framed photograph of Peter from the mantelpiece. He looked so carefree and happy, the light in his eyes caught in a way that made him look so alive.

'What should I do, Peter? Please, love. I'm frightened. Tell me what to do.'

The Phoney War limps on. Unbearable without the children (even the poor dog is off his food), but better safe than sorry, and they seem happy enough when they write (their little kisses at the end of their letters break my heart). Latest news is that the draft will extend to all men aged 18–41 in the new year. Anyone in a reserved occupation will get a pass. Everyone else will get their papers. Waiting is awful; wondering, worrying, imagining the worst. Sometimes feel I'm going mad. War does funny things to the mind.

Mass-Observation, Diarist #6672

5

Kent. May 1940

Alice sat in the window seat in her bedroom, her hair still wet from a disappointing bath in the few inches of water now permitted. She tried to settle to her book, but her mind wouldn't rest, turning over the devastating images of the previous day. The mangled body of the pilot. The tangled wreck of the plane. Her body itched – physically itched – to be somewhere else, to do something other than sit in her childhood bedroom, surrounded by silly little ornaments and fussy home comforts while the world spun wildly and cruelly on. Eventually, she gave up on the book and made her way downstairs to the sitting room. She switched on the wireless and paced up and down the Persian rug as Anthony Quinn MP set out the details of his overseas evacuation scheme.

'*Parents will not be permitted to travel with children being evacuated under the CORB scheme, so applications are now sought from teachers, clergymen, healthcare workers, and those in other suitable professions who are willing to act as volunteers to escort the children during their long voyage. Enquiries should be submitted in writing to the Children's Overseas Reception Board at 45 Berkeley Street, London. Successful applicants will be invited for interview and a full medical examination.'*

Alice stopped pacing. Like a sea fog lifting, everything was suddenly clear. This, she could do. Children, she understood. And while she'd always found the open ocean daunting, she felt an affinity with the sea, a pull of possibility in its never-ending expanse. Yes, crossing the Atlantic came with its own risks, but so did staying in Britain. '*You have to back yourself, Alice . . . Real life is lived in all the messy difficult bits.*'

'Still crowing about evacuation.' Alice's mother stalked into the sitting room and switched off the wireless. 'Cowards, the lot of them, if you ask me.'

Alice wanted to say that nobody *had* asked her, but, as she so often did with her mother, she bit her tongue. There was no use in trying to change her opinion, or in trying to alter who she was. Alice had long ago accepted her mother's many faults.

'Any mother considering evacuation should be ashamed. If the royal princesses are staying in England, I don't see why anyone else should send their children away. We might as well wave the white flags and put up the swastikas now.'

Alice didn't have the energy for a fight. 'You're right, Mother. They're all horrid little cowards running away. I can't understand why any mother would possibly want to keep their children safe by sending them overseas.'

A disgruntled harrumph followed Alice as she made her way upstairs, and paused outside her father's study. She pressed her hand against the dark oak door before turning the handle and peering inside. It was a room full of memories, a room full of ghosts. She'd spent so many happy hours here as he'd patiently taught her to play chess. Sometimes she'd pretended not to understand, or had stalled when she'd already worked out her next move, so that the lesson would last longer. 'We don't always see the solution straightaway, Alice. It takes practice and patience. But the best move will reveal itself eventually.' And so it was with the question of what she could do to play her part in the war.

Kitty was right. Their mother had taken advantage of her for far too long. As a young girl, forced to grow up quickly beneath the shadow of grief, it had been Alice who had taken the maternal role in the family, their mother unable to cope without a husband whose sudden loss exposed her many failings. But Alice accepted that her mother was right, too. There *was* a role for her, a way to do something useful to help the war effort, and she would have to leave Willow Cottage, and England, in order to do it.

Alice closed the study door, went upstairs and wrote her letter of application. The next chapter in her 'narrow little life' would now be determined by the few words sealed inside an envelope that she would drop into the postbox on the village green. She felt a quiet sense of destiny as she slipped the envelope into her skirt pocket. A moment of calm. A change in the weather.

She spent the rest of the day at the harbour with Walter, partly to avoid her mother, but mostly because she enjoyed Walter's company and steady assurance, and she needed both.

As the sun began to sink toward the horizon, they cycled back to Walter's cottage, but as they turned the final corner, Alice pulled her bicycle to a stop. COWORD was daubed in bright red paint across the front wall.

Walter leaned his bicycle against the gate. 'Idiots can't even insult me properly. You'd think they would at least learn to spell the word "coward" if they intend to go around accusing people of being one!'

For all Walter's nonchalant good humour, Alice knew the cruel taunts and disdainful looks hurt him. They hurt her, too. They made her furious. Walter didn't deserve them.

'I know it bothers you,' she said. 'You don't have to brush it off for my benefit.'

Walter rolled up his shirtsleeves. 'Brush it off is exactly what we're going to do. You can grab a paintbrush and give me a hand.'

They worked quickly, covering the paint with a thick layer of limewash, but the intention behind the insult wouldn't be so easily removed.

'I hate this,' Alice said as she slapped limewash roughly onto the wall. 'I hate that they do this to you.'

'Do what? Sticks and stones. They're not *doing* anything to me. They might think they are, but that's up to me.' Walter tapped his head. 'I decide whether I let it in.'

'Can I ask you something?' Alice said. 'And please don't hate me for it.'

'Let me guess. You want to know if I wish I'd signed up instead of putting up with this. Am I right?'

Alice nodded, ashamed to have even considered asking.

He pushed his hair from his eyes and leaned back on his heels. 'Honestly? I haven't regretted my decision once.' He stood up to check their work and declared the job done. 'They call me a coward because they think I'm afraid of dying to protect our country. But it isn't *my* death I'm afraid of. I'm afraid of bringing death and grief to someone else's life. We know how that feels. If that makes me a coward, so be it.'

Alice thought about how he'd run toward the injured pilot without a thought for his own safety, how respectfully he'd closed the young man's eyes, how calmly he'd told the local Red Cross volunteers about the casualty and taken them to the crash site. Walter wasn't a coward. Far from it. He was the best of them all.

'I can't stop thinking about him, Walter.' She imagined her Liberty silk scarf draped across the pilot's face, a piece of her buried with him. The thought of it haunted her. 'I can hear him, asking for his mummy. I hate that we couldn't save him.'

'I can't stop thinking about him either, but at least he didn't die alone. I like to think there was some comfort for him in that.'

They both stood in silence for a moment. Thinking. Remembering.

'Do you remember when the dog had puppies and the runt died?' Walter asked.

Alice nodded. She remembered it all too clearly. 'Father said the depth of our sadness when someone dies is a measure of our love for them. Those few words gave my sadness a purpose, a reason.'

For a moment, Alice was a ten-year-old girl again, playing chess with her father on a quiet Sunday afternoon. White knight takes black knight, a proud smile, and then a look of shock – or was it fear? – on his face, his hand frozen in mid-air, the sickening thud as he fell to the floor.

'Father didn't waste his words,' Walter said. 'Whatever he said, he said for a reason. I also remember him saying that we can't save everyone. That no matter how desperately we want to, or how deeply we care for them, we can't save them all.'

'But that doesn't mean we shouldn't try, does it?'

'Of course not. That's why I ran to the pilot, even though I was terrified of what I would find. No matter how afraid we are, or how impossible it might seem, if there's a chance to save someone or help them, even in some small way, we should always try.'

Alice smiled. 'That sounds like something Father would have said, too.'

Walter put his arm around Alice's shoulder. 'You'd better remember it then. And you can think of me when you do.'

6

London. June 1940

The weeks wore on. Each day the children went to their makeshift school in the local church hall, Lily went to work, and in the hallowed halls of Westminster, the government talked about the matter of evacuation. Some days, the war was quiet. Distant, despite the proximity of Hitler's army. But the lull never lasted long, and Ministry leaflets kept coming with their alarming information and warnings. The bold black lettering on a particularly sinister leaflet that arrived on a muggy June morning stopped Lily in her tracks.

She perched on the armchair in the sitting room and read the instructions with her heart in her mouth:

IF THE INVADER COMES – WHAT TO DO, AND HOW TO DO IT

Stay put if the enemy invades by parachute; do not attempt to run away as the invader may fire on civilians using machine guns from the air, as happened to Belgian and Dutch civilians.

It was more like fiction than fact, and it was the starkest indication yet that the government believed the Germans really would invade that summer.

Lily smoothed the paper on her knee. How could she possibly keep the children in London with the threat of machine guns being fired at them? The first time the children went away, it had felt inevitable. They would go to the countryside, and that was that. This time, it came down to individual choice.

But how to choose when both options were so frightening? Keep them close, but in almost-certain danger from Nazi oppression and bombs – a danger that would last until war was over – or send them away on a potentially perilous ocean crossing, but with a chance of reaching safety. It was the greatest puzzle Lily had ever tried to solve. She could hardly bear that she had to do it without Peter's gentle assurance.

Think, Lily, think.

It was impossible to know what the months ahead would bring. So she turned to the one constant unfailing thing that she trusted – numbers. She turned probabilities over in her mind – invasion, bombs, the risk of a U-boat strike, the agony of separation. Which was the greater risk? What was the solution? She could hear Peter say: *What are the odds, Lil?*

A quietness fell over her, a clarity of thought. That was the answer, wasn't it? To play the odds. And to do that, she had to apply to the CORB scheme in the first place.

A decision was made.

But the problem was far from solved.

The sultry June heat drew a flush to Lily's cheeks as she stood outside the CORB offices on Berkeley Street a few days later.

The limestone walls of the imposing Georgian building dazzled in the sun and gave her a headache. She felt out of place, out of sorts, the fourteenth person in a queue of hundreds patiently waiting to fill out the paperwork to send their children away as if they were a birthday gift for a distant relative.

She felt sick to her stomach as she leaned out of line again to count the people ahead of her. She was definitely fourteenth. She returned her gaze to the pattern in the tired-looking tea dress of the woman in front of her. Where other people saw flowers and leaves, Lily saw repetitions, symmetry, sequences. Never-ending repeating patterns. It made her mind spin if she thought about it too much.

The woman in front lit a cigarette and fanned her face with a Wedgewood-blue linen cloche that had clearly seen better days. Lily wondered if their places in the queue that June morning would have any bearing in the weeks to come. Thirteenth. Fourteenth. She imagined Peter beside her, smiling at her funny superstitions and the way she saw everything in patterns and numbers. He'd often teased her about it. Not in an unkind way, but in that affectionate familiar way that comes with twelve years of marriage and many more years of friendship before that. He'd joked that they would have to spend their thirteenth wedding anniversary apart in case something bad happened. In the end, they'd been parted by something far worse than an unlucky number.

Across the road, people went about their business at the barbers and poulterers, at Barratt's shoe shop and the wine merchants. Great piles of sandbags stood against the windows of the Palace picture house and other shop fronts. Billboards shouted about the need to save paper. A passing omnibus advertisement declared that Guinness was good for you. Across the street, a large sign indicated the nearest air-raid shelter. Life went on, and yet life was unrecognizable. Behind Lily, the line of anxious parents wound on and on, until it disappeared around the corner. She took some reassurance in seeing so many others make the same impossible decision as she had.

The summer morning still carried the muggy heat that had kept Lily awake all night. The fabric of her dress stuck to the back of her neck and made her skin itch. She fidgeted and sighed and fanned her face with a *Woman's Weekly* she'd bought to pass the time, but she was far too agitated to read instructions for knitting a balaclava helmet or making 'a sturdy apron' out of old tea towels. Her mouth was dry. Her stomach churned in nauseating knots of doubt and guilt. More than once, she convinced herself to forget the whole idea, catch the bus home, collect the children from Mrs Hopkins and sit in the shade of the laburnum tree in the backyard while they played hopscotch in the street. But she remained in her spot. Fourteenth. Part of a pattern she couldn't break.

After what felt like an age, she tapped the woman in front on the shoulder. 'Excuse me. Do you have the time?'

The woman jumped, startled by the interruption. She checked her wristwatch. 'Just before ten, love. Good job we came early.' She nodded at the long line behind Lily. 'They'll close the doors before half of them have even made it round the corner.'

'I wish they'd hurry up,' Lily said. 'The longer I stand here, the more tempted I am to forget the whole thing and go home.'

'Go home! Why on earth would you do that? This is our chance to send our kiddies to safety. A chance for the likes of us to do what them with money have been doing for months.'

The likes of us. The working class.

'Still,' the woman added, 'it won't be easy to say goodbye. I've five to send off. Four girls and a boy.'

'Five! You must have your hands full.'

'I do indeed.' She lowered her voice. 'We took the boy in from the children's home, but you love them all the same, don't you?

No matter how they arrive. Poor little bugger. Unwanted goods, like scrap left out for the rag and bone.'

Their conversation was interrupted as a church bell began to strike ten. A ripple of anticipation passed down the line, a gathering of thoughts, a stiffening of shoulders and resolve. Moments later, a pretty young woman in a smart uniform of navy skirt and cream blouse opened the doors to what was previously Thomas Cook Travel Agents. Lily watched as the woman pulled up a window shutter, wound down a striped awning, and placed a potted pink geranium on either side of the door. It all felt wrong: the flowers, the neat uniform, the drawn-out business of opening up. The cheerful red-haired, red-lipped young woman ushering everyone inside seemed more suited to boarding holidaying passengers onto an ocean liner than to the serious business of the Children's Overseas Reception Board.

'Punctual at least,' the woman in front said. 'Hope it won't take long. We've to be at the doctor at eleven. We spend more time in that bloody surgery than we do at home! Sometimes a bad start in life never leaves you, does it? Well, good luck to them, and to you Mrs . . .'

'Nicholls. Lily Nicholls. And good luck to you as well, Mrs . . .'

'Fortune. Ada Fortune.'

Lily hoped Ada Fortune was aptly named when it came to sending her five children away.

The heat inside the CORB offices was even worse than outside. There wasn't a breath of air and not a window open. A nause-ating cocktail of stale cigarette smoke, cheap Woolworth's perfume and Johnson's polishing wax turned Lily's stomach as she approached the front desk. A woman with flushed cheeks and a clipboard instructed her to take a form, a pen, and a seat.

'Anywhere?'

The woman looked at Lily as if she had three heads. 'Preferably on one of the seats, dear.'

Fifty identical chairs were neatly arranged in five rows of ten. The thirteen women ahead of Lily had dutifully filled the first thirteen chairs, one beside another, but Lily made her way to the back of the room. She needed privacy.

She fussed and fidgeted and shifted her weight, crossing and uncrossing her legs to try to get comfortable, but the lining of her skirt stuck to the back of her legs whichever way she sat. Balancing the paper form on top of the *Woman's Weekly* on her knees, she began to fill out the necessary information for Georgie and Arthur: full name, date of birth, address, school attended, medical history, religion. There were boxes to be ticked, declarations to be signed, small print to be read. She hesitated over the section that asked for her marital status. She hated the word 'widow' and what it meant, hated the blunt finality of it. She ticked the box and moved on to the occupation of the parents. *Housewife and domestic help* was simple enough, but what should she put for Peter? She settled on *Signwriter*, and added (*deceased*). The word reminded her of a corpse laid out, bookended by a head and feet.

She carried on with the rest of the form, crossing out and correcting silly mistakes, her mind a turmoil of decision and indecision, action and inaction.

Tear the form up, Lily. Walk out and go home.

Fill the form in, Lily. It's for the best.

The office was uncomfortably quiet, the monotonous click-clack of typewriter keys, and the occasional cough the only sounds as Lily completed the form and then read it over, twice, to make sure nothing had been missed, or misunderstood. Even then, she sat for a while, waiting for a moment of absolute certainty, but like so many other things, certainty was in short supply during a war. The best she could manage was a sense of resignation to finish what she'd started and try to make her peace with it.

She walked back to the front desk, conscious of the damp patch of sweat on the back of her skirt, and handed the paperwork to the young woman who'd opened the office doors. A badge pinned to her blouse introduced her as Katherine King. She offered a warm ruby-lipped smile and told Lily she was lucky to have got ahead of the queue.

'They'll close the doors well before lunchtime at this rate,' she said as she applied an official stamp to Lily's form with a sickening thud. 'Never seen anything like it!'

'Is that it?' Lily asked. Her hands fell to her sides as all the tension she'd carried with her from Clapham that morning dissipated like air from a burst tyre.

Miss King was already reaching behind Lily for the next person's form. 'Yes, that's it, Mrs . . .' she cast a cursory glance at the paperwork, 'Nicholls. That's all. You'll be notified in writing if the application is successful, and you'll be advised of further procedures then. Next there, please.'

That's it, Lily thought as she made her way back out into the glaring sunlight. That's all.

'All done, Mrs Nicholls?' Ada Fortune was already outside, smoking a cigarette beneath the welcome shade of a plane tree.

'Yes, all done.' Lily walked over to join her.

'Have to hope for the best now, I suppose. I haven't told the kiddies yet. Don't want to get their hopes up, just in case.'

Lily thought about the many conversations she'd had with Georgie and Arthur about evacuation. Georgie especially was desperate to head off somewhere exciting, like her schoolfriends' well-off cousins. Arthur just liked the thought of being a seavac and being on a real ship.

'I wish they would let parents go with them,' Lily said. 'It would make it all a lot easier to stomach.'

Ada Fortune laughed. 'Not for me! I get seasick just looking at the Thames! Besides, they won't want their mothers fussing over them all the time. The escorts they're hiring will be much better suited to the job. More functional. Less emotional.'

Lily couldn't agree. There could surely be nobody better suited to travel with the children than their own mothers. 'But what are we supposed to do in the meantime?' she said. 'What's *our* job until the children come back?'

Ada Fortune stubbed out her cigarette with the toe of her scuffed shoe, patted Lily's arm, and looked her straight in the eye. 'Our job is to stay alive, love. Our job is to make sure we're still here when they come back.'

The words crept along Lily's skin like a chill. That was the thing that terrified her the most, because people didn't always come back, even when they promised, even when you wanted them to more than anything in the world.

That night, Lily dreamed that the children were trapped beneath the rubble of their bombed-out home. She woke in a sweat and instinctively reached for Peter's hand for reassurance. She flinched at the touch of the cold bed sheets. *It's freezing, Lil. Go inside and get warm. I'll write when I'm at the training camp.*

She could still hear the familiar squeak of the garden gate as he'd closed it behind him. The squeaky gate was as much a part of their marriage as the rings on their fingers. 'I'll fix that when I get back,' he'd said, just as he did every day when he went off to work. It was a joke they shared. A pattern, repeating. But unlike on every other day, Peter wouldn't come home that evening. His papers had come through. He was headed to war. He hated the thought of it with every bone in his body, hated what it had done to his father after he'd returned from the Somme, and what that, in turn, had done to him and his mother, but he refused to object like the pacifists and COs. Peter couldn't bear the thought of killing another man, enemy or not, but he believed it was his duty to fight, just as it was his father's duty before him, and his grandfather's before that.

People like Mrs Hopkins, who'd lost husbands and loved ones of their own, said time was a great healer, but the more Lily tried to adjust to life without Peter, the more present he became. Everywhere she went, he was there. Everything she thought, he thought too. Every question she asked, he answered. He was everywhere and nowhere. She was Mrs Peter Nicholls and Lily Elizabeth Harris, plaits swinging at her back as she played hopscotch in the street, a smile on her lips as the boy called Peter walked by, because she knew he would ask her to marry him one day, and she knew she would say yes.

Wedding anniversary! Opened the Christmas sherry, danced in the kitchen, made love like young fools (one benefit to the children being evacuated) and promised that whatever happens we'll always dance and make love and drink the Christmas sherry in November. Life can't stop just because there's a war on. Moments and memories and days like this are surely what we're fighting for.

Mass-Observation, Diarist #6672

7

Kent. July 1940

'There's a letter here, addressed to you, Alice. It looks rather formal. Who on earth would be writing to *you*?' Alice took the envelope from her mother. She opened it, read the letter inside once over, returned it to the envelope, and excused herself from the breakfast table.

'Where are you going? Alice! You haven't even finished your porridge. *Alice!*'

Her mother's capacity to screech was one of many things Alice was eager to escape. Ignoring her, she grabbed her sunhat from the back of the pantry door.

'Where are you going in such a rush? We're supposed to be planning the fundraising lunch together. What on earth's got into you this morning?'

'I'm needed early at the library, Mother. I'll see you later.'

It was true. She *was* needed early at the library. A delivery was due from London and it was all-hands-on deck to get everything catalogued and stored. Alice always looked forward to opening the wooden packing crates to see what had arrived. She loved the musty smell of old leather-bound volumes, the crackle of the pages, the embossed lettering beneath her finger-tips, but the items she handled that day didn't hold their usual charm. She was distracted and made silly mistakes, her thoughts preoccupied by the letter in her pocket:

I am very pleased to inform you that your application for the voluntary position of escort with the CORB evacuation scheme has been approved, further to a satisfactory interview and medical examination which will be conducted at the CORB offices at the time and date specified below . . .

Maud could tell there was something on Alice's mind. 'You're either in love or in trouble,' she said.

Alice reassured Maud that it was neither. 'I don't want to say too much, because it might all come to nothing yet, but I applied as a volunteer with the new overseas evacuation scheme. There's a chance I might be escorting the seavacs.' It felt strange to say it out loud. She felt immensely proud, and more than a little nauseous.

Maud put down the pile of books in her arms and grabbed Alice's hands. 'That's marvellous news! I can't think of anyone better.'

'Really?'

'Yes! Really! I'll miss you terribly, but this is perfect for you, Alice. To be honest, I think you're wasted here, stuffing books on shelves. You're a natural with children. You're exactly the sort of person I'd want to keep my kiddies safe if I was a parent.'

It was the vote of confidence Alice needed. 'Actually, would you mind if I popped out for a bit? I haven't told Walter yet.' She needed his steady reassurance now more than ever.

Maud insisted she go and tell him immediately. 'And I don't want to see you back here again today. Go and have fun with your brother. This lot can wait.'

She found Walter repairing a fence at the far end of the farm. He read the letter from CORB with a grin on his face. 'Blimey! You're off on the high seas then. What does Mother have to say about it?'

'Haven't told her yet. She'll only find a way to spoil it. Besides, there's no point saying anything until the formalities are done. Just in case.'

'Surely even Mother won't be able to find anything disagreeable about this. She's been on at you for an age to *do* something. I think it's bloody brilliant.'

'So you think I should go? It's all a bit daunting now that it's official.'

Walter smiled at her in that lopsided way that was so like their father. 'I think you're already halfway there. As for daunting? Show me anything worthwhile that isn't.'

As usual, he was a rock of common sense. Alice took the letter from him and read it again. It was so matter of fact for something that felt so significant.

'You're braver than you think, Alice,' Walter added, sensing her hesitation. 'I wouldn't be at all surprised if you turned out to be the bravest of us all.'

She nudged Walter's shoulder. 'Don't be silly.'

'I'm not being silly. I'm deadly serious.'

Alice pulled her cardigan around her shoulders as the breeze picked up and sent a chill down her back. She didn't feel brave. If she were being honest, she would tell Walter she was terrified. Over recent weeks, she'd read the newspaper with an increasing sense of dread. Churchill's Battle of Britain had begun in earnest, with dramatic aerial dogfights now taking place over the English Channel and across the south coast counties. Casualty numbers were creeping up on both sides, yet the newspapers and the BBC wireless reports kept the news cheery and hopeful, talking of victories and celebrating 'our brave boys in blue'.

'I'll miss you though,' Walter added.

It was the second time that morning she'd been told she would be missed. Alice had been in Whitstable, at Willow Cottage, for so long that she'd never given anyone a reason to miss her, although she understood all too well the ache of absence, the unfathomable void left behind by those departed.

After a frustrating delay, the final confirmation of Alice's appointment as a CORB escort eventually arrived at the end of a difficult week at the library. Three entire shelves of books in Gardening had been damaged by a burst water pipe, and then an unpleasant woman borrowing several romance novels had felt it necessary to remind Alice how ashamed she should be of her brother, and that, 'he should be up there, fighting with the rest of them'. That was the thing about war. It was everyone's business, a uniquely shared experience, and it made personal responses to it everybody's business, too.

As the Battle of Britain intensified over the English Channel and Kent's orchards, Alice's days were accompanied by the background noise of aerial dogfights. The brave RAF pilots, scrapping it out with the Luftwaffe, were idolized by the local boys who couldn't get enough of the Hurricanes and Spitfires looping and turning with such speed and dexterity. It was thrilling Boy's Own stuff, and Alice hated it: the ominous hum of approaching enemy planes, the *rat-a-tat-a-tat* of machine gun fire, the rising pitch of an engine as another damaged plane plummeted to the ground. The sound haunted her.

She checked the post every day, but still nothing arrived from CORB. She'd passed her medical with a perfect bill of health, and had got along well with the lead escort during a rather nerve-wracking interview, but when Kitty had told her that sailings were indefinitely postponed due to a shortage of naval escort ships, Alice had almost given up on the evacuations going ahead altogether. So, when the final acceptance letter arrived, it felt less like an obligation to play her part in the war, and more like a very welcome invitation.

Her heart raced as she read the instructions. She was required to report to the ballroom of the Grosvenor House Hotel in London on the tenth of September, where she would be given further information about the ship and the route she would be sailing on. It was all unexpectedly thrilling, and although it felt wrong to be enthusiastic about escorting children away from their homes and families, Alice couldn't suppress her good mood. Finally, she had a sense of purpose, a clear direction to travel in. There was just one obstacle remaining: her mother. And that was a threat of an entirely different kind.

She decided to announce her news over dinner that evening. Walter was coming over, and he would help take some of the sting out of their mother's inevitable response. To take her mind off it until then, she busied herself in the garden and cleaned out the chicken coop, smiling to herself as she thought about Kitty holding her nose and calling it the smelliest job in the world. Dear Kitty. Alice would miss her terribly.

'Surprise!'

Alice jumped and turned around. 'Kitty! What are you doing here? Did somebody die?'

'I came to see my family. Is that so very odd?'

'Yes! You never visit unless you have to.' Alice stepped out of the chicken coop, brushed herself down, and gave her sister a hug. 'It's lovely to see you.'

'And it isn't so lovely to smell *you*!'

Kitty was a vision in mint green. Alice felt like a dock worker beside her in her scruffy old boiler suit. 'There is a war on, you know, Kitty. You could at least try to look thrifty.'

Kitty laughed, but there wasn't the usual brightness to her.

'Actually, your timing is perfect,' Alice said. 'I've something to tell you.'

'I've something to tell you, too.' Kitty hesitated. 'You go first. Mine can wait.'

'I suspect you might already know.' Alice pulled the letter from her pocket and held it up. 'I'm a fully approved CORB escort. Shipping out in a few weeks!' She waited for Kitty's reaction and was disappointed when it didn't come. 'Well? What do you think? It was partly because of you telling me to listen to that wireless programme with Anthony Quinn. I listened, applied, and—'

Kitty burst into tears and threw her arms around Alice's neck.

'Kitty? Whatever's the matter? I thought you'd be pleased.'

'I am pleased. You'll be perfect! I hoped you would apply but I didn't want to suggest it, in case you thought I was interfering like everyone else. You'll be marvellous!'

'Then why are you crying?' It really wasn't like Kitty to be so emotional.

Kitty brushed the tears from her cheeks. 'Ignore me. I'm being silly. I'll miss you, that's all.'

Alice smiled. 'No you won't. You're far too busy having fun in London with Terry, or whatever his name is. Come on. Let me get tidied up and we can go for a stroll along the harbour. Mother will be delighted to see you.'

Kitty looped her arm through Alice's. 'I'm not so sure about that.'

Before dinner, Alice took a moment alone in her father's study. She opened the heavy oak door and stepped inside. The sun didn't reach that side of the house until late evening and the room retained a coolness, even on warm days. Despite the many years that had passed, the air still carried a trace of him, the unmistakeable scent of pipe smoke and Swan's shoe polish. It was a room suspended in time, a museum exhibit to be displayed but never touched. The chessboard was still set up for a new game. It was almost twenty years since Alice had moved one of those precious pieces, and yet part of her was still an impatient little girl, studying the board, waiting for her father to make his move.

She walked around the desk and bent down to look through the old telescope, its lens still trained toward the northern sky. What magic he'd taught her as they'd explored the heavens together. She turned to the bookshelves then, running her fingers over the embossed spines of leather-bound medical journals and encyclopaedias, and the novels she'd devoured as a child – *Moby Dick*, *Treasure Island*, *Swallows and Amazons*, *The Complete Nonsense of Edward Lear*, *Gulliver's Travels*, *Alice in Wonderland* – her imagination captivated by stories and rhymes about distant lands and vengeful whales. Those stories had whispered to her of possibility and adventure, but a whisper was all they remained.

As she admired these favourite old books now, her fingers settled on her treasured clothbound edition of *David Copperfield*. She'd adored the book the first time she'd read it as a young girl, and loved it more with each re-reading. She knew the opening lines by heart. *Whether I shall turn out to be the hero of my own life, or whether that station will be held by anybody else, these pages must show* . . . Unlike David Copperfield, Alice had always thought she would prefer to become the hero of someone else's life; to make a quiet difference to someone she perhaps didn't even know. But it was the inscription inside the front cover she treasured the most: *25 December 1921, To my darling Alice, Happy Christmas! Be the hero (heroine) of your own life. Always, your Papa x*. She'd often thought of the book as her father's last gift to her, but it wasn't. The gift of reading, a love of books, was something she would have forever, could take with her, wherever she went. She took the book from the shelf. *David Copperfield* would be a welcome companion on the unfamiliar journey she was about to embark on.

As she walked from the study, the old floorboards creaking beneath her feet, she thought of her father, and wondered what he would say. He'd always encouraged her to stretch her wings; to try new things, even when she was reluctant and afraid. 'We are only limited by what we fear, Alice. Fear nothing, and you can do anything!' She closed the study door behind her, took a deep breath, and prepared to announce her news.

Unsurprisingly, her mother was searingly critical of the whole idea. 'It sends the entirely wrong message to the enemy, but I can see that your mind is made up, and I suppose it's better than stamping library books, so there's no point in my saying anything else about it. Is there?'

'Do you know where you're going?' Walter asked. 'Or can't they say?'

'They'll only tell us at the last minute. Careless talk costs lives, and all that. I hope I'm on the shorter route, to Canada. Three weeks sailing to Australia sounds like such a long time!'

Alice's mother tutted. 'Being choosy already, I see. You do realize there are active U-boats in the Atlantic? A civilian ship was sunk by a torpedo recently. I read about it in the newspaper.'

Kitty gasped dramatically. 'Goodness, Mother. Is that a hint of *concern* in your voice?'

'Don't be facetious, Kitty.'

'They've given repeated assurances about safety,' Alice said. 'Evacuee ships will be under naval escort and will sail in convoy.' She sounded more convinced than she felt. 'Anyway, it's no more dangerous than staying here, waiting for the Luftwaffe to blow us all up, is it?'

There was very little anyone could say to that. Even her mother had nothing to add.

Kitty raised her glass. 'To the good ship *Alice* then. And all who sail with her!'

Everyone raised their glass in response. 'To Alice.'

They continued their meal without mentioning CORB, or evacuation, again. Alice noticed how quiet Kitty was, and when Walter remarked on the beef being 'good and bloody' in the middle, Kitty put her hand to her mouth and ran from the room.

'What on earth's the matter with her?' he said. 'She's been skittish all day.'

'Probably the whelks we had for lunch,' Alice said. 'I'll go and check on her.'

She found Kitty with her head down the toilet. She was positively green as Alice passed her some tissues.

'Better out than in. It'll be my turn next. Heave ho, me hearties!'

Kitty shook her head.

'What is it, Kitty? You haven't been yourself all day.'

Kitty looked at Alice and paused, long enough for the grandfather clock to chime, for their mother to rap on the door and tell them to hurry up, for the dog to bark at the cat. Long enough for Alice to know that whatever Kitty said next was going to be far more serious than eating a bad portion of whelks.

'I'm expecting, Alice. I'm pregnant.'

For a moment, Alice couldn't respond. Whatever she'd thought was bothering Kitty, it certainly wasn't this. 'Are you sure?'

'The doctor confirmed it.'

'Oh, Kitty.' Alice squeezed her sister's hand. She didn't know what else to say. 'Does he know? The father? Is it . . .'

Kitty nodded. 'Terence. He doesn't know. He's very high up in the Admiralty, and very married, so he can never know.'

Her words made Alice furious, but now wasn't the time to discuss the injustice of things always being left to the woman to sort out. 'How long?' she asked. 'How far gone are you?'

'Not exactly sure. I've missed two monthlies.' Kitty threw her arms around Alice and burst into tears. 'I'm such a bloody idiot.'

'You're not an idiot. You've got yourself in a bit of trouble, that's all. And you're still ever so pretty, even when you cry.' Alice passed Kitty a handkerchief to wipe away the rivers of mascara streaming down her face. 'Although, maybe not so pretty after all.'

Kitty broke a watery smile. 'This is more than a bit of trouble, Alice. Promise you won't tell Mother. She'll die from the scandal and shame.'

Alice promised. 'Do you know what you're going to do?'

Kitty shook her head. She had no easy answer, no matter how much she considered the options. They both understood how difficult life was for unmarried mothers, shunned by society, and cast aside by their families. But they also knew how dangerous the alternative solution could be.

Their mother knocked on the door. 'Are you two ever coming out of there?'

'Yes,' Alice called back. 'Kitty has an upset tummy. We're coming now.' She straightened Kitty's hair and helped her look presentable. 'We'll talk about it later, but try not to worry.' She almost echoed their father's favourite phrase, 'worse things happen at sea', but there were few things worse than this.

A weekend of dog walks, picnics, and jazz on the gramophone eventually restored Kitty to something like herself, but she was unusually reflective as Alice walked her back to Whitstable train station, where Kitty was the only civilian passenger on the platform. She boarded the train, pulled down the compartment window and leaned out to kiss Alice on the cheek as the shrill blast of the conductor's whistle made them both jump.

Alice pressed her hands to Kitty's. 'Everything will be all right, Kitty. I promise.'

Kitty returned a thin smile. 'It won't. But thank you for pretending.'

As the train pulled away, Alice's heart sank, because she didn't know how to make this all right. This was far more serious than Kitty's usual relationship dilemmas and silly mistakes at work. This wasn't a problem that could be easily fixed with a well-written letter of apology, or a new dress to lift her mood. Whatever decision Kitty made, there would be difficult weeks and months ahead. Weeks and months when Alice would be further away from her sister than she'd ever been, at precisely the time when she needed her the most.

8

London. 7 September 1940

The first wave of enemy planes arrived over England just after four o'clock on a warm Saturday afternoon. The war had been officially declared a year ago, but still the attack took everyone by surprise.

In Whitstable, on the north-east Kent coast, Alice and her mother watched in horror as a swarm of Messerschmitt aircraft flew in formation across the Channel. In Poplar, in the East End, Ada Fortune was on her way back from the fishmonger when the air-raid siren sounded. She assumed it was another false alarm and hurried home, reluctant to spend hours in a bomb shelter with a bag of mackerel. Kitty was already running late for her four o'clock appointment at a rather grim-looking building in Southwark where she'd been assured that her 'procedure' would be carried out safely and discreetly. She hurried past and headed straight to the nearest shelter. In Elm Street, Lily called the children inside.

'Is it real this time?' Georgie asked.

'I'm sure it's just another false alarm, but we still need to go to the shelter.'

The children were well-rehearsed in air-raid drills. They calmly grabbed their gas masks and shelter bags, and followed Lily to the brick surface shelter that stood in the middle of Elm Street. Lily hated it and was sorry now that she'd watched it being built. Arthur took more care over his sandcastles at Chalkwell Beach.

She stalled at the entrance.

'Get a move on, Lil. I don't fancy being target practice.'

Lily stood aside to let Mrs Hopkins go ahead. 'Sorry, Mrs H. After you.'

Georgie and Arthur followed Mrs Hopkins into the shelter. Lily took a deep breath and stepped inside.

There wasn't a scrap of space to spare. The children crammed into one of the makeshift bunk beds, along with four other children. Lily squashed herself onto one of the narrow pallet benches at the back.

Mrs Hopkins shoved in beside her. 'Hope we're not stuck in here for long. I've a casserole in the oven.'

Lily buttoned her coat. Her thoughts were a long way from casseroles.

The atmosphere was stoic and calm. Everyone assumed it was another false alarm and expected to be back home within the hour. People took out knitting, or played card games. Lily sat quietly with her thoughts until the all-clear sounded just after six. Two hours in the shelter was just about tolerable. The residents of Elm Street gathered up their things, emerged into the fading afternoon light and made their way home.

From an upstairs bedroom window at The Beeches on Richmond Hill, Isobel Carr noticed that the sky was glowing a peculiar shade of orange over the East End. She remarked that it looked like one of the gasworks had exploded. Molly was too enraptured by her new doll's house to take any notice.

Just after blackout at eight that evening, the siren went off again. Lily glanced at the kitchen clock. They'd never had two raids in such close succession. It made her uneasy.

She woke the children, told them to put their coats on over their nightclothes and hurried them outside. Georgie stopped to look up at the searchlights that criss-crossed the sky, almost in time to the rise and fall of the siren. Lily urged her along. War had brought so many new sights and sounds to the children's lives. She wished it would all go away. Wished it had never started.

Unlike during the earlier raid, the atmosphere in the shelter the second time that day was tense and restless. Some tried to make light of the situation, joking about there being nothing worth bombing in Clapham anyway. Some people slept. Others resumed their knitting or games of cards. The children whispered and giggled. To them it was all a great adventure. Lily sat on the rough wooden bench and stared at the scuff marks on the toes of her shoes. She tried not to think about the thin brick walls that stood between her and the children and Hitler's bombs.

Hours passed, and still the all-clear didn't come. Midnight came and went. The nervous residents of Elm Street huddled in the cramped shelter as the bombers came again and again. Too anxious to sleep, Lily flinched at each awful thud and thump as bombs found their targets. Several people wept. Everyone was terrified by these alarming new sounds. Lily desperately needed the loo, but she held it in rather than use the buckets behind the curtain. The smell made her retch, and it was humiliating to spend a penny in front of your neighbours. She counted backwards from a hundred to take her mind off it.

'Listen to this, Lil.' Mrs Hopkins was reading the newspaper to pass the time. '*In the few weeks since the new CORB evac-*

uation scheme opened its doors, some two hundred tho
applications were received for just twenty thousand places.'

'Two hundred thousand? Surely you mean two thousand?'

'Definitely says two hundred thousand.' Mrs Hopkins read out the rest of the article: '*The head of the CORB programme, Anthony Quinn, MP, earlier confirmed that no further applications will be accepted, and that those who had already submitted the necessary paperwork should expect to hear the outcome in the coming days.*'

Lily's stomach heaved at the thought. She dreaded the snap of the letter box; dreaded learning the outcome of her application. What if they said no? But what if they said yes? Because despite everything, despite everyone's reassurance that it would be for the best, she still didn't know if she could put Georgie and Arthur on a ship and send them halfway around the world to live with people she'd never met.

'You'll know what to do when the time comes,' Mrs Hopkins said, as if reading Lily's thoughts. 'You'll know what to do for the best. If you ask me, it was silly of them to plan for so few children to go. Every parent in Britain will wish they'd applied if these bloody bombing raids get any worse.'

As if to emphasize the point, a distant thud of another bomb added a horrifying sense of urgency to the issue of staying or going.

Just after four in the morning, the continuous singular tone of the siren signalled the all-clear. Lily let out a long sigh of relief. She felt as if she'd been holding her breath all night.

'You'd think they'd have come up with something a bit more cheerful,' Mrs Hopkins muttered as she gathered up her things. '"Land of Hope and Glory", or "The Charge of the Light Brigade". That bloody siren is enough to turn your insides funny.'

Arthur yawned as Lily gently woke him and hitched him up onto her hip. 'Have they gone, Mummy?'

'Yes, love. They've gone.'

Lily clasped Georgie's hand in hers as they trudged home, the skies over London silent once again. At first glance, Elm Street looked entirely unchanged, but the aftermath of the night's raids was evident in the tang of cordite that tainted the air, and in the fine particles of brick dust that caught at the back of Lily's throat and made her cough.

'Why is the sky orange?' Georgie asked.

Lily looked up at the strange amber glow from the distant fires. 'It must be the sunrise, love.'

'Already? But we haven't properly been to bed yet.'

As Lily tucked the children in tight beneath their bed covers, she didn't feel relief in the silence, or in the undamaged houses of Elm Street. She felt only a profound sadness. Something had changed that night, and Lily had a terrible feeling that it was only going to get worse.

She kissed the children's foreheads, and sat on the end of Arthur's bed, watching over them both until they were asleep.

For forty-eight hours, Londoners endured heavy bombardment. Each night, the siren went off at eight, just after blackout. Each night, Lily dragged the children from their beds and hurried them into the shelter. Each night, she felt certain their luck was about to run out. She watched for the post each morning, her sense of dread and urgency fuelled by awful headlines in the newspapers. Specific damage and casualties were reported in scant detail, the newspaper editors careful not to give any encouragement to the enemy. BLITZ BOMBING OF LONDON GOES ON ALL NIGHT. *Mothers and children among casualties. Damage considerable, but spirits unbroken.* Photographs were carefully chosen to portray a sense of community and defiance in the face of death and destruction, but Lily could see the truth for herself. Lives and homes were shattered. People's spirits *were* broken. Everyone was exhausted.

Lily hated it all. The wail of the air-raid sirens, the claustro-phobic tomb-like compression of the shelter, the sense of sitting there, waiting for the inevitable. Awful stories began to emerge about brick surface shelters collapsing from bomb blast, so that every time Lily went into the Elm Street shelter, she felt as if she was stepping into her own grave.

'Don't be sad, Mummy,' Arthur said as Lily tucked him into bed when they returned after the fourth consecutive night of raids. 'The bad men always lose.'

To Arthur's young mind, war was an adventure story in which good always defeated evil. Lily kissed him goodnight and hoped to God he was right.

Within the hour, the siren went off again.

The bombing that night was relentless and seemed ever closer, the impact of the bombs shaking the Elm Street shelter walls. Everyone looked to one another for reassurance, their eyes carrying the same unspoken fear: Will the next one find us?

'Sounds like that one landed Islington way,' someone offered.

'Sounded more like Tooting direction, to me,' someone else disagreed.

'Does it bloody matter where they've landed,' Mrs Hopkins snapped, 'as long as it isn't on us?'

Again, Elm Street was spared. Neighbouring streets weren't so lucky.

Later that morning, Mrs Hopkins brought the terrible news that the Ingrams' house had taken a direct hit, along with several others in the street.

'Thank goodness they were in the shelter,' Lily said. 'Do they have anywhere to stay? Beth can stay with us until they get themselves organized. I'll pop round later with a few bits.'

Mrs Hopkins reached for Lily's hand. 'But that's the thing, dear. They didn't go to the shelter last night.'

Lily's heart filled with dread. 'What? Why?'

'Mrs Ingram had heard of one nearby collapsing and crushing everyone inside, so they sat out the raid at home.' Mrs Hopkins brushed a tear from her cheek. 'The brick shelter held. The poor things didn't stand a chance.'

'No! Oh, Mrs H. No.' Lily's hands instinctively covered her mouth as if she didn't want to share her reaction, didn't want to make it real. This wasn't a list of casualties in a newspaper report. These were people she knew well; her daughter's best friend. Tears fell in steady ribbons down her cheeks as she sat down in disbelief. It was devastating proof, if any were needed, that war was cruel and indiscriminate. Her distress quickly turned to anger, and somewhere within her rage, she found the courage and certainty that had eluded her.

As if in reply to her renewed sense of desperation, the letter from CORB arrived that morning. Lily's heart thumped as she opened the simple brown envelope – such an ordinary thing, and yet she felt as though her next breath was held inside it. She unfolded a single typed page, longing for the words she'd once dreaded.

Further to your application, I am pleased to inform you that your children, Georgina and Arthur, have been accepted for evacuation with the CORB programme, subject to satisfactory medical examination. They will proceed to the port of embarkation on Tuesday, 10 September and will be included with a party going to Canada. You should accordingly proceed to make preparations at once, along the lines of the instructions set out below . . .

Lily glanced at the kitchen calendar, then back at the letter. The tenth was tomorrow.

War arrived just after four on Saturday afternoon. The East End was burning by five. Black Saturday, they're calling it. Unimaginable destruction. Hundreds dead and wounded – many women and children among them. Nothing else to say. No words can ever capture what we have seen.

Mass-Observation, Diarist #6385

9

Kent. 10 September 1940

The London train was unusually punctual. Alice watched with her heart in her mouth as it approached. This was it then. She was really going.

Around her, people began to say their farewells, but Alice stood alone on the station platform. She'd insisted she didn't want anyone to see her off, or to make a fuss. She'd never liked goodbyes, always found the business of extracting herself from gatherings and parties embarrassing and awkward. She'd popped her head into the library to say goodbye to it, and to Maud, but she'd even kept that brief as her emotions had threatened to get the better of her. She'd left rather abruptly, a snivelling Maud in her wake, the little bell above the door jingling a poignant au revoir.

She was glad to slip quietly into the second-class compartment, place her small suitcase on the luggage rack overhead and take her seat. Others around her pulled down the windows and exchanged emotional farewells with loved ones as the locomotive lurched forward with a hiss of steam and a cloud of smoke. In the seat opposite, a red-faced woman flapped a newspaper frantically at a painted lady butterfly trapped inside the compartment. Alice pulled down the window to let it out and blinked back a tear as she took her seat again, conscious of the echo of her own release from her 'narrow little life'.

'Always sets me off,' the woman said, dabbing at her eyes with a handkerchief. 'There's something so sad about a train pulling away from a station, isn't there? Especially during a war. Everything feels so final.'

Alice nodded and bit her lip as she stared intently at the passing hedgerows, because the woman was right. Everything was intensified by the war. Everything was so much more because there was a chance it could become so much less, that the people and things left behind wouldn't be there when – if – you returned. Entire communities were being decimated now, homes demolished, shocked and shattered people left to search for what bits of their lives they could salvage from the rubble that remained, and when it came to evacuating the nation's children from the cities and towns most at risk, there wasn't a moment to lose. Alice felt the momentum build as the locomotive gained speed, her heart racing in her chest, her breathing matching the rattle and thrum of the wheels on the tracks.

The glorious Kent countryside soon gave way to the hard industry and architecture of London. As the train pulled into Victoria station, Alice took a deep breath, gathered her things and double-checked the information she'd been sent. She was to report first to the CORB assembly point at Grosvenor House Hotel in Mayfair, then to Euston Station, from where the group would depart for Liverpool at 1500 hours. She'd hoped to see Kitty before she left, but the strict schedule didn't allow for such sentimental nonsense as saying goodbye to your sister.

Alice left the train station and set out to walk along Grosvenor Place, past the Wellington Arch and up Park Lane. Her palms were clammy. Her small suitcase banged awkwardly against her legs as she picked her way past damaged buildings, and looked for alternative routes when a street she needed to go down was impassable. Shocked by the sight of sandbags everywhere and of the barrage balloons dotting the sky, she kept a close eye on the nearest air-raid shelter as she walked. She hadn't been in a shelter yet, and hoped her first experience wouldn't be during a raid on the nation's capital. The smell from open pipes and damaged sewers was nauseating. Alice put her hand over her nose and hurried on, wishing she were back in the hushed familiar walls of Whitstable library, listening to Maud singing Gracie Fields as she made the tea.

She was relieved to finally reach the calm interior of the hotel where a sign in the lobby directed her to CORB ASSEMBLY, Grand Ballroom. She took a moment to compose herself before making her way up a flight of crimson velvet stairs. There was no turning back now.

She hadn't fully appreciated the scale of the CORB operation until she entered the opulent ballroom, once used for elegant dinner dances and now transformed into something resembling a postal sorting office and a field hospital for broken hearts. The atmosphere was tense, the air thick with emotion. Children snivelled as they clung to their mothers' skirts. Some openly bawled. Several played contentedly on the floor, unfazed by the prospect of leaving, or too young to fully understand what was happening. Ashen-faced women consoled and reassured one another. The few men present lingered awkwardly at the side of the room, chain-smoking cigarettes and desperately trying to maintain an air of composure. One young father burst into tears as he told his son to be brave and to look after his little sister. Alice looked away. She had a job to do. She couldn't let herself become emotionally involved.

Seeing a sign for Escort Registration, she made her way over to a rather formidable-looking woman wielding a clipboard. She recognized her as the woman who'd conducted her interview.

'Hello. I'm here to register as an escort? Alice King?' She couldn't conceal the uncertainty and hesitation in her voice.

The woman looked up briefly, nodded, and studied a list attached to her clipboard. 'King. Yes, here you are.' She added a tick beside Alice's name, stuffed the clipboard under her arm and thrust out a hand. 'Eleanor Heath. Lead escort. Welcome aboard, Miss King! Delighted to have you!'

Alice thought her arm would be pulled off, it was shaken with such vigour. 'Delighted to be here.'

'Everyone will be fully briefed when we reach Liverpool. For now, it's a matter of rounding 'em all up, and I'm afraid you've two to collect from their home. Bit of an inconvenience, but we did offer the choice, so needs must.' Eleanor gave Alice a piece of paper with an address in Clapham. 'Georgina and Arthur Nicholls. There's a bus stop outside. The number eighty-eight will take you there. We'll see you at the train station, departing at fifteen-hundred hours sharp, and Miss King . . .'

'Yes?'

'Two things. We mustn't show any favouritism, or become emotionally attached. And we *will* leave without you if necessary.'

Alice assured her she wouldn't be late.

'Excuse me. Am I in the right place to register for escort duty?'

Eleanor Heath looked up from her paperwork as Alice turned to the voice to her right. Both women stared at a very tall, rather striking man, a hopeful smile on his face.

'Howard,' he added. 'Howard Keane.' He took a piece of paper from his coat pocket. 'I think I'm in the right place. Either that or there's been a terrible muddle and I'm supposed to be somewhere in France.'

Alice laughed. She could listen to his Irish accent all day.

Eleanor Heath studied her paperwork again. 'Keane, Howard. Ah, yes. Here we are. Welcome aboard, Mr Keane. All your young charges are being brought to the hotel, so there's no chance of us leaving without *you*. Grab a cup of tea – if you can call it that – and I'll direct your evacs to you as they arrive.' She turned to Alice. 'Still here, Miss King?'

Alice jumped to attention and checked the address again. 'On my way. Thirteen Elm Street, Clapham. I'll see you at the train station.'

Howard Keane offered an encouraging smile and wished Alice good luck.

Eleanor Heath tutted. 'She doesn't need luck, Mr Keane. She needs to get a move on.'

But there was one more thing Alice needed to do.

She found a public telephone box across the road from the hotel. She hadn't telephoned Kitty at work before and hoped she would be able to talk. If anyone could settle her last-minute nerves, Kitty could.

'Alice! Is everything all right? I'm not supposed to take personal calls at work, but they said it was urgent.'

'It is. I wanted to talk to you, before I leave.'

'You're not nervous, are you?'

'A little. But I didn't call to talk about me. How are *you*? How are . . . things?'

Kitty paused before answering. She lowered her voice so that Alice could hardly hear her. 'I made an appointment, a few days ago.'

'Oh, Kitty. You should have said. I'd have come with you. Was it awful?'

'I didn't go in the end. There was an air raid.'

'And? Have you rescheduled?'

There was another pause. 'Not yet, but I think . . .'

The pips started to go. Alice fumbled in her purse for another coin, but she dropped it as she tried to put it into the slot. The line went dead before she could find another. Her parting words, 'I'll miss you, Kitty,' were never heard.

Unlike many other streets Alice passed on the bus, Elm Street was remarkably undamaged. She felt calm and purposeful as she walked down the red-brick terrace, following the numbers displayed in the fanlights until she reached number 13. The generous autumn sun cast a golden glow over the olive-green front door. The garden gate squeaked as she opened it and walked up the narrow path. The house looked a little careworn. The small patch of front garden needed weeding, and the hydrangeas could do with deadheading. She lifted the knocker and rapped gently twice. She could sense the neighbours twitching at their net curtains.

After a moment, the door was opened by a tall narrow-framed woman, mahogany hair pin-curled into waves, olive-green eyes that matched the colour of the front door, a look of Katharine Hepburn about her.

'Mrs Nicholls?'

The woman nodded. 'Lily.' She held out a hand.

Alice shook it. 'Alice King. With CORB. I've come to . . .'

'I know.'

Two children appeared in the hallway behind Mrs Nicholls. The boy hid behind his mother's legs. The girl smiled broadly as she joined her mother on the doorstep.

'Hello! I'm Georgina, but you can call me Georgie. What's your name?'

'Georgie! Manners.' Lily placed her hand on the child's shoulder.

'I'm Miss King.' Alice held out her hand. 'Very pleased to meet you, Georgie.' The child carried an air of confidence. A Girl Guide, no doubt. Through her years in the classroom, Alice had developed a knack for marking out those she could rely on to help, and those who would cause trouble. Georgie was definitely a helper.

'And this is Arthur,' Lily said as she gently encouraged the boy to step forward.

'Hello, Arthur.' Alice shook his hand. 'I'm very pleased to meet you.' She tried to keep her voice bright and friendly despite her own nerves.

Arthur didn't share his sister's confidence, but he shook Alice's hand anyway. 'This is Small Lion,' he said, producing a small stuffed animal. 'He's coming on the ship with me.' Like Arthur, Small Lion had an evacuee label tied around his neck.

Alice shook Small Lion's paw. She suspected Arthur was the sensitive type. Eager to please, but vulnerable. He would, no doubt, be terribly homesick. She would need to keep an eye on him.

The two women spoke for a few moments, both of them painfully aware that the need for small talk and pleasantries only made the situation worse. Lily made sure the children's cases were securely fastened and their labels firmly tied through the buttonholes of their coats.

'Promise me you'll wear your coats at bedtime,' she said. 'It's very important, to make sure you're nice and warm if you have to go up on deck suddenly in the middle of the night.'

The children solemnly promised.

Alice understood that the reason for Lily's insistence was her fear of a U-boat attack.

'Would you take this, Miss King?' Lily pressed an envelope into Alice's hand. 'It's a lucky talisman, a white feather, to keep the children safe. A silly superstition really but, would you mind?'

A little bemused by the notion of lucky talismans, Alice took the envelope and slipped it into her jacket pocket. 'Of course.'

The girl was anxious to leave. The boy dallied at his mother's side. Alice hated to rush them, but she was conscious of the time and Eleanor Heath's stark warning about leaving without them.

'We really should be going,' she said.

Lily nodded, took a deep breath, gave the children a firm hug and a kiss on the forehead and told them to remember their manners and to be on their very best behaviour. There was a quiet strength about her, a determination not to give in to whatever emotions were raging inside.

'SS *Carlisle*,' Alice whispered. 'Departing from Liverpool.'

She wasn't meant to know, and certainly wasn't meant to say, but she'd seen the name of their ship on Eleanor Heath's list, and thought Lily Nicholls should know.

Lily nodded. 'Thank you.' Her voice was a whisper, as if she didn't have the emotional wherewithal to make any greater sound.

Alice ushered the children ahead. The gate opened and closed with another squeak and they set off down Elm Street, their small suitcases in one hand, their other hand grasped firmly in Alice's. She told the children not to look back because it would only upset their mother, but she chanced a quick glance herself.

The olive-green door was already closed.

Whatever was happening behind it was for Lily Nicholls to know.

At Euston station, Alice registered the two Nicholls children with a very flushed Eleanor Heath, who, despite her authoritative exterior, now seemed a little harried by the endless line of escorts and children who had questions for her or needed something from her. They were a significant group. CORB evacuees had come from right across London, collected up like scrap left out for the rag and bone man. They all looked so small beneath the great railway station arches, their shoelaces already undone, their bewildered little faces pale and tear-stained as they wondered what on earth they'd done wrong to be sent away from their mothers.

'You made it back in time then?'

Alice turned to see Howard Keane, the man she'd met earlier at the hotel. 'And with time to spare!'

Howard was keeping his young evacuees entertained by pretending to pull a coin from behind their ears and making it disappear again.

'You're very good with them,' Alice said.

'Learned everything from my da. With seven of us to keep out of trouble, he always had a trick or two up his sleeve.'

Alice wondered why a healthy young man like Howard wasn't away fighting. She remembered reading something about men from Northern Ireland being excluded from conscription. Or perhaps he was a CO, like Walter. Whatever the reason, she knew better than to make assumptions. War was complicated. Assumptions were usually wrong.

Thankfully, the Liverpool train was on time. Alice was eager to get out of London. The bombing raids usually started at blackout and she didn't fancy a night in a London bomb shelter with children who were already upset enough as it was.

'Ready for the off, Miss King?' Eleanor Heath went around the group, checking everyone off her list one last time.

'Ready for the off,' Alice confirmed.

'Ready for the off,' a small voice beside her echoed.

She looked down at a scrappy little boy who'd strayed from Howard's group. Shoelaces undone, his cap falling over his eyes, grazes on his knees.

He pulled a marble from his coat pocket. 'My best shooter,' he said. 'Bet they've never seen one this big in Canada!'

Alice bent down to inspect the marble, a clear glass orb with a swirl of aquamarine running through the centre. She checked the identification label tied to the buttonhole of the boy's coat, picked a small white feather from his sleeve, pushed his cap back from his face and smiled. 'I'd keep that in your pocket if I were you, Billy Fortune. And I think this belongs to you, too.' She held out the feather.

'That'll be from the pigeons. I'm looking after them for Father while he's away. Their bleedin' feathers get everywhere.'

Alice noticed that the boy's breath caught a little when he talked. The remnant of a stutter, perhaps, or maybe just excitement. She knew Billy's type instantly. A hard worker, a charmer. He would become everyone's friend.

He slipped the feather and the marble into his coat pocket, wiped his nose with the back of his coat sleeve and reached for Alice's hand. 'Have you brought any marbles, lady?'

'No, dear. Grown-ups tend not to play with marbles.'

Billy thought about this for a moment, a frown on his face, as if he couldn't understand that you would ever reach a point in life where you didn't play with marbles. He wrapped his fingers tight around Alice's. 'You can borrow mine if you like.'

Alice looked at Billy Fortune, and swallowed a lump of emotion. Until then, she'd focused on the practical aspects of her role – dates, times, lists, and instructions – but in that instant, with a small hand in hers, something shifted. As she looked around the station platform, at Georgie and Arthur Nicholls, and dozens of other children whose welfare and safety she and half a dozen other escorts were now responsible for, she felt a crack in her heart. Despite Eleanor Heath's warning not to get emotionally attached, Alice quietly accepted that she already was.

IO

London. 10 September 1940

That night, Lily's dreams returned. This time, she was trapped beneath rubble, pinned down by heavy masonry. A woman with a Scottish accent spoke quietly and calmly. A white *W* was painted onto the front of her steel helmet. 'You're at the ARP station, my love. UXB. One of the smaller bombs, thankfully.' A casualty label was threaded through a buttonhole on Lily's plum-coloured wool coat, the relevant lines struck out to indicate the severity of her injuries. 'The children?' she asked. 'Where are the children?' The woman shook her head and held Lily's hand. 'I'm sorry, dear. I'm very sorry.' It was all so raw, so vivid, that when the air-raid siren woke her, it took a moment to leave the nightmare behind.

Half asleep, she went to the children's bedroom to wake them, and stopped at the sight of their empty beds. She pulled the door gently to behind her. She never fully closed it because Arthur was afraid of the dark.

The siren was especially loud that night, wailing out across the cloudless sky.

'Bomber's moon,' Mrs Hopkins said as the two of them hurried to the shelter. 'London will be lit up like a West End stage for them tonight.'

The thud of a distant explosion emphasized her point.

A wave of dread placed a vice around Lily's chest so that she could hardly breathe. She laid a hand against the shelter wall and leaned forward, her breaths thin and shallow.

Mrs Hopkins steered her to one side to make room for those coming behind. 'They're better off away from all this,' she said, understanding the reason for Lily's distress. 'Better to be sound asleep on their big ship than scurrying into bomb shelters in the middle of the night.' She added an encouraging pat to Lily's hand, a salve of compassion and empathy.

It didn't help. Nothing could make it better. The children hadn't even been gone a full day and already it felt like weeks.

Lily looked at her neighbour through the light of the moon. 'Thank you, Mrs H. For everything. You've been so kind since Peter . . .' Always a pause, a trailing off. She couldn't bear to finish the sentence.

Mrs Hopkins tightened the belt of her housecoat and waved Lily's gratitude away. 'Don't be starting with that sentimental nonsense or you'll have me all asunder. Think of them as swallows migrating for the winter. They'll be back in the summer, full of chatter and stories, and a foot taller no doubt! That's not so bad, is it?'

Lily said no, it wasn't so bad. But it was. It was all terrible, and she couldn't shake the nagging worry that they might forget her; might not want to come home in the summer, or whenever it was safe for them to return.

The shelter was busier than usual. Men, women and children

huddled together on the low benches made from packing crates and pallets. The smell of Mr Kettlewell's beef tea infused the musty air as the sounds of whispers, laughter and snoring filled the uneasy silence. There was a neat order to it all, everyone slotting into place, like washed cutlery put away after tea. Lily stepped over the tangle of stockinged legs and bags of knitting and rows of cards stretched out in games of Solitaire. She nodded a brisk greeting to neighbours she now knew by distinct traits: the snorers, the sleep-talkers, the helpers, the shirkers, the busy-bodies and worriers. Lily wondered how she was perceived, aware that people viewed her with a mixture of pity and scorn and that they talked about her behind her back. *Did you know him? Did you hear what happened? They said it was an accident, but it all sounds a bit fishy to me . . .*

At the back of the shelter, Lily stalled. Two children sat on the bench in Arthur and Georgie's places. An attractive woman – presumably their mother – sat beside them. Lily stared at the woman's copper victory rolls, her crimson Cupid's bow and pencilled eyebrows, the delicate apple-green tea dress beneath her navy-blue wool coat. She looked out of place, dressed for the theatre more than an air raid.

Noticing Lily's hesitation, the woman lifted the children onto her lap. 'We have to make room for the lady,' she said as they grumbled and complained. 'Plenty of room for everyone, see.'

Lily squeezed into the thin gap. She felt like overworked pastry beside this extravagant dessert of a woman. The children in her arms only emphasized the awful absence of Georgie and Arthur. She wished she'd sat somewhere else and wondered if it would be rude to move.

'Dreadful business, isn't it?' The woman budged up a bit more so that her thigh didn't press against Lily's. 'I'm Elsie, by the way. Well, not Elsie By-The-Way!' She laughed at her joke. 'Elsie Farnaby.' She held out a hand.

'Lily. Nicholls.' Lily wiped her hand on her coat and shook Elsie's.

'This is William, and this is Mary,' Elsie continued. The boy scowled at Lily. The girl buried her face in her mother's fur-trimmed coat.

'I haven't seen you here before.' Lily didn't mean to be curt, but then again, perhaps she did.

'Only moved in this morning. Our house was bomb-damaged last night, out Finsbury High Street way. Still standing, thanks be, but structurally unsound according to the fire warden.' Elsie rolled her eyes, as if to imply that the fire warden didn't know what he was talking about. 'We're staying with my mother-in-law for the time being.' She nodded toward an older woman opposite. She was asleep and snoring loudly.

Lily recognized the woman who lived across the road. Old Mrs Farnaby, as she was known to everyone.

The distinctive scream of a falling bomb saw everyone brace and pray for it to fall on some disused wasteland. Lily pressed her hands to her ears as the sound drew closer, and she breathed a sigh of relief at the muted distant thud. The shelter shook with the impact. A fine film of dust settled on coats and hats.

'No little ones of your own?' Elsie asked. 'Don't blame you. These two are a proper handful! Never give me a minute's peace.'

'Two, actually. Georgie and Arthur.'

'Two boys! More than a handful!'

'One of each,' Lily corrected. 'Georgie is my daughter. It's short for Georgina. She's named after my husband's father, George. Arthur is named after my father.' She was a burst dam, desperate to talk about them, to keep them beside her in words if not in physical form. 'They're being evacuated overseas.'

She waited for the tut of disapproval, aware that women who'd sent their children away were generally considered cowardly and unpatriotic by those who'd kept their children at home.

'Ah! Seavacs!' Elsie said without a hint of judgement. 'They'd closed applications by the time I got round to doing something about it. Seems they could have filled the ships ten times over.' The thump of another explosion, closer this time, pierced the tentative hush of the shelter. 'Maybe they'll send more if this keeps up. You were lucky to get your two away.'

'I don't think any of us could be called lucky, Elsie.'

Lily's thoughts strayed beyond the shelter walls as the Farnaby boy kicked his sister's shin and the girl complained that her brother was breathing too loudly. Lily didn't hear Elsie say that she thought Lily was ever so brave for sending her children overseas, and that she worried, every day, if she'd done the right thing in keeping hers in London, what with the bombs falling every night, more and more of the bloody things. Lily's mind was already far from the shelter, following the train tracks north toward Liverpool, to the boarding school where the children would sleep before setting out on their long Atlantic crossing to Canada.

It was probably just as well she'd had such short notice in the end. Just a day to pack their suitcases according to the strict CORB instructions. *Warm coat + mackintosh, hat/beret/cap, 1 pair gloves, 1 suit (boys), 1 pullover, 2 shirts (coloured), 1 warm dress or skirt and jumper (girls), pyjamas, 1 towel, comb, 6 handkerchiefs, face flannel, toothbrush and paste, 1 suitcase, Bible or New Testament, ration card, identity card, stationery and pencil, sanitary towels, sewing kit*, on and on. She didn't know how she'd ever managed to tie the identification labels onto their coats, as if they were goods to be displayed in a shop window. She ached for them. Physically ached.

'Did you meet their escort?' Elsie asked. 'I heard it was unbearably sad at the hotel where they all assembled.'

Lost in her thoughts, Lily took a moment to realize Elsie was talking to her. 'I did. Yes.' She was glad she'd asked for the children to be collected from home; glad she'd been able to close the front door and sink to her knees in the hallway, to process her anguish in private.

'People are very kind, aren't they?' Elsie continued. 'To go all that way with other people's children. Very brave. Not sure I'd be up to it.'

'Yes, very kind,' Lily agreed. 'Very brave.'

She'd only exchanged a few brief words with Alice King, but Lily hadn't stopped thinking about her and the quiet, almost apologetic, way she'd taken the children. Now, as Lily listened to the whistle and boom of distant bombs beyond the shelter walls, she wondered what unsettling sounds Alice King was listening to, and who she was worrying about in the middle of the wretched night. She was the bridge connecting Lily back to her children, which was why, despite knowing hardly anything about her, Alice King was now one of the most important people in Lily's life.

'Suppose we should try to get some sleep,' she said, although she knew she wouldn't sleep at all. The barrage of bombs was relentless. They fell in strings of three, each one seeming to land closer to Elm Street.

Elsie yawned. 'Suppose so.'

Lily pushed her hands into her coat pockets where her fingers found the magpie feather Arthur had picked up a few days ago. The phrase 'One for sorrow' perched in her mind. She imagined Peter saying, *Two for joy!* She'd found the feather in the shoebox beneath Arthur's bed while she was packing the children's suitcases. So many precious little treasures she was always too tired or too busy to stop and admire. In the uncertain dark of the shelter, Lily made a silent promise that when the children came home she would always make time to listen to their eager little soliloquies about found feathers and special sticks, because all that stretched before her now was an infinite sprawling sequence of quiet hours and hushed weeks; an empty calendar; an aching void.

The all-clear finally released them just before five. Outside number 13, halfway down the street, Lily saw Mrs H safely inside, and paused for a moment with her hand on the garden gate. Across the street, William Farnaby stamped on the flowers in Old Mrs Farnaby's front garden. Lily frowned as she watched him, but she didn't see William, she saw Arthur, knees bent as he picked a few blooms for a posy, and there was Georgie beside him, inspecting the same flowers for the insects that fascinated her.

'Makes you feel guilty, doesn't it?' Elsie said as she caught up, having stopped to tend to a howling Mary who'd fallen and cut her knee. 'Knowing others have lost everything during the night, and here we are, about to walk through the front door as if we didn't have a care in the world!'

For a moment, Lily couldn't reply. Elsie's words carried such casual disregard for her own quiet agony, and stirred a deep sense of resentment. She gripped the top of the gate to steady herself. 'I suppose it would be nice to have nothing to worry about. To have your children beside you. Not to have a care in the world.'

Elsie was shocked by the edge to Lily's reply. Lily was also surprised by the depth of her anger.

Elsie pulled her daughter into the folds of her coat. 'I just meant . . . I *do* have things to worry about . . . I just don't . . .'

Lily didn't have the energy for an argument. 'I'm very tired, Elsie. I'll no doubt see you later.'

The familiar rasping squeak of the garden gate was almost too much to bear. Aware that Elsie was watching, Lily walked briskly up the moss-covered path, turned the key in the lock, and stepped inside. Behind the closed door, she rushed to the kitchen and thew up in the sink.

She fell asleep at the kitchen table and was woken by the snap of the letter box. She sat up, stretched out her neck and shoulders and splashed cold water on her face at the sink. She didn't hurry to pick up the post. The year had brought nothing but bad news and she approached the doormat with a sense of trepidation. But it was just another Ministry leaflet, Mrs Sew-and-Sew, advising on how to darn holes in socks and pull-overs. It was a pity Mrs Sew-and-Sew didn't have any advice for how to repair a broken heart. Lily tore the leaflet in half and added it to the basket beside the fire.

Suddenly ravenous for hot buttered toast, she lit the gas and put two slices of slightly stale bread under the grill. She wondered what the children would eat on the ship. She hoped Arthur wouldn't run everywhere, and that Georgie wouldn't encourage his antics. Her thoughts clattered about with all the things they might do, and might need, and might forget, and there was nothing she could do about any of it. The CORB escorts were responsible for them now, and then a different woman in Canada would dry their tears and patch up their grazed knees and remind them to wash their hands.

She took the butter dish from the pantry and groaned as she remembered she'd used the last scrapings yesterday teatime. She glanced at the clock. She still had a couple of hours before she needed to leave for The Beeches. Plenty of time to pop to the corner shop. She didn't get waylaid as she used to. Nobody knew what to say to her now, so they pretended they hadn't seen her, or just ignored her.

She pulled on her shoes, coat and hat, grabbed her purse and ration book and headed out.

At Fletcher's corner shop, Mrs Fletcher wrapped a miserably small cube of butter in brown paper as Lily's eyes strayed to the front pages of the morning papers. Stark headlines declared HORROR IN HULL! and SCENES OF DEVASTATION! from recent bombings across the country. Photographs depicted bleak images of lives and homes destroyed.

'When are you expecting them to arrive, dear?'

'Sorry?' Lily stared at the web of scarlet thread veins that patterned Mrs Fletcher's cheeks. For a moment she couldn't remember what she was doing there.

'The children?' Mrs Fletcher tilted her head to one side the way people did when they were explaining something complicated. 'When will they arrive?'

'A week or so. It depends on the weather mostly.' All she knew was that they were scheduled to depart on the twelfth. A book she'd found in the library had stated that the average sailing time from England to Canada was eight days. Lily placed her hands to her chest, their absence like a stuck lozenge in her throat.

Mrs Fletcher shook her head. 'Poor things. So far from home. But you must be relieved they're going somewhere safe.'

Was she relieved? Was there a sense of relief in any of this? The truth was, she felt as scraped out as the butter dish. She slipped her change into her coin purse. 'I'll be glad when the war is over and they're safely home, where they belong.'

She took the long route back to Elm Street, past the duck pond, and sat for a while on the bench, imagining Georgie and Arthur beside her, shrieking with joy as the ducks pecked at the crumbs around their feet. She thought of all the times Peter had arrived home in his paint-spattered overalls to find the potatoes not peeled and the meat pie waiting to go in the oven. 'We got distracted!' she'd say, as he pulled the children onto his knees and asked them to tell him all about their day, and instead of a hot dinner they would have a picnic in the front room, and they would want for absolutely nothing because they had each other, and it was enough.

It was everything.

Lily did up the top button on her coat as a brisk breeze sent ripples dancing across the duck pond. She watched a young boy squeal with excitement as his toy boat was tossed around dramatically in the small waves, but as the breeze strengthened, the boat tipped onto its side and sank in the middle of the pond. The mother scooped up the distraught child, his forlorn little body cocooned against the curve of her hip as she carried him home.

Lily walked on, lost in her thoughts as a fire engine rushed past, bell clanging. She took no notice. Fire engines were ten a penny these days. But as she turned the corner at the top of Elm Street, she stopped. A crowd was gathered in the road, their faces staring up at a column of thick black smoke billowing from one of the houses halfway down the street. A house with an olive-green front door.

Lily dropped her basket, and ran.

1 January 1940

(Happy?) New Year. Rare sense of optimism about today. Everyone glad to see the back of '39 and hopeful that we'll soon see the end of Adolf bloody Hitler, too. Lovely to have the children back home, but forgot how noisy and messy they are. Keep threatening to send them back to the countryside! (Won't – obviously.)

Mass-Observation, Diarist #6672

11

Liverpool. 13 September 1940

In a fusty dormitory bedroom of a boarding school on the outskirts of Liverpool, Alice lay awake on a lumpy mattress and stared at the ceiling. Her mind was too busy thinking about the journey ahead for her to sleep. In the bed beside her, Beryl Barnes, another CORB escort, snored loudly. Alice threw a pillow at Beryl, pulled the bedcovers over her own head, and waited for daylight.

Their departure had been delayed due to unexploded mines being discovered in the Mersey. It wasn't the most auspicious start to their long journey across the Atlantic, and while Alice wasn't usually superstitious, she couldn't help dwelling on the fact that they were now scheduled to depart on a Friday, the thirteenth, in the middle of a war. At least they'd been spared the disruption of another air raid, unlike the first night. The children were unsettled enough as it was, and air raids certainly didn't help.

'Bad luck isn't it, to set sail on a Friday?' Beryl said as they herded their respective groups of children to Liverpool docks later that morning. 'Old sailors' lore, or something.'

Alice's already heightened sense of trepidation wasn't helped by Beryl's grim contribution. 'Well, if I wasn't worried before, I am now. Don't let the children catch you saying such things.'

Beryl laughed and said Alice worried too much.

Alice said there was a lot to worry about.

The day was bright and calm. The ninety children held hands in pairs, or in threes, and walked in groups of fifteen, topped and tailed by an escort at the front and back. The sight warmed Alice's heart, and broke it at the same time. She tried to focus on the process and practicalities, the importance of getting the children to safety in Canada, but it was impossible not to be moved by the sight of so many children leaving their families and homes, not to mention all the worry and despair they would leave in their wake.

As they turned a corner, the ship they would sail on loomed large in front of them.

'Bad luck or not, we're here now,' Beryl said. 'No going back, as they say.'

The children gasped at their first sighting of SS *Carlisle*, the impressive steamship that would be their home for the next week. They tipped their necks back as they gawped up at the smokestacks and pointed out the portholes and the immense anchor chain, as thick as a tree trunk. Alice was pleased to see them wide-eyed in wonder, their faces bright, their young minds excited by new sights and sounds, their reason for being there momentarily forgotten until Billy Fortune pointed out the guns that were fixed to the deck.

Alice was like a child herself, fascinated by the vibrant collection of people waiting to board the ship. Until now, she'd focused on the CORB evacuees, but of course there were hundreds of other passengers, a mixture of young and old, from all classes of society, British accents mingling with American, Eastern European and others she didn't recognize.

'I hadn't expected so many people,' she said to Beryl, who wasn't listening, having stopped to attend to a little girl who had tripped and grazed her knee. 'You'd wonder where everyone is going in the middle of a war.' It was reassuring to see so many people considering it safe to travel, despite the risks.

The arrival of the evacuees caused quite a stir and all eyes turned to them. Such a large group of children would have been a spectacle in any event, but was even more so in the particular circumstances of their departure. Their arrival brought a spontaneous cheer from the gathered crowds, and cries of 'Good luck' and 'Best of British!' Several immaculately turned-out children boarding via the first-class steps stared at the CORB group. One young girl, walking with the aid of a crutch, tugged on the arm of the woman she was with and whispered something into her ear which made them both laugh.

Eleanor Heath ticked the name of each child off the list on her clipboard as they made their way aboard. 'Really, it's enough to stir the heart of a stone statue,' she said as Alice passed. Even unflappable Eleanor Heath was teetering on an emotional precipice.

Alice encouraged her girls to wave and smile to the gathered well-wishers. She'd learned their names and was beginning to know their individual personalities: the carer, the jester, the teacher, the child. Georgina Nicholls had quickly established herself as the leader of her group. She was an exuberant girl, eager to help. Despite their many differences, collectively they were simply known as seavacs, a tidy label for a generation being sent away to ensure their proud nation would endure, whatever the next few months might bring. As the girls waved and smiled at those who'd come to see them off, Alice recalled her mother's scathing opinions on the matter of evacuation. These weren't horrid little cowards running away, or rats leaving a sinking ship. They were Britain's young ambassadors, and Alice was enormously proud of them.

Once aboard, the children were encouraged to explore the ship, to expel some energy and get their bearings. They gambolled around the deck like spring lambs, absorbing their lavish new surroundings, their excited chatter and bright laughter a balm to the butterflies that danced in Alice's stomach.

Eleanor Heath remarked on what a gift their parents had given them. 'Such freedom already and we've not even left Liverpool. If their parents could see them, any doubts about sending them away would be gone in a flash.'

Alice thought of Lily Nicholls at number 13 Elm Street. Something about the woman's quiet composure had left an impression on her. She wished she could tell her how excited and carefree the children were, wished she could see their smiles for herself.

When a further short delay to their departure was announced, the children were called back to their escorts and encouraged to each write a letter home.

'It's a useful way to fill the time, and it will be nice for your parents to receive a few words from you,' Eleanor said as she handed out paper and pencils.

Alice thought it might upset the parents to hear from their children when they were already halfway across the Atlantic, but she didn't want to appear difficult, so kept her thoughts to herself.

'And one for you, Auntie.' Georgie Nicholls passed Alice a sheet of paper and a pencil.

It still caught Alice by surprise that escorts were called auntie and uncle by the children. She couldn't quite get used to it.

'I think it's just the children writing letters, Georgie,' she said.

'But don't you want to write to your mother and father? I'm sure they'd like to hear from you.'

Alice smiled and took the paper and pencil. 'Of course.'

With the children quietly occupied and the breeze ruffling the hem of her skirt, Alice's pencil hovered over the page. She looked at the water beckoning her on, and wished, with all her heart, she could tell her father what she was about to do.

So she did.

Lost in her thoughts, she jumped when Eleanor clapped her hands and announced that the last of the mines had been cleared and they were, finally, ready to depart.

A fizz of anticipation passed among the children. A mixture of anxious and hopeful glances were exchanged among the escorts. The children's letters were collected and given to a crew member who was leaving the ship and would arrange for them to be posted on to their parents. Three blasts of the ship's whistle indicated that they were ready to raise anchor and set sail.

Alice remained on deck with her group of girls. The children waved back to the dock workers and well-wishers who raised their hats and cheered loudly as their mighty ship of hope slipped anchor and set out with its precious cargo. Alice swallowed a lump of emotion as the Three Graces of Liverpool's waterfront – the Renaissance-style Cunard Building, the soaring clock towers of the Liver Building with their mythical birds, the Port of Liverpool Building – disappeared behind a light sea mist. As the coastline slowly shrank away, Alice wondered what sort of England the children would return to, and when they would return. War didn't come with an end date. Evacuating the children was all anyone had talked about. Bringing them home again felt like an afterthought, a matter for someone else to worry about, at another time.

The engines were stoked and the sea breeze picked up, tangling Alice's hair and bringing goosebumps to her arms, but she found she didn't want to go inside. A thrill ran along her spine as the island she'd lived on her whole life drew further away and the ocean took over, pulling her on. It was invigorating up on deck, the sea churning beneath the ship's hull, the wind blowing colour into her cheeks. Once clear of the Mersey and out in the open water of the Irish Sea, they were met by their impressive naval escort of a destroyer and two sloops. The eighteen other vessels in their convoy also joined them, forming the nine columns they would travel in, headed by SS *Carlisle*, the striking convoy leader at the front of the centre column. It was surely a sight to deter any U-boat commander considering an attack.

That evening, after a delicious dinner in an ornate wood-panelled dining room, and with the children all in bed, Alice was pleased to have a little quiet time alone in the ship's small library. She opened one of several books she'd brought with her and was soon lost in Dickens's world of *David Copperfield*, but the motion of the ship was more obvious now and after a few chapters she began to feel queasy. She joined Beryl for a stroll on deck, glad of the fresh air and a barley sugar. When Beryl found the breeze too chilly and made her way back inside, Alice stayed at the railings, her gaze fixed on the horizon, as they'd been advised in the onset of seasickness.

'I hope *you're* the Alice I'm looking for! I've already drawn a blank with three others!'

Alice recognized the voice behind her. She offered a weak smile as Howard Keane appeared at her side. 'Hello again!'

'Oh dear. You look a bit green.'

'I feel a bit green.'

'Well, if you *are* the right Alice, this might cheer you up.' He held out her treasured copy of *David Copperfield*.

Alice hadn't realized it was lost. 'Goodness! Did I leave it in the library?'

'On a lamp table. I was sure Alice would be keen to be reunited with it. Inscribed books are very special. Fathers too, if you're lucky.' He pushed his hands into his pockets.

There was something about his smile, his lilting voice, the distinctive fleck of amber in an otherwise perfectly green iris that caught Alice off guard, so that all she could do was mutter a thank you in reply.

'It's a bit chilly out here. Bracing, I believe the term is!'

Alice pulled her thin cotton jacket around her shoulders. 'It is, a bit.'

Howard smiled and said he was about to take coffee in the lounge, and whether to fill the silence or for some other reason neither of them yet understood, added, 'I don't suppose you and *David Copperfield* would care to join me?'

12

London. September 1940

In the front bedroom of 14 Elm Street, Lily couldn't sleep. The mattress was too firm. The unfamiliar creaks and cracks of a strange house sent her imagination racing. She stared at the edge of the blackout curtain, willing daylight to wash over Elm Street as her thoughts tumbled back through the events of the last few days. Of course it was Elsie who'd seen the smoke and raised the alarm; Elsie who'd insisted Lily stay with her while the damage was repaired.

She didn't want to stay with Elsie Farnaby, but she didn't want to impose on Mrs Hopkins either. 'If you're sure you don't mind,' she'd conceded, too tired to battle against Elsie's greater will. Elsie had said she didn't want to hear another word about it. 'That's settled then. I'll make up the bed in the front bedroom.'

But nothing was settled at all. Everything was in a terrible disarray.

Lily had never done anything so forgetful and dangerous. The fireman had explained how the flames from the grill had caught on a tea towel that was left on the cooker top, and how that had set a pan of cooking oil alight. 'If your neighbour hadn't seen the smoke and alerted us, it could have been much worse.' Mostly, she was embarrassed to have nearly lost everything because of a forgotten piece of toast and things left lying about, not washed and put away as they would usually be.

She tossed and turned, her mind a jumble of worry, questions without answers. Were the children homesick? Had she packed everything they would need? Would Georgie remember what to do if she got a nosebleed? She imagined a woman in Canada, also lying awake in the middle of the night, wondering about the British guests who would arrive shortly. As difficult as it was to send the children away, Lily imagined it wouldn't be easy to bring a stranger's children into your home. Whoever she was, Lily hoped she was kind. She thought of the few lines she'd written and placed in an envelope inside Georgie's suitcase:

Thank you for giving my children a home during our time of great need. They are well-behaved and will help around the house. Arthur needs help to tie his shoelaces. Georgina has a funny reaction to strawberries. I'm sure you'll discover their likes and dislikes in time. Perhaps we'll meet, one day, when the war is over. Until then, I can't thank you enough.

It was the hardest letter she'd ever written, part thank-you note, part instruction manual; a desperate plea from one woman to another.

The bed sheets were stiff with starch, and cold against Lily's feet. She tucked her knees up to her chest and pulled the eiderdown up to her nose, but she couldn't get warm. She wished she could tell Peter about the kitchen fire, and so many other things. She missed having someone to chat to, to share a joke with, and a pot of tea, and a bed. She missed being half of something so effortlessly whole. She was officially a widow now on forms and paperwork, but she hadn't only lost her husband, she'd lost her best friend, her childhood sweetheart, and a part of herself. There wasn't a special word for that.

Giving up on sleep, Lily got out of bed, walked to the bay window and pulled aside the heavy blackout curtain. Beams of anti-aircraft searchlights criss-crossed the sky like ghosts. Across the street, number 13 was shrouded in darkness. One by one, it had ejected them. First the dog, then Peter, then the children, now her. There was an almost apologetic look about it, as if it were sorry for not keeping them safe. She leaned her head against the window and smiled wistfully as she remembered Peter pushing the gate open and shut, mimicking the squeak of the hinge with an exaggerated, 'Hel-lo, Li-ly!' She'd been so happy there. They all had, most of the time. Only she knew about Peter's 'troubles', as he called his nightmares and brooding thoughts, the lingering shadows cast by the previous war that had raged on in his demobbed father's tormented mind, and had brought a different kind of war to Peter's young life.

She let the blackout curtain fall back into place, pushed her feet into her slippers and padded downstairs to make tea, only to find that Elsie had already had the same idea. Lily didn't have the energy for one of Elsie's conversations and wished she'd stayed upstairs.

'Can't sleep?' Elsie put down her pen and turned over the sheet of paper she was writing on.

Lily shook her head. 'Not a wink.'

'Me neither. There's tea in the pot. I'll grab you a cup.' Elsie stared at her. 'You're ever so pale. Are you eating properly? I sometimes forget, what with all sense of routine gone haywire.'

Now that Elsie mentioned it, Lily realized she hadn't eaten much at all in the last twenty-four hours.

'A bit of something in your tummy will help you sleep,' Elsie pressed. 'Bread and dripping will have to do, I'm afraid.'

Lily sat obediently at the small kitchen table and watched Elsie potter about with first-thing-in-the-morning industriousness as she set out a china cup and saucer, and filled a rose-patterned jug with milk.

'We'd be as well to take this into the shelter,' Lily said as Elsie poured tea from the pot. 'We'll no doubt end up in there at some point during the night.'

'That bloody siren sets my teeth on edge. I don't think I'll ever get used to it, no matter how many times I hear it. David says there's no point lying in bed worrying about it. He says if your number's up, your number's up and that's all there is to it.'

'Where is your husband? Is that who you're writing to?'

Elsie glanced at the kitchen dresser and the photograph of a handsome man in uniform. 'He's at sea. Royal Navy.' She spoke with a thick layer of pride, the way everyone did when they told you where their men were, and what a terrific job they were doing. 'He's leading a naval convoy in the Atlantic, escorting supply ships. I worry about him terribly, but he's never happier than when he's at sea.'

'The children must miss him.'

Elsie nodded. 'William, especially. He's been a bit of a handful since David left. Not the same boy at all. But we're managing as best we can.'

Lily was ashamed to think how rude she'd been to Elsie, and how she'd considered her children unpleasant, spoilt things. They were missing their father. More young lives disrupted by war.

'Anyway, David's due a period of leave after this trip. HMS *Imperial* should be almost back to Scotland by now.' Elsie clamped her hand over her mouth. 'Oops!'

'Didn't hear a thing,' Lily said.

'Never could keep a secret. You don't look like a German spy anyway!' Elsie pulled her chair closer to Lily's. 'You must be missing the children terribly.'

Although she was tired, Lily was glad of the invitation to talk about them. 'I just feel so helpless, and so far away from them. I'm sure I'll relax a little when I know they've safely arrived.'

'Hundreds of ships cross the Atlantic every week,' Elsie said as she poured more tea. 'And the ship your kiddies are on will have the protection of a naval escort and a convoy. That's what my David does. He escorts outgoing vessels to the limit of convoy, then he meets incoming supply ships and comes back. He's in and out of Liverpool as often as the tide!' She passed Lily the milk. 'They'll be fine,' she said. 'Having a wonderful adventure, no doubt. Try not to worry.'

But Lily did worry. 'Civilian ships have been hit in the Atlantic,' she said as she sipped her tea and spread a thin layer of dripping on her bread. She was hungrier than she'd realized.

'*Unescorted* civilian ships,' Elsie countered.

'An evacuee ship was hit a few weeks ago.'

'An awful shock, but everyone survived. Lifeboat drills were followed and everyone was picked up within a few hours. You're tormenting yourself, Lily. Imagining the worst when the worst rarely happens.'

Part of Lily knew Elsie was right. There was no point worrying. They would be on their way now and were in safe hands. But part of her couldn't stop fearing the worst.

'You must miss your husband, too,' Elsie added. 'Where did you say he was?'

Lily was so used to shutting down questions about Peter that it had become an automatic response to deflect the conversation elsewhere. She could never explain in a way that made any sense, or that changed the opinion of those whose minds were firmly made up about people like Peter Nicholls. Mrs Hopkins said as long as Lily knew the truth, that was all that mattered. But sometimes she wished everyone else knew the truth about him, too. She wanted to tell Elsie what a wonderful man Peter was, how shocking and awful it had been, how unbearable it was without him.

She took a deep breath. 'My husband died. Earlier this year.'

For once, Elsie was speechless. 'I'm so sorry. I had no idea. What a nonsense I am, going on and on.'

'You weren't to know. People assume he's away fighting. It's easier not to correct them.'

'I hope he didn't suffer. You hear such awful things, don't you? You poor dear. And with two young children.' Elsie shook her head and reached for Lily's hand as the rising wail of the air-raid siren cut through the silence.

The two women looked at each other.

'Best get our things,' Elsie said.

Lily nodded. 'Best get our things.'

The dreaded papers arrived. Can't stop looking at them, can't actually believe this is happening. The cold weather and short days don't help. Might as well be in blackout the whole day. Even the snowdrops were late this year. Find myself wondering if I'll see them come up next year – and other murky thoughts. Picked a few to put on the spot where the dog was buried, and had a good cry. We've agreed not to cry in front of the children. I spend a lot of time outside.

Mass-Observation, Diarist #6672

13

SS *Carlisle*. September 1940

Alice was surprised at how readily she accepted Howard's invitation. It somehow felt like the most natural thing in the world to have coffee with him, as did their agreement to meet again after lunch the next day. Being at sea lent a lighter air to conversations that might otherwise have been weighed down with expectations and awkward arrangements. The fact that they were on a ship made it almost impossible *not* to meet again.

Talking to Howard was easy and uncomplicated and took Alice's mind off the magnitude of her task. He was full of amusing anecdotes and interesting facts. The children were especially charmed by his seemingly endless repertoire of games and magic tricks to cheer them up when they were glum. Everyone loved Uncle Howard. Eleanor Heath got in a flap whenever she spoke to him, and Beryl Barnes flushed scarlet if he so much as looked at her, but Alice felt strangely calm in his company, as if she'd reconnected with a long-lost friend. They discovered they had lots of things in common: both schoolteachers, both the middle child, both bookworms. She lived in Whitstable in north Kent. He lived in Whitby, North Yorkshire, 'although originally from Portrush in Northern Ireland,' he said. 'But let's not allow that to spoil the symmetry!' They found the coincidences amusing. Alice found the easy connection between them increasingly hard to ignore, although when Beryl remarked on it she scoffed, insisting they were just enjoying each other's company.

'He's very charming, but I'm too busy with the children for "romantic inclinations", as you put it.'

Beryl didn't believe her. Alice wasn't entirely sure she believed herself.

As the wind strengthened during the first two nights, seasickness among the evacuees kept all the CORB escorts busy. For most of the children, it was their first time at sea, and the rolling motion of the ship saw them laid up in their cabins, a bucket within reach. Barley water was dispensed with abandon by the escorts, even though many of them were suffering too, Alice especially.

'The up and down isn't so bad,' Alice said as she offered Howard the ginger biscuit that had been served with her coffee. She couldn't stomach it herself. 'It's the side to side that gets me.'

'It's the swell,' he explained. 'The continuing motion of waves, like the ripples you see when you drop a stone into water.' He moved his hands in exaggerated dips and curves to emphasize his point.

Alice's stomach turned somersaults. 'Would you mind if we went outside?'

The bracing sea air helped a little. She stood at the railings and took deep breaths, her eyes on the horizon.

Howard stayed with her. He didn't suffer himself and found everyone else's seasickness mildly amusing. 'It's some feeling though, isn't it? Steaming across the Atlantic. The wind in your hair. The power of the ocean all around you.'

Alice understood the sentiment, despite her nausea. The static nature of her life in Whitstable already felt so stifling in comparison. The continual sense of forward motion was invigorating, even if her stomach couldn't keep up.

Howard rubbed his hand over the iron railings. 'She's a good ship, this one. A gentle old soul.'

Alice laughed at the notion of a ship having a soul. 'You'll be telling me it has a family next!'

'I'm serious! And it probably does have a family – a sister ship, at least. All ships have a personality. Some are tormented. Others are like unruly children. This one feels like a kind grandparent, as if it knows it is taking children from danger to safety.'

Alice's gaze strayed to the reassuring lights from the other vessels in their impressive convoy. 'I hope this old soul keeps us safe.'

'You're not nervous, are you?'

'A little.'

'Don't be.' Howard nodded toward the large naval destroyer on their left flank. 'We're in very safe hands. The might of the Admiralty watching over us.'

His voice was calm, reassuring. He was right. They were very well protected.

'Do you mind me asking why you volunteered?' he asked. 'I spectacularly failed my conscription medical. Seems that I have a weak heart. And flat feet, although they don't worry about that as much as they did in the other war.'

'I'm sorry,' Alice offered. 'About your heart. And your feet.'

It sounded so funny, they both laughed.

'I'm not sorry. I'd rather be here than over there, although I probably shouldn't admit that. Not quite the right thing to do, is it? Admit to being afraid of fighting.'

Alice thought about Walter and felt a sudden pang of home-sickness, for him and Kitty.

'Well?' Howard prompted. 'What about you? Don't tell me you have flat feet as well!'

Alice stalled. There were so many reasons that had led her here. 'I felt that it was something I could do, something I'd be suited to. And because . . .'

'Because?'

She took a deep breath. 'It sounds silly, but I wanted to do something different. Something unexpected. Something brave.' She heard the echo of Kitty's words as she looked at Howard. 'And here I am, trying not to lose my dinner over the railings! Not so brave after all.'

Howard laughed. 'Nonsense. You're here, aren't you. That makes you brave in my estimation.'

She didn't know what to say to that.

Reluctantly, she let go of the railings. 'We should probably get back to the flock. Pity I can't stay out here until we get to Canada.'

'Pity we have to turn around and sail straight back to England when we get there. I've always wanted to see Canada. The Rockies. Niagara Falls. In fact, maybe I will, when we've shipped all the evacuees across the Atlantic, after the war.'

Alice smiled to herself. Another coincidence. A painting of Niagara Falls hung in her father's study. He'd promised he would take her there one day.

'What will you do?' Howard asked as they made their way back to the deck door. 'After the war? When things get back to normal?'

Alice couldn't think that far ahead. Her plan to apply for a teaching position at a prestigious boarding school now felt like a barely heard whisper. Her other, intensely private, ambition to own her own bookshop, now nothing but a fanciful dream. 'I can hardly think beyond tomorrow! It's impossible to think about life after the war when we don't even know how long the war will last, or what the outcome will be.'

'Ahh. A pessimist! Finally, we discover a difference. I'm entirely the opposite. War makes me impulsive. It makes me want to plan and do things I've always wanted to. I refuse to let it make me bitter and angry. If we do that, they've already won.' He pointed towards the ocean. 'There's a whole remarkable world out there, Alice. Let's make a pact.'

'A pact?'

'That we won't go back to the lives we've left behind, that we'll stay curious, keep moving forward. "If adventures will not befall a lady in her own village, she must seek them abroad."'

Alice smiled at the quote. 'A fan of Austen, I see.'

'A fan of my sister. She must have read *Northanger Abbey* at least a dozen times!'

The look of wild enthusiasm on Howard's face was so unexpected and exhilarating and infectious that Alice laughed, and agreed to his pact. There were so many things she couldn't be sure of, so many questions without answers, but for once she shushed all the uncertainty and doubt and embraced the possibility of better things and happier times to come. The wind buffeted her cheeks as the *Carlisle* steamed ahead and, for a brief perfect moment, as she looked toward the path of moonlight on the horizon, the sounds of war were silenced and Alice's heart thrummed to the tune of adventure and hope.

By their fifth day at sea, the majority of adults and children were finally free of the debilitating seasickness. With renewed energy, the children spent most of the day on deck, playing games of quoits and shuffleboard. Their high spirits lent a real sense of optimism to the day, and yet there was intense discussion among the adults. Overnight, their naval escort had left. Everyone had become so used to the reassuring sight of the Royal Navy destroyer and the two smaller warships flanking them as they progressed into the mid-Atlantic that their absence was quickly noted, and not without concern.

'Nothing to worry about,' Eleanor asserted when Beryl Barnes mentioned it at the daily escort briefing. 'Evidently, we are now beyond the point in our journey where the threat of U-boat attack was believed to be the greatest. We are, I am told, some six hundred miles from land. We are now in safer waters, beyond any recorded U-boat activity. Hence, the need for the escort is lessened.'

Beryl was satisfied with Eleanor's explanation, but Alice wasn't as easily reassured. She'd presumed the naval escort would see them all the way to Canada, but at least the other vessels in their convoy were still in their columns, travelling parallel to them. SS *Carlisle* was the lead vessel, or 'convoy commodore'. She had to trust those in charge.

'Given that the immediate danger has passed, we can allow the children to change into their nightclothes this evening,' Eleanor added. 'I expect they will be very pleased to hear it.'

Alice's girls were delighted. They'd found it uncomfortable to sleep fully clothed as they'd been required to so far. Georgie Nicholls said she would still sleep in her overcoat because she'd promised her mother. Some of the children had new nightdresses and pyjamas and couldn't wait to put them on.

Their enthusiasm was infectious. As the day progressed, Alice stopped worrying about the absence of the naval escort, and started to think about their arrival in Canada. There would be a lot to do to match up the children with the many host families. It would be hard to say goodbye to her young charges, but there were plenty more children in England waiting for the next sailing. According to news from home, relayed by the captain, there was no sign of any let-up in the nightly bombing raids, despite the

RAFs success in suppressing the Luftwaffe's most intense aerial attack yet, two days after they'd set sail. While a land invasion had been prevented, bombing from the air had not.

Free of her nausea, Alice finally found the appetite that had eluded her since Liverpool and rather indulged herself with food and wine at dinner that evening. Emboldened by two glasses of Burgundy, she was unusually vocal during a vibrant debate about Schrödinger's thought experiment involving a hypothetical cat being simultaneously alive and dead in a box.

Eleanor Heath couldn't get her head around the concept at all. 'Of course the cat is dead if you leave it in there long enough!'

Howard found her consternation amusing. 'But until you open the box, Eleanor, how can you be sure? Therefore, the cat is alive until such time as the box is opened and its demise has been confirmed.'

Declaring it a nonsense experiment, Eleanor moved the conversation on to the more familiar matter of disembarkation procedures once they reached Canada.

The conversation, the wine, the opulent surroundings of the dining room, and the company left Alice light-headed, happy in a way she hadn't quite experienced before. As desserts were finished and dinner wound up, she hoped Howard might ask her to join him for a nightcap, but Eleanor had other plans.

'It was an interesting conversation, Mr Keane. Most frustrating, but enjoyable nevertheless. Miss King, coffee and a stroll on deck?'

Alice said that would be lovely and suddenly felt very tired. Eleanor clearly hadn't noticed (or had chosen to ignore) the friendship developing between her and Howard.

Howard politely excused himself. 'I look forward to continuing our conversation tomorrow, ladies. I'll wish you goodnight and leave you to enjoy your coffee while I retreat to my cabin with the delightful *David Copperfield*.'

'How are you finding it?' Alice had insisted Howard borrow the book after he'd admitted he'd never read it.

'It's terrific! Young David and I have just met Uriah Heep. I suspect we are in for some trouble.'

They held each other's gaze a moment longer than was necessary.

'Goodnight then,' he said.

'Goodnight,' Alice replied.

But neither of them moved, and it was Eleanor in the end who asked Mr Keane if he was ever going to leave, at which he laughed and wished them both a goodnight again.

Alice smiled into her coffee cup.

'I do hope you're not becoming *distracted*, Miss King.'

So Eleanor *had* noticed. 'Of course not.'

'Good. Mr Keane is disarmingly pleasant, but we have an important job to do. Now, how about that stroll on deck? A blast of cold air might do you good.'

The winds had freshened again during the evening. Word was that another storm was headed their way.

14

London. September 1940

Lily yawned, rubbed a film of condensation from the window of the omnibus and stared numbly out at the bomb-damaged houses and the sandbags piled against shop fronts. She'd barely slept last night, restless in an unfamiliar bed, and then restless in the shelter. She certainly wasn't in the mood for Isobel Carr, but it was better to keep busy and take her mind off things.

As the bus rumbled on, Lily's gaze strayed to young women walking past, dressed in smart skirts and blouses, making their way to offices and typing pools. She imagined herself walking with them, arm in arm, laughing about something or other, successful women who'd fulfilled the potential of the promising young students they'd once been, surrounded by maths books and calculations. But like the omnibus as it picked its way around London's bomb-damaged streets, Lily's life had taken a different route, and while she wouldn't change her life with Peter, Georgie and Arthur for anything, sometimes, just sometimes, she wondered what she might be doing and where the bus might be taking her if things had gone in a different direction.

She yawned again, picked up a newspaper someone had left on the seat beside her, and completed the crossword. Her mind craved the challenge, but she savoured the distraction just as much. As she worked through the cryptic clues and plucked obscure words from her vocabulary, she momentarily forgot about the children and evacuation. A welcome reprieve.

When she'd finished, she tore the page from the newspaper, folded the completed crossword and put it in her handbag for future reference. Behind her, a man cleared his throat and tapped her on the shoulder.

'Excuse me, miss. I couldn't help noticing how quickly you finished that crossword. Do you always complete them?'

She nodded. 'Mostly, yes.'

He studied her a moment before pulling a business card from his jacket pocket. 'We're looking for the brightest minds in Britain. No obligation, but come along if you're interested in finding out more.'

Lily looked at the card with an address in Baker Street, and laughed. 'Thank you, but if you're looking for the brightest minds, I'm afraid you're looking in the wrong place!' She passed the card back to him.

He didn't seem surprised. 'Of course. But if you change your mind, go to 64 Baker Street and tell them Wimborne sent you. Tell them you're interested in the Stately 'Omes of England.'

To be polite, Lily said she would, and turned back around in her seat. She was glad to reach her stop a few minutes later.

As the omnibus pulled away, the man smiled and tipped his hat at her. Lily buttoned her coat, and thought no more about it.

From Richmond town centre, she made her way to the river, following the path toward the incline up Richmond Hill. She passed a group of women and children asleep beneath the arches of the bridge that crossed the Thames, and others, huddled like piles of washday laundry on the banks of the river, but her head was too full of other thoughts to pay much attention.

At the top of the hill, she stopped to look out over Petersham Meadows toward the city. The view she'd often admired was so different now, the amber glow from the fires in the East End rusting the sky, the barrage balloons like ink blots. As the church clock struck the hour, she pushed her hands into her coat pockets and carried on up the hill. One foot in front of the other. Sometimes, it was all she felt capable of.

Mrs Carr was waiting at the boot room door, her face pinched and anxious. 'Thank goodness you're here, Lilian. We're in a bit of a predicament I'm afraid. We've been infiltrated.'

'Oh dear. Rats?' Lily took off her coat and hung it up.

'Of a sort, yes.' Isobel placed her finger to her lips and led Lily down the back stairs. At the bottom, she pointed toward the staff kitchen.

Lily peered around the door to see a dozen or so women and several children sitting around the table, a few bags and small cases strewn across the floor. They all looked exhausted.

'Evacuees,' Mrs Carr whispered. 'From the East End. Arrived last night in their hundreds. Boats and barges full of them. Susie let these in. I've already had words with her.'

Lily now understood the huddled groups she'd seen under the bridge. 'Poor things must have been terrified. Imagine having to leave your home and everything you own. You can still see the fires burning from here.'

'Yes, but they can't *stay*.'

'Why not?'

'Why not! Because this is my home, Lilian, not a poor house. According to the gardener they're swarming all over Richmond, knocking on basement doors. Some are even sleeping in the picture house. We'll be inundated if word gets out. There must be a communal shelter they can put them in, or something.'

Or something.

Lily looked at the bewildered women and children, and thought about the three Carr girls, shipped away to safety with their very best dresses and favourite toys, given the finest first-class accommodation. 'Surely you could let them stay for a few days? Until they get themselves organized.'

Mrs Carr huffed and folded her arms. 'I don't really have much choice, do I? I'll look uncharitable if I send them away now.'

Lily bit her tongue. She imagined Peter beside her. He'd thought Isobel Carr was an insufferable snob and hated that Lily worked for her.

'Anyway, I suggest you get on,' Mrs Carr continued with a dramatic prolonged sigh. 'We apparently need extra beds to be made up for a start.'

Lily stepped into the kitchen. The poor things hadn't even been given a cup of tea.

A woman resting her head on the table sat up. Lily remembered her – the Wedgwood-blue linen cloche, the patterns and swirls in the tired-looking tea dress.

'Mrs Fortune?' The name had stayed with her. 'Ada?'

The woman stared at Lily blankly. 'I'm Ada Fortune. Do I know you?'

'I'm Lily Nicholls. We met a few months back. In the queue to sign the children up for evacuation.'

The woman shook her head. 'I'm sorry, love. I don't remember.'

She was hardly recognizable as the lively woman Lily had spoken to just a few months ago. Her face was tired and drawn, her eyes spoke of loss and unimaginable things.

'I remembered your name,' Lily said. 'Fortune. I hoped it would bring your children good luck.'

'Everything's gone,' Ada said. 'The house, the pigeons, every-thing. Nothing but a pile of rubble and feathers.' Tears slipped down her cheeks and dropped onto the table. She was too exhausted to brush them away.

Lily didn't know what to say, except how sorry she was. It was such an odd word – sorry – an apology dressed up as sympathy. It never felt enough. 'Your children? Did they get a place on the seavac ships?'

'Yes, thank the Lord. All of them. Gone off to Canada.'

That was something, at least.

Lily couldn't bear to leave Ada sitting in the staff kitchen, considered as nothing better than vermin. She led her gently to one side of the room. 'You can stay with me,' she said. 'Come with me when I finish up this afternoon.' As she made the offer, she remembered she wasn't even staying in her own home. Maybe it was time she went back to number 13. What did a bit of smoke damage matter when other people's houses had been flattened?

Ada shook her head. 'You're very kind love, but I wouldn't want to put you to any trouble. The maid said we can stay here for the time being. To be honest, I'm too exhausted to go anywhere. I'll sleep right here on the floor if needs be.'

Lily grabbed a piece of paper and a pen from a drawer in the dresser, scribbled down her address and handed the paper to Ada. 'Come if you need anything at all. I don't have much, but you're welcome to share it with me. My children have gone away, too. I'd be glad of the company.'

Ada took Lily's hands in hers. 'You're a good woman, Mrs Nicholls. Thank you.'

She folded the paper and put it in her pocket, but Lily sensed she was only being polite and was far too proud to take her up on her offer.

Lily's anger simmered all day as she ironed bed sheets and plumped pillows for the East End evacuees to sleep on that night.

She was glad they'd come to The Beeches, glad that Mrs Carr had been forced to confront the reality of war up close. Maybe, if she saw for herself the people whose lives had been upended by something far more devastating than pulling up a few rose bushes, she would put aside her privilege and welcome these poor souls into her home.

Before she finished for the day, Lily knocked on the door of the Rose Room where Mrs Carr was taking her afternoon nap.

She startled when Lily walked in. 'Lilian? What on earth—'

Lily cleared her throat. 'Sorry to disturb, but I wanted to remind you that there are thirteen desperate women and five terrified children downstairs, and I think you should let them stay as long as they want.' Her hands trembled in her coat pockets.

Mrs Carr stared at her. 'Was that all?'

'Not quite.' Lily took a deep breath. 'You know, the bend in the river out east might determine someone's status in life, but it doesn't make them any less deserving of a chance to keep their children safe. Those women downstairs are mothers and daughters and wives, just like you. They want the best for their children, just like you.'

At this, Mrs Carr laughed. 'I can assure you, those *creatures* downstairs are *nothing* like me. We are hardly even the same species.'

Lily bristled. 'No, you're right. They *are* nothing like you. They're far better than you.'

Mrs Carr stood up. 'Well! I have never—'

'I'll see myself out.'

Lily walked out of the austere room, along the polished maple floors of the entrance hall, and, heart pounding, left by the main entrance, her shoes crunching satisfyingly over the pristine stones of the carriage circle.

Her heart was still racing, her body fizzing with adrenaline and anger as the omnibus took a detour around Putney High

Street to avoid a burst water main. Lily leaned her head against the window. The government's message that the people of Britain were 'all in this together' wasn't true, even if Her Majesty did think she could face the East End now that Buckingham Palace had been hit. Until the bombs started to fall on the grand houses in Richmond and the wealthy mourned *their* children, there would always be one war for the poor, another for the rich.

'I brought the milk in for you,' Elsie said as Lily told her about the evacuees from the East End after supper that evening. 'Hope you don't mind, but it was under assault from the sparrows. You should pop over again yourself. Air the rooms and check for post. I can come with you if you like? See how things are? The smell of smoke should have gone by now.'

Lily said she would go first thing in the morning. She'd put it off for too long. She hadn't intended to stay at number 14 for more than a night or two, but despite finding Elsie's relentless chatter exhausting, a bit of company was a welcome distraction. It was certainly preferable to the stark silence waiting for her across the road.

'I'm sure there's nothing urgent anyway,' she said. 'All I seem to get in the post these days are bills and leaflets from the Ministry.'

Elsie nodded and, for once, left the conversation there and returned to her pen and notepad.

Right on cue, the siren went off just after eight.

After the all-clear several hours later, Lily found herself, once again, lying awake in a stranger's bed, alone, and yet surrounded by memories. She'd always liked patterns and routine, but now they only emphasized the things that were missing. It was so hard sometimes to keep going, to wake up and get dressed and go about her day knowing that it would end the same way: without Peter, and now without the children, too. Sometimes it felt too hard to make a meaningful life out of what was left.

Eventually, she slept, but her dreams that night were especially chaotic, the children shouting for her, someone calling for help, until she sat up with a jolt, panicking because the children weren't in her arms and she was sure she'd grabbed them both. But they were never in her arms. It was only a dream.

She let out a long tense breath. The children would be in Canada any day now, the dangers of their journey behind them. A rare bud of optimism unfurled in her heart as she lay back down, and settled in for her now nightly vigil, watching the edge of the blackout curtains, waiting for the release of morning.

15

SS *Carlisle*. 17 September 1940

It was two minutes after ten when the torpedo hit.

Alice had just finished her after-dinner stroll with Eleanor and said she would turn in for the night when the violent shudder of the impact knocked her sideways. The deck vibrated beneath her feet as she gripped the railings.

'What was that? You don't think . . .'

Eleanor pushed her shoulders back. 'Most likely hit a whale. Go and get your life jacket then check on the girls. I'll see what I can find out. And Alice . . .'

'Yes?'

'No need to panic.'

Alice checked her wristwatch as she made her way to her cabin. It felt important to make a note of the time. She walked quickly, passing other people who were grim-faced. Nobody spoke, afraid to acknowledge what they all suspected.

In her cabin, Alice grabbed her life jacket and hurried on along the corridor, her only thought to get to the children. As she made her way down a set of stairs, a loud siren started up. Three sharp shrill blasts. She thought back to the emergency drills, but couldn't remember whether it was three blasts or a continual siren that meant abandon ship.

She pressed on, but found the stairwell to the girls' cabins blocked by a sickening tangle of shattered wood and twisted metal. Dark churning water already licked at the bottom of the steps. The ship gave a sudden lurch to the right as more water gushed into the lower compartments with appalling force and speed. Whatever had hit the ship must have caused serious damage. Alice stared at the terrible scene in front of her. The violence and noise of the water was terrifying. She began to shake, her body reacting to the shock. She had to get to the children, but she couldn't possibly go any further.

As she turned to try and find another way down to the cabins, a woman – a maid? – rushed past, struggling against the increasing incline of the corridor. 'Get up on deck, miss!' she shouted. 'Get to your muster station.'

Alice followed the woman, praying that the girls in her group were already on deck, but her progress was hampered by the bulky life jacket and the list of the ship, so that she walked like a drunk, staggering suddenly to one side. As she emerged onto the boat deck, wild gusts of wind snatched her breath away and lashing sideways rain made it almost impossible to see. Above the wind, she could hear panicked shouts and desperate cries. This was nothing like the calm order of the lifeboat drills she'd attended. This was a ship in crisis.

Head down, Alice stumbled toward the muster station for lifeboat seven where she found a dozen girls gathered, with Beryl Barnes instructing them to keep calm as they climbed into the lifeboat.

'Girls! Beryl! Thank goodness!' Alice frantically counted seven girls from her group.

Beryl's eyes were wide with fear. 'Torpedo strike. She's going down.'

Alice nodded as she tried to steady her breathing and ignore the clattering of her heart in her chest. 'Make sure your life jackets are securely fastened, girls,' she said, shouting to be heard above the noise. Bewildered faces stared back at her, small bodies shivering in paper-thin nightdresses. Only one of the girls wore an overcoat. 'And don't worry,' Alice added. 'The other ships will come to help.' As she spoke, a distress flare sent a burst of light into the sky above.

To Alice's right, a lifeboat jammed on its davits as it was being lowered. She looked on in horror as it swung wildly from left to right, then tilted sharply down and hung for a moment until a cable snapped and sent everyone inside spilling into the water like pennies thrown into a wishing well. The girls screamed. Alice turned her face away. Memories raced through her mind: the dying pilot crying for his mother, Walter draping her silk scarf over the young man's bloodied face, the sea breeze in Kitty's hair as she told Alice she wished she would do something unexpected and brave, the lifeless form of the runt of the dog's litter. *You can't save everyone, Alice. You can't save them all.*

'I'm going back for the others,' she said.

Beryl grabbed her arm. 'It isn't safe, Alice! You have to get into the lifeboat.'

'I can't leave them!'

Before Beryl could say anything else, Alice turned and made her way back to the door she'd just come through.

Inside, the ship creaked and groaned ominously. Alice hurried back along the corridors, passing people going the other way. Driven by a primal instinct to help, at the stairwell to the cabins, she pulled desperately at the shattered wood and the steel beams that blocked her way. She gasped at the shock of ice-cold seawater against her stockings and shoes.

A passing crew member saw her. 'You have to go up, miss! Torpedo strike. Captain's orders to abandon ship.'

Alice pulled and kicked at a stubborn beam. 'There are children down there! I have to help them.' Her words were drowned out by the persistent wail of the siren.

The young man looked at the impossible tangle of metal and wood. 'You can't save the dead, miss, but you can save yourself. Get to a lifeboat before it's too late!'

Alice couldn't bear to walk away knowing children were trapped below. *We can't save everyone, Alice. No matter how desperately we want to, or how deeply we care for them, we can't save them all.* She pulled at the beam once more, wishing she were stronger, wishing Walter were there with his great arms. The water was now at her knees and rising fast. She let out a panicked cry and, choking back tears, hurried back to the muster station, but lifeboat seven had already launched.

She looked around wildly. All the lifeboats had gone.

As a crew member rushed past, she grabbed his arm. 'I was supposed to take lifeboat seven! What shall I do?'

'There's one boat left,' he said. 'Forward port. Lifeboat twelve.'

Alice hurried to the front of the ship. All around her, lifeboats swayed wildly on their ropes, dangling over the side of the great ship like puppet show props. Three were quickly overturned by the strength of the waves. Too many people were in the water.

SS *Carlisle* already sat dangerously low in the ocean. Alice peered over the railings. Some seven feet below, the last lifeboat to be lowered was just reaching the water. It was now, or never. The wind was so strong it snatched her breath away, leaving her gasping for air as she half-stumbled, half-jumped, and fell, face down, against the boards in the bottom of the boat. She tried to pull herself up, but the lifeboat pitched violently as another monstrous wave smashed into them and threw Alice into a woman beside her. The woman lost her grip on the rain-

slicked mast, and tumbled, with extraordinary grace, into the
dark ocean, her white nightdress unfurling around her, spinning
and twirling as if she were a ballerina in a pirouette. Too shocked
to respond, Alice couldn't look away.

'Miss, can you help them?'

Alice turned to see a tall man in plaid pyjamas emerge through
the rain. He grabbed the mast to steady himself as he pointed
toward something at the other end of the lifeboat.

'Miss! *Miss!* Can you help the children?'

Part Two – Absence

16

SS *Carlisle*. Mid-Atlantic. 17 September 1940

Alice hears the crack and snap of wood and metal, the broken bones and wounded flesh of their dying ship. The boy in the coat grabs her arm tight as a low metallic groan slices through the dark.

'What's that noise?' he asks. The chilling sound comes again, adding to the howl of the storm and the clamour and confusion of panicked voices that fill the lifeboat. 'Is it another torpedo?'

'It's the *Carlisle*,' Alice says. 'She's going down.' It is the sound of despair, she thinks. The sound of mothers and fathers sinking to their knees as they learn the fate of the ship that was supposed to take their children to safety. The finality of it is horrifying.

The boy can't comprehend that a ship as big as the *Carlisle* can possibly sink. 'All of it?' he asks, his tiny piping voice so misplaced among such brutal turmoil. 'The smokestacks, and everything?'

Alice holds his hand. 'Yes, dear. All of it. Everything. Even the smokestacks.'

He nudges a boy beside him. 'It's going down, Billy! And all your marbles with it.'

The boy, a bedraggled scrap of a thing, hugs his knees tight to his chest and shrugs. His silent acknowledgement is devastating. So many little treasures lost, so much so violently destroyed.

It takes Alice a moment to recognize little Billy Fortune, the boy from the station platform in London, shoelaces undone, cap falling over his eyes, a prized marble in his coat pocket. The boy in Howard's group. 'A real character,' he'd said.

Billy pats the pocket of his pyjama top. 'Still have my best shooter though. Stinking Nazis can't have everything.'

Alice could cry at his staunch defiance.

The lifeboat pitches and rolls erratically in the swell caused by the slip and suck of the sinking ship. Alice braces herself as cries and screams rise up from those around her. A group of six men, who seem to have taken charge, shout urgent instructions to each other to row away, to pull hard to starboard. Alice shouts above the noise to tell the children to hold hands as the *Carlisle*'s proud stern plunges beneath the waves, and disappears.

It is unfathomable to Alice that the pristine restaurant she'd drunk coffee in that evening, the linen-draped tables, the bone-china cups and saucers, every breakfast bowl and butter knife, every gilt-framed seascape and polished brass handrail, every library book and reading chair and table lamp are now lost to the ocean. She focuses on fixtures and fittings because it is impossible to acknowledge the questions that sit like stones dropped into her heart and send ripples of dread coursing through her: What *has* happened to everyone else? Where are they all?

Another huge wave hits them sideways. Alice gasps, certain they are going over this time and that this is how she will die. Not by a bomb from the Luftwaffe's air raids, but by drowning in the mid-Atlantic. At the front of the lifeboat, a man stands up and grasps erratically at the iron handles that are used to steer the boat. He shouts something about going back to help. As those closest to him scream at him to sit down, the lifeboat lists heavily and he loses his balance and falls overboard. He is instantly swept away by the swell. The first thought that crosses Alice's mind is that he was wearing an overcoat and hadn't offered it to the children when she'd asked. Behind her, another man clutches his chest and slumps to his knees saying he can't breathe. A well-spoken man attends to him as best he can in the cramped conditions. The bulky life jackets they all wear make movements clumsy and awkward. To Alice's right, an American man says something about keeping the children warm and throws a knitted sweater to her. Two of the boys huddle inside it.

Amid the chaos and the dark, Alice searches for memories of her quiet gentle life; precious moments she wants to remember if this is where it all ends: jumping over the waves with Walter; her cheek resting against her father's shoulder as he pointed out the constellations in the inky blue skies of late summer; Kitty helping her to save a baby bird thrown from its nest in a spring storm.

Billy Fortune wraps his arms around Alice's legs and sobs. 'When will it stop, Auntie? Please make it stop.'

'Soon, Billy. Very soon.' Help will arrive at any moment. She is sure of it. The other ships in their convoy will rush to help them.

The girl starts to cry.

A bigger boy tells her crying isn't going to help anyone.

The boy in the coat tugs on Alice's sleeve. 'I'm afraid of the dark, Auntie.'

Alice had found it endearing the way the children called the escorts 'uncle' and 'auntie'. It had lent a sense of family and familiarity to the unsettling business of evacuation, but now she feels suffocated by the word 'auntie', smothered by the profound responsibility it carries in the face of such danger.

We can't save everyone. We can't save them all . . .

But that doesn't mean we shouldn't try . . .

A rush of nausea washes over her. She turns away from the children and retches violently over the side of the lifeboat.

Conditions worsen as the night presses on and the storm intensifies. Alice wraps herself into a tight cocoon, her body wracked with convulsions, her mind a jumble. Still, nobody has come to their aid. Still, the ocean threatens to capsize them with every thunderous wave. She thinks about Kitty and Walter, Maud, her mother, the girls in her group, none of whom are in this lifeboat. She prays that Eleanor and Beryl and the other escorts are safe. And what of Howard?

To her right, someone whimpers. To her left, someone prays. Behind her, someone inexplicably plays a harmonica. Just ahead, two men attend to another who is injured. In front of them, the same scene is repeated. The man she'd seen clutching his chest seems to have recovered a little and is being reassured by the well-spoken young man in evening dress. At the other end of the lifeboat, the man in the plaid pyjamas, and three other men, search through the emergency supplies beneath the thwarts. There is a sense of urgency and industry, a lot of movement and noise, scraps of shouted conversation that are snatched away by the wind before Alice can make any sense of them, and all the while, the children cling to her, only the whites of their eyes visible through the murk. They remind her of a sack of kittens waiting to be drowned, all tangled up in each other in their narrow space at one end of the lifeboat. Prow? Stern? She can't remember. It's hard to believe they are the same children who'd galloped about the boat deck earlier that day, finally free of the seasickness that had plagued them since they left Liverpool. They are such frightened things now, their prize marbles lost, their mothers many hundreds of miles away, all talk of their Canadian adventure forgotten.

Alice tells them to hold hands, to link arms, to sit close together. 'Help is on the way. They'll be here soon.'

Several of the children are seasick. The girl vomits onto her nightdress, and then onto Alice's shoes. Two men have an argument which ends in one punching the other. People step on each other's hands and feet, elbows and knees knock awkwardly into those of strangers, legs are buckled and bent in what small scrap of space people can find. The smell of brine and vomit sticks to the back of Alice's throat and all the while the storm rages and wave after wave smacks into them with such ferocity that she wonders how much longer the lifeboat can withstand it.

There is a small moment of relief when the man in the plaid pyjamas brings the children an emergency blanket each. 'There aren't enough for the adults,' he explains, noticing Alice's disappointment. 'We'll have to take it in turns.'

Like Alice, most of the adults in the lifeboat are still dressed in the clothes they'd eaten dinner in shortly before the torpedo strike. Others are in flimsy nightclothes. There hadn't been time to return to the cabins for sensible things like overcoats and shoes.

The man grabs the gunwale to brace himself. 'How are they doing? The children?'

'Well. Considering.'

'And you? How are you?' His manner is brusque, but his intention is kind.

'I'm fine.'

He nods, understanding that Alice is far from fine but is doing her best to hold it together. He places a hand on her shoulder. 'We've eight of *Carlisle*'s crew on board, and a dozen or so reasonably fit men. Only a handful of casualties. We could be in worse shape.'

She nods. It is something, at least.

'Jimmy,' he says. 'Ship's cook.'

'Alice,' she replies. 'Why aren't the other ships coming to help us? There were eighteen ships in our convoy. Where are they?'

Jimmy glances at the children before responding. 'Rules of convoy.'

'Rules of what?' Alice can hardly hear him above the roar of the wind.

'Convoy. Following orders to scatter. Ships in convoy can't attempt a rescue while there are U-boats in the area. Normal procedure.'

'Normal procedure?' Alice repeats. 'You mean, they deliberately left children to drown?'

She can't believe this is happening. Can't believe they've been abandoned.

Jimmy runs a hand through his sodden hair and shakes his head. 'Rules of convoy,' he repeats. 'They'll come at first light, as soon as it's declared safe.' He staggers and stumbles his way to the other end of the lifeboat.

Behind Alice, the man with the American accent says exactly what she is thinking. 'We'll all be dead by first light. They'll be too late.'

17

London. 20 September 1940

The olive-green front door of number 13 shines in the soft sunlight of early morning. The stained-glass sunburst in the fanlight reflects the light back so that it shimmers on the flagstones at Lily's feet.

As she picks up the milk, Mrs Hopkins's cat appears, winding around her ankles, looking for food.

'Come on then,' she says, glad of the company. 'Let's see if I can spare a drop for you.'

Inside, things aren't as awful as they'd first seemed when she'd popped over a few days earlier. There is still a lingering smell of smoke, and the kitchen is in a sorry state, but it doesn't overwhelm her. She sees manageable individual jobs rather than the dark unwelcoming mess the house had become in her mind. She pours a splash of milk into a saucer, rolls up her sleeves and gets to work, making her way methodically around the house, taking down the blackout blinds, opening windows to let in some fresh air. The cat trails around after her, until it finally settles on Arthur's bed.

Hours pass in busy concentration. Around mid-morning, Lily hears the squeak of the front gate and the snap of the letter box. She spends another twenty minutes tidying the front bedroom before she makes her way downstairs and picks up a single buff-coloured envelope from the doormat. She kicks the draught excluder back against the bottom of the front door, and straightens the lace curtain.

The cat follows her as she walks into the kitchen and sits down at the table. That is when she notices the black edges of the envelope.

She falters.

The cat miaows.

Hands trembling, Lily opens the envelope and removes a single sheet of paper, neatly typed. She glances at the official crest at the top of the page, starts to read, and stops. All the air seems to be sucked from the room, words and sentences blurring on the page as she tries simultaneously to grasp their meaning and throw them away – *very distressed . . .the* Carlisle *. . . torpedoed . . . your children* . . . It is a horrifying, terrifying muddle of things she can't understand, doesn't want to believe.

A rush of blood fills her ears. White spots in her eyes distort her vision as she stands up and backs away from the table, from the letter, distancing herself from the unbearable news sitting there in black type. A high-pitched ringing in her ears grows louder and closer as she lifts her hands to her face, but it is more than her hands lifting up, it is her soul, her whole being, pulling away from the kitchen, from number 13, from Elm Street, because she doesn't want to be there, doesn't want to be Mrs P. Nicholls who has just read the devastating news that the ship carrying her children to safety has been hit by a torpedo and has sunk in the Atlantic.

She leans forward against the table and reads the letter again, absorbing the impossible information with a gut-wrenching gasp as everything she's ever known comes crashing down around her and a terrible, unimaginable future roars into her present.

She sinks to her knees, unable to breathe, unable to draw air into her lungs. She claws desperately at the floor, grasps at the chair leg, but she can't get up. She is made of lead, and the floor is cold against her cheek. She is made of liquid, drowning in grief as the cat dabs playfully at the frayed ends on the ties of her apron.

Later, Elsie Farnaby will tell Lily that the sound she heard through the open window of number 13 that morning was like no human sound she'd ever heard before. What Lily hears in the moment is a bellow, a deep guttural roar as her heart shatters and a smothering suffocating darkness engulfs her.

18

Mid-Atlantic. 18 September 1940

Day One

The power of the open ocean is shocking, the ferocity of the wind appalling as it tosses the lifeboat around like a child's toy. It is nothing like the winter storms Alice has felt batter the north Kent coast. This storm is a monster. It cares nothing for her distress.

Even the first hint of daylight on the horizon seems afraid to show itself too clearly as Alice watches the ominous sky. With so little in their favour, there is relief and hope in the faint smudge of grey. They've survived the torpedo strike and the awful hours in the lifeboat through the violent black of night. Today, they'll be rescued and their ordeal will be over.

Wide awake despite her exhaustion, Alice rubs Billy Fortune's bare feet. She'd been around all the children several times during the night, warming frozen fingers and toes, remembering her father doing the same after she'd played too long in the snow.

'Look, Billy. Daylight. It's the morning.'

The boy's eyes flicker open. 'Will they rescue us now? Can we go home?'

He wheezes when he talks, the cough he'd carried with him from Liverpool still evident in the catch of his voice. 'Yes,' she says. 'They'll rescue us now and then we can go home.'

In front of Alice, in a space no more than three feet across, the children huddle beneath the tarpaulin canopy Jimmy had put up in the night to give them some protection from the storm. They cling to each other as one miserable mass, lurching and swaying as the ocean rises and falls, so that one minute the lifeboat seems to be touching the sky, and the next it is plunging down into a deep trough, surrounded by curtains of seething water. The tarpaulin and blankets that were found in the emergency supplies in the night, and the heavy sweater the American man had given them, offer meagre protection for children dressed only in their nightclothes and with iron-hard rain landing on them like nails. Alice asks again for everyone to give the children anything they can manage without. An extra layer, a pullover, a hat. Anything. She has already given Molly her jacket.

The boy in the coat says he wishes his sister were here. 'Have you seen her, Auntie?'

Alice peers at him through the rain. His cheeks and lips are horribly pale. He resembles a sliver of ice that might melt at any moment.

'Have you seen her?' he repeats.

Alice shakes her head. 'I'm afraid I haven't, but I'm sure she's safe in another lifeboat, no doubt wondering where you are. Try not to worry.' She attempts a reassuring smile, but her face is frozen with cold and guilt. His sister is one of the girls in her group. She should be here, with her. All the girls in her group should be with her.

The boy tucks his knees up to his chest and starts to sob. 'I want my mother. My hands are cold.'

Alice takes the boy's frozen hands in hers and rubs vigorously, first his left hand, then his right. 'You were very sensible to wear your coat.'

He rubs water from his eyes. 'Mother made us promise. She said it would keep us warm if we had to go outside in the night.'

'Then your mother was very clever, Arthur.' Alice thinks about his mother's devastating composure as she'd kissed him and his sister goodbye.

Arthur nods firmly, as if it is the only thing of which he can be certain. 'Do you think she'll mind if I share my coat with Billy?'

'I think your mother would be very proud to know that you offered to share.'

Alice sees Lily Nicholls so clearly: a tall, narrow-framed woman, mahogany hair pin-curled into waves, olive-green eyes that matched the colour of her front door. A look of Katharine Hepburn about her. She'd given Alice an envelope. Something about a white feather. 'A lucky talisman,' she'd said. A silly superstition, to keep the children safe. The envelope was still in the pocket of Alice's jacket, the jacket which was now draped around the young girl.

In scrappy fragments of conversation, shouted between the crash of the waves and the howling wind, Alice learns that in addition to Arthur Nicholls (seven and a half, from Clapham) and Billy Fortune (six years old, from Poplar, in the East End), the other boys in the lifeboat are Brian Walsh, Robert Beck and Hamish Mackie, that they vary in age from nine to twelve, and come from Liverpool, Sunderland and Scarborough. Brian is in shock and can only offer these essential bits of information about himself. Hamish considers it all a great adventure and asks Alice if the newspapers will want to take their picture when they get home. She says she doesn't know, and silently hopes not. Robert is desperately worried about his two brothers, having promised his mother he would look after them. The girl tells Alice that she is nine years old, from Richmond in London, and was travelling in first class with her nanny, Birdy.

'And what's your name?' Alice asks.

'Molly Carr. I should have been in Canada weeks ago with my sisters. I shouldn't have even been on that stupid ship. My father will be furious.'

She bursts into tears and buries her head between her knees.

Billy stares at Molly for a moment and announces that his father keeps pigeons. 'One's a British champion. Our Tom says they might use her to send secret messages into France.'

Every minute feels like an hour as the first fragment of daylight slowly expands, and the wretched survivors gradually unfurl from their hunched, cramped forms. Alice counts thirty people in total, excluding herself and the children. It is a fraction of the several hundred who'd boarded the ship in Liverpool. Some exchange words of reassurance or share concern for loved ones, several quietly pray together, others are too distressed to interact at all. Six men busy themselves with tasks to keep the lifeboat seaworthy.

'Where's everyone else, Auntie?' Arthur peers out at the vast expanse of ocean. 'Where's Georgie, and all the other lifeboats?'

His question echoes Alice's own, because for all the relief daylight has brought, it has also confirmed the terrible fact that they are entirely alone. There are no other lifeboats nearby. No other ships from their convoy. Not one bit of debris. It's as if the *Carlisle* had never existed. Ninety evacuees had boarded SS *Carlisle* in Liverpool. Ninety hopeful faces had stared up in wonder at the magnificent ship that would take them to Canada, far away from Hitler's wicked bombs and the looming threat of invasion. Alice looks at the six children in front of her now and tries to ignore the sickening sense of dread that sits in her stomach.

'I'm sure we'll see the other lifeboats soon, Arthur. When the sky brightens a little more.' And yet Alice had seen many lifeboats quickly overturned by the strength of the waves, and so many poor souls thrashing in the water, crying for help. 'How about a game to pass the time – Simon Says? Molly, you can be Simon.'

As the children play a half-hearted game, Alice fixes her gaze on the horizon, lost in her thoughts, until a voice behind her catches her attention.

'Anyone order a Scotch? Neat?'

The harmonica-playing American is holding a bottle of whisky toward her. He resembles a slab of rain-soaked granite, chiselled from the contours of the murky morning light. He is dressed in summer slacks and a knitted polo shirt. Water drips from the brim of his tweed cap.

'Found the liquor in the emergency stores,' he says. 'Or should I say, "booze". Captain Nemo over there says we're each to take a wee dram to warm us up.' His voice is deep; gravelly. It reminds Alice of pebbles washed by the tide.

'He's called Jimmy,' Alice corrects. 'He's a cook on the *Carlisle*.'

'Jimmy to you. Captain Nemo to me.' He waves the bottle of Scotch around. 'Has to be neat, I'm afraid. Bartender is all out of ice.'

Alice glances toward the children, reluctant to drink in front of them. She twists around on the thwarts to face the other way.

The man fills the cap of the whisky bottle with a splash of amber liquid. 'Tastes like shit, but it'll warm you up. Knock it back.'

She tips her head back and drinks quickly, remembering how Kitty laughed when they first tried their father's whisky. Now, as then, the sharp burn of alcohol makes her cough, but a welcome warmth spreads from her chest to her stomach.

She passes the bottle cap back to the man. 'Thank you. I think.'

'Owen Shaw,' he says, jabbing his hand toward her.

'Alice King,' she replies. His grip is firm and cold. He is a man of stone.

Owen narrows his eyes as he studies her. 'Let me guess. Teacher? Librarian?'

'Both, actually.'

He nods. 'Have that look about you. All earnest and twitchy. You're one of the escorts. With the seavac kids, right?'

'Yes. You?'

He fixes his gaze on hers, his face inscrutable. 'Stowaway.'

Alice isn't sure whether to believe him. What does it matter anyway? A stowaway or the ship's captain, first class or third, they're all the same now. 'Stowing away *from* something, or *toward* something?' she asks.

'Is there a difference?'

'If you're stowing away *from* something, I presume you're in trouble. If you're stowing away *toward* something, I presume you're in love.'

At this, he laughs. 'A teacher of philosophy, I see.' But he doesn't answer the question. 'Here. Take this.' He passes his tweed cap to her.

'You've already sacrificed your sweater.'

Owen drops it into her lap. 'Give it to one of the kids, 'til we're rescued at least.'

Too tired to argue, Alice wrings it out and puts it on Billy's head. It offers him little protection from the rain, but the simple act of kindness, the quiet normality of the exchange amid such chaos, brings her great comfort.

She looks at a point straight ahead, partly to quell her familiar seasickness but mostly to watch for any signs of an approaching rescue ship. She tells the children to do the same, to shout as loud as they can if they see anything. But the hours pass and there is nothing to see but the endless ocean.

By mid-morning, the storm eases. There is a sudden industriousness, a sense of regaining control of a situation that was so desperate and chaotic through the night. Jimmy and the other crewmen from the *Carlisle* hoist the lifeboat's sail. Containers are brought up from the emergency supplies beneath the thwarts, the items inside carefully counted and organized: tins of salmon, corned beef, condensed milk, pineapple; canisters of water; medical supplies; ship's matches; bailing buckets. Alice's mouth is paper dry. Arthur announces that he's proper starving, and parched. Brian sits quietly, his knees tucked up to his chest. Billy, Robert and Hamish talk about what they'd most like for breakfast when they're rescued and lick their lips at the prospect of sausages and bacon, fried eggs and slices of thick buttered toast, their eyes fixed firmly on the tins of food being organized. Molly retches into the bailing bucket Alice had given her in the night.

'The seasickness will pass, Molly,' she says, even though her own stomach heaves with the see-sawing motion of the lifeboat. 'The sea is a bit calmer now. Try to keep your eyes on the horizon.'

The poor child is green. Alice wishes she had some ginger or barley sugars to give her, but all her remedies are in her cabin, and her cabin is now at the bottom of the ocean.

Nobody has eaten since dinner on the *Carlisle* the previous evening, the last of their three lavish meals of the day served on gilt-edged tableware by staff in crisp uniforms. How quickly they'd become accustomed to the luxury. Only yesterday, Beryl Barnes had joked that the *Carlisle* would sink beneath the added weight they were all gaining. There were no food shortages at sea, it seemed.

'Don't people eat each other when they're shipwrecked?' Hamish says. 'What's it called again?'

Molly puts her hand in the air. 'Cannibalism. I read about it in one of my father's books.'

Owen Shaw interrupts. 'Don't worry, kids. We'll be rescued long before any of you would even consider nibbling someone's ear.'

His remark makes Billy and Arthur giggle. The sound is an unexpected gift, but Billy's laughter morphs into a prolonged coughing fit that almost makes him vomit.

'I'm so hungry I'd definitely eat an ear for breakfast,' Hamish adds, his expression implying he is entirely serious.

Molly stares at him. 'You sound silly when you talk.'

'People from different parts of the country speak with different accents, Molly. Hamish is from Liverpool, so he talks with the local accent, the same way you talk with the Received Pronunciation you've learned in school,' Alice says.

Molly shrugs. 'He still sounds silly.'

'I think *you* sound silly,' Hamish says. 'So now we're the same.'

Molly scowls at him. 'We are *not* the same. I have a first-class ticket.'

'Hey! You! Princess Polly.' Owen whistles between his fingers to get Molly's attention. 'First class or last damn class, nobody could give a crap. Apologize to the boy, or I'll throw you into the sea. Maybe that'll teach you some manners.' His voice is harsh.

'Mr Shaw! Nobody will be throwing anyone in the sea!' Alice glares at him.

The children stare at Molly, then at Owen, equally shocked and fascinated by him.

Molly bursts into tears. 'Sorry! I'm sorry!'

Owen nods. 'There's no room for airs and graces here, young lady. There's no room for anything much, but especially not that.'

He isn't wrong. Daylight hasn't only revealed how alone they are on the vast ocean, but also how little space there is in the lifeboat. Elbows and knees knock awkwardly against each other. Legs that would dearly love to be stretched out remain buckled and bent. Everyone is uncomfortable and restless. Alice notices cuts and bruises on her forearms that, now she's aware of them, sting and ache. One man, bleeding heavily from a leg wound, drifts in and out of consciousness. Another, suffering from influenza, seems to be worsening by the hour. Lifeboat twelve has collected able seamen, a teacher, six children, a stowaway, and a dozen other competent and willing individuals, but one thing it doesn't have is a doctor or a nurse. For those in anything less than perfect health, every hour at sea is an hour too long.

'Sorry for butting in, Teach,' Owen says as the children settle down to a game of I Spy With My Little Eye. 'But that girl needs to learn some manners.'

Alice looks at him. 'Perhaps. But threatening to throw her into the sea was a bit much.'

'I'd have jumped in after her. I'm not a complete monster.' He picks up his harmonica. 'Any requests?'

Alice shakes her head. She finds his relentless playing jarring.

Owen shrugs. '"When the Saints Go Marching In" it is then.'

After what feels like hours, Jimmy announces the arrangements for distributing the emergency food and water. 'We'll err on the side of caution for now,' he says. 'Better to have plenty left over than . . . Well, let's just see how we go, shall we?'

The meagre portions of food are prepared in an atmosphere of grim resignation. All eyes are fixed on Jimmy and a younger crewman, Bobby, as they slice painfully thin strips from a tin of corned beef and carefully place each strip on a ship's biscuit. Almost reverentially, the portions are passed from one person to the next, first to the children, then to those suffering the most, and finally to everyone else. Each temporary custodian passes the biscuit along with the greatest of care as the lifeboat lists and sways.

When it's Alice's turn to eat, the smell of the corned beef makes her gag. The ship's biscuit is so dry that it sticks to the roof of her mouth, but with the children watching, she has to set a good example. What she really needs is a long cool drink of water to wash it down.

As with the food, Jimmy has calculated careful rations for the water supplies. He announces they'll have two servings of water each per day, although Alice isn't sure why he's talking about days when they'll be rescued at any moment.

'How much is a serving, Cap?' Owen asks.

'Six ounces. And there's no need to call me Cap. Jimmy will do.'

'Six ounces! Are you kidding me?'

Alice wishes Owen hadn't asked. Six ounces isn't even a full teacup. Less than two teacups of water a day? Surely Jimmy's calculations are wrong.

The water is passed out in a steel dipper, a few inches tall, with a long handle. Alice makes sure the children have the first drink. When her turn comes, she holds the cool liquid on her tongue, washing it around her mouth before swallowing. It is so satisfying, and yet it only makes her desperate for more.

Molly asks why they can't just drink the seawater since there's so much of it.

Alice explains that it is too salty. 'It could make you poorly.'

Overhearing them, Jimmy asks for everyone's attention. 'Nobody is to drink seawater, no matter how thirsty you are. It causes dehydration and can be extremely dangerous.'

Arthur says it tastes horrid anyway. 'I swallowed a whole mouthful once. And then I was sick in the bucket I was using to build sandcastles.'

The brief interlude of the food and water is a welcome distraction, but it leaves Alice with a horrible sense of settling in. Their immediate crisis has extended beyond the first terrifying night, and the new morning is already slipping toward afternoon. She was so sure they would be rescued at first light. Surely the danger of U-boats has passed by now. Her initial fear turns to anger as she thinks of all the ships in their convoy. Not one of them had insisted on turning back, despite the desperate situation. Didn't any of the ships' captains have a conscience? Didn't any of them have children of their own? How quickly Britain's so-called young ambassadors had been abandoned by those who'd promised to keep them safe. She will tell Anthony Quinn, MP, exactly what she thinks of his CORB programme when she gets home.

When the children grow restless again, Alice distracts them with guessing games and songs in rounds until their attention wanders. To her relief, Owen interrupts a half-hearted game of Mother, May I to suggest something else.

'Anyone know how to talk in Pig Latin?' he asks.

Alice is encouraged to see how easily the children can be distracted and entertained, but they quickly become distressed again, worrying about their brothers and sisters, and the new friends they'd made on the *Carlisle*.

'I do hope our Georgie's all right,' Arthur says. 'And Uncle Howard.'

Alice falters. 'Uncle Howard?'

'Me and Billy were in his group. He was terrific fun. He could make a coin appear from behind our ears!'

The mention of Howard opens a door Alice has tried to keep closed since the torpedo strike. She pushes him from her mind, and pulls the emergency blanket around her shoulders, glad to have her turn again.

The lifeboat plunges on. Afternoon turns toward evening and the day shrinks below the horizon. The children enjoy a small tin of Carnation milk each for supper, but the treat is fleeting, and a renewed sense of anxiety settles over the lifeboat as their world dims and darkens, and the dense black of night consumes them again. This time, they know there aren't any ships close by waiting to rescue them at first light, or other lifeboats nearby carrying their family and friends. This time, they know they are entirely, terrifyingly, alone.

20 September 1940

Terrible news. An evacuee ship has been torpedoed and sunk in the Atlantic. Many children are dead. Can't stop crying. Turned the wireless off long before the air raid tonight. Seems wrong to listen to silly comedy sketches when there's so much sadness. It feels like we've all lost a child on that ship. What on earth are we doing to each other?

Mass-Observation, Diarist #6385

19

Mid-Atlantic. 18 September 1940

Day One

The darkness makes everything worse. In the absence of
light, noises intensify and morph into something new and
disturbing. The ocean doesn't even sound liquid. Beneath
Alice's feet, deep booms knock against the keel of the lifeboat.
She flinches at every sound, certain the timber will splinter and
see them waterlogged, or worse.

Nightfall has also brought the return of high winds. The salt
spray whipped up from the water makes Alice's eyes sting, so
she keeps them closed as much as she can. She urges the children
to hold hands, to stay close together. She checks that their life
vests are properly secured, but her fingers are numb from the
cold and she fumbles with the fastenings as the lifeboat plunges
steeply down and the nauseating swell heaves and undulates.
Everyone clings to something or someone as the unrelenting

desperation of their situation consumes them all over again. Alice leans over the side of the boat and retches violently.

Somewhere around midnight, through a brief break in the clouds, Alice assesses the condition of the children. Billy and Arthur doze and wake in short bursts. Their emotions swing erratically – remarkably calm one moment, crying for their mothers the next. Billy's cough comes and goes. He complains of his ribs hurting from the exertion. Molly's seasickness worsens again. Brian is silent and withdrawn. Even Hamish is quiet, all his earlier talk of adventures at sea replaced by a visceral fear of the dark. Robert, the oldest child, frets about his brothers.

'I promised Mother I'd look after them,' he says, his distress palpable. His hair is plastered to his forehead. Streams of water thread down his face and neck. His knees shake from the cold. 'I promised I'd stay with them if anything happened.'

'Try not to worry. I'm sure your brothers are safe in another lifeboat.' Alice hears the hollow ring to her reassurance. How can she – how can anyone – be sure of anything anymore?

Restless hours pass beneath wild gusts and wicked squalls. Jimmy arranges a rota for manning the Fleming gear, the iron handles that operate a rudder to keep the lifeboat parallel to the swell and prevents them being sideswiped, and capsized. Alice insists on taking her turn, even though Jimmy says she isn't expected to, being a woman. She shuffles stubbornly forward to take her place. The iron handles are icy cold, the metal slippery to the touch. Spindrift hits her in the face. Her hands are so numb she can hardly tell which way to pull.

Owen Shaw works the handle beside her and sings a chaotic version of a children's nursery rhyme. 'Row, row, row, your lifeboat, roughly 'cross the sea! Life is but a dream, Alice. But. A. Dream.'

Alice doesn't know what to make of Owen. The children respond well to his spontaneity, but his wild unpredictability unsettles her.

'Where are we rowing to anyway?' she asks, partly to stop his mad singing and partly because she is increasingly convinced they're rowing away from help, not toward it.

'Ireland, according to Captain Nemo. Welcome aboard, begorrah. Tis a grand soft day, so it is.'

'Ireland? But that's miles away! Days away!' They'd sailed past the coast of Antrim and Donegal on their first day at sea. Howard had talked so enthusiastically about the Giant's Causeway and Dunluce Castle that she'd promised to visit when the war was over. 'We can't possibly row to Ireland,' she says.

Owen nods toward Jimmy. 'Just repeating what the big man said. That we should set a course for Ireland, in case help doesn't arrive. He reckons it'll take eight days, if the currents are favourable and the winds prevail.'

'EIGHT DAYS!' Alice is horrified. She'd set her mind on toughing it out until daylight on the first morning. They were now halfway through a second dreadful night. She couldn't possibly endure being in the lifeboat for six more days. And the children certainly wouldn't. None of them could. It was absurd to even think about it.

Owen shrugs. 'Don't shoot the messenger.'

Alice decides Owen must have heard wrong. She works the iron handles, pushing her desperation into the movement of the rudder beneath the water.

When her turn is over, she crawls back to her small space at the end of the lifeboat and tucks her knees up to her chest.

'Will they rescue us soon, Auntie?' Arthur asks.

'My leg hurts,' Molly says. 'And I feel sick.'

'I'm hungry,' Billy adds.

'I'm thirsty.' It is the first thing Brian has said since telling Alice his name.

On and on the children's questions and demands come, and Alice doesn't have an answer for any of them. She tells them to watch the sky for shooting stars and rescue ships and the first sign of daylight.

'Shout if you see anything,' she says. 'Shout as loud as you can.'

But as the darkest, bleakest hours drape themselves around the lifeboat, there is nothing to see, no reason for anyone to raise the alarm.

It is now over thirty-six hours since she'd last slept, but despite her exhaustion, Alice fights the pull of sleep, afraid that one of the children will fall out if she isn't fully alert. Sometimes she thinks she's dreaming. Other times, she is pin-sharp and alert. Memories come and go. Voices past and present merge into a muddle of nonsense. She sings show tunes to herself, incomplete verses and half-remembered choruses, so that she sounds demented.

As she huddles against the side of the lifeboat, unable to stop shivering, her earlier fear and anger are replaced by a bone-deep ache of grief and despair. She thinks about how purposeful and hopeful she felt as the *Carlisle* pulled away from the docks in Liverpool. Now, with every wave that drenches her, she feels as if she's being washed away, eroded by something far more powerful and prevailing than a fleeting sense of hope. What a fool she was. What fools they all were to think they could ever outrun the war and Hitler's wicked weapons.

Eventually, she sleeps.

Sometime in the night, she is woken by a gentle shake of her shoulder. She opens her eyes to see a man's face close to hers. For a moment, she thinks it's her father. *Come and see the full moon, Alice. It's magical!* But then she recognizes the man. He was the one who'd reached for the woman in the water during the first frantic moments in the lifeboat.

He bends forward and presses a blanket and a life jacket into Alice's arms. His hands tremble. 'You must get the children home, to their mothers,' he says.

His voice is so quiet that she can hardly hear him above the storm. She is too drowsy and confused to make any sense of it. Perhaps she is dreaming. Everyone around her is asleep.

'You will do that for me, won't you? Get the children back to their mothers, whatever it takes.'

'Yes,' she says. 'Yes.'

She watches in a sort of trance as he shuffles a few paces to the left, swings his legs over the edge of the lifeboat and slips into the water with barely a splash.

Alice is so shocked that, for a moment, she can't respond.

A moment is all it takes. In seconds, he is carried away by the swell, far beyond the lifeboat, far beyond the path of moonlight that seems to light his way. By the time Alice manages to cry out for help, he is gone.

20

Mid-Atlantic. 19 September 1940

Day Two

The shocking news of someone going overboard in the night passes around the lifeboat as people begin to wake. A balding man, who doesn't have very good English, accuses Alice of having left the poor soul to drown. Bobby insists it wasn't Alice's fault, and that the ocean swell would have carried him away in seconds. Jimmy, who was the first to respond to Alice's cries for help, says she mustn't blame herself, but she is tormented by the echo of another time when her cries for help had come too late.

'Did he say anything, before he . . .?' Jimmy can't finish the sentence. The strain of their ordeal is already evident in his bloodshot eyes.

Alice shakes her head. 'He just gave me his blanket and life jacket and asked me to promise to get the children home to their mothers. That was all. It happened so quickly. There was nothing I could do. I don't even know his name.'

Jimmy rubs a hand across his beard and dips his head. 'His name is William. Bill.' He looks out at the ocean, and then back at Alice. 'But I called him Dad.'

'He was your father? Oh, Jimmy. I'm so sorry. I couldn't . . .'

'He wanted to be with her. Couldn't bear to be without her.'

'Her?'

'My mother. She fell into the water just after we launched the lifeboat. We tried to reach her, almost did, but the swell swept her away.'

Alice remembers the falling woman, the white nightdress pirouetting into the water, the pale hand reaching out of the water during those first frantic minutes. 'I'm so sorry.'

Jimmy shakes his head and wipes a tear from his cheek. His quiet anguish is unbearable. 'They say drowning is a peaceful death. That you don't feel any pain.' His voice cracks with emotion. Alice gives him a moment to compose himself. 'They were married for forty years. He couldn't bear the thought of being without her, even if it meant following her to his own end. Imagine loving someone so much that you'd rather die than live another day without them.'

Alice looks at the water, so cold and deep and dark. She knows she couldn't do it, no matter how desperate she was, or how deeply in love. She'd had no experience of such profound devotion, not from her parents' marriage, or in her own life. Maybe a connection like the one shared by Jimmy's parents was a form of madness. Maybe it was possible to literally love someone to death?

Again, she says she's sorry.

Jimmy nods. What else is there to say?

Alice barely registers the change from night to day as a grey morning dawns and the now familiar strangers around her begin to stir: Bobby, the young British crewman from the *Carlisle*; Mr Harlow, a retired classical pianist, travelling to stay with his cousin in Vancouver; Mr Sherwood, returning to Canada after a family wedding in the Lake District; Thomas Prendergast, recently engaged to a Canadian actress and attired in evening dress having just finished dinner in the first-class accommodations when the torpedo hit, his fiancée, Helene, sleeping off a migraine in their cabin at the time, and not seen since. So many lives and stories, so many different reasons for making the journey to Canada, and yet no particular reason for any one of them to have been travelling on SS *Carlisle* rather than on one of the hundreds of other ships that crossed the Atlantic every week and arrived safely at their destination. War was unpredictable; indiscriminate. As Walter had said just a few weeks ago, 'We're all a target until the aggressor is disarmed.' Alice had somehow believed herself to be immune. Things like this happened to other people, not to her. Except now she *is* the other people.

Her head pounds, the pain exacerbated by the incessant whine of Owen Shaw's harmonica. Every muscle in her body aches from sitting in the same huddled position, from bracing against the bucking motion of the boat, from pushing and pulling the Fleming gear. She longs to stretch her legs and spine, to stand up and walk around, but such simple actions are impossible now. The foul smell that hangs over the lifeboat only adds to her headache, a stomach-churning cocktail of body odour, urine, vomit, and damp.

Finally, Owen puts down his harmonica. 'On the plus side, there's one less mouth to feed.'

Alice can't believe he can even think such a thing. 'That's a terrible thing to say.' Her manner is tense, her nerves on edge.

'Just stating facts.'

'Well don't. You don't know anything about him. You don't know anything about any of us.'

She didn't mean to raise her voice, but she's exhausted, and distressed by the night's events, and she finds Owen's casual attitude infuriating, not to mention his insistence on playing the harmonica morning, noon, and in the middle of the bloody night.

'Tell me then, Miss King. Or is it Mrs? Is there a Mister King at home, keeping the bed warm? Tell me everything, so I don't make any more assumptions and get you all mad at me.'

Alice tells him to shut up. 'Just stop it,' she snaps.

He raises an eyebrow. 'So the mouse has a squeak after all.'

Overhearing the conversation from his seat a few feet ahead, Jimmy turns around. 'He bothering you? We can easily send another one overboard.'

The men's growing dislike for each other makes Alice anxious.

The day staggers on in long restless hours and small controllable routines: a guessing game to distract the children, taking a turn at the Fleming gear, having a blanket, not having a blanket, taking the next meagre serving of food and water, watching the horizon for a plume of smoke from a rescue ship that never comes. The sun struggles to break through the cloud, the dull sky echoing the mood in the boat as heavy rain and strong winds come in unpredictable squalls. Even the children are miserable. Like toppling dominos, their moods affect one another. Having been so brave and resilient over the first forty-eight hours, they are now desperately cold, hungry and thirsty, all the promises of imminent rescue having being washed away. Alice can hardly bear to look at them. They should be in Canada having the time of their lives, not fighting to stay alive, their faces wind-reddened, their lips cracked, their eyelashes gritty with salt.

After the meagre rations of food and water, the bucket is passed around for anyone who needs to use it. The boys aren't shy, but Molly insists that everyone look away while she's going. The cramped conditions in the lifeboat leave no room for dignity. It is almost impossible not to see and hear everyone's private business. The sight of grown men, squatting over the small bailing bucket, makes Alice deeply uncomfortable. A few torn pages from a newspaper someone found in their pocket are used as paper. Alice has avoided using the bucket so far, but she can't put it off much longer.

Being the only woman in the lifeboat, she is afforded as much privacy as possible. Owen tells everyone to turn the other way as Alice bundles her skirt around her hips and positions herself into an ungainly squat. She doesn't have the energy for the gymnastics required to pull down her knickers, and with everything already soaked it hardly makes any difference anyway. The relief is so immense that she doesn't care who sees, or hears. When she's done, she empties the bucket over the side of the lifeboat, rinses it out, and passes it back to the front. The whole thing only takes a few excruciating minutes, but she is exhausted by the effort and her legs tremble from squatting. Thankfully, it won't be something she has to worry about repeating too often. With so little to eat and drink, there is nothing much for their bodies to expel.

Another hour passes in quiet contemplation and occasional conversation. The children play another round of I Spy, but there is a limited amount to spy when the only thing for miles around is water and sky, and they soon run out of ideas and enthusiasm. Alice leads a rendition of the hokey-cokey, until she realizes there is no room for them to put their arms and legs in and out. It amuses them nevertheless, their *whoah-oh the hokey-cokey* matching the rise and fall of the lifeboat.

While the children are distracted, Jimmy asks Owen to help him with something at the front of the lifeboat.

'Everything all right?' Alice asks when Owen slots back into his space behind her.

He makes a slicing gesture across his throat. 'Strike two. Bad dose of the flu. Canadian man. Last night finished him off.'

Their numbers are dwindling too quickly. 'What have they done with him?' she asks.

'Sailor's funeral. Wrapped him in a bit of sacking and sent him off to feed the fish. I told Nemo we should have kept him. Y'know. Just in case.'

'In case what?' Alice has barely asked the question when she realizes what Owen is hinting at. 'I hope you're not serious.'

'So do I.'

Jimmy, Bobby and the other men from the *Carlisle*'s crew conduct their regular inspection of the lifeboat from their various positions aft and fore, port and starboard. Every decision and action now revolves around keeping the lifeboat watertight and ensuring the sails are working to maximum efficiency, and that the Fleming gear is operational. Without a functioning lifeboat, the emergency supplies are irrelevant.

'We're tilting too far to port,' Jimmy announces. 'We need to redistribute the weight to even it out.' He doesn't need to say that the loss of two heavy men has left the lifeboat unbalanced.

Owen salutes. 'Aye, aye, Herr Kapitän.'

Jimmy fixes Owen with a glare. 'We'll get through this much better if we have a bit of discipline and order aboard ship.'

At this, Owen bursts into laughter. 'Aboard ship? We're in a lifeboat, not on the fucking *Titanic*!'

The wind and the waves seem to stall as everyone stares at Owen, shocked by his outburst.

Alice puts her hand on his arm. 'Can we just let him get on with it? Please.'

'My mother doesn't allow swearing,' Billy announces. 'She says bad language is for those who don't know any better, not for decent sorts like us.'

'And she's right,' Alice says. She reminds Billy to cover his mouth when he coughs. 'There are more than enough words in the English language without resorting to . . . that.'

Owen holds up his hands in apology. 'Sorry for swearing, Billy the Kid. Your mother is right. Scouts honour, I won't do it again.'

He turns to Alice and apologizes again. 'Sorry, Teach. I'm an ass.'

Alice can't disagree with that.

Jimmy instructs Alice, Owen, the six children, Mr Harlow, and Mr Sherwood, to stay where they are. Several other people move into their new positions until he is happy there's no list to port or starboard. It is a precarious procedure that requires small movements and care, so as not to send them all spilling into the ocean. But despite the loss of two people and the rearranged seating, the confined space is taking its toll, and it isn't just Owen and Jimmy who find cause for disagreement. A palpable sense of frustration threads its way around the lifeboat as petty arguments and disagreements replace the polite discipline of the first day. It seems to Alice that for all that the weight is more evenly distributed, the emotional ballast in the lifeboat is wildly off balance.

After a second serving of corned beef and ship's biscuit, and a second meagre dipper of water, the children have an earnest conversation about whether it would be better to be bombed in England, or torpedoed at sea. They conclude that being torpedoed at sea is far more impressive.

'Do you think they *will* put a picture of us in the newspapers when we get home?' Hamish asks.

His question prompts Alice to wonder how news of the disaster will be shared. What will the newspapers say? Will the *Carlisle's* passengers and crew be reported as missing, or dead, or missing presumed dead? She imagines the children's parents lifting buff-coloured envelopes from their doormats, unaware, for a few precious moments more, of the devastating words inside. What will they do, these poor women and men, when they learn the fate of the *Carlisle* and their children? How will they ever leave the small patches of worn lino near their front doors as they absorb the impossible news? Alice wants to scream out into the dark. 'We're here! We're still alive. Why isn't anybody coming to help us?' As if to echo her despair, the ocean pounds its fists against the keel of the lifeboat.

'They might want us on the newsreels!' Arthur adds. 'We might even meet the king!'

Alice is glad their minds can turn tragedy to adventure so easily. Most of all, she envies their stoic belief that this dreadful present will become their past, because as they limp toward a third night in the lifeboat, she isn't so sure.

As the hours pass, the children ask Alice question after question. 'When will the navy come?' 'Will we still go to Canada?' 'How far away is England?' 'Are we lost?' 'Why haven't they rescued us yet?' On and on until she feels she'll go mad.

'It's a pity I don't have a book to read you a story,' she says.

'My father used to make stories up,' Arthur says. 'From his head. Will you make a story up from your head?'

Arthur is such a tenacious little thing. He reminds Alice of her Jack Russell, Stoker, the dog she'd found as a puppy wandering along the train tracks and carried home in her sunhat. She misses her. She misses so many things.

'I can tell you about Owen Chase and the *Essex*,' Owen offers. 'The whaling ship that—'

'Inspired Melville to write *Moby Dick*,' Alice interjects.

'What's *Moby Dick*?' Billy asks.

'It's a story about an enormous white whale,' Alice replies. 'And about revenge, and lots of things.'

Brian peers out from beneath the tarpaulin. 'Will you tell us the story of the white whale, Auntie?'

Finally, something has drawn him out of his stupor.

'I'm afraid I don't have the book with me, Brian.' She pictures the novels she'd carefully chosen for the journey, all lost to the ocean, including the precious copy of *David Copperfield* that she'd lent to Howard.

'I bet you can still remember the story though,' Owen prompts. 'Even without the book.'

Alice doesn't have the energy, but the children plead, and she is keen to keep Brian engaged.

'Very well,' she says. 'I'll do my best.'

Billy shuffles forward an inch or two to make sure he's as close to Alice as possible. 'How does it start?'

Molly scowls at him from beneath her sodden fringe. 'All stories start with "Once upon a time", Billy. Everyone knows that.'

The girl looks a little peaky. Alice is concerned that her seasickness still hasn't lifted. 'Actually, that's not true, Molly. *Moby Dick* doesn't start that way.'

She clears her throat and leans forward, just as she had so many times in the classroom, a group of eager children gathered cross-legged at her feet. 'Call me Ishmael,' she begins. 'Some years ago – never mind how long precisely – having little or no money in my purse, and nothing particular to interest me on shore, I thought I would sail about a little and see the watery part of the world . . .'

The words catch in Alice's throat, the familiarity of them evoking such clear memories of her father reading the book to her over long autumn nights. She can almost feel the low vibration of his voice, hear the crackle of the pages turning. And just as she was as a young girl hearing the story for the first time, her audience is instantly spellbound.

She keeps going, adding action and pauses where required, giving the characters distinct voices and accents, and still the children sit, enraptured, and she realizes that this ability to capture their imaginations is as precious as the tinned pineapple and flasks of water they've found in the emergency supplies. This, too, must be rationed, kept in reserve for when they need it the most.

'And that's all for today.' She closes the invisible book.

A groan of disappointment rises up from the children.

'Please, Auntie! Please read some more!' Billy begs.

'To be continued,' she says.

'Later?' Molly asks.

'Tomorrow?' Arthur guesses.

'Soon,' Alice confirms.

'Right, kids. The Yank will take your next lesson.' Owen taps Alice on the shoulder and indicates that they should swap places.

Grateful to let someone else take over for a while, Alice sits quietly. Her thoughts return constantly to the awful moments immediately after the torpedo strike. She replays the images, over and over in her mind like a Sunday cinema reel at the picture house. She thinks about her family, too, especially Kitty. She can't bear to think that she might never know what decision she has made, or that whatever she decides, she'll have to deal with it on her own. Kitty is resilient, but raising an illegitimate child, facing society as an unmarried mother, will be impossibly hard.

At the other end of the lifeboat, Jimmy and Bobby sing 'Eternal Father, Strong to Save', the final poignant words settling over the lifeboat like a lament. '*O hear us when we cry to Thee, For those in Peril on the sea.*' To Alice's right, Mr Harlow and Mr Sherwood discuss the evacuation from Dunkirk. In front of her, between coughing fits, Billy tells Arthur about his pigeons. Molly rambles on about Birdy and her ballet teacher and her mother's roses. Robert complains about his feet. Behind Alice, Owen plays 'It's a Long Way to Tipperary' on his harmonica. This is what war looks like then: terrified children separated from their mothers, people lost and injured and afraid. It is nothing like the images in the patriotic posters that encouraged men to fight and encouraged mothers to send their children away. As she sits in the dark, the awful thought occurs to Alice that this lifeboat, this restless ocean, these strangers surrounding her, might be the last things she'll ever know.

Amid the cramped conditions and noise, she craves silence and solitude. In her mind, Stoker is barking outside the wardrobe door in her grandmother's bedroom and Alice is huddled inside, her hands over her ears, desperately trying to block out the sounds coming from downstairs; the sounds of a family, and a house, in grief. She closes her eyes and covers her ears and clings to the tattered fragments of hope that tear and fray beneath the restless wind. She thinks about the envelope Lily Nicholls had given her, and the white feather, to keep her children safe. Alice feels for the envelope in her jacket pocket, and remembers she'd given her jacket to Molly. What use is a lucky charm anyway? The only thing that can help them now is being rescued, but still nobody comes, and still the lifeboat plunges wildly on as the children retreat beneath the tarpaulin and their blankets and the unimaginable nightmare of a third night in the lifeboat begins.

We all think a lot about the past, the simple comforts of family life we took for granted. War makes everyone nostalgic. I think about the children when they were small, the silly things they've done and said, the little sticks and feathers they find, the names they've given to rocks and worms in the garden. I've started to write it all down because there's a lot I forget, and I want to remember. I want to remember everything.

Mass-Observation, Diarist #6672

21

London. September 1940

Lily stares at the cup of tea in front of her. She watches the bubbles on the surface, the small whirlpool formed from the spoonful of sugar Mrs Hopkins has vigorously stirred in, 'for the shock'.

She reaches for the letter and reads it again. Her hands shake. Her breaths are fast and shallow.

Dear Mrs Nicholls,

I am very distressed to inform you that in spite of all of the precautions taken, the ship carrying your children to Canada was torpedoed on Tuesday night, 17 September.

Your daughter, Georgina Nicholls, is confirmed among the list of survivors and is recovering on HMS *Imperial* en route to Scotland.

I am, however, afraid to tell you that your son, Arthur Nicholls, is not reported among those rescued and I am informed there is no chance of there being any further survi-

vors from the torpedoed vessel. The Children's Overseas
Reception Board wishes me to convey its very deep sympathy
with you in your bereavement. Like so many other parents,
you were anxious to send your children overseas to enjoy a
happier and safer life. You courageously took this decision in
the interest of the children . . .

She can't bear to read any more.

Was she courageous, or would it have been braver to keep
the children with her in London, like Elsie Farnaby? Even in her
profound distress, Lily knows the question will haunt her until
she takes her last breath. What if she'd walked away from the
CORB offices that muggy June morning? What if she'd told Alice
King she'd changed her mind and the children would be staying
in London with her after all? They tell her Arthur is not reported
among those rescued, that there is no chance of finding any more
survivors, but what if there *are* other survivors? What if he is
hurt and afraid and alone?

What if? What if? What if?

'What if he's still out there? People can survive for weeks at
sea, and it's only been a few days.' She speaks to the knot in
the kitchen table, picks up the teacup and takes erratic sips
before putting it down and picking it up again. She stares into
the cup but what she sees isn't tea but a vast ocean, and her
little boy, crying out for help as he clings to the teaspoon, reaches
up to the rim of the cup, desperate to clamber to safety. He is
all she can think about, all she can see, in everything.

She rushes to the sink and retches. 'I can't stand it, Mrs H! I
can't bear it!' She shivers violently despite the blanket that has
been placed around her shoulders. 'They have to keep looking
for him.'

Mrs Hopkins rubs Lily's back. 'I know, love. I know. It's such
a terrible terrible thing.' She brushes tears from her cheeks and

shakes her head, as if she cannot imagine something so awful could ever happen.

Lily feels the echo of a moment just like this, when the news arrived about Peter. Now, like then, she doesn't know how long her neighbour has been there, doesn't remember her arriving. Everything is distorted by shock and the bone-deep agony of grief. She grips the hard stone edge of the Belfast sink. 'I need to know where he is, Mrs H! I have to know where he is!'

It is the appalling void, the absence of facts and certainty that is so utterly unbearable. Lily can't get the words 'there is no chance' out of her head. There is always a chance. There has to be. And she cannot – *cannot* – stand the thought of Arthur, alone and frightened, trapped in the sinking ship. Or worse, floundering in the water, his eager cries for help unheard. She has nightmarish visions of him crumpled on the sea bed like a pile of discarded rags, his hair stirred by the motion of the water. She feels as if she is going mad because some primal part of her is certain Arthur isn't dead. She has felt death stand at her shoulder, knows that chilling whisper of departure, and this is not the same. Arthur is alive, and she should be doing something to find him.

She returns to the table, leans forward and presses her palms hard against it as a low moan erupts from deep within her. It is a sound of excruciating, eviscerating grief. She runs her hands through her hair. She pulls so hard she thinks she might tear it all out, great clumps of it, one after the other. Anything to release her anguish. Anything to stop the ghastly visions in her mind.

'I have to do something!' Eyes wide, she fixes her gaze on her neighbour's. 'They're my children! He's my boy!' It is ridiculous that she is drinking tea in her smoke-charred kitchen, while Arthur is out there, cold and frightened, and Georgie is on some other ship, with nobody she knows, traumatized by what has happened to her. Lily grips the edge of the table so hard she is sure she could snap it in two if she tried. 'I have to *do* something. He's my little boy!'

A miaow at her feet takes her by surprise. The cat stares up at her as if it understands something of her losses. She lifts it up and cradles it to her shoulder, just like she used to hold the children to wind them after a feed. The steady purr against her chest is a welcome reminder of life among so much talk of death.

Tears fall in steady ribbons down Mrs Hopkins's cheeks as she gently encourages Lily to sit back down.

'I'm sure they did everything they could, dear. I'm sure they did their best.'

'Their *best*? They told us it was for the best to send our children away!' Lily puts the cat down and rushes to the kitchen drawer, rummaging inside until she pulls out the packet of correspondence from CORB and spreads it out on the table. 'They promised us they would be safe, that they would sail in convoy, that they would be escorted by navy warships. What good did any of that do? What difference did it make?'

She lifts her cup to take another sip of tea, but it slips from her hand and crashes to the floor. She stares at the pale brown puddle as it spreads over the parquet floor, watches with numb detachment as Mrs Hopkins grabs a dishcloth, wipes up the tea, sweeps up the fragments of broken china and puts them in the dustbin outside. Lily feels as if she is staring through the window of a doll's house, observing the chaotic lives of the miniature people inside. What does it matter if there's an entire ocean of tea sloshing around at her feet? Who cares if all the cups are smashed and broken on the kitchen floor? The only thing that matters now is bringing Georgie home and finding Arthur.

'Why don't you let me take you over the road, dear? Mrs Farnaby should be back from the shops by now.'

Lily shakes her head.

Misunderstanding the gesture for forgetfulness, Mrs Hopkins tries again. 'She went to get smelling salts, remember? For the shock? Let me take you over.'

Lily stands up. 'I'm staying here. There might be news. I have to be here when they find him. I have to be here, Mrs H. My job is to be here when my children come home.'

Mrs Hopkins follows Lily into the front room. She hovers in the doorway as Lily takes a photograph of Arthur from the mantelpiece.

'Did I ever tell you he nearly died when he was born? The cord was wrapped around his neck. I saw him turn from blue to pink, right there in front of me. He's a survivor, Mrs H. Arthur knows what it takes to live. He's *eager* to live, full of life and questions. Always in a hurry . . .' She clasps her hand to her mouth, incapable of finishing the sentence, her voice smothered by the reality of what she's saying.

Mrs Hopkins takes a tartan blanket from the back of a chair and leads Lily gently to the sofa. 'Try to get some rest, dear. It's hard to think straight when you're tired, and you've had such a dreadful shock.'

But Lily *is* thinking straight. She is certain Arthur is alive, despite what the letter says. He has to be alive, because how will she ever bear it if he isn't?

Long hours pass in agonizing minutes. Mrs Hopkins brings a pan of soup and lights a fire in the grate. Other neighbours arrive with their deepest sympathies and a bit of something to eat for when she feels up to it. Lily stares at them and closes the door before they've finished speaking. She doesn't want their pity or their pies, because every offer of condolence makes the nightmare more real, and it isn't, it can't be.

She goes to the children's bedroom, plumps Georgie's pillows, smooths Arthur's bedspread. She picks up his toy rabbit, left behind with great consternation in favour of Small Lion. She rubs the nap of the worn velvet in Rabbit's ears as she lies down on the bed and stares at an old water stain on the ceiling. She wonders and imagines. Which part of the ship was struck? How many children survived? What does it feel like to drown? There is a morbid fascination in her need for details, no matter how grim. In the absence of any information, she conjures the worst imaginable scenarios until reality can't conceivably be any worse.

Sometime in the afternoon, Elsie Farnaby arrives. She lets herself in and bursts into tears when Lily appears at the top of the stairs.

'Oh, Lily. It's the most terrible news. I've been putting off coming over. I don't know what to say.' She dabs at her nose with a handkerchief.

'There's nothing you can say, Elsie. There's nothing anyone can say.' Lily makes her way wearily downstairs.

'David's ship picked up the survivors.' Elsie blurts out the information. 'He sent a telegram. HMS *Imperial* is on the way back to Scotland now.'

Lily's hand stills on the banister. 'Georgie? Georgie is on his ship?' A hundred questions fly through her mind as she rushes down the remaining steps and grabs Elsie's arm. 'Is she hurt? Is anyone with her? What did he say?'

Elsie shakes her head. 'I don't know very much, I'm afraid. All he said is that *Imperial* was the first on the scene and they'll arrive in Scotland in two days.'

Lily sinks down onto the bottom step. 'I don't understand why they've stopped searching already. Why don't they send another ship to keep looking?' She doesn't even know where the *Carlisle* went down. There's so much she doesn't know.

'I'm so sorry, Lily. All I know is that David and his crew will have done their best.'

The words fall on Lily like bullets. Why does everyone keep saying they've done their best when their best hasn't found her son? 'I'm very tired, Elsie. Maybe you should come back later.'

'Of course. But promise you'll come over if you need anything at all. I hate to think of you here, all alone.'

'I'm not alone, Elsie.' The children are in every room, in every chipped cup and cracked plate and scuffed skirting board and sticky fingerprint. 'The house is full of them. Full of memories of them.'

Elsie nods, bursts into tears again and heads back across the road. Lily watches through the side panel of the front door as Elsie goes inside. She sees her go to William and Mary who have been watching through the window of the front room. She looks on, numbly, as Elsie wraps both children in her arms. Lily lets the net curtain fall back into place.

Frantic in her need to go back over every detail, she returns to the packet of CORB correspondence spread out on the kitchen table. She doesn't need tea and sympathy, she needs facts and information, shipping routes and wind speeds, locations, times and dates. She needs to know where the ship went down, and where Arthur might be. She needs to do what she's good at: solve the problem. She studies every line of every letter, searching for any small scrap of information until she reads the words, *'The ship in which your children will sail will travel in convoy and will be under the protection of a Royal Navy escort . . .'*

The words 'convoy' and 'escort' remind her of something Elsie had said about David's job escorting supply ships. Something about a 'limit of convoy'. The words prod and poke at her. She checks the letter again. There is no mention of any limit.

She drops the pile of correspondence and runs across the street. She pounds on the door of number 14.

'Elsie! Elsie! Are you there?' She doesn't care that she sounds hysterical, doesn't care that she looks demented in her slippers and housecoat.

After a moment, Elsie opens the door. 'Lily! Whatever is it? Is there news?'

'What did you mean?' Lily grabs Elsie's hand. There is an urgency to her voice. 'You said something about David's escort ship reaching a limit of convoy. What does that mean?'

Elsie pulls her cardigan around her shoulders. 'It means that outbound convoys are escorted to an agreed limit.'

'And then?' Lily grips Elsie's hand tighter.

Elsie hesitates. 'And then the escort ships meet the inbound convoy and the outbound ships proceed.'

'On their own?'

Elsie nods.

'Unescorted? Unprotected?'

'Yes, they proceed unescorted.' Elsie takes a breath, a beat, before she meets Lily's gaze. 'They proceed unprotected.'

Lily feels dizzy with the weight of this vital piece of information. 'They abandoned them? They abandoned our children? *My* children?'

Had she been told this would happen? Had she missed something that would have warned her the escorting naval warships would leave the *Carlisle*'s convoy before they reached Canada?

Her mind racing, Lily goes back home and looks through the CORB correspondence again. She scrutinizes every letter, but all she can find is the gradual progression of information, detailed lists and reassuring instructions gathering momentum like a stone dislodged and sent tumbling down a hill. There is no mention of any limit to the convoy escort. No mention of it at all.

Concerned for her neighbour, Elsie follows Lily across the street. She hovers in the kitchen doorway, unsure of what to do, or say, as Lily tosses pages aside and spreads papers out erratically on the table. She places a gentle hand on her shoulder. 'Lily?'

'I need to go,' Lily says as she rushes into the hallway and grabs her coat.

'Go where?'

'To the CORB offices. I need to talk to someone. I need them to tell me how this was ever allowed to happen.'

22

Mid-Atlantic. 20 September 1940

Day Three

A golden orb of light rests against Alice's cheek, blooming and spreading inch by inch as it traces a path across her lips, then her nose, her eyes, her forehead. She is awake, but keeps her eyes closed to better absorb the sensation of light and warmth. The relentless damp and cold have made icicles of her bones, but now she begins to thaw as the brittle tension in her body eases.

The air is still. The silence, a gift.

Above, the sky is robin-egg-blue, immense and beautiful. Alice draws in a deep breath, fills her lungs with the brackish air, infuses her soul with hope. This will be the day. The break in the weather will, at last, bring help.

She reaches for Arthur's hand. 'Look, Arthur! The sun is shining.'

He sits up and blinks against the dazzling light of the shimmering ocean, his face ambered by the morning sun. Beside him, Billy places his palms together in prayer and says it is like one of Jesus's miracles. Hamish says it looks like the sky has been painted in the night.

Alice is astonished by their gentle grace and steely resilience, their ability to find beauty amid the dismal horror of their situation. They look so small and vulnerable beside the vast ocean, yet they are Titans; brave warriors battling on. She feels so fiercely protective of them, prepared to do anything to keep them safe. Maybe this is the devotion Jimmy spoke about.

She sets the children a task to see how many different colours they can observe, and how many different words they can find for reds and yellows and oranges.

'Does marmalade count as a colour?' Arthur asks.

'Of course.'

Robert adds butter. Molly suggests golden syrup. Brian and Hamish shout, 'Honey!' at the same time.

Alice scoops up a handful of water from one of the pools that have formed in the bottom of the lifeboat. 'Imagine, children. This is the same water you paddle in when you're at the beach back home in England. Here, touch it.'

Her father once told her all the world's oceans are connected, that a Pacific wave is made of the same water she splashed in at Whitstable Beach. *Water has a memory, Alice; a soul.* The concept is as magical to her now as it was to her curious young mind.

'Is it really the same?' Arthur dips his fingers into the cold liquid in Alice's hands. 'The same water I swallowed on Chalkwell Beach?'

Alice smiles. 'The very same. And it knows the way home. It remembers.'

As others wake to the calm sunlit morning, a round of applause rises up from the lifeboat. Robert sings 'The Sun Has Got His Hat On', accompanied by Owen on his harmonica. Mr Harlow plays the notes on an imaginary piano. Hamish emerges from beneath the tarpaulin and joins in. Even Brian sings along, quietly at first, and then louder. Molly is still asleep. She's been unusually quiet over the last twenty-four hours. Alice observes the scene, conscious of the need to pay attention so that she can tell the parents about these extraordinary days in their children's lives. Buoyed by the bright morning, she gathers up the tattered fragments of hope the storm had torn from her in the night, and stitches them together into a patchwork of determination and belief; a blanket of courage big enough to cover them all.

The mood in the lifeboat shifts that morning, everyone revived by the improvement in the weather. Robert and Hamish are interested in sailing and ask Jimmy the proper names for each part of the lifeboat: thwarts, footings, gunwale, rowlocks, stanchion, prow, stern and keel. Socks and other smaller garments are wrung out and hung over the thwarts to dry. Bobby finds a comb in his pocket and passes it around for everyone to pull the knots and tangles from their hair. Torn garments become makeshift socks and shoes for those who don't have any. Buttons are ripped from clothes, and sucked to stimulate saliva in desert-dry mouths. Thomas Prendergast's moustache wax is rubbed onto cracked lips and the tips of painful, swollen ears. They are resourceful and organized, the lifeboat infused with a collective urge to endure, despite their many physical and emotional struggles.

But there is one person in the lifeboat who doesn't relish routine and instruction. For all that Owen Shaw does to keep the children entertained, Alice still doesn't quite trust him. She watches him carefully, wondering what unpredictable or disruptive thing he'll do next.

She doesn't have to wait long.

After the midday rations have made their way around the lifeboat – with an extra tin of Carnation milk each for the children in celebration of the good weather – Owen stands up, strips down to his underpants, raises a hand to his forehead in salute, and swan-dives elegantly over the side of the lifeboat.

For a moment, everyone is too shocked to say, or do, anything.

Alice is the first to raise the alarm. 'Man overboard!' she cries. 'Man overboard!'

Bobby is about to jump in when Owen resurfaces, laughing as he treads water.

'It's glorious! Couldn't stand it any longer, being tied up in knots. Had to stretch my legs.'

Bobby leans forward and reaches out an arm. 'For God's sake, man. Get back in.'

'Get out!' Alice shouts. 'Get back in the boat!'

'Get out! Get in! What's this, the hokey-cokey?' Owen tips his head back and floats, arms and legs splayed like a starfish.

'You're being ridiculous!' Alice is furious, and frightened. She can't believe he's jumped into the ocean; can't believe he'd even contemplate such a thing. The lifeboat is the only thing keeping them safe. The thought of being outside it is terrifying. 'You'll give the children ideas.'

'Good. Much better for them in the water than sitting in that bloody boat all day, folded up like an ironing board.' Owen dives beneath the lifeboat and surfaces on the other side, much to the children's delight. He tumbles and turns for them like a performing seal. 'Can any of you kids swim?'

They all raise their hands, except Billy who says he's never tried.

Thomas Prendergast leans over the side of the lifeboat and holds out a hand. 'I think that's enough fun for one day, old chap. Best get back in the lifeboat now.'

Jimmy isn't so polite. 'Get back in the damn boat, Shaw. You're frightening people.' His wind-reddened face is further flushed with anger.

Owen ignores him. 'If you all want to rot away in there, crammed together like gone-off fish, go ahead. I'd rather have a bit of exercise when the weather allows. It's good for the soul.'

Realizing he isn't going to talk Owen out of it, Jimmy throws his hands in the air and leaves him to it. 'Drown then, you bloody idiot. See if I care.'

Arthur shouts out, 'Mustard! We forgot mustard for yellow!' Nothing makes sense anymore.

Alice watches Owen carefully, partly in anger, partly out of caution, but mostly in silent envy. He swims around the boat for fifteen minutes, slow steady laps, before hauling himself out. He looks so alert. The children are even more in awe of this loud American who does mad impulsive things.

Robert asks Alice if he can have a turn. 'I'm a strong swimmer. I swim in the public baths back home. Just once around the boat? Please, Auntie?'

'Absolutely not. The Atlantic Ocean isn't the public baths, Robert. And you need to save your energy.' She glowers at Owen. 'See? Now they all want a go.'

Owen rubs his skin dry with his polo shirt. 'So? Let them. *You* should try it. Live a little. If not now, when?'

'Just stop it.' Alice can't keep the anger from her voice. 'None of us wanted this to happen and you're just making it worse.'

'Swimming a few laps around the boat is making *this* worse?' He shakes his head. 'You need to let go, Alice. Stop being so prissy and perfect. Take a few risks.' He takes his seat on the thwarts behind her. He smells of the ocean; fresh and alive.

'I did take a risk,' she snaps. 'And look where that got me.'

Infuriatingly, Owen doesn't say anything in reply.

Certain that the better weather will bring the help they so desperately need, they spend the rest of the afternoon taking turns on watch for signs of an approaching ship. Fleeting moments of hope come and go as someone cries 'Over there!' when they think they've spotted a column of smoke, only to discover they're looking at a cloud.

Alice joins Jimmy at the mast, glad to stand up and stretch her legs while the weather is calm. 'Do you think we might be the only survivors?' she asks. 'It doesn't make sense, but I don't understand why we haven't seen any other lifeboats.'

'The swell that night was the biggest I've ever seen,' he says. 'It's entirely possible the other lifeboats went down in the storm.' His hair is matted, his eyes bloodshot and tired. Alice wonders if she looks as bad. 'We were the last lifeboat to leave the *Carlisle*,' he continues. 'We had a relatively clean entry into the water having the shortest distance to lower. Maybe we were the only lifeboat left seaworthy. Maybe we were the only ones capable of rowing away when the ship sank and tried to pull us down with it.'

It is unbearable to think that out of the hundreds of passengers and crew, they might be the only ones to have made it through that first dreadful night.

'They'd have sent an SOS though, wouldn't they? Before everyone abandoned ship.'

Jimmy nods. 'Whether anyone responded in time to help those in the water is another matter.'

Alice can't shake the image of the poor panicked souls, thrashing in the water like fish struggling in a net. Perhaps they were people she knew, people she was responsible for, people she cared for.

'We will survive this, Alice. At times we'll doubt it, but we've enough supplies to see us to Ireland if we're careful, and if the wind and the ocean are on our side.'

Alice appreciates the words of encouragement, but when she looks at the endless expanse of water over Jimmy's shoulder, and as another afternoon passes without any sign of help, she is increasingly certain the wind and the ocean are not on their side at all. And still the question torments her: why does nobody come to help them? The only answer she can find is that Jimmy has made a mistake in his calculations. By being organized and taking regular turns at the Fleming gear, they have purposefully rowed away from the site where the *Carlisle* went down. But what if that is precisely where the rescue ships have been directed? What if their efforts have taken them away from help, rather than toward it?

Alice returns to her space beside the children and reads another imaginary chapter of *Moby Dick*. Her dry mouth and swollen tongue make her sound as if she has cotton wool stuffed in her cheeks. The children sit at her feet, transfixed. They don't notice her muddles or hesitation, or if they do, they don't care.

Before the light fades fully, Jimmy prepares the second of the day's rations. It is a complicated business for something so basic. People have to move to give him access to the emergency stores beneath the thwarts. Crates are opened, the correct number of tins chosen, the portions carefully divided. The dipper of water seems to shrink with each serving so that when Alice sips the precious liquid, she feels a sort of madness in her desire for more. With everything so bland and inedible, a rare sweet treat of a slice of pineapple brings a smile to jaded faces. Alice savours every sticky bite, holding the soft fruit between her teeth, letting the juice reach every corner of her mouth before swallowing it. Molly is still too seasick to eat anything. Alice encourages her to have some water, at least. She is increasingly concerned about the girl's lethargy.

'Will there be more pineapple tomorrow?' Arthur sucks his fingers to make sure he's got every last drop of juice. 'It's so delicious.'

'I've never had a pine apple before,' Billy adds. 'They're my favourite apples now.'

Molly turns to Billy, but whatever she is going to say dissolves on her tongue and she tells him they're her favourite apples, too.

Hamish begs Alice to let him drink from the ocean. '*Why* can't we drink the seawater, Auntie? There's so much of it. Just a mouthful?'

'It isn't safe, Hamish,' she says. 'I know it seems cruel, but the salt in the water can damage your insides and make you terribly sick. Suck one of your buttons and try to think about something else.'

Hamish turns his back to her and folds his arms around his knees. 'It isn't fair. You're mean.'

'I'm sorry, Hamish, but if your mother were here, she would say the same thing.'

He mutters something over his shoulder.

Alice leans forward. 'What did you say? I didn't hear you.'

Arthur places his mouth to Alice's ear and whispers. 'He said his mother is dead.'

Without any wind, the sails hang limply at the mast and the lifeboat drifts, carried along on the whim of the ocean currents. Alice slips in and out of sleep. She dreams about the boats in Whitstable Harbour, the breeze singing through the rigging, the cry of the gulls. She dreams she's in her father's fishing boat, catching cod for supper. He knocks the floundering creatures on the head with a stick. The pope, he calls it. 'One good whack and they don't know anything about it.' But when Alice looks into the bucket of fish, they are all gasping for breath. 'They're still alive!' she shouts as she tips the day's catch into the water. 'They're all still alive!' But they float lifeless on the surface. Walter is there. He shakes Alice's arm. 'You can't save them all, Alice. You can't save them all.'

She wakes to Arthur shaking her arm.

'Auntie! Auntie! Wake up.'

The children stare at her. Fish in a bucket, gasping for breath.

She doesn't have the energy for more of Arthur's questions. 'Try to rest, Arthur. You need to rest to keep up your strength.'

'But Molly is all twitchy. Look.'

Alice turns her head. Molly is slumped in the bottom of the lifeboat, her arms and legs jerking in spasms.

'Molly?' Alice crawls forward and lifts the child's head. 'Molly? It's Auntie. Can you open your eyes?'

The child is delirious.

'What's wrong with her?' Arthur asks. 'Is she dying?'

Alice's mind races. 'I don't know, Arthur. She needs help.' She looks up and calls out. 'I need help! Can somebody help me?'

23

Mid-Atlantic. 20 September 1940

Day Three

Alice feels the first drops of rain on her face as Molly murmurs and moans in her arms. Jimmy stumbles and clambers his way toward them, stepping on sore toes and banging his knees against shins as people cry out in protest and pain. 'Oi! Watch where you're standing!' 'Look where you're going!'

'What is it?' he says as he reaches Alice. 'What's wrong?'

'It's Molly. She's convulsing and keeps vomiting. I thought she was just lethargic from seasickness, but I think it might be something worse.'

Jimmy inspects the child. 'Molly? I need you to sit up.' She is like a ragdoll one minute and rigid the next. 'Molly? Come on now. Try to open your eyes.' He glances at Alice and lowers his voice, aware that the other children are listening. 'Don't like the look of her, to be honest.'

He shouts to Bobby to pass down a dipper of water for the

child, but the request creates immediate dissent and disagreement. Everyone is desperately thirsty. The suggestion that even a drop of water might be taken out of turn isn't well received.

'Tell him to get lost,' someone shouts back. 'We'll stick to the rations, and that's that.'

Other voices mutter in agreement.

Alice doesn't care about rations. 'What is wrong with you all? The child is sick and needs water! Bobby, ignore them.'

As Bobby takes a container from beneath the thwarts, two men stand up and try to wrestle it from him.

Brian tugs on Alice's arm, deflecting her attention from the quarrel.

'Maybe the water made her sick, Auntie.'

'It isn't the water, Brian. The water is helping to keep us ali—'

'Not *that* water.'

'What do you mean?' Alice turns to him. 'Brian? What do you mean?'

His face crumples. 'I promised not to tell.'

She grabs the boy's hands. 'You're not in trouble, Brian. It's very important that you say. Molly is very sick.'

He whispers, so that Alice can hardly hear him. 'Molly drank the sea. I told her not to, but she kept drinking it.'

Alice is horrified. 'Dear God. How much?'

Jimmy looks at Alice and shakes his head. 'Bloody hell. Silly girl. Silly silly girl.'

Brian points to one of the empty tins of Carnation milk. 'She kept filling it up when you weren't looking. I told her not to. I told her she would get into trouble.'

'How often?' Jimmy asks. 'How many days has she been doing it?'

'I don't know.' Brian starts to cry. 'I can't remember. I shouldn't have said. I promised not to tell.'

Molly vomits into the bottom of the lifeboat.

Arthur puts his arm around Brian's shoulder and asks him if he wants to play a game of Who Am I?

'What can we do?' Alice stares at Jimmy. 'How can we help her?'

Jimmy shakes his head. 'Her sodium levels will be high. Looks like hypernatraemia has already set in.'

'What does that mean?'

'Salt poisoning. If she's drunk enough seawater, she could slip into a coma.'

'And then?'

His silence gives Alice all the information she needs.

Up ahead, the three men continue to tussle with the water canister.

Alice has seen enough. She stands up unsteadily, clambers toward them and grabs the canister with Bobby. 'For God's sake. The child needs a drink!' She and Bobby pull hard to try and wrench the canister from the two other men.

One of them lets go. 'Take the bloody lot then. Who cares? We're all going to die anyway.'

The sudden release of tension sends Alice stumbling backwards. As if in slow motion, she loses her balance, feels momentum take over as she windmills her arms, grasping helplessly at thin air as she falls, sideways, into the water.

The sound comes first, the heavy splash of her fall followed by a terrifying muffle as she goes under. The cold comes next, sending her body into shock. She kicks and resurfaces. Hears another splash. Goes under again. She tries to cry out but the cold water takes her breath away. She can't breathe. She kicks again. Loses a shoe. Her arms and legs are so heavy as she thrashes wildly at the water, and then something pulls her up, and she is floating, and someone has their arms around her and then she is being told to reach up as Bobby and Jimmy grab an arm each and she is hauled back into the lifeboat and blankets are placed around her.

'Where's Shaw?' Jimmy shouts. His voice sounds panicked and urgent. 'Shaw? Owen?'

Alice sits up. She can't stop shaking. 'Where's Owen?'

'He went in after you,' Bobby says. 'Then he went for the water canister.'

Alice peers out into the water. Where is he? 'Owen! Stop messing around. Owen!'

For what seems like an age, they watch the water, and then Owen's arms reach up, and Jimmy and Bobby pull him back into the lifeboat.

'It's gone,' he says. 'I tried to grab it, but the swell took it. The water's gone.'

It is a devastating blow. A third of a canister of water – a whole day's rations – lost to the ocean. Without saying a word, Alice knows everyone is thinking the same thing, that perhaps their chance of survival has been lost with it.

'I'm sorry,' she says. 'It's my fault.'

Owen slumps onto the thwarts beside her. Ribbons of water drip from his hair. 'It isn't your fault. You were only trying to help the child. If it's anyone's fault, it's those selfish idiots' up there.' He glowers at the two men who'd fought over the water. They sit in sullen silence as Jimmy takes a dipper of water from the remaining canister and passes it down the boat for Molly.

Alice encourages Molly to drink as she cradles the child in her arms. She wants to say something to Owen, but doesn't have the words or the emotional strength. Too shocked to fully process what has just happened, she shuts down her own emotions and focuses on the child instead.

The dim light of evening turns toward the dense black of night. Still soaked to the skin, Alice sits with Molly as the child drifts in and out of lucidity and takes small sips of water from the dipper. Nobody says anything more about it. All they can do now is hope she doesn't get any worse.

The boys are shocked by Molly's illness and the drama of Alice going overboard. They are also impressed by how quickly Owen jumped in to save her.

'You've made quite the impression on them,' Alice says as they sit quietly after the light has faded. 'You're like a character from one of Hamish's adventure stories. A real-life hero.'

Owen dismisses the notion. 'Heroes are for fiction. Made-up nonsense. I'm not a hero. Far from it.'

Alice turns to face him. His profile is just visible beneath the intermittent moonlight. She thinks back to the first morning when he'd offered her the whisky, how she'd thought of him as a man made of granite, gruff and outspoken, provocative and foul-mouthed. But his hard edges have worn away, eroded by the wind and the struggle to survive.

'Thank you,' she says. 'For earlier.'

He shrugs. 'No big deal. Fancied a swim anyway. I didn't go in just for you, you know.' He smiles.

Alice smiles back. 'Definitely not a hero then.'

'Definitely not.'

'You're not really a stowaway either, are you?'

He takes a deep breath. 'Not exactly.'

'So, what are you then? *Who* are you?'

'You wouldn't believe me if I told you.' He takes the blanket from around his shoulders and passes it to Alice. 'Here. Wind's picking up again.'

'It can't be my turn already. You've only just been given it.'

'And now I'm giving it to you. Looks like we could be in for another rough night. Try to get some rest. You've had an eventful day. I'll watch the girl.'

Alice is grateful, relieved, exhausted. 'Thank you.'

He offers a thin smile. 'Pleasure, neighbour.'

The children become fretful as they feel the pronounced sway of the lifeboat and the rising strength of the wind. They know this sensation now, know these sounds.

Afraid of the dark and the returning storm, the children huddle together. Billy presses up as close as he can to Alice's side and holds her hand. Arthur clambers onto Alice's lap and wraps his arms around her neck. He is nothing but a feather, and yet the weight of responsibility she feels for him is immense. She looks at the identification label still attached to his coat and imagines Lily Nicholls at her kitchen table, labelling her son like a post office package. Evacuation was unbearably cruel. It had been presented as such a selfless, honourable thing, a patriotic act to protect the next generation and secure Britain's future. Alice thinks about the footage she'd watched on the newsreels at the picture house. 'There go Britain's young ambassadors, smiling and waving as their ship departs!' What she sees in those images now isn't children proudly waving goodbye, but children desperately crying out for help as they drown. War is an ugly, brutal business. Walter was right to want nothing to do with it.

She closes her eyes and squeezes Billy's hand with one of hers as she rests her other against Arthur's cheek, pressing strength and reassurance into them both. They are both so cold, their skin brittle and crusted with salt. Like barnacles, they are stuck to her now, their fates, and their lives, permanently entwined.

24

London. September 1940

Like a moth drawn to light, driven by an instinctive urge she isn't fully in control of, Lily returns to the place where it had all started on a warm June morning.

She steps off the bus at the top of The Mall, buttons her coat and points her feet in the direction of Mayfair and Berkeley Street, but she can't make herself move. She stands on the spot, swaying like a daffodil blown by a stiff breeze as people side-step around her and hurry past. It's the first time she's been into the West End since the Blitz started. She finds the bustle and noise brash and intrusive. There's an arrogance here, an unpleasant air of 'Britain will prevail' superiority. She hates it, shouldn't have come, isn't thinking straight, but she can't get the phrase, 'limit of convoy' out of her head. It had been Lily's understanding that evacuee ships would be escorted, in convoy, all the way to Canada. If they weren't under naval escort when the torpedo hit, that changes everything. The need for answers propels her on.

She doesn't feel fully within herself as she begins to walk, everything muffled and distant, as if she is underwater. She passes flirtatious women in uniform, arms linked, laughing as they share a cigarette and try to catch the attention of a soldier in front of them. She doesn't understand how they can be so carefree when there's a war on and children are being blown out of their beds by German torpedoes. She blinks back gritty tears and hurries on, head down, certain that everyone she passes can sense her erratic state of mind and see the grief etched on her face.

She heads toward Green Park, and on, until she reaches the CORB offices. She stops. For a moment she is back in the sweltering heat of a June morning, the fabric of her dress sticking to her skin. 'Walk away, Lily. Turn around. Go home.' It is three months since she'd signed the children up for the scheme. It feels like three years.

She approaches cautiously, mistrusting her emotional state. Anger has summoned her back, but now she is here she feels only an unfathomable sorrow that circumstances ever brought her here in the first place. Outside the office doors, the once bright geraniums are now withered brown sticks in their pots. The sign is turned to closed. The blackout blinds are pulled down. She remembers the ease with which the neatly turned-out woman behind the counter had taken her completed application form. It had all been made to feel so straightforward, so simple. A minor inconvenience to send your children away. And now, just like Arthur, the ruby-lipped women with their forms and clipboards and authoritative stamps have vanished. It's as if the entire scheme never existed. The empty building left behind hangs its head in shame and remorse.

The church clock chimes the half hour as Lily sinks down onto the cold stone steps, a wretched broken thing as her grief overwhelms her again. She feels a tightness in her chest, her breathing restricted by the lump of grief lodged there like a boulder. She shouldn't have come. She isn't ready to confront this, any of it.

'I'd be closed too if I'd sent all those kiddies to their deaths.'

Lily looks up. A woman stands in front of her.

'I don't know what to do,' the woman says. 'Don't know where to go. I just keep wandering around, wishing things were different. I don't even know why I came here, or what I hoped to find. Someone to blame? Someone to tell me why it happened?' She dabs a handkerchief to the tears that spill down her cheeks as she looks at Lily. 'What can we do?'

'We can demand answers,' Lily says.

'From who?'

'From those in charge.'

'What does it matter? It won't bring our children back.'

Lily stands up and bangs on the door. 'Maybe not. But someone has to be held accountable. Someone has to take responsibility for what's happened.'

She is about to leave when the door opens slightly. A pale-faced woman peers out at Lily. 'I'm afraid we're closed until further notice.'

'I want to speak to Anthony Quinn, or someone in charge.' Lily's grief solidifies into anger again, a rod of resolve to get answers for her children. 'I want to know if the escort ships were still with the *Carlisle* when it was hit.'

The woman looks at Lily, then at the woman standing beside her, and bursts into tears. 'I'm so sorry. We're all so terribly sorry. There'll be an official announcement in the newspapers. When all the parents have been informed.'

Lily finds the words chilling. 'All the parents.' How many lives have been shattered by this terrible news?

'I don't care about an official announcement,' she says. 'I want to know where my son is, and why nobody is looking for him.'

Behind Lily, someone hurries up the steps, heels clacking against the granite. Lily recognizes her face, but can't remember why.

The woman perched in the doorway gasps. 'Kitty! Oh, you poor love. I'm so sorry. You shouldn't have come. It's all so terrible.'

The young woman glances at Lily as she hurries past. Lily lunges toward her and grabs her arm as she reaches the doorway.

'Kitty is it? Can *you* help me?' She is desperate now to be heard, to be listened to. 'Please, can somebody help me!'

Kitty gently removes Lily's hand from her arm. 'What's your name?'

'Lily. Lily Nicholls. My children are Georgina and Arthur.'

Kitty nods. 'Go home, Mrs Nicholls. Please. We are still trying to understand exactly what happened and what condition the survivors are in.'

'Did the escort ships leave the convoy?'

The question prompts an uncertain glance between the two CORB women. The one called Kitty asks Lily what she means.

'I know about the limit of convoy escort. I want to know the truth. I want to know if the escort had left the convoy before the torpedo hit. And I want to know where my son is.'

Kitty looks at Lily. 'We are all so sorry, Mrs Nicholls. The best thing you can do for your son now is to go home and let us do our jobs. We'll be in touch if there is any further news.'

Lily hears the echo of her conversation with Ada Fortune, here, on these very steps, not three months ago. *Our job is to stay alive until they come back.*

She has no more energy to argue and fight. She just wants her children home.

Defeated, deflated, she turns and walks away.

Time seems suspended now, paused in the moment when she first read the devastating letter from CORB. She hangs her coat and hat on the stand in the hall, uses the outhouse, kicks off

201

her shoes and pads through to the kitchen, her stockinged feet flinching against the chill of the quarry tiles in the hallway. She imagines Georgie hopping from one square to the next, insisting it is bad luck to step on the lines. Superstitious, just like her mother.

She bundles up all the CORB paperwork on the kitchen table and pushes it back into the drawer along with all the odds and ends of life that have accumulated there over the years: balls of string, birthday candles, matches, spare buttons, fuses, nails and screws. Before she shuts the drawer, she rests her hand on the Huntley and Palmers biscuit tin pushed to the back. She thinks about the things inside it, placed there for safekeeping, too painful to read, too precious to ignore. *Go back inside, Lil. It's freezing. I'll write when I get to the training camp.* She misses Peter's calm voice more than ever, but she shuts the drawer anyway. It sticks on its runners and needs a shove with her hip. She doesn't need to read what's inside the biscuit tin. She already knows every word.

Utterly exhausted, she sinks into a chair at the kitchen table and leans forward, her palms pressed against the rough wood that anchors her to this place. It was her mother's table before it became hers, her grandmother's before that. An island of family life, where three generations of women had eaten, laughed, loved, and wept. It lends her some comfort, a sense of life continuing, with all its impossible sorrows and gentle solace.

Her head in a cradle of folded arms, she eventually sleeps. She dreams she's a feather, floating on the surface of the ocean as someone – Peter? – tries again and again to scoop her up, but she keeps drifting away, carried by the shifting waves, always just out of reach.

Try to find a moment of quiet and calm in each day. Not always easy (mostly impossible), but I try to be grateful for all the wonderful things I have, instead of being angry about what has been taken from me. It's lonely being surrounded by memories and worry and doubt. They don't have a leaflet with instructions for that. That bit, we have to work out for ourselves.

Mass-Observation, Diarist #6672

25

Mid-Atlantic. 21 September 1940

Day Four

Alice reaches for Molly's hand as the first pale brushstrokes of a new day stretch across the horizon. The girl's skin is cold to the touch.

'Molly? It's Auntie. It's the morning.'

She doesn't move.

Alice shakes her gently. 'Can you hear me, Molly? Move your hand if you can hear me.'

Molly's fingers stir. Alice breathes a sigh of relief. She has survived the night, at least.

Alice leans back against the thwarts. She is light-headed and dizzy, her body weak, her mind losing its grip on reality. Painful cramps and pins and needles come and go in her arms and legs. A fog of exhaustion sits across her forehead like a vice. She'd sat up with Molly all night, encouraging her to take sips of water, wrapping blankets around her to keep her as warm as possible, calming her when she became delirious. Even when Owen and others had taken their turn to watch the child, Alice couldn't rest.

Beneath the thin light of dawn, while others still sleep, she idly scrapes a fingernail against the fine layer of salt that has formed on her teeth. She inspects it briefly, both disgusted and fascinated by it, before wiping it on the edge of her skirt. She lifts her arm and sniffs her armpit, repulsed by the sour odour of damp and sweat that clings to her. She breathes onto her hand and places it to her nose to check her breath. The smell of fish and decay turns her stomach. Her skin is spongy and pale, like well-proved bread dough that leaves little indentations when she presses her fingers into it. She doesn't recognize the way her body looks, or feels, or smells. She is disgusting; stripped of everything but the most basic human needs to survive.

Eventually, the children begin to wake; a gaggle of scruffy urchins peeling wayward limbs from each other as they emerge from beneath their tarpaulin shelter and begin the chorus of greetings that now marks the start of each day.

Billy looks at Molly, so still and lifeless beside him. 'Did Molly die?'

They are all obsessed with death. Are they going to die? Will somebody else die? Will they be buried at sea if they die?

Alice assures Billy that Molly is just resting. 'That's the best thing for her now. Rest and water.'

Rest and water are all they can offer the poor child. Alice prays it will be enough. For all of them. Billy's cough has worsened again, the rasping wheeze now thick with phlegm that he spits out over the side of the lifeboat. Every hour, their situation seems to deteriorate. Alice feels demented in her despair and frustration. Why haven't they been rescued? She doesn't, cannot, understand.

Exhausted after her sleepless night, Alice feels her patience with the children wearing thin. Sometimes she thinks she's going mad, hearing voices from her past, seeing things that aren't there. She has seen Kitty and Walter waving to her from the other end of the lifeboat, and her father telling her to come and look at the moon, and she is certain she can see a dark shape in the water, just off the bow of the lifeboat.

She ignores it at first, convinced it is a trick of the light or another vision conjured from her muddled mind, but then a plume of spray arcs across the water and a slick blue-grey back breaks the surface.

'A whale!' Alice whispers, afraid she'll startle it if she shouts out. 'There's a whale.'

Owen sees it at the same time. 'Christ! Was that what I thought it was?'

'Yes!' Alice laughs, a little hysterical. 'A whale!'

As if to silence any doubt, the creature dives and its enormous tail flukes rise gracefully out of the water.

Alice gasps. It is so shocking, so immense, so close to the lifeboat, but she doesn't feel the slightest bit afraid. 'It's beautiful!' Tears spill down her cheeks as she holds her hands to her chest. 'It's wonderful!'

'There's another! Look!' Arthur points to a second smaller whale as it surfaces beside the first with a loud puff from its blowhole.

Everyone who is awake watches the whales in awed silence. Those who are asleep are gently encouraged to wake up. Even Molly briefly revives a little. The children kneel up and grip the gunwale, their faces full of wonder as the enormous creatures swim parallel to the lifeboat and then dive, their tail flukes spreading like great black wings across the water. For twenty minutes, maybe more, tired gritty eyes are soothed by the mesmerizing presence of something so big and alive when their world has become so small and lifeless. Then the whales dive one last time, and are gone.

Alice sits quietly with her thoughts as others talk about what they've just seen, and what it might mean: a portent of good luck, or perhaps a sign that they are close to offshore feeding grounds.

Owen sits down beside her. 'Sure beats that lifeless skeleton in the Natural History Museum.'

Alice brushes a tear from her cheek and shakes her head in disbelief. '*That's* your response? Do you ever just see the beauty in things, or does everything have to boil down to a clever remark?'

Owen leans forward to stretch out his back. Alice waits for a reply, but, infuriatingly, none comes.

26

London. September 1940

Lily is woken by a knock at the front door. She opens her eyes. The knocking comes again, three quick raps followed by a fourth, after a beat.

She sits up and takes a moment to adjust to the light. Her head thumps, her eyes are pools of sand, gritty when she blinks, and her nose is sore from being constantly dabbed at with a handkerchief. She wishes she were still asleep, wishes she didn't have to remember that the *Carlisle* has sunk and Arthur is missing, presumed dead. The phrase sits like a lump of granite in her heart, the name ARTHUR PETER NICHOLLS chiselled onto it in thick block lettering. She gasps, unable for a moment to catch her breath.

The knocking comes again, followed by a voice through the letter box.

'Hello? Mrs Nicholls? Are you there?'

The voice is clear and purposeful. It doesn't belong in this place of dread and grief.

Lily drags herself up from Arthur's bed. She feels as thin and hesitant as the strand of light that edges around the blackout screen at the window. She remembers the air-raid siren last night, remembers going to the shelter, remembers Mr Kettlewell's sympathy and his anger at what the enemy had done. She doesn't recall the all-clear, or coming upstairs, or unlacing her shoes, but there they are, neatly paired beside the bed. The covers on Georgie's bed are disturbed, the pillow gently hollowed. Then she remembers. Elsie had brought her home. She'd insisted on staying until Lily fell asleep.

Head pounding, Lily pushes her feet into her slippers and makes her way downstairs, gripping the banister, not fully trusting her feet to find the next tread. At the bottom, she catches her reflection in the mirror beside the coat stand. The woman staring back at her looks so broken that she bursts into tears.

The knocking comes again. 'Hello? Mrs Nicholls?'

Lily wipes the tears from her cheeks with the cuff of her cardigan and opens the door to a woman with green eyes, red hair, crimson lipstick. She is so vibrant and vital, a sharp contrast to the pitying looks and anaemic pies everyone else has arrived with. Lily is reminded of the moment in *The Wizard of Oz* when the film changed from black and white to Technicolor and the children shrieked with excitement.

'Mrs Nicholls?' The woman is speaking. 'Lily Nicholls?'

There's an intensity to her voice, an urgency in her manner. Something about her is familiar. Did she call yesterday?

Lily starts to close the door. 'I'm not speaking to reporters.'

Elsie had warned her about that: 'They'll twist things you say. Be careful who you talk to.'

The woman places a hand against the door. 'I'm not a reporter, Mrs Nicholls. I work for the Children's Overseas Reception Board. We met yesterday, at the offices.'

The words land on Lily like a splash of cold water to the face. She remembers her now. A sultry June morning. A breezy smile. *You're lucky to have got ahead of the queue . . .* The same woman whose arm she'd grabbed yesterday at the CORB offices. *The best thing you can do for your son now is to go home and let us do our jobs. We'll be in touch if there is any further news.* Slowly, the pieces of the puzzle fall into place. Lily understands why the woman is here.

'They've found him, haven't they? They've found Arthur!' Her voice is thin; fragile. She holds her hand to her mouth to stifle a sob. 'Is he safe? Is he hurt? Where is he?'

The woman looks at the ground and shakes her head. Why is she shaking her head? Lily grips the edge of the doorframe to steady herself.

'I'm so sorry, Mrs Nicholls. I don't have news of your son, but I *am* here about the *Carlisle*. My sister was also on the ship, as a volunteer escort. My sister is Alice King. She collected your children.'

Alice King. The name is so familiar to Lily. She has thought about her every day since the children left, and yet she knows hardly anything about her. Certainly not enough for her sister to be standing on the front doorstep.

'You said something yesterday, at the CORB offices,' the woman continues. 'Something about a limit of convoy.'

Lily's mind is a whirl. She can barely remember what day it is, hardly remembers going to the CORB offices yesterday. Everything is shrouded in a fog of grief. 'Why are you here?' She is too tired to be polite.

The woman steps forward. 'It might be easier to talk inside?'

Too exhausted to question the whys and wherefores, Lily opens the door fully and stands to one side.

'Thank you.' The woman extends a hand as she steps inside. 'Kitty King. Katherine, actually, but everyone calls me Kitty.'

Kitty King fills the narrow hallway of number 13 with the heady aroma of expensive perfume. Lily watches in a sort of trance as Kitty pulls off her gloves and hangs her coat on the stand with the confidence and familiarity of someone who visited her regularly.

'I'm so desperately sorry about your son, Mrs Nicholls.' Kitty places her hand on Lily's arm. 'Is it all right to call you Lily? Such a pretty name.'

Lily nods. 'Your sister? Alice. Is she . . .?'

Kitty shakes her head and takes a deep breath. 'Alice wasn't listed among the survivors.' All the colour drains from her face as she looks at Lily. 'And she wasn't among the names of those they . . . recovered.'

Lily notices the red tinge to Kitty's eyes; the glisten of tears. 'I'm sorry.'

Kitty dabs a handkerchief to her nose. 'I keep talking about her, telling people, but I can't believe it's real. I don't want it to be real.'

This, Lily understands. 'You'd better come through.' She leads the way through to the kitchen. 'Ignore the mess. There was a fire.'

'Incendiary?'

'Toast, actually.'

The reply is so ridiculous that they both laugh. It is a tired attempt to conceal their pain.

Kitty sits in Peter's chair and places her handbag on the table. 'I'm so sorry to turn up like this in such awful circumstances. You must think me very odd.' She takes a packet of cigarettes from her handbag. 'Do you mind?'

Lily says she doesn't mind, although she does, a little. She grabs a saucer for an ashtray.

Kitty's hands tremble as she lights her cigarette. 'I really shouldn't, but in a time of crisis, and all that. You don't smoke?'

Lily says no, and wishes she did. She fills two glasses with water from the sink and sits in the seat opposite Kitty at the table. She guesses Kitty is in her early twenties, although she carries an air of heaviness that seems to age her.

'How did you know my address? And that I'd met your sister?'

'I knew Alice had come here because I checked the records after we spoke yesterday. Georgina and Arthur Nicholls were listed as a home collection for Alice King.' Kitty opens her handbag and takes out some papers. 'I came here because of what you said about the limit of convoy. How did you know about that?'

'A neighbour. Her husband is in the navy.' Lily needs an aspirin. Her head feels like an iron bomb about to explode. 'I just want to know if the *Carlisle*'s escort was with them when the U-boat fired the torpedo. I want to know if my children were sailing under the protection we were promised.'

Kitty blows a ribbon of smoke toward the charred ceiling and crushes her almost-full cigarette into the saucer. 'Your question prompted me to look through the Atlantic shipping records for the past few days. I'm Mr Quinn's private secretary now, since poor Gloria caught one in a raid, so I get access to lots of official records and reports.'

'And?'

Kitty hesitates.

'I've already been told my son is dead, Miss King. There isn't anything worse you can possibly tell me.'

Kitty lets out a deep breath. 'The naval escort for SS *Carlisle*'s convoy dispersed early on the morning of the disaster, at longitude 17 degrees west, around five hundred miles out, the range at which it is widely believed U-boats don't operate. Also known as the limit of convoy. From that point on, all outbound convoys proceed unescorted.' Kitty looks at Lily. 'You were right. The escort ships weren't present when the U-boat fired the torpedo.'

Lily's head feels as if it will burst. 'So they abandoned them. They sent our children halfway across the Atlantic and abandoned them.' She stands up. She feels like screaming. 'I wouldn't have sent them if I'd known! I thought they were being escorted all the way to Canada. Protected until they arrived.'

'I suspect everyone thought the same. Alice certainly did. We talked about it over dinner not long before she left. There will be dozens of grieving families who'll want to know why the naval escort left, and why it took twelve hours for a rescue ship to reach survivors, and why the other ships in the convoy didn't go immediately to the *Carlisle*'s aid. There are so many questions, Lily. I think we deserve some answers, don't you?'

Lily hardly knows what to think, what to do with this awful new information. She sips her water and wishes she had something stronger.

'I'm sorry to burden you with all this, Lily. I don't know you at all, but when I saw you at the offices yesterday, I realized you were the first person I'd met with a personal connection to the *Carlisle*. I had to do something other than sit in my flat and cry. I came here purely on instinct. There isn't any logic in grief, is there?'

Lily understands the need to act, to follow instinct. 'I have to find Arthur,' she says. 'I should be doing something, not sitting here discussing naval escorts and longitudes.'

'Did you know that only seven CORB children were picked up by HMS *Imperial*, your daughter included? Just seven out of the ninety who boarded in Liverpool.'

The number is impossibly small. Lily doesn't know what to say. 'I didn't know that. I hardly know anything.'

Kitty pulls some more papers from her handbag and spreads them out on the table. 'According to official reports, SS *Carlisle* was hit just after ten on Tuesday night. She sank within half an hour, with all lifeboats launched. A supply vessel in the convoy, HMS *Eagle*, was also hit, and the crew abandoned ship in a lifeboat. In the force nine gale that night, those who made it off the *Carlisle* faced terrible conditions and many of the lifeboats were capsized. One hundred and forty-eight survivors were picked up by HMS *Imperial* around noon the next day, close to the wreckage. They conducted a search pattern to check for other survivors, but without success. Two hundred and fifty souls were lost. Only fifty bodies were recovered.'

Lily absorbs the facts, stark and terrible as they are. Until Kitty arrived, it had been a tragedy of two. Now, it expands and amplifies, the scale of it overwhelming, the devastation immeasurable. She grabs the kitchen calendar. 'What day is it today?'

'Saturday. There'll be an official announcement in the newspapers tomorrow, when they're sure all the parents have been contacted. There are a few we are struggling to locate, having been bombed out of their homes. There'll be a national outcry when people hear.'

Lily's mind is a jumble of dates and times. Arthur has been lost for four nights. Starved of details, she is suddenly desperate for any information Kitty can give her. 'You said something about a search pattern?'

'Yes. When looking for survivors at sea, rescue ships use a grid system. They traverse back and forth over a set distance – a mile say – and then move onto the next one-mile square in the grid, and so on, sweeping the surface of the ocean.'

'And when do they stop searching?'

'When they reach a point beyond which a lifeboat or any wreckage could feasibly have travelled, given the tides and wind speed and direction. Things like that.'

'So, if a lifeboat had drifted just outside that grid, it would be missed? The rescue ship wouldn't see it, but it could still be there, just beyond the search pattern?'

'I suppose so, but it's extremely unlikely. The rescue ship wouldn't have left the search area unless the captain was certain they'd accounted for all the lifeboats and, given the conditions that night, it seems improbable that anyone else could have survived beyond the twelve hours it took the rescue ship to reach the site. Impossible, even.'

Lily puts her head in her hands. 'I still don't understand why they've already given up looking. Why not search in a new grid? There *must* be other survivors; other children. And I know Arthur is alive. I can feel it.'

Kitty's cheeks turn suddenly pale. 'Do you mind if I use your outhouse?' She rushes outside before Lily can answer.

When she returns, Lily refills Kitty's glass of water. 'You don't look very well.'

Kitty says she's fine. 'Bit of an upset tummy, that's all.'

'It's the shock. I've felt nauseous since I heard.'

'Me too. Are you sleeping at all?' Kitty asks.

'Not really. You?'

Kitty shakes her head, takes a handkerchief from her pocket and dabs at her tears. 'I can't stop thinking about her. She was so proud to be accepted as an escort. She thought she'd finally found something she could do, and do well. Why did it have to be Alice's ship that was hit? She wouldn't hurt a fly.'

Lily looks at Kitty and feels so sorry for her. They are both as lost as each other.

Kitty starts to return the paperwork to her handbag. 'I want to know why her ship was abandoned and why survivors were left in the water for twelve hours. I want to know who is responsible. When I saw you at the CORB offices yesterday and you asked about the limit of convoy, I presumed you were looking for answers, too. Perhaps I was wrong.'

Lily places her head in her hands. 'I'm not interested in finding someone to blame, Miss King. I just want to find my son.'

Kitty leans forward and reaches for Lily's hands. 'Then perhaps we can help each other after all.'

27

Mid-Atlantic. 21 September 1940

Day Four

For the second day in succession, the survivors in lifeboat twelve are blessed with blue skies, calm seas and bright sunshine. The bone-rattling cold of the first few days slowly lifts and everyone uses the spell of calmer weather to rest and recover, to tend to minor injuries and ailments, to patch up their tormented minds and restore their fractured optimism. The strain of the confined space and lack of water is taking its toll in frequently cramping muscles and increasing aches and pains. Everyone has a headache. Everyone has cracked lips and a sore throat and a dry mouth. Several people are suffering from something Jimmy calls immersion foot, their skin withered and wrinkled, as if they've stayed too long in the bath.

The children are in good spirits, full of chat about the whales, and how they were certain they would tip the lifeboat over and how they'd never seen anything so big. They are now even more interested in the tale of *Moby Dick* and beg Alice to continue the story. It is almost impossible now, her memory increasingly foggy, her lips swollen and crusted with salt. But she knows how much they enjoy story time, so she does her best, even though she stumbles over her words and remembers things out of sequence. The children are enthralled, but the words that circle through Alice's mind, over and over, are those that come towards the end. *And I only am escaped alone to tell thee.* She looks around the lifeboat and wonders which of them, alone, will be left to recount their tale.

'Do you feel sad today, Auntie?' Arthur asks. 'You look sad.'

He is a perceptive child, unusually concerned with how others feel. Alice wonders how you do that, as a parent. How you instil in your child all the good things, and avoid the bad.

'I'm just tired, Arthur,' she says. 'That's all.'

'I felt sad in the night,' Robert says, joining the conversation. 'I cried a bit, but I didn't want to bother anyone.'

'You should have told me, Robert. You should never feel sad on your own.'

'I didn't feel sad for me. I was sad for my mother. She'll be so worried about me and Tom and Mattie.'

Hamish agrees. 'When our dog went missing for two weeks it was the worst thing ever. Not just that he wasn't at home, but that we didn't know where he was, or if he was hurt and frightened. My father cried every day. He went out to the shed, but I still heard him.'

'Did your dog come back?' Billy asks. 'Pigeons come back all the time.'

Hamish nods. 'Turned up one morning covered in mud. We *all* cried then. My father didn't even go out to the shed.'

Alice wishes there was a shed she could go to, to process her emotions in private, although she barely has the energy to cry. She feels her despair as a deep, invisible melancholy, a quiet agony.

After story time and a short game of Simon Says, Alice reminds the children to wash their hands and faces in preparation for grace and the midday rations.

Owen finds it laughable the way she insists on these small mealtime routines. 'They're not exactly about to take afternoon tea at the Ritz, are they? Who cares if they have grubby hands?'

'*I* care! And the children care, even if they don't realize it.' Alice understands that these small, apparently insignificant things have become big things, vital drops of oil to keep the mechanism of hope turning. 'If we stop hand washing and saying grace before we eat, it means we've given up.'

Alice notices that Owen says grace with them all for the first time before their midday meal that day.

They each take a dipper of water and a slice of tinned peach in quiet gratitude, but the fact doesn't go unnoticed that the minuscule amount of water they've tolerated so far has been further reduced since the loss of the canister. Jimmy has recalculated their rations. With the rainwater they've managed to collect, they have just enough for the remaining days he expects it will take to reach Ireland. Not for the first time, it strikes Alice how much effort and organization is involved in the act of survival. It is, in itself, a thing to be endured.

When everyone has taken their share, Owen peels off his clothes and, once again, dives into the water. To avoid the panic he'd caused previously, he'd announced his intention to swim twice a day, weather permitting, five laps around the boat, for as long as he is able.

'Anyone who wants to join me is welcome. It's a big pool for one.'

Alice leans against the gunwale and watches Owen as he swims around the boat, lap after lap, one arm over the other, slow and steady. He looks so peaceful and free. She envies the cleansing wash of water over his body, but the terrifying experience of falling in has left her increasingly wary of the ocean, and all she can think about when she watches Owen now is the cold and fear she'd felt.

'Where do you find the strength?' she asks as he swims past. He taps his head. 'Mind over matter.'

He is the only one among them still showing any real signs of vigour and, without doubt, is one of the most valuable people in the lifeboat. Where everyone else has become listless and weak, Owen has retained an air of stubborn resilience. Alice still finds him a curious man, certainly like nobody she has ever met before, but for all that he is opinionated and loud-mouthed, there's an energy about him that's impossible to ignore. His ability to get the children to snap out of a moment of despair or self-pity is admirable. His unpredictability, while unnerving, is exciting. What might he say next? What might he do? Sometimes, he turns around and lets out an almighty, 'Boo!' at the children, drawing them out of their stupor, bringing them back to life. He is the spark they all need, and although Alice finds him unfathomable and infuriating and argumentative, she also finds him impossible to dislike.

After his fifth lap, Alice expects him to haul himself out of the water as he usually does. But instead of climbing out, he hangs onto the side of the lifeboat.

'Right then, kids. Who's for a quick dip?'

Jimmy lifts his head. 'You're not serious?'

'Never been more serious. Look at them. Withering away like rotten apples. It'll do them good. It might shock them back to life if nothing else.' He looks to Alice for support. 'What do you say, Teach?'

Alice is too exhausted to say much at all. She looks at the children and thinks of how peaceful Owen looks in the water. What harm can it do? The ocean is flat calm and they've been so still and cramped for so long now. She imagines the relief it will give their bodies to unfurl.

'Will you hold them?'

'Won't let go for a second.'

'Just a very quick dip?'

'A very quick dip.'

She nods her head.

Owen needs no further encouragement. 'Right then. Who's first?'

One by one, the children peel off their blankets and life jackets and strip off the flimsy nightclothes they've worn for the last five days. Robert goes first. He looks like a skinned rabbit, so pale and wrinkled as Jimmy lifts him carefully over the side of the lifeboat into Owen's arms. He shrieks as the cold water wraps itself around him, but the initial shock quickly passes and a wide smile fills his face as he relaxes against Owen's embrace.

Owen holds the boy in his arms, lies back in the water and kicks, until they are both floating alongside the lifeboat.

'Can I look down?' Robert asks. 'I've never been in water this deep.'

'I have him,' Owen says before Alice can protest. 'I won't let go. I promise.'

He tilts Robert forward until the boy's chin dips beneath the surface. Robert draws in a breath and puts his face into the water. Alice holds her breath with him. She counts – three seconds, four, five, six. Just as she's about to shout to Owen to get him up, Robert re-emerges.

'It goes down for MILES!'

His excitement is infectious. He stays in a minute longer and even takes a few strokes alongside the boat, but he is cold and needs to come out. Alice wraps him in two blankets and Owen's thick sweater. He trembles beside her, but he looks so alert, so alive, for the first time in days.

Molly is still too weak and poorly to swim, but she watches with a smile as Brian and Hamish take their turn to have a quick dip. Like Robert, they are revitalized by the sensation of freedom and the chance to move in the water. Arthur isn't as confident as the other boys. He hesitates before taking off his life jacket and coat.

He stands at the edge of the lifeboat and grips Alice's hand tight. 'Does it really go down for miles, Auntie?'

She squeezes his hand. 'Not really. Think of it as a nice cool bath. That's all.'

'Come on in, kid.' Owen calls from the water. 'I'll have hold of you all the time.'

Arthur looks at Alice once more for reassurance.

'He won't let go,' she says. 'You'll be perfectly safe.' It is only when she's said it that she realizes how much she trusts Owen to keep the children safe.

A rare sense of peace washes over her as she watches Arthur in the water, his arms and legs spread wide, his face a wide, gap-toothed smile. For a moment, he is just an ordinary seven-year-old boy, free from the extraordinary circumstances he has found himself in.

Finally, it is Billy's turn. Alice isn't sure he should go in the water at all. 'You have a nasty cough, Billy. I don't want you to catch a chill.'

'Please, Auntie! Just for a minute.'

Jimmy says they should let him go in. 'I don't see how he can get much colder than he already is. Look at him, soaked to the skin.'

It is a fair point, but Alice is still reluctant.

Billy takes the marble from his pyjama pocket and hands it to her. 'Will you keep it safe for me?'

She studies the clear glass orb, a swirl of aquamarine running through the centre. It reminds her of the ocean, and of a stoic little boy on the station platform, ready for the off.

Alice can't bear it. 'Yes, I'll keep the marble safe for you. Just a very quick minute though. That's all.'

Stripped of his clothes, and standing just in his underpants, Billy is nothing but a bag of bones as Jimmy lowers him into Owen's arms. He gasps as his narrow shoulders slip beneath the surface, his legs and arms instinctively kicking into life.

He laughs and cries at the same time, euphoric in his delight. 'I'm flying!' he says, his reedy voice amplified by the water. 'I'm floating! Look!'

It is a gift to see him – all of them – being children again. Alice wipes a tear from her cheek, her need to protect them now so urgent and profound, the need to trust and encourage herself, just as strong. She remembers Kitty's words when they'd skimmed stones together in Dover: *I want you to do something, Alice. Something reckless and unexpected. Something brave.*'

By the time Billy is back out of the water and dressed, she has made up her mind.

In a sort of madness, she unzips her skirt, unbuttons her blouse, and in only her underwear, she edges forward on the thwarts, swings her legs over the side and dips her toes into the water. It is cold, but it is also smooth and inviting. She pushes her fear to one side as she thinks of the pact she'd made with Howard Keane to stay curious, to keep moving forward.

'Come in. I'll catch you,' Owen says.

Alice slips into the water with a gasp, the cold snatching her breath away as she briefly goes under. She starts to panic and reaches for the side of the boat, but her grip is weak and she can't hold on.

Owen loops his arms around her. 'I have you,' he says. 'Relax. I have you.'

She steadies her breathing, leans back into Owen's arms and lets the water wash over her. Her teeth chatter with cold, but the sensation is exhilarating. The once furious ocean is a balm, a sheet of silk that drapes itself around her battered body. She feels so free and light, all the pain and discomfort eroded by the gentle lapping of the ocean. But it is more than that. She feels a spiritual response as well as a physical response, a cleansing of more than her skin; a washing away of the past, a letting go.

'What made you change your mind?' Owen asks as they float effortlessly beside the lifeboat.

Alice can't respond for a moment because the answer is overwhelming. It feels impossible to her now that she'd thought her steady quiet life in Whitstable would be hers for as long as she wanted it, that nothing would ever change, or that she would ever want it to.

'Everything,' she says, eventually. 'Everything made me change my mind,' and whether Owen understands the depth of her answer or not, she feels his cheeks widen in a smile.

Too soon, he guides her back to the boat and Jimmy helps to pull her out.

'How was it?' he asks.

'Cold, and wonderful!' She looks at the ocean as she shivers beneath an emergency blanket. 'It's so unpredictable, isn't it. Constantly changing. Terrifying one day, beautiful the next.'

'Much like life,' Jimmy says.

Alice nods. 'Yes. I suppose it is.'

Before the torpedo strike, she'd taken life for granted. Now she knows it is a gift to be cherished, and as she stands in the lifeboat, impossibly lost in the middle of the Atlantic Ocean, she has never felt closer to the whisper of death, or more acutely aware of the insistent thrilling roar of life.

28

London. September 1940

Kitty's arrival, although unexpected, lends shape and structure to Lily's grief. Now, with facts and information, her sense of helplessness shifts toward action and purpose.

'Tell me everything you know. I'll put the kettle on.' But as she stands up to light the stove, she remembers she's out of milk. 'Actually, would you prefer something stronger? I'm sick of tea.' She rummages in a cupboard, pulls out an almost empty bottle of sherry and pours two small glasses. 'The Christmas trifle can do without this year.'

Lily drinks her sherry in one satisfying gulp.

Kitty takes a sip and puts her glass down. 'Right. Let's start at the beginning.'

The facts, while hard to hear, offer vital ballast to Lily's floundering hope. She clings to the details, desperate to find Arthur somewhere among the rigid lists of dates and shipping records as Kitty sets out everything she knows about the last movements of SS *Carlisle* and its convoy and naval escort. Lily takes a sheet of paper and maps out known locations, distances, wind speeds and the span of the search grid. Her mind craves information while her heart longs to find a solution to the most important puzzle she's ever faced. But as Kitty speaks, Lily's thoughts drift and wander. She imagines Peter at the kitchen table, quiet in his grief, but determined to find their son, to bring Georgie home, to understand how this terrible tragedy ever happened. *Make them keep looking*, he says. *Make them go back for our bright-summer-breeze of a boy.*

Peter had a way with words, his creativity – and his trauma – expressed through his poetry as well as his sketching. He couldn't hide the physical marks of his father's temper, but those who knew him as happy-go-lucky Pete Nicholls didn't see the mental scars he also bore. Only Lily knew the truth. Although she was too young to fully understand it at the time, when they'd played together as children, she'd seen the reality of life for a boy whose father carried the emotional trauma of the Somme in his fists as well as in his mind. It was no surprise to Lily that Peter grew up to hate everything about war, the violence it provoked in some men, the narrative of heroes and cowards, the senselessness of so many lives lost, including, eventually, his own.

Some accounts of the incident said Peter's rifle misfired during a training exercise. Others said he hadn't followed safety instructions and was entirely to blame. However it had happened, the awful fact remained: a young man was dead, killed by a bullet fired from Peter's rifle. It was all the war Peter could bear. Lily stares at the knots in the table, as if she might find a different outcome there. His response wasn't just the act of a man irreparably traumatized by guilt, but that of the frightened young boy he'd never fully outgrown. The next time he fired his rifle, he did so with fatal intent.

'A terrible act of war, with tragic consequences.'

Lily looks at Kitty. 'Sorry? I was miles away.'

'I was saying that the official line from the Ministry of Shipping is that the loss of the *Carlisle*, like the *Lusitania*, is a terrible act of war, with tragic consequences. Word is that the king will mention it in his next address to the nation.'

Lily couldn't care less about the king's stuttering speeches. 'Even the king can't bring them back though, can he?' She turns her attention back to Kitty's documents. 'I still don't understand why it took so long for help to arrive. Why didn't the other ships in the convoy go to help straightaway?'

'Ships in convoy are always instructed to scatter in the event of a torpedo strike,' Kitty says. 'They can only return to assist when the threat of danger has passed.'

It is the sense of abandonment Lily finds so unfathomable, the active decision of the other ships' captains not to return when they knew the *Carlisle* was carrying children. 'In other words, they deliberately left them to drown.'

For a while, the two women sit in brooding silence. The facts are too unbearable to accept. Lily feels Kitty's anger and anguish, as well as her own.

'What is she like?' Lily asks. 'Your sister? Alice?' She refers to Alice in the present tense, aware of how impossible it is to put a person you love in the past. She still can't talk about Peter that way.

Kitty smiles. 'She is wonderful, although she doesn't know it. Alice never looks for praise or attention, like I do. She just quietly gets on with things. She's always rescuing things: baby birds that have fallen from their nests, bumblebees from cobwebs, lambs caught on wire fences. Where most people wouldn't even notice, Alice sees a creature in need of help.' She takes a moment to compose herself. 'We lost our father when we were children. I was only three, so I hardly remember him. Alice was ten and absolutely adored him. She was alone with him at the time and has always blamed herself for not being able to help him, or

226

save him. I think that's why she always looks for ways to save everything else.' She takes a deep breath and rests her hand on her stomach.

'How is your mother taking the news? She must be heart-broken.'

'My mother would require a heart in order for it to break.' Kitty offers a tired smile. 'They sent a very nice letter, said lots of kind things about Alice. Deepest regrets and sincere condolences, expressions of gratitude for her sacrifice and devotion to duty. She would be horrified if she knew. Alice hates a fuss, hates being the centre of attention.'

'Will you get into trouble?' Lily asks. 'For coming here and talking to me?'

'Probably, but I don't care. They've suspended CORB sailings for the time being, but I suspect they'll resume as soon as possible. There are thousands of children still scheduled for evacuation, and this can *never* happen again. If mistakes have been made, I want to make sure they're found.'

Kitty's sense of injustice and determination is infectious. Lily pores over the paperwork again: official Admiralty documents, typed reports from the Ministry of Shipping, memos on CORB letterhead, numbered lists of lifeboats and names of survivors recovered. No matter how many times she sees the facts set out, or how clearly her head tells her it is impossible for anybody to have survived this long, the possibility that she will never see Arthur again is the much harder thing to believe. 'What can we do to make them keep searching?' she asks. 'A mother's intuition and instinct isn't enough, is it?'

Kitty takes another small sip of sherry. 'You could come to Scotland with me.'

'Scotland?'

'I'm travelling with Mr Quinn to meet HMS *Imperial* when she arrives. You should be the first to see your daughter, not some stranger from the government. Come to Scotland and make them listen to you.' Kitty picks up a pile of papers from the table. 'Make them look you in the eye and explain all this to you themselves.'

Every bone in Lily's body wants to be there when Georgie arrives. 'I could never afford the train fare.'

'You don't need to. I was supposed to travel with a secretary to a newspaper editor we've invited – there's always a scoop – but she was injured in a raid last night. You can take her place. Nobody ever pays attention to the secretaries. Nobody will even notice. The train leaves at nine tomorrow morning, from Kings Cross.'

'Tomorrow?' Lily's mind races. 'But what about Arthur? What if there's news?'

'Then we'll hear it together. Come with me, Lily. There's nothing you can do here. Think about it while I use the loo.'

As Kitty uses the outhouse again, Lily looks back through the documents to check the information one more time. Something nags at her, a piece of the puzzle is missing, she is sure. Just as Kitty comes back into the kitchen, Lily remembers something.

'You said a supply vessel in the *Carlisle*'s convoy was also hit. HMS *Eagle*? You said the crew abandoned ship, in a lifeboat. What happened to them?'

Kitty studies the list of survivors. 'Here it is. Yes, thirteen crew of HMS *Eagle* are listed among the recovered survivors. They were also picked up by HMS *Imperial*.'

'And what about their lifeboat? Was that also recovered?'

Kitty checks again. 'I presume so, but it doesn't specify.'

The information forms a pattern in Lily's mind. A connection of facts and possibility. 'And it says a total of twelve lifeboats were recovered from the site where the *Carlisle* sank. But if the *Eagle*'s recovered lifeboat was mistakenly counted as one of *Carlisle*'s lifeboats, then . . .'

Kitty looks up, her eyes wide and alert. 'They might have missed one.'

Lily's heart races as they double-check the list of recovered lifeboats.

'Lily! You're right. There were twelve lifeboats recovered from the site, but that must have included one from the *Eagle*. The *Carlisle* had twelve lifeboats, so . . .'

'So there could be another, still out there.'

Kitty grabs Lily's hand. 'Yes. There could be another lifeboat still out there.'

They are interrupted by a knock at the door. Lily ignores it, frantic in her need to check over the information one more time, to make sure.

The knocking continues.

'Shouldn't you answer that?' Kitty prompts.

'It'll only be Elsie with another casserole.' Eager to dispatch her, Lily hurries along the hall and opens the front door.

But it isn't Elsie.

Ada Fortune stands on the doorstep, ashen-faced as she pulls a handkerchief from her coat pocket and wipes her eyes.

'I didn't know where else to go, and you said I could come. They're gone, Mrs Nicholls. All five of 'em, gone.'

Sick and tired of the raids but don't like to grumble because lots of people have it much worse. Had a dream last night that the Germans were bombing us with potatoes – skins on, of course, because a peeled potato (Heaven forbid!) is almost as shocking as an iron bomb at this stage. 'The Kitchen Front' has become 'The Potato Front'. Everything must be made from the bloody things: potato pastry, potato salad, baked potatoes, potatoes, potatoes, potatoes. I'll turn into a potato at this rate.

Mass-Observation, Diarist #6385

29

Mid-Atlantic. 22 September 1940

Day Five

Alice wakes with a sense of quiet optimism. Since the encounter with the whales and the reviving thrill of the swim, and with a gradual improvement in Molly's condition, there is plenty to feel hopeful about. It seems to Alice that others feel the same, that despite their inevitable physical deterioration, the tense atmosphere of previous days is slowly lifting. But Billy's worsening cough still worries her. Like a lioness watching her cubs, she keeps a close eye on the boy. She asks him to recite his times tables so that she can assess his lucidity while she presses her hand to his forehead to check his temperature.

'Your face is a bit warm, Billy. How do you feel?'

'I'm so thirsty, Auntie.' His voice rasps, his throat bone-dry and sore from coughing.

'I know, dear. Try to think about something else. The pigeons back home. All the new marbles you'll play with after we're rescued.'

When the midday meal comes around, Alice turns away so that nobody can see as she quickly gives Billy her ration of water. 'I don't feel thirsty today, so you can have mine. But let's keep it a secret, just between you and me.'

Billy presses a finger to his lips and promises not to tell.

It is then Alice's turn on watch. They still follow the lookout rota they'd established on the first day, when everyone was convinced a rescue ship would reach them at any moment. They continue it now as something to do, rather than out of any real expectation of seeing anything. The false alarms are fewer now that everyone has adapted to their surroundings and can better distinguish a low cloud from a potential plume of steam from a ship's funnel, but the actual sighting of a ship that they so desperately long for continues to elude them.

Alice scans the horizon, ever hopeful, but her thoughts drift far beyond the point at which the ocean meets the sky, retracing the many miles they've travelled, until she is back on the deck of the *Carlisle* and Howard is returning her mislaid copy of *David Copperfield*.

She sees the wild exuberance in his eyes, his head tipped back in laughter as the lively debate about Schrödinger's cat passed around the table during their last meal together. He had such a bright mind, such a warm soul, that the few days she'd known him felt like months. Time expanded. Emotions heightened. Beryl Barnes had said Howard reminded her of a hero from an Austen novel. Alice had pointed out that some of Austen's most memorable heroes were not like Howard at all. They were the exact opposite, in fact.

'So, what *is* your story then, Alice King? What really makes someone like you volunteer to sail across the Atlantic in the middle of a war?'

Alice stirs from her thoughts, and looks over her shoulder. Owen has a habit of launching into a conversation without any prelude. 'Someone like me? Someone boring, you mean?'

He smiles. 'I wouldn't exactly call *this* boring. You just seem like the quiet, serious type. The type to stay at home and settle with some sensible young chap from the village. The headmaster, perhaps. Or the vicar's son. And don't tell me some charitable nonsense about doing your bit. I mean, what *really* made you volunteer to escort the CORB kids? Because I know there's a story. There's always a story.'

Alice doesn't answer his question immediately. There were so many reasons, all falling into place like a line of toppled dominos, one event and decision leading to the next until destiny had swept her up and spat her out in an Atlantic storm.

'It was a chance to do something other than stamping library books, something useful I felt I could do well. And it gave me a chance to get away.'

'From?'

She takes a deep breath. 'From the war. And from me, I suppose.'

Owen offers a rueful smile. 'How's that working out for you?'

'Not particularly well.'

'It isn't so easy is it, to change *who* we are by changing *where* we are. The past has a nasty habit of following us around. I believe it's called regret.'

'My father said we should always look forward, not back, that you can't change the past, but the past can change the future, if you want it to.'

'Sounds like he talks a lot of sense.'

'He did.'

'Ah. Past tense. Sorry.' Owen pulls the blanket around his shoulders. 'You want to talk about it? Him?'

Alice shakes her head.

'Another time then. Over a decent bottle of whisky. Whenever we get out of this crappy lifeboat.' He holds a hand out to Alice. 'Deal?'

She shakes his hand, even though the prospect of a time when they aren't in the lifeboat feels like the greatest work of fiction ever written. She hardly dares to think about other days at all. Life has been reduced to fragments – a few inches of space, a dipper of water, a sliver of food. She inhabits minutes and hours now, anything bigger impossible to grasp. And yet she must imagine a time beyond the lifeboat; another life, a second chance. Without that, without hope, she may as well slip into the water now and let it carry her away.

A pair of gulls follows the lifeboat as the sun rises high in the afternoon sky, dripping warmth and light onto the lifeboat like honey from a spoon. Alice watches the birds for a long time as they soar overhead, their calls and cries a balm to ears that have heard nothing new for days. Alice wishes she were a bird, wings spread wide as she launches herself from the lifeboat and glides effortlessly into the sky, her bones light as air, her aches and pains diminished. Like the whales, the gulls also offer fresh hope, a sign that they're within reasonable distance of land. For a while, the gulls settle on the water, a short distance from the lifeboat. As Alice watches them, a white feather drifts toward her. She reaches carefully over the side of the lifeboat and scoops it up. It reminds her of the envelope Lily Nicholls gave to her. *A lucky talisman . . . A silly superstition.*

Molly is still wearing Alice's jacket. The girl is sleeping; recovering. Careful not to disturb her, Alice checks the jacket pockets and finds the sodden envelope, the words *CORB escort* written in smudged black ink on the front. Inside the envelope, she finds a bedraggled white feather, and a single damp sheet of paper. The writing is barely legible, the ink smudged.

Thank you for escorting my children on their long journey. I would be very grateful if you could write a few lines to me at the address below, about where the children are staying in Canada, and who with. It is unbearable not to know. With my sincere thanks, Lily Nicholls, mother to Georgie (10) and Arthur (7½).

Alice folds the soggy page into a small square, returns it to the envelope and puts it back in her jacket pocket. She looks at Arthur Nicholls, aged seven and a half, and wishes she could somehow tell his mother that her son is alive. Alice presumes that Lily will have been given the dreadful news by now that her son didn't survive, and yet there he is, in front of her, and very much alive. She is reminded of Howard's thought experiment and how like Schrödinger's cat they are as they drift across the Atlantic, simultaneously dead and alive.

She is so lost in her thoughts that when a shrill cry of, 'Ship! There's a ship!' cuts through the lethargic silence, she hardly stirs.

But the cry comes again.

'Look, Auntie! There's a ship!' Arthur nearly loses his balance in his sudden excitement as he shakes her shoulder. 'There's a real ship! Over there.'

Alice sits up straight and looks around in every direction. 'Where, Arthur?'

Behind her, Owen clambers to his knees.

Jimmy leaps up from his place at the front of the lifeboat. 'Bloody hell. He's right. There *is* a ship!'

Dead ahead, a large vessel steams into view. Alice fixes her gaze on the plume of smoke billowing from one of the smoke-stacks. It is unmistakable this time. Not a cloud, but a real ship. And it is headed straight for them.

Everyone is suddenly frantic. From a state of listless stupor, all is noise and movement. Whoops and cries of 'Help! Over here!' join a banging of tins and a wild waving of arms. Bobby sets off the single flare they have left. In their excitement, Robert and Hamish lift up their tarpaulin shelter and toss it into the ocean.

Soon the ship is close enough for Alice to make out the small but definite forms of people on deck. It is almost too much. She can't find any words. Can't believe their prayers have been answered.

Cautious relief spreads around the lifeboat as everyone looks for a way to catch the crew's attention.

'We need a flag. Something bright to help them see us,' Jimmy says.

Alice wriggles out of the pink slip she's wearing beneath her blouse. 'Here. Use this.'

Jimmy ties the slip to the rope on the mast and hoists it up.

Owen stands beside Alice, and laughs. 'Who's ridiculous now?'

Alice looks up at her underwear, flapping madly in the breeze and can't help laughing herself.

Everyone who can, cries out and waves, desperate for someone to confirm they've been seen. A signal of some sort, a whistle, a flare.

'Can't they see us?' Robert asks. 'Why don't they signal?'

A minute passes, two minutes, three. Still they wait for an acknowledgement that they've been sighted. Their first euphoric cries of celebration become more urgent. 'Over here! We're over here!'

And then the unthinkable happens.

'Why is it turning around?' Billy asks.

'I don't know.' Alice pulls him close to her. 'I don't know.'

Arthur reaches for her hand. 'Where's it going, Auntie?'

'It's leaving,' Robert says. 'Why is it leaving us?'

More urgent shouts go up from the lifeboat, everyone frantic now in their desperation to be spotted. Alice waves her arms above her head and joins the cries for help. 'Over here! We need help! *Please*! Over here!'

The ship doesn't respond.

Alice's cries for help become tears of despair as she sinks down onto the thwarts, dizzy from her efforts, distraught as she leans against the gunwale and watches the ship sail away, her cries for help unheard, just as they were once before.

She closes her eyes and sees a chessboard in front of her. She is ten years old. She can hear the sea through the open window of her grandmother's sitting room, and she bites her bottom lip as she always does when she is concentrating. Her father leans back in the chair opposite her, rubs his moustache, and smiles.

'Your move, Alice. Take your time. Think it through. Remember to always look ahead.'

Chess is their favourite game. Nobody else in the family plays and Alice is glad to spend time alone with her father while Walter is fishing with friends and her mother and grandmother take Kitty to the doctor to get something for her cough. Alice enjoys the mental challenge of the game, the quiet puzzling of possibilities, the anticipation of what her opponent might do in response to her actions.

Finally, she makes her move. White knight takes black knight. She lifts her father's piece triumphantly.

He smiles and nods, acknowledging a smart move, but as he looks at Alice there is a shift, a pause as his smile morphs into an expression she has never seen before. His hand freezes in mid-air and then he slumps over the desk and falls, with an appalling thud, to the floor.

'Daddy! Daddy!'

The voice, the screams, are hers, but they seem to come from someone else, from somewhere else – a different place and time when she is still playing chess and not watching the terrifying flood of viscous crimson that spreads from her father's nose and ears onto the Persian rug.

She crawls beneath the desk and shakes him gently. 'Daddy? Daddy, wake up. Please, wake up.'

His silence, his stillness, is terrifying.

She runs to the sitting room door and shouts for help, but there is nobody home. Afraid and alone in a house that isn't hers, she runs back to her father, the man who always keeps her safe, who always knows what to do. She doesn't know how to help him. 'What should I do, Daddy? I don't know what to do!' She drapes her arms across him, rests her head on his back and tells him it will be all right, not to be frightened, just as he has done for her so many times when she's been afraid during a thunderstorm.

For a long time, there is silence.

She doesn't know how long she is there, or who finds them.

All she remembers is hiding in the back of her grandmother's wardrobe, her hands pressed against her ears so that she can't hear the awful commotion downstairs, doors opening and closing, cries and shouts, voices and footsteps coming and going, rushing, rushing, rushing, until she hears Walter calling her name. 'Alice? Alice, where are you?'

Stoker yaps and barks at the wardrobe door, until Walter finds her and carries her out into the muted light of early evening. The black knight is still gripped in her hand. Walter says there was nothing she could have done, that the doctor said the aneurysm in his brain was fatal, his death instantaneous, but she doesn't believe him. Her father is dead because she didn't know what to do, and her cries for help weren't heard.

After all the chaos and noise, the house is infused with a dense silence; an absence of life, an emptiness. Everyone speaks in whispers. Alice doesn't cry. She is numb and withdrawn. The doctor tells her she's had an awful shock, that it will take time to recover, but she knows she never will because the only person who can possibly comfort her is the very person for whom she is grieving.

'Alice?' Owen is shaking her shoulder. 'Alice!'

She opens her eyes and looks at him, uncertain for a moment where she is, and then she remembers the ship turning around, sailing away from them.

'You slept for ages. Dinner is served, madam.'

She pushes his hand away.

'You have to eat,' he says. 'Keep your strength up.'

She shakes her head. Closes her eyes.

There have been many dark moments since the *Carlisle* first trembled beneath Alice's feet, but having watched the ship sail away from them, she feels a new level of despair engulf her. She looks at the children, so pale and thin. She has no answer to their questions as to why it sailed away. No words of reassurance to offer. She'd made a promise to Jimmy's father to get the children home to their mothers, but stories and games and hope can't keep them alive indefinitely. There was, surely, only one miraculous end to their story, only one ship that would save them, and it has gone, taking thirty-five lives with it.

30

London. September 1940

Lily's stomach lurches as the train pulls away from the station platform at King's Cross. Once again, she feels torn in two – desperate to be in Scotland when Georgie arrives, but reluctant to leave London in case there is news of Arthur. She'd always told the children that if they got lost when she took them to see the Christmas windows in the West End, they should stay where they were when they'd last seen her, and not go wandering off to look for her. She is breaking her own rule.

She takes some comfort from the fact that Ada Fortune has agreed to stay at number 13 for the time being. She'd come to Elm Street after learning the fate of the *Carlisle* through a hysterical Mrs Carr. Lily was shocked to discover that Molly Carr was on the ship with her nanny, and that neither was listed among the survivors. Like Lily, Ada had been to the CORB offices where she was told that none of her five children had survived. It was devastating news. Lily felt terrible to leave Ada in such distress, but Elsie and Mrs H promised to take good care of her. There was no end, it seemed, to the suffering 13 Elm Street would bear witness to.

The train compartment carries the hush of early morning. Lily rests her cheek against the window and watches London's grey industry give way to a tapestry of berry-rich hedgerows and furrowed fields. Beside her, Kitty presses Pan-Cake to her cheeks and nose. She looks a little green and says she doesn't travel well on trains. Across the compartment, sleepy passengers and weary soldiers on leave quietly read newspapers or doze in the gentle autumn sun. Lily holds Arthur's toy rabbit in her hands and strokes the patches in the velvet ears where his fingers have rubbed away the nap. The agony of not knowing what condition Georgie is in, or where Arthur is, hits her in waves, but there is purpose in the momentum of the train, a sense of moving forward rather than sitting in her kitchen like a stagnant pond.

The possibility that a lifeboat from another ship in the *Carlisle*'s convoy was counted among the twelve recovered from the site of the sinking has given Lily real reason to hope. Kitty has brought more documents and charts which Lily studies to try and work out the direction a missing lifeboat could have sailed in. Instinct and hope are fragile things. Facts and calculations lend them structure and rigidity.

Somewhere outside York, the train stops to take on water and coal and to change drivers.

'I sometimes wish life would pull into the sidings,' Lily remarks as she watches the firemen and stokers work. 'That you could pause to take stock; prepare yourself for the next stage of the journey.'

Kitty adjusts the bobby pins in her hair, holding them between her lips as she finds the exact place for them among her carefully managed curls. 'I don't want life to pause. I want to get on with it. I'd especially like to get to the part where we aren't in a war.'

'But don't you ever wish you could stay exactly where you are, with the people you're with, doing whatever it is you're doing? Just stay in that moment for a while rather than hurtle on to the next thing?'

Kitty fixes the last pin and leans her head against the back of the seat. 'Honestly, I can't say I've ever had a moment I'd want to stay in. Most of the time, I'm desperate for things to speed up, for the clock to reach five so I can leave work, for the weekend to begin, for the song to end so the man I'm dancing with will buy me another gin. If you have a moment you'd want to stay in, you're lucky.'

Lily does have a moment. Many, in fact. But one is especially clear in her mind, a moment in which everything she'd ever wanted was right there, and after which life would be forever changed.

'I hope you find a moment, Kitty. I hope there are many moments ahead, for both of us. Since Peter . . . Since he died, I seem to have stumbled from one crisis to the next, and the worst thing is that Peter isn't there to comfort me, or cheer me up. I still talk to him all the time. Ask for his advice and opinion. Do you think that's silly?'

'Not at all. I think it's lovely. I've talked to Alice a lot in the last few days. I find it comforting.'

Lily likes Kitty. Although they come from very different backgrounds, she wonders if they might have become friends in different circumstances; gone dancing together, swapped dresses and lipstick, gossip and boyfriends. If things were different, maybe *she'd* have taken a job in a government department when war broke out. Her maths teacher had said she could do very well if she worked hard, even go to university. Not for the first time, she wondered about the woman she might have been, and what she might have done if she were young and carefree, like Kitty King.

Kitty turns to face her. 'Do you mind me asking what happened? To your husband?'

Lily feels the familiar wall build around her, bricks of grief cemented with the inevitable questions and judgements that follow. 'I'd rather not talk about it if you don't mind.' She's learned that not all deaths are treated with the respect they deserve, that some, like Peter's, are tainted with suspicion and shame.

'Of course. It's none of my business anyway. People used to ask my mother all the time after our father died, desperate to find out the gruesome facts. I hated the pitying way everyone looked at us, at Alice especially. I always felt they were secretly delighted by the great tragedy of it all, that it gave them something to gossip about with their friends.'

Lily knows something of odd looks and funny stares. She hated the way people pretended not to see her, or whispered about her as she left the corner shop. At a time when everyone spoke of the honourable deaths of brave heroes, Peter's death was a messy tangle of tragedy and blame. What did you say to a woman whose husband had not only killed a man, but had then taken the coward's way out and killed himself? Even the words used on the official paperwork spoke of the criminal act Peter had committed in taking his own life.

'My husband was a good man,' she says. 'He was the very best of men. That's all anyone needs to know.'

In the seat opposite, a man pulls a newspaper from his coat pocket. The headline glares back at Lily in large black type. MURDER AT SEA!

Kitty notices it at the same time. 'The news is out,' she whispers.

Lily nods. She feels numb.

'The official press release went out late last night,' Kitty explains. 'Press, newsreels and radio have been given permission to interview and photograph survivors and their families.'

'What if we don't want to be interviewed?'

'I'm afraid that's never bothered the press.'

Opinions are exchanged between the man and his colleague. Remarks about 'the bloody Huns' and 'callous inhumanity' pass between them. Rightly, they blame the Nazi leaders, but they also blame the U-boat commander who ordered the torpedo to be fired. Lily hasn't thought about him until now. She's focused all her anger on the CORB programme and Hitler – she at least had a face to put to that hateful man's name – but of course there was another man, faceless and nameless to her, who'd given the instruction to fire at the *Carlisle*. She has been so angry with the man who organized the execution, she'd forgotten about the man who pulled the trigger.

'I wonder who he is,' she says. 'If he has a wife, and children.'

'Who?'

'The U-boat commander.'

Kitty tuts. 'I doubt he even has a heart, let alone a wife and children.'

When the man opposite finishes with the newspaper, Kitty asks if she can take a look. Lily can hardly bear to read the account of the tragedy, but a deep maternal compulsion forces her to acknowledge the terrible facts set out in black and white. The names of the seven surviving CORB children are listed, Georgina Nicholls among them. Lily stares at her daughter's name, and at the gap beside it. Since Arthur came along, Georgie and her brother have always been a pair. Two coats on the stand. Two pairs of wellingtons at the back door. Two bowls at breakfast, two egg cups, two spoons. It is impossible to imagine one without the other. It has always been Georgie and Arthur, always in that order. There is a rhythm to it, a flow. And now the pattern is broken.

Kitty reads from the report:

'*With details emerging that the naval escort had left the convoy earlier that morning, the question must be asked: Was SS Carlisle* convoyed far enough out to sea? While the CORB programme proudly states that some three thousand children have been successfully evacuated without a single casualty, this does not mitigate the loss of these eighty-three young lives. More must surely be done to prevent such a tragedy ever happening again. They'll have to hold an inquiry,' she says as she folds the paper. 'You may be asked to give a statement.'

'Good. I'll give them a statement.'

But despite the forcefulness in her reply, Lily doesn't have the energy for inquiries and statements and official reports. All she cares about is seeing Georgie and finding Arthur.

The train rushes on, the gentle rocking motion willing her to doze, but she can't sleep, can't stop her thoughts from drifting from the English countryside to the mid-Atlantic. *Go faster*, she thinks as she picks up the rhythm of the wheels on the tracks. *Faster, faster, faster*, the clickety-clack mirroring the beating of her heart.

'You must be excited to see your daughter,' Kitty says, as if she can sense the urgency in Lily's thoughts.

Lily isn't sure how she feels. Her heart is such a muddle of relief and despair, anticipation and anguish. 'I'm very anxious to see her.'

Kitty reaches for Lily's arm. 'I'm sorry. Of course you're not *excited*, given the circumstances. I'm so stupid sometimes. I'll be a terrible mother.'

Lily looks at her. 'Mother?'

Kitty takes a deep breath and points to her stomach. 'Not planned. All a bit of a shock. Nobody knows, except Alice, and now you. I made an appointment to . . . you know . . . but there was an air raid so I didn't go, and then I started to think about all the lives being lost.' She takes another deep breath. 'I don't know how I'll manage, and I know I'll be treated like dirt without a husband, but I've decided to keep it. I can't even keep house-plants alive.'

'Everyone thinks they're going to be a terrible mother until the baby arrives and then it turns out we are the best mothers in the world. I found out I was expecting when I was only seventeen, and I was absolutely terrified. I thought my mother would throw me out, but she was surprisingly supportive. Maybe yours will be, too.'

Kitty laughs. 'I doubt that very much.'

'Sadly, I lost that baby, but I didn't regret continuing with the pregnancy, or marrying Peter in a hurry. Georgie came along a few years later, and Arthur not long after that.'

'It sounds as if you were very brave.'

'I was young, and in love. For what it's worth, I think *you're* very brave, Kitty. You'll find a way to manage. We all do. Somehow.'

'Is that your special moment? Your wedding day? Or when Georgie and Arthur were born?'

'Those were wonderful moments, but my favourite moment came later. Quite recently, in fact.'

As the train hurtles on, Lily closes her eyes and remembers. It is so clear, so vivid. She can feel Peter reaching for her hand as the opening strains of the national anthem crackle through the wireless cabinet, and the dog jumps up from its basket and stands to attention at her side. She sees Peter cover his mouth, trying not to laugh, but it is too late. His shoulders shake, despite the solemn moment.

Lily nudges him. 'Peter! You did hear him say we are at war with Germany?'

'Sorry! I know I shouldn't laugh. It's just . . . the dog stood up, right when the national anthem started!' He doubles over, tears streaming down his cheeks.

For a moment, Lily isn't sure if he is laughing or crying, or both, and then she starts to laugh, too.

Then Georgie laughs.

Then Arthur. 'Why are we laughing, Daddy?'

The dog barks and runs around in giddy circles as Peter lifts Arthur into his arms and tickles his knees.

'I don't know, Artie. I don't know! But if we can't laugh, what's it all about, eh? What's it all for?'

The four of them collapse onto the sofa, clutching their sides and telling the others to stop, that it isn't funny, but the dog jumps up to join them and Peter laughs even more.

Lily remembers the sound of laughter, the sensation of sharp little elbows digging into her sides, the touch of Peter's hand in hers, so much life and love in his eyes when he looked at her. She remembers how she'd absorbed it all deep into her soul, into her bones, as some distant future part of her understood that she must treasure the memory, that whatever dark and difficult days lay ahead, she would always have this perfect moment to return to.

It is hers now, to keep. Come what may.

31

Mid-Atlantic. 22 September 1940

Day Five

Alice can't stop thinking about the ship sailing away. The fact that it almost reached them and turned away is far worse than if they hadn't seen it at all. Nobody can quite believe what has happened, or understand why. Jimmy thinks the only plausible explanation is that the ship had mistaken them as a lure for a U-boat attack.

'It has happened before,' he says. 'Small ships and boats are used to draw in a bigger ship and then the torpedo is fired.'

Alice hardly cares for the reasons why. The ship has gone. That is all that matters. She had seen the tiny figures of people on deck, so surely they were able to see the lifeboat. It doesn't make sense. Once again, she feels utterly helpless and alone, but she also feels abandoned, more certain than ever that nobody is coming to save them. It is up to them now to save themselves, or die trying.

Even the children stop talking about being rescued, their belief that adventure stories really can come true, now cruelly shattered. Apart from Owen, nobody has any enthusiasm for keeping watch. Nobody else scans the horizon. Instead of looking outward for help, Alice shifts her focus inward to the few pitiful things within her control. Whatever's happening outside their small wooden island is of little relevance.

Alice dozes and wakes as the lifeboat shuffles on through another windless afternoon, the sail hanging limp on the mast. She drifts in and out of lucidity, sometimes awake and entirely focused on the children, then distant and withdrawn, images and memories cycling through her mind until she isn't sure what is real and what is imagined: her father pointing out the stars of Orion's Belt, Walter teaching her how to make grass sing, her mother bringing in the apple harvest, Maud telling her not to be so serious, Howard's invitation to have coffee, Kitty telling her she is expecting. It is the thing that saddens her the most. Not that people will never know what happened to her, but that she will never know what happened to everyone else, what they did with their time, what they became. She's always hated the awkwardness of goodbyes. Now, all she wants to do is say the things she never has to those she cares for the most.

To add to their woes, Bobby makes the awful discovery that during the two days without wind, they have drifted off course. Instead of tracking east towards Ireland, they have drifted two days further south. Everyone understands that this means the water and food will run out two days before they'd hoped to reach land, assuming they've been sailing in the right direction the rest of the time. Even Jimmy's unremitting resourcefulness and optimism are replaced by a brooding sense of despair.

'What if we *are* the only survivors?' he says, to no one in particular. 'If we don't make it home, they'll never know anyone survived. It'll be like the *Carlisle*, and everyone on it, just disappeared.' He mutters chaotically to himself as he rummages through the remaining supplies. 'Half a sardine and a dribble of water. For what? What's the point when we're all going to die anyway?'

His words are unsettling, his emotions raw.

Mr Harlow admonishes him. 'You really mustn't speak like that in front of the children. You might think it, but there's no need to say it. We may be losing our minds, but there's no need to damage morale as well.'

Mr Sherwood suggests they all sing a song to lift their spirits, but nobody has the energy or enthusiasm.

The tension in the lifeboat is palpable.

Alice ignores their petty squabbles and disagreements. Her greatest concern lies with the children, Billy especially. His cough and temperature haven't improved and he is increasingly listless. She makes a cold compress from a handkerchief and sponges him down as she watches Owen swim around the lifeboat. He is either stubborn or demented, she isn't sure which. Either way, he is determined to carry on with his daily exercise, despite their dire situation. The other adults are too weak to swim; the younger children too sullen and dejected since the disappointment of their failed rescue. Only Robert has the energy to swim with Owen now. Alice has noticed how Robert looks up to him, and how good Owen is with the boy. He is good with all the children, but with Robert especially. She wonders if he has sons of his own. She wonders a lot about Owen Shaw. Who he really is, what he has left behind, and why.

When Owen gets out of the water and takes his place behind her, she doesn't shuffle and shift away from him as she did at the start of their ordeal when she was uncomfortable with the forced physical closeness. She doesn't care now that Owen's body presses against hers, or that she sometimes wakes with her head on his shoulder. If anything, she finds the physical contact comforting.

'You should probably tell me who you really are before it's too late,' she says. 'I hate not knowing the end of a story.'

Owen looks at her a moment, weighing up his response. He nods his head to one side, indicating that they should turn to face the water, so the others can't hear.

'You really want to know?'

'Yes. Really.'

He leans closer and whispers into her ear. 'Richard Heath. Pleased to meet you, Alice King.'

'You're English!' The gruff gravelly-voiced Yank she knows is instantly replaced by a softly spoken Englishman.

He presses a finger to his lips, reminding her to lower her voice. 'As English as roast beef and Yorkshire puddings. My father was a proud Yorkshireman, but I was born on the Isle of Wight. That's where I live now, in a lovely little cottage above the coloured sands. Or lived. Apparently, I now live in a lifeboat.'

Alice is stunned. 'Are you a spy?' she asks. 'British intelligence?'

He shakes his head. 'Nothing quite as impressive, I'm afraid.' He leans even closer, his voice barely audible. 'I'm a deserter, Alice. I'm running away to Canada to avoid having to go up there again.'

'You're with the air force?'

He nods. 'Wing Commander Heath. *Ex*-Wing Commander Heath. I can assure you I look an awful lot better in my uniform.'

Even his face seems to soften as he talks about his real life, becomes his real self.

Alice is astonished, her already fogged mind barely able to make sense of what Owen – Richard – is telling her.

'So, Owen Shaw isn't real? He's just someone you made up? A cover story?'

He nods. 'In part, yes. Although a lot of what you've seen is the real me, I'm afraid. It's hard to pretend when you're fighting for your life.'

'Why did you desert? Was it awful?' Alice thinks about the dying pilot and the downed planes she's seen. Of course it was awful.

'Took a couple of bad hits and had to eject. I was lucky. Many others weren't. It scared the hell out of me. Couldn't stand the thought of going up there again, so I took a chance, a risk. I thought I could start again, become someone else. Let's just say, it didn't quite work out as I'd imagined.'

'I'm sorry.'

'So am I.'

They sit quietly for a moment. Alice isn't sure what else to say, what to think.

'What will happen, if we're ever found?' Alice asks eventually. 'Will you be arrested?'

'Probably. Maybe they'll show a bit of compassion, given the situation. At least they've abolished the death penalty for desertion. And now you probably hate me and think I'm the worst sort of coward.'

'I don't actually. My brother is a CO.'

'You understand then, why I can't shoot down another enemy plane, or pull another colleague's burning body from the wreckage of his downed plane.'

'I don't think anyone can understand unless they've been up there in a dogfight, but I know you have to be very brave. And I also know you have to be brave to object, to say no.'

Their conversation is cut short by a noise at the front of the boat. Alice turns around to see Jimmy shouting and gesturing wildly at the ocean.

'What the hell are they playing at? Surely to God someone picked up the SOS. All the military might of the Royal Navy and they leave us to rot like discarded fish.'

Alice watches as he pulls off his boots and hurls them into the water in a looping arc, accompanied by a demented bellowing roar.

'I HATE THIS STUPID OCEAN! I HATE IT!' He sinks to his knees and puts his head in his hands, repeating over and over, 'I hate it. I hate it,' as he weeps like a child.

Nobody knows what to do, where to look. They can't even leave him alone, to spare his dignity. They can't fetch him a cup of tea, or tell him it will be okay. There is no comfort to be offered here. It is horrible to see.

Molly bursts into tears. Arthur clings to Alice's arm. Even Owen looks rattled. The ocean has stirred a madness in them all. Like the delicate parts of a clock, each needs the others to function, every one of them necessary to the survival of the group. Alice is terrified that if one of them cracks, they will all fail.

Her thoughts drift back to the first moments after the torpedo strike, when she'd tried to access the lower cabins and faced the terrifying reality of what had happened. Perhaps it would have been better to die in the immediate impact rather than endure this interminable nightmare, suspended in a sort of half-life. As she looks at the now familiar faces in the lifeboat, a dreadful thought occurs to her: not which one of them death will take next, but who it will leave until last.

Another afternoon is washed away and the honeyed hue of gentle evening light settles over the lifeboat. Too tired and weak to question the how and why of things anymore, Alice feels a sense of inevitability wash over her. She doesn't feel the urge to rail and roar at the ocean like Jimmy. There is a peacefulness in quietly accepting her fate. Not giving up, but letting go.

'What are you thinking about, Auntie?' Arthur asks. 'You look sad.'

She reaches for his arm, but her vision is intermittently blurred and she misjudges the distance and grabs his leg instead.

'I'm thinking about home, Arthur,' she says, her words muffled and tired. 'About my father, mostly.'

'My daddy died,' Arthur says. 'He went to sleep and didn't wake up.'

'I'm very sorry to hear that. My daddy died, too.'

'What did he die of?'

For the first time, Alice finds the words. 'Something went wrong in his head. Nobody knows why. I was ten years old. The same age as your sister.'

She still can't fathom how someone you love so much can be talking to you one minute, and the next, like a candle blown out, they're gone. All that life, extinguished.

'My daddy wrote Mummy a letter. She said all the soldiers write one when they go to war and it is sent home if they die. Did your daddy write a letter?'

Alice shakes her head. She wonders what he would have said if he'd had the chance. What do you say, when it's the last thing you'll ever write? How do you say your very last goodbye?

'*We* should write a letter,' Robert says. 'A message in a bottle. People always do that when they're stranded on a desert island, or lost at sea.'

Owen stirs. His American persona back on display. 'Hey. That's not a bad idea, kid. We have the empty whisky bottle. Does anyone have paper? Anything to write with?'

'I have paper.' Alice asks Molly to look in the pocket of her jacket where she finds the letter Alice had written to her father while they were delayed in Liverpool. 'Here.' Alice hands the paper to Owen. 'Use this.'

'And we are writing with invisible ink, I presume?'

'Somebody must have a pen, or a pencil. Something.'

But nobody does.

Then Alice remembers the gull feather she'd fished out of the ocean. She takes it out of her skirt pocket. 'Could we use this? Like a quill. Is there something we can dip it into? Anything in one of the supply tins?'

Hamish suggests blood. 'Pirates always use their blood to write with.'

Owen says it isn't the worst idea.

'What would we write?' Alice asks.

Jimmy has calmed down a little. He likes the idea of sending a message, to let someone know they'd survived. 'We should write the name of the ship. The number of adults and children in the lifeboat. The date. The direction we're sailing in.'

Owen makes a nick in his thumb with the edge of an empty tin of Carnation milk. Jimmy does the same. Dipping the end of the gull feather into the beads of blood that form on their skin, Owen slowly writes the words *SS Carlisle, Lifeboat 12, 6 ch/29 ad*, and the date which, according to the notches he's marked in the wood on the gunwale, is 22 September. He adds the words, '*Remember us*', then rolls up the page, pushes it carefully into the whisky bottle and screws the cap back on.

'Who's doing the honours?' he asks.

Alice suggests Robert, since it was his idea.

Everyone counts to three, and Robert drops the bottle into the ocean.

It bobs alongside the lifeboat for a while before slowly drifting away. The final chapter of thirty-five lives captured in a few short words, a final act of hope that, one day, somebody will know they were here, that they mattered, that they tried.

That night, the stars dazzle in a cloudless sky and the water shimmers beneath the steady forward motion of the lifeboat.

'Bioluminescence,' Alice says, struggling to enunciate the word as she explains it to the children. 'The light you can see is from millions of tiny creatures.'

The children are mesmerized by the way the water lights up when they trail their fingers over the side of the lifeboat. Alice encourages them to see the beauty that surrounds them. She feels a childish sense of wonder herself, astonished by the

255

unfathomable magnitude of the universe as she leans back and looks up at the sky.

'Look up, children,' she says. 'Look how beautiful it is.' The children stare up as she points out the constellations: the plough, Orion, the clear spiral of the Milky Way. 'How lucky we are,' she says as she reaches up a hand and imagines her fingers touching each source of light. 'A ship full of miracles, beneath a sky full of stars.' She counts thirty-nine stars before her eyelids flutter and close. Beside her, Arthur reaches seventy-three. And then there are no more stars, no more words, as Alice gives in to the pull of sleep, and lets herself drift away.

32

Glasgow. September 1940

Lily wakes in a small bedroom of a guesthouse perched above Greenock harbour. Too exhausted to put up the blackout screen when they'd arrived last night, she'd fallen into bed in the pitch dark. Now, from the iron bedstead in the middle of the room, she can see the calm waters of the Clyde glistening beneath the morning sun. She imagines Georgie waking to a similar view, pictures her waving from the deck as HMS *Imperial* approaches. They must be close now. She can feel it in the rush of blood that thumps against her chest, drawing her daughter to her like a magnet. Hurry up. Bring her home.

And Arthur? What is he looking at? What does he see when he wakes? Lily closes her eyes and pictures him in a lifeboat, his pale cheeks kissed by a gentle sun. He looks so content, so at peace, but he is so still. Too still. She wills him to move, urges him to fight against the weakening flutter of his little fledgling heart. She places her hands to her chest and wills the steady thud of her own heartbeat to become his. She breathes in and out, slow and steady, breathing life into him. 'I'm coming, Arthur,' she whispers. 'Hold on a bit longer, love. We're coming.'

She prepares for the day ahead in small, steady increments. She washes at the sink of the shared bathroom across the landing, brushes her teeth, teases out her finger waves and smooths her hair into side rolls. A hat will cover the rest. She pulls on her last half-decent pair of tan stockings, zips up her buttercup-yellow dress – Georgie's favourite – throws a moss-green cardigan over her shoulders, pinches her cheeks to bring a bit of colour to her washed-linen complexion. Inside, she feels colourless and weak, but she needs to be strong and bright, for Georgie.

The breakfast room is at the front of the guesthouse, over-looking the harbour. Lily feels horribly self-conscious as she makes her way across the faded crimson carpet to join Kitty at a table beside the window. Ancient floorboards creak and squeak beneath her footsteps as if announcing her arrival. *Look, everyone! She's one of the parents.* She doesn't want to draw attention to herself, especially in a room full of newspapermen. There is a sharp air of anticipation among the murmured conver-sations and the occasional clatter of teapots and cutlery.

Kitty wishes Lily good morning as she takes the chair oppo-site her. 'Did you sleep?'

'Not much. You?'

Kitty shakes her head. 'Sat up all night, reading reports and correspondence about the *Carlisle*. It's front-page news every-where. People are demanding an inquiry.'

At tables around the room, government officials and news-paper reporters speak in hushed, urgent voices over plates of congealed egg and cold toast. Like Kitty and Lily, they pore over the morning newspapers, digesting the latest details of the tragedy, speculating about the inevitable questions and recriminations and demands for Churchill to retaliate. It seems to Lily that everyone in the guesthouse is there because of the imminent arrival of the *Carlisle*'s precious few survivors. She wonders if other parents have made the journey to Scotland, or if she's the only one.

'You look nice today,' Kitty says as she nibbles a triangle of toast. 'When the reporters realize who you are, they'll want to ask questions and take your photograph. The newsreels might even want to take some film.'

'I couldn't give two figs how I look for their photographs and newsreels. I want to look nice for Georgie. That's all.'

Lily pushes a poached egg around her plate. She has no appetite. Her stomach is as knotted as the coils of old fishing rope she can see on the wharf beyond the window.

Kitty kicks her under the table as Anthony Quinn enters the room and takes a seat with two other gentlemen at a table beside the fireplace. 'That's him. The one just sitting down.'

'Are you sure he doesn't know who I am?' Lily keeps her voice low and pours tea from a pot. It dribbles and leaves a stain on the white tablecloth. She covers it with her napkin.

Kitty shakes her head. 'If anyone asks, you're with the *Express*. They're all so caught up in their explanations and excuses, he won't even notice you.'

Lily sips her tea and studies Mr Quinn. She'd expected someone much more impressive. The wiry-haired man across the room seems too wishy-washy to have held such enormous responsibility in his anxious little hands, too inconsequential to have become such a devastating part of so many lives. He pushes his spectacles onto his nose and consults some paperwork as he sips a cup of tea. His calm demeanour grates on Lily's nerves. He *should* notice her. Maybe she will make him notice her.

'Lily! Look at this.' Kitty pushes a newspaper toward her. 'It says here that one of the lifeboats recovered by HMS *Imperial* was from HMS *Eagle*. One of *Carlisle*'s lifeboats *is* unaccounted for, just as you said.'

Lily reads the newspaper report with a sense of anger and urgency and a sickening pulse of fear. The confirmation renews her hope for Arthur, but also stirs a lingering sense of dread. The thought of him, lost and alone and afraid, is unbearable. Her stomach churns. Constantly on the brink of tears, and certain she will vomit if she so much as looks at the egg on her plate, she fights to maintain her composure.

'You're a little pale,' Kitty says. 'Maybe you should get some fresh air.'

Lily is about to make a dash for it when the opening strains of the national anthem blare from the wireless cabinet in the corner of the room. Everyone stands up. Lily thinks of Peter and the dog, as she always does now when she hears the first bars of the music.

The king's broadcast spreads around the small room. The sound of an air-raid siren wailing in the background is a poignant reminder to Lily that the war, and the Blitz, goes on, even if she is now far away from it. She thinks about Mrs H and Elsie Farnaby and poor Ada Fortune and wonders how they're getting on. The king's monotonous tone is steady and calm for a full ten minutes, then the familiar stutters and pauses return. '*And here, I want to tell, the following parents, how deeply we grieve for them, over the loss of their children, in . . . in the ship torpedoed, without warning, in mid-Atlantic. Surely, the world could have no clearer proof, of the wickedness against which we fight, than this foul deed.*'

Lily feels as if he is speaking directly to her, as if he is standing beside her, telling her how terribly sorry he is, and that he shares in her sorrow.

As the broadcast ends, two men at a table behind Lily speculate about revenge and reprisals. At another table, someone becomes an expert on the subject of hypothermia. Someone else asks the waitress if there's any chance of more tea and toast. Lily feels her grief and distress meld into anger. How can everyone just sit there, enjoying their breakfast, while dozens of children have died and Arthur is missing? She refuses to count him among the dead.

As Mr Quinn leaves the room, Lily stands up.

Kitty asks her where she's going.

'I have to talk to him, Kitty. I can't stand it, sitting here like a porcelain statue.'

She grabs Kitty's documents, and her own paperwork with her notes and calculations, and walks as calmly as she can across the crimson carpet as she follows Mr Quinn from the room.

'Excuse me. Mr Quinn? Could I have a word?' Her heart thumps beneath her dress.

He turns and looks at her, then at his pocket watch. 'Who are you with?'

'Sorry?'

'Which newspaper?'

'The *Express*.'

'Two minutes.' He steps into a small reading room off the entrance hall and indicates two chairs beside a large window. 'Fire ahead.'

Lily takes a deep breath and perches on the chair opposite him. She clutches the papers to her chest, thinks about her children, Ada Fortune's children – all the CORB children – and wills herself to find the courage to speak.

'I want to know why the naval escort abandoned the *Carlisle*.'

Mr Quinn peers at her over the bridge of his spectacles. The bluntness of her question has clearly disarmed him. 'Well, that's simply not true. There was no "abandoning". The naval escort left the convoy, as planned, to rendezvous with an incoming supply convoy from Canada. It is always the way.'

'Yes. The "limit of convoy escort", I believe.'

Mr Quinn picks a hair from his jacket and straightens a cufflink. 'That is correct.'

'Something you failed to mention in your correspondence to parents. You told them the ship their children would sail on would be escorted, and in convoy. There was no mention of any limit.'

Lily looks at him. Challenging him.

'I see you've done your homework.' He leans back in the chair and studies her. 'At the limit of convoy, escort ships depart and the convoy proceeds unescorted because it is considered safe to do so. The threat of U-boat activity is greatly reduced beyond that limit.'

'Reduced, but not eliminated. And there *have* been recent reports of U-boat activity beyond the present limit of convoy, haven't there? And yet the limit wasn't revised. Also, not one ship from the convoy went to assist the *Carlisle*. Not one, out of eighteen. Not one, while children drowned. Why?'

Mr Quinn shuffles uncomfortably in his seat. He looks flustered; rattled. 'It is a profoundly distressing tragedy, but the fact remains that we are a nation at war against a ruthless enemy. There is no absolute guarantee of safety. There never was. I made that perfectly clear in one of my first broadcasts. It was always a decision for the parents to take, having weighed up the relative risks. Everything else – limits of convoy, instructions to disperse – is merely detail, Miss . . .'

'Nicholls. Mrs Nicholls.' Lily feels heat rise in her cheeks. Her breathing is sharp and shallow. 'And my children are NOT merely details!'

'Your children?'

She takes a deep breath. 'I'm not with the *Express*. I'm a mother, Mr Quinn. One of dozens of mothers whose children are missing, or dead. Your "merely details" are my last hope of understanding how this could ever happen. We trusted you. We put our children's lives in your hands when all we ever wanted was to keep them in our own. How can we ever make peace with that, Mr Quinn? How can we *ever* be at peace?'

Her words, her grief, fill the small room so that she thinks she might suffocate beneath the weight of it all.

He looks at her, ashen-faced. 'I'm so sorry, Mrs Nicholls.'

'My children are—'

'Georgina and Arthur.' He nods. 'I remember. I remember every name. Your daughter, Georgina, was picked up by HMS *Imperial*. Your son, Arthur, was not found.' He leans forward and puts his head in his hands. His eyes glisten with tears when he looks up. 'I am so terribly sorry, Mrs Nicholls. I wish there were something I could do to ease your suffering. Truly, I do.'

'There *is* something you can do. We know a lifeboat from HMS *Eagle* was miscounted as one of *Carlisle*'s twelve lifeboats. There is still one lifeboat unaccounted for. I want you to keep searching for survivors.'

Mr Quinn shakes his head. 'It's impossible. Nobody could have survived this long.'

Lily picks up the papers covered in her pencil marks and carefully laid out notes, and pushes them toward him. 'It *is* possible. I've studied the tides and the wind direction for the hours and days immediately after the *Carlisle* sank. Assuming the missing lifeboat was in a seaworthy condition and sat high in the water after it launched, unlike most of the other lifeboats, it is possible that it travelled beyond the initial search grid. I've done the calculations, Mr Quinn. It's all there.' She grabs his arm, anchoring herself to him until he understands. 'What's impossible is that I might never see my son again, never know what happened to him. *That* is impossible.'

Mr Quinn stacks the papers back into a neat pile. 'Can I ask where you obtained all this information?'

'A friend.' She refuses to say anything further.

'A friend who seems to know an awful lot about our operation.' He steeples his hands and leans forward, pressing his fingertips to the bridge of his spectacles.

Lily's heart thumps beneath her dress. 'So? Will you order another search?'

He shakes his head. 'I'm sorry, Mrs Nicholls. I understand your agony, but we are already struggling to requisition sufficient vessels to escort supply convoys. Resources are stretched tight. It isn't simply a case of sending HMS *Imperial* back. It is already assigned to another convoy.'

Lily feels her cheeks flush with anger. 'Then at least redirect a ship already out there. There must be some way to keep looking.' She points at the papers in front of him. 'The location is right here. Send the RAF. Just *do* something. Please. I'm begging you.' Lily grips his arm again, more tightly than she'd intended, her despair like a vice. 'Do you have children, Mr Quinn?'

He looks at her and nods. 'A boy.'

'Then forget about the charts and calculations. As a father, as a parent, I know you understand. As a mother who has lost *her* boy, I am begging you to help me.'

He stands up and lets out a long sigh. 'Very well, Mrs Nicholls. I will look at your calculations with my superiors and, if it is indeed possible that a remaining lifeboat could have passed beyond the search grid before HMS *Imperial* arrived, I will arrange for one more search attempt. In the meantime, I believe your daughter's arrival is imminent. We should leave for the docks.'

Lily begins to make her way from the room.

'One more thing, Mrs Nicholls.'

'Yes?'

'For what it's worth, I would have done exactly the same, in your position. I wouldn't rest until my child was found.'

'Well, for what it's worth, *I* wouldn't have done the same in *your* position, Mr Quinn. I would have been honest from the start. I would have told parents the exact arrangements for escorting their children. But that's the difference between people like you and people like me. I have decency and integrity. All you have is power and ambition and letters after your name.'

She shuts the door behind her and closes her eyes as she takes a moment to compose herself and catch her breath.

'Lily? Is everything all right? What happened?'

She is relieved to see Kitty. 'I'm not entirely sure.'

'We should go down to the harbour. They'll be here soon.' Kitty reaches for Lily's hand. 'Are you ready?'

Lily pushes her shoulders back and takes a deep breath. What matters now is her daughter. 'Yes. I'm ready.'

Over two weeks of bombing and still no let-up despite the air force inflicting heavy losses on the Luftwaffe. Some say Hitler won't invade after all. Hope they're right. Feel very war-weary. For now, we count our dead and our blessings because there's always someone much worse off. Even felt guilty putting on lipstick today, but they tell us to keep our spirits up, so Spitfire Crimson it is (beetroot juice sounds so rural). Going dancing later. Haven't a thing to wear.

Mass-Observation, Diarist #6385

33

Mid-Atlantic. 23 September 1940

Day Six

A new day dawns beneath moody skies and a sludgy grey ocean. Sunlight or storms, it is all the same now.

Alice watches the water, mesmerized by the undulating motion, in awe of its power. She stays like this for a long time, drifting in and out of sleep, watching the waves as the lifeboat rocks gently, up and down, up and down. Everything is so quiet, so calm, that when a juvenile whale surfaces beside the lifeboat, Alice doesn't cry out or try to get everyone's attention as she did before. She stays exactly as she is, quietly observing.

The creature studies her for a moment, its jet-black eye fixed on hers, telling her to hold on, that there is still hope, that there will be a life beyond this. It is so beautiful and intense, so peaceful and serene. It moves closer. Alice reaches out an arm, desperate to touch it. She stretches her fingertips as far as she can, leans forward until she is almost there. Someone says something behind her, but noises are muffled and strange now and she can't understand what they're saying. She reaches out further until she is hanging over the side of the lifeboat. The whale stays perfectly still, as if it is waiting for her, and as the ocean pushes the lifeboat forward, Alice feels cool flesh beneath her fingertips. She runs her hand across the whale's smooth skin, reaches out further, but somebody is pulling her arm back and somebody else is pulling her waist and the whale, startled, suddenly dives, and there is so much noise and commotion as Alice slumps into the bottom of the lifeboat.

Owen is staring at her, his eyes wild and intense. 'What the hell are you doing? Nearly lost you overboard.'

Jimmy runs his hand through his hair. All the colour has drained from his face. 'That was too close for my liking.'

'I was looking at the whale,' she says, confused by their reaction. 'I wanted to touch it. Did you see it?'

The children stare at her. Arthur looks away, embarrassed.

'What's the matter? Why are you all looking at me like that?'

Owen helps her to sit up. 'There wasn't a whale, Alice.'

'There was! The juvenile came back. It was right there, beside the boat.'

Jimmy shakes his head. 'You're seeing things, Alice. Hallucinating.'

'How did you not see it? I touched it!' She can't understand what they're saying. She'd seen it look at her, she'd felt its skin beneath her fingertips. She turns back to Owen. 'You must have seen it!'

He says he didn't. 'I'm sorry, Alice. It wasn't there. There wasn't a whale. It was all in your mind.'

Upset and confused, she leans forward and curls into a ball, her head in her arms. They are wrong. She had seen it; felt it. They are all wrong.

A little while later, Arthur shuffles up beside her. 'There wasn't a whale, Auntie. You leaned out of the boat and dangled your arm in the water. We thought you were going to fall out. You won't, will you? Promise you won't leave us.'

Alice brushes Arthur's hair from his forehead. 'I won't leave you, Arthur. I promise. We've come this far together, and we'll go home together. You've been ever so brave. Really, I think you are all the bravest children I will ever know.'

She rests her head on the gunwale as the ocean breathes in and out against the lifeboat, and the haunting sound of whale song reaches out to her from the fathoms below. In her mind, she sees her father, a finger to his lips, a smile in his eyes. 'Come and see,' he whispers. 'It's a Hunter's Moon. It's so close you can touch it.' In her slippers and dressing gown, she pads downstairs, her hand in his, and they sit together on the old bench in the garden and look up. She reaches out her hands, either side of the great orb in the sky, so that it looks as if she is holding the moon. 'What does it feel like?' he asks, and she makes up stories about how it feels soft and warm like butter, or hard and cold like ice and they sit, telling stories about the moon until she falls asleep and he carries her back inside, and in the morning she won't be sure if she'd dreamt it, or if it was real, but she'll know for certain that her father is the most wonderful man she's ever known.

Alice sleeps, wakes, watches the children. She sees faces and shapes in the gathering clouds.

Someone recites the Lord's Prayer. Someone sings 'Pack Up Your Troubles'. Owen's harmonica catches the haunting melody. Alice moves her lips in time to the chorus. 'Smile, smile, smile.'

The midday dipper of water comes around. Alice knows she can't keep giving Billy her water, but she quietly gives him half of her ration and sucks on a slice of tinned peach, drawing as much liquid from it as she can. Owen watches her carefully to make sure she eats. Small scraps of food. Little routines. The only things they can rely on now.

Mr Harlow sees two phantom ships that day, conjured from the play of light on the horizon and his delirious mind. Robert spots land, but it is just a cloud, hanging low in the sky. Imagined things. Nothing is real anymore.

At Alice's feet, little Billy Fortune is restless. His cough has worsened again. When she touches her fingertips to his forehead, he feels hot, and yet he shivers. She reapplies the cold compress, dipping the rag into the puddles of seawater in the bottom of the lifeboat as she wills him to cool down, to be well again.

She sleeps, wakes, watches the children. The lifeboat moves up and down with the rise and fall of the ocean, up and down until Alice's breathing matches the rhythm of the boat and she becomes the ocean.

A breath in. A breath out.

Up, and down.

Up, and down.

'Alice. Alice! Wake up!'

She opens her eyes. Owen is crouched beside her. She stares at him, confused for a moment as to who he is, where she is. And then she remembers. His name is Richard, but she doesn't know why.

'Are they here? Are we safe?'

He shakes his head. 'It's the boy. He's in a bad way.'

'Which boy?' Her words are muffled by her swollen tongue. She wishes she could rip it out, wishes she could be free of the thick useless lump in her mouth.

'Billy.'

She sits up. Every part of her is in pain. Her bones feel heavy and yet spongy at the same time. She retches at the stench of damp and stale sweat that clings to her clothes. The lifeboat is rotting and decaying, and she is decaying with it.

Billy is laid out on the thwarts, delirious with a fever.

270

Alice crawls over legs and feet to sit beside him. 'It's all right, Billy. Auntie is here. What's all this noise?' She tries to comfort him, calm him, rubs his hands and reassures him.

He scrabbles at her like a wild animal. Between heart-wrenching wails he coughs so violently that his tiny body bucks and jerks. When Alice places her hand to his skin, he is burning up.

Little Billy Fortune, who captured her heart the moment he reached for her hand on the station platform in London, is now suffering the most. His fevered body convulses in dreadful spasms.

'Nearly home now, Billy,' she says as she holds him in her arms. 'Nearly home to see your mother, and your father's marvellous pigeons.'

He cries for his lost marbles, and reaches for the one in his pocket.

Alice assures him it is safe.

'We'll buy you some new marbles when we get home,' Owen says. 'The biggest and best we can find. How about that, Billy the Kid?'

Another coughing fit takes over.

Alice wraps her arms firmly around him and tells him to hold on. There is nothing else she can do.

As afternoon drifts into evening, the last of the day's water is handed out. After that, everyone sucks their buttons to try to stimulate a little saliva. When that doesn't work, they suck the sodden sleeves of their pyjamas and the damp edges of their blankets, crazed in their desperation to drink more.

Alice stumbles her way through the final parts of *Moby Dick*, a gory muddle of harpoons and smashed boats and sailors tossed into the sea, until Ishmael is floating on Queequeg's coffin and he is rescued by a whaling ship.

'And I only am escaped alone to tell thee. The End.' She repeats her closing words twice, reluctant to finish, for the story to be over. Arthur is pleased that Ishmael was rescued, but Alice's heart is heavy. There is no pen poised to write them out of *their* ordeal, and their end is surely not far away now. As she shuts the imaginary book, she notices that the wind is picking up again.

Over the next hour, dark, ominous clouds gather. The increased rocking of the lifeboat is impossible to ignore.

Not long after sunset, the first heavy drops of rain begin to fall.

The seventh night in the lifeboat, and another storm, begin.

34

Glasgow. September 1940

A murmur of expectation ripples through the crowd gathered on the wharf. Hundreds of spectators have arrived, eager to see the few precious survivors for themselves, but Lily hardly notices anyone else. She is silent and still, alone in her desperation to have her daughter safely in her arms.

She shields her eyes from the sun and peers into the distance. It takes her a moment to locate the plume of smoke from HMS *Imperial* as it steams toward them. She takes in a breath and clenches her hands together at her chest, as if in prayer.

Kitty stands on Lily's right, Mr Quinn stands beside Kitty. He is pale and quiet, his impervious gaze giving away little of whatever emotions simmer beneath his carefully controlled demeanour. He brushes off reporters' questions with a firm, 'Not now, gentlemen. There will be ample time for questions later.'

The enormous ship moves agonizingly slowly. Each minute feels like a hundred more, until Lily is just able to make out figures beside the railings, and then she can see people clearly

– the crew, waving. Then, individual faces become distinct. She scans them quickly, searching wildly. Where is she? Where are they? There is still a faint trace of stubborn hope in Lily's heart that Arthur will be with his sister, that the authorities have made a mistake and the two of them will walk off the great ship together, hand in hand.

Everything moves in slow motion as the ship comes to a stop alongside the wharf, dwarfing every vessel beside it. The ropes are thrown and secured, protocols and procedures diligently followed despite the exceptional circumstances of this ship's arrival and the growing sense of anticipation among the restless crowd.

A group of adults leaves the ship first. Men and women, young and old. Lily sees the same haunted expression on every face. She wonders what horrors they've seen, what unimaginable events they've been through. Some are reunited with loved ones in moving scenes of tender relief. Others seem to just melt away into the crowd, their ordeal over, and yet in many ways only just beginning. She notices a tall man hesitating as he approaches the gangway, and then sees the reason for his pause: children are beginning to emerge through a doorway.

Lily's pulse quickens. Goosebumps run along her skin. Her eyes dart from one face to the next, looking, searching as the man bends down and says something to each child in turn before giving them a hug or a handshake or tousling their hair. Three boys walk, unaided, down the ramp. At the bottom, they are met by Mr Quinn and Red Cross volunteers and a barrage of newspaper reporters and cameramen with popping flashbulbs and loud commanding voices. Lily is heartened by the fact that the boys seem to be in remarkably good spirits. Even the two girls who are carried off the ship on stretchers manage to wave to the crowds and lift their heads to smile before being taken away by ambulance.

Shock and relief thread among the assembled crowds. These few surviving souls are the first visible evidence of the tragedy that has unfolded so far away. Yet their arrival brings as much pain as joy; a reminder of the many others lost.

'Where is she? Where's Georgie?' Lily says the words out loud, but speaks only to herself. What if they've got it wrong? What if she hasn't been rescued at all?

After what feels like an age, two more figures emerge through the doorway and stand on the deck beside the tall man. A boy Lily doesn't know. A girl she does.

'Georgie!' The name falls from Lily's lips in a gasp. 'My Georgie.'

She is here.

All the noise around her fades away. All the reporters and spectators disappear. There is nothing and nobody else, just her daughter, her beautiful brilliant girl. Seeing her now is like seeing her for the first time, when the midwife placed the impossibly tiny bundle in her arms. Lily looks at Georgina now the way she'd looked at her then, with wonder and disbelief, and an overwhelming sense of love.

She moves forward, pushing her way past people, propelled by a powerful rush of relief and love. 'Let me through. That's my little girl. That's my daughter.'

She can't get to her fast enough, can't catch her breath through her tears as she calls Georgie's name again and again so that her words come out in snatched gasping fragments, and then Georgie sees her, and Lily hears her cry out, 'Mummy! Mummy!' and she is moving towards her, and they are both running and stumbling until, in a dizzying whirl of joy and relief, Georgie is in Lily's arms.

She is in her arms.

She is in her arms.

Lily sinks to her knees.

For a long time, they stay locked in an embrace in the autumn sunshine as Lily absorbs every part of her daughter, the sweet scent of her hair, the thump of her heart against her own. There isn't a mark on her. Not a scratch or a bruise. It is, without doubt, a miracle.

Georgie sobs and sobs and tries to say something, but her words come out in great gulps and it takes Lily a moment to understand what she's saying.

'I don't have him, Mummy! I don't have Arthur. I'm sorry, Mummy. I'm sorry.'

'It's all right, love. I know. It's all right.' Lily presses her cheek against the top of her daughter's head. She refuses to let herself cry. She has to be strong, for them both. 'You're safe now. You're safe.' She draws in a long deep breath. 'You're safe.'

'How does it feel to have your daughter home?'

'When did you and your husband first hear the news?'

'What do you want to say to those in charge of the evacuation programme?'

The reporters' questions land on Lily like arrows. She wants to tell them she is beyond grateful to have her daughter back, but that her son is still missing and her heart is still broken. But that's not the story they want to hear. They don't want sorrow and grief; they want reunions and survival. They want to focus on the happy ever after, not on the recriminating questions that linger.

'I'm very glad to have my daughter safely home.' It is the best she can manage. 'If you'll excuse us, we'd like some time alone. In private. There's a lot to catch up on.'

As Kitty had warned her, such a public tragedy demanded a public response, and as a representative from the government steps forward and introduces himself, it is immediately clear to Lily that she will not be permitted the quiet time of healing and recovery she so desperately wants.

'Ed Atkinson. Ministry of Shipping.' He gives Lily a bewildering set of instructions: places to be, names of people Georgina will be asked to talk to. 'We've arranged a welcome reception for the CORB children. They'll be given an opportunity to speak to the newspapers, and there'll be some formal photographs.'

Lily couldn't care less what has been arranged. 'We don't wish to speak to the newspapers, thank you. We just want some time alone. My daughter has been through a terrible ordeal.'

Mr Atkinson is a little taken aback. 'But everything has been arranged. We have a car waiting to take you to the hotel. It shouldn't take long.'

'You should go,' Kitty says, stepping in discreetly. 'Get it over with. They'll only hound you otherwise.'

'But what about Arthur? I need to speak to Mr Quinn again. He promised he would order another search.'

Kitty places her hand on Lily's arm. 'I've already spoken to him. He confirmed that a supply ship already in the Atlantic has been instructed to resume the search, given the new information we have. You have your daughter to focus on now. I'll meet you at the hotel in a while.'

A weight lifts from Lily's shoulders. They are going back. There is nothing else she can do now, except wait and pray for another miracle. Kitty is right. She must focus on Georgie, but she won't rest until she has both her children in her arms.

Lily holds Georgie's hand tight as the car takes them to the hotel. There are so many questions Lily wants to ask her, about what she'd endured that dreadful night before help arrived, about how Arthur was during the journey, and when Georgie had last seen him, but Georgie only wants to tell her about how nice the *Carlisle* was, and how friendly the other girls were, and how much food they'd eaten at every meal. She seems to have blocked out the sinking and her ordeal in the storm. Lily's questions will have to wait.

'Auntie was ever so kind,' Georgie says.

'Who's Auntie, love?'

'Auntie Alice. The lady who came to collect us. We called the escorts auntie and uncle. She was in charge of my group. There were fifteen of us.'

Lily had only seen three girls return on HMS *Imperial*. The losses are unimaginable. 'Was Auntie Alice in your lifeboat?'

Georgie shakes her head. 'I saw her on the deck just as we were getting into the lifeboat, but she rushed off again. One of the other escorts, Auntie Beryl, said she'd gone back to help people trapped in their cabins. Auntie Beryl looked after us in the lifeboat until the rescue ship came.'

Eventually, Georgie talks a little about the night of the sinking, how she made it to the muster station and got into lifeboat seven, but fell out as it was being lowered down. 'It tipped right up, Mummy. Lots of people fell into the sea and it was so cold and dark and I thought I was going to die until I was pulled out of the water.'

Lily can't bear to think about the fear and panic, or whether Arthur was one of those children thrown into the water. 'Who pulled you out, love? Do you remember?'

The driver comes to a stop outside the hotel. 'It was that man, over there.' Georgie points to a tall man talking to a group of newspaper reporters. 'He pulled me and two other girls into the lifeboat. Can we go inside for the sandwiches now?'

'Yes, love. We can go inside for the sandwiches. Do you remember the man's name?'

'Yes! He was everyone's favourite. That's Uncle Howard.'

35

Mid-Atlantic. 23 September 1940

Day Six

The storm approaches slowly, like a predator stalking its prey. Dark clouds snuff out the stars, one by one, until all that is left is a shroud of intense, impenetrable black draped above the lifeboat. Fat raindrops turn to painful hailstones as the temperature drops and the wind gusts and howls, and great waves wash over the gunwales again and again. Those who have the strength bail desperately to keep the lifeboat afloat. Those who don't look on helplessly.

Alice encourages the children to sing the hokey-cokey, just as they did before – she can't remember when – but they are afraid and weak and after the first verse and chorus their tentative singing is replaced with frightened whimpers. It is distressing, but it is also reassuring. It is their silence Alice dreads more than their despair.

Everyone clings to something or somebody as the lifeboat pitches and rolls violently. This is it then, Alice thinks. This is surely the end. Images flash through her mind, snapshots of the life she has already lived, glimpses of the one she might have known. She sees a cottage on a clifftop, overlooking a stretch of coloured sand that leads to the sea. She is sitting on a bench in the garden, surrounded by an arch of white roses, a book in her hands. Someone is walking toward her, but her eyes are dazzled by the sun, her visitor a faceless silhouette. She is so happy there, so free and invigorated.

But it is just an illusion.

A dream.

A suggestion of what might have been.

A huge wave washes over her and tosses the image overboard.

Stripped of everything, Alice gives in to her terror and despair and weeps for all that she was and all that she might have been and for the unwritten stories of thirty-five lives that will never be told.

The children scream with each dramatic plunge. It is like the first night all over again, but this time it is worse, the winds wilder, the rain harder, the terrifying pitch and toss of the lifeboat more pronounced. This time, they are starved of food and water and hope. This time, nobody has the strength to handle the Fleming gear. Nobody believes a rescue ship will appear. Nobody expects to survive.

There is so much noise and fear that when Alice is thrown forward and bangs her head on the thwarts, there is a moment before she loses consciousness when she is grateful for the numbing silence. 'I can sleep now,' she thinks. 'I can slip away. I did my best.' And through the retreating roar of the wind, she hears her father tell her about the constellation of Orion. *Look, Alice. Look how beautiful it is.* And a golden light reaches out and she lifts her hands to meet it, and her father is there, smiling at her. *Your move, Alice. Take your time. Think it through. Remember to always look ahead.*

36

Glasgow. September 1940

Inside the stuffy formal rooms of a rather tired-looking hotel, Lily leads Georgie to the buffet. She can't eat a thing herself, but Georgie is delighted by the spread that has been put on for them, 'In the middle of a war, and everything!' After all she has been through, she is still just a little girl, easily impressed by a few sandwiches and cakes, ready to see the good in everything and everyone. Lily wishes she could be so easily distracted.

She reaches for Georgie every few minutes, responding to an urge to hold her daughter's hand or smooth her hair, to keep her close to her side. She reluctantly agrees to let her go to the lavatory with another girl, and tells her to come straight back. She is anxious and restless. The formalities and photographs are tiring. The muted air of relief sticks in her throat as she stares at the buffet and tries to find something she can bear to eat. Everything is beige and dry-looking, and her stomach is in knots. For all that Georgie is wonderfully here, her return has made

Arthur's absence more pronounced. He should be here, with them. Everything is mismatched and uneven without him.

Lily adds a few triangular sandwiches to her plate so as not to look impolite. Peter always laughed at sandwiches cut into triangles. He thought they were complete nonsense. 'Silly things they put out at weddings and funerals. When I go, promise you'll give people sandwiches cut into halves. Give people something decent to bite into!' There weren't any sandwiches for Peter in the end. She'd blamed rationing, but it was sympathy and mourners that were really in short supply.

Peter's cousin conducted the small private service in the local Methodist chapel. There were only a handful of mourners. A blackbird sang while he was buried. Wet grass soaked through a split in the seam of Lily's shoe. The children went to play at the Ingrams' afterward. On the wireless that evening, there was talk about the threat of German invasion and a second wave of evacuation, overseas this time. J.B. Priestley delivered his regular Postscript, and then Peter delivered his own.

A letter, and a diary, were enclosed along with his personal effects. He'd written the letter on the way to the training camp. It was the letter every soldier hoped would never find its way to their loved ones.

My darling Lil,
They said we should write a letter to be sent home in the event of the worst happening. This is my fifth attempt because how can I possibly say goodbye to you? I can't, so I won't. This isn't a goodbye letter. It's a love letter, to my sweetheart . . .

'Excuse me. Do you know what's in these?' A man to Lily's right peels back the top slice of bread on one of the sandwiches on his plate and inspects the contents. 'Meat paste, perhaps? Cement? It's hard to tell these days. Maybe I'll stick to tea and biscuits.'

Lily doesn't have the stomach or the energy for a conversation about limp sandwiches. 'Probably wise.'

He puts the sandwich back. 'You're not with the newspapers, are you? I'm not entirely sure who it's safe to talk to.'

'Don't worry. You're safe. I'm with my daughter. Georgina.' She nods her head toward Georgie, who is happily playing Cat's Cradle with one of the other children. 'I still can't believe she's here.'

'You're Georgie's mother?'

'Georgie Nicholls. Yes.'

'Howard,' the man says, holding out a hand.

Lily recognizes him now. He is the man Georgie pointed out as they arrived at the hotel. '*Uncle* Howard?'

A brief, self-conscious smile crosses his lips. 'Howard Keane officially, Uncle Howard as I've been known recently. I was – am – an escort with CORB. I'm very pleased to meet you. Georgie talked about you such a lot.'

Lily grips his hand tight. 'I'm so pleased to meet *you*. Georgie told me you pulled her and two other girls out of the water. I can't thank you enough, Mr Keane. You saved her life. I can't even begin to imagine what you've all been through.'

'You don't have to thank me, Mrs Nicholls. I only wish we could have saved them all.'

Lily dabs at her nose with a handkerchief. 'I'm sorry. It's just all very difficult. My son is still missing.'

'Would you like to sit down?'

They find a couple of chairs beside a fireplace and sip weak tea as Lily keeps a close eye on Georgie.

'She's a credit to you,' Howard says. 'She was incredibly brave. They all were.'

'It sounds as if you were the one who was brave, Mr Keane.'

He shakes his head. 'Anyone would have done the same. Raw instinct takes over in the moment. A primal need to help. To

283

survive. We assumed help would arrive immediately from the other ships in the convoy, but not one of them came back.' He pauses for a moment, as if to catch his breath. 'It was twelve hours before HMS *Imperial* arrived. Many didn't make it through the night. I find that the hardest to accept, that they made it off the *Carlisle* and into a lifeboat, and still didn't survive.'

Lily puts her cup down. Part of her wants the details, but it's too painful to imagine Arthur as one of those desperate souls waiting for help to arrive.

Howard reaches for her arm. 'I'm so sorry, Mrs Nicholls. I shouldn't have gone on. Georgie talked about Arthur a lot. She was desperately worried about him.'

Lily nods through her tears. 'They're going to search again, for more survivors. It seems they might have missed a lifeboat, but it's been such a long time now, and he was only wearing his cotton pyjamas.' This small detail torments her. Georgie had told her the children were allowed to change into their night-clothes for the first time the night of the torpedo strike. 'I told the children to wear their coats,' Lily says. 'Just in case. I can't help thinking that Arthur might have been weighed down, that he struggled in the water . . .'

'Try not to upset yourself.' Howard runs his hands through his hair. 'I feel so guilty for surviving when so many didn't. Children, especially.' He pulls a handkerchief from his breast pocket, and removes a book with it. He sits quietly for a moment, his anguish overwhelming him.

Lily can't think of anything else to say and is glad to see Kitty make her way over to them.

'Sorry to interrupt, Lily, but I'm afraid Georgie is needed for another photograph.'

Lily sighs. 'Does she have to? Surely she's done enough.'

'Just one more. For *The Times*.' Kitty's attention is caught by the book on Howard's lap. 'Excuse me. Where did you get that book?'

Lily finds the question a little abrupt. 'Kitty, this is Mr Keane. He saved Georgina from the water. He's an escort with CORB.'

Howard looks at Kitty and offers a weary greeting as he turns the book over. 'It was lent to me by a friend on the ship. She said I must read it. She was quite insistent! I was reading it when the torpedo hit. I'd got all the way to the boat deck before I realized it was still clutched in my hands.'

Kitty reaches for it. 'That's Alice's book! A Christmas gift from our father.'

Howard looks astonished. 'You know Alice? Alice King?'

Lily answers for her. 'Kitty is Alice's sister. This is Kitty King.'

Howard looks at Lily and then at Kitty as he hands her the book. 'I'm so sorry, Miss King. Please, take it.'

Kitty's eyes fill with tears as she looks at Howard, opens the book to the title page and reads the inscription. 'She insisted you read it?'

'Yes.'

A thin smile edges Kitty's lips. 'That sounds like my sister. You knew her?'

Howard nods. 'I was getting to know her, yes.' He pauses. 'I'm so sorry, Miss King. For your loss.'

Kitty pulls up a chair and sits beside him. 'How was she, on the ship? Was she happy? Homesick?'

Howard smiles. 'She was very seasick, but not homesick. She was, I think, very proud of her appointment as an escort, and a natural with the children. She found the ocean freeing. Said it made her see things differently.'

Lily listens to their easy conversation. She notices Kitty's manner change, the burden of her grief lightening a little as she talks about her sister with someone who'd spent those last happy days with her, and who clearly admired her.

She excuses herself and takes Georgie for the photograph. Thankfully, the photographer is quick, and doesn't stage the children as rigidly as the previous photographers. Lily watches from a discreet distance. The small group of evacuees looks so lost in the large room, too few in number by far, and as the photographer encourages them to smile, Lily's gaze passes beyond the five children present, and settles on the empty space to her daughter's left. The empty space where her son should be.

37

Mid-Atlantic. 24 September 1940

Day Seven

The storm passes and Alice wakes to the most beautiful sunrise she has ever seen; the sky an orchard of peach and lemon trees. Or perhaps she is dreaming. She imagines herself climbing the ambered clouds, picking ripe fruit for winter preserves. It is so peaceful, so calm, the only sounds the gentle wash of the ocean against the lifeboat and Arthur telling Brian about some small matter of great importance to young boys. Above her, the sail hangs in lifeless folds against the mast. The boat barely moves, just a gentle rise and fall, up and down, in and out, to match the rhythm of her hand rising and falling on her chest. A breath in, a breath out. That is all she needs to do. Keep breathing. Beside her, the five children wake. One by one, they emerge from beneath their blankets. Five little miracles. Too full of life not yet lived to give in to the pull of death.

Five children?

There should be six.

Alice sits up. Her head pounds. Did she bang it? Had she fallen? She feels dizzy with the sudden movement. 'Where's Billy?' She shouldn't have slept. She should have stayed with the boy. She casts her gaze wildly about the lifeboat. 'Where is he? Billy!'

Arthur tells her he's sleeping. 'He's very tired. Uncle Owen has him.'

Alice turns to see Billy asleep in Owen's arms. He looks so frail and small. He desperately needs fluids and something for his chest infection, but all they can give him is gentle reassurance and their increasingly anxious prayers.

'How is he?' she asks as Owen catches her eye.

Owen's face is pale and drawn, his expression grim. He shakes his head.

Alice closes her eyes and prays.

An hour later, maybe two, Owen takes his morning swim, although he doesn't stay in the water as long as usual and he struggles to haul himself out. The children talk about what they'll do when they get home. The adults sit in stupefied silence.

At midday, everyone takes their dipper of water, the children unaware it is their last. Alice insists that Billy takes hers. She doesn't long for it the way she had during the first few days. Drinking and eating are purely mechanical things now. Open your mouth, swallow, stay alive a bit longer. She refuses the offered chunk of tinned salmon. She can't bear the thought of chewing something solid, afraid she'll choke if she forces it down her dry, swollen throat. The children dip their fingers into the last of the pineapple juice.

Nobody pulls the Fleming gear. Nobody talks about direction or distance. The active fight to survive has become a quiet struggle to endure whatever time they have left.

The sun is full and warm against Alice's face. She thinks about her promise to Howard to visit Ireland – the Antrim coast, the

Giant's Causeway, Dunluce Castle. She closes her eyes and sees a cottage on a clifftop, an arch of white roses, coloured sand, a face silhouetted against the sun. A peaceful place.

She trails her hand over the side of the lifeboat. It is a gentle day, a good day to slip away, to go quietly into the water.

Hours pass. A distant hum drifts through the air. Alice thinks of summer afternoons, the bees in her uncle's hives, lavender-scented honey on thick slices of freshly baked bread. It is a soothing sound, familiar and yet somehow out of place.

She opens her eyes, sees the ocean, closes them again.

Another minute passes.

The bees return, closer now. Just over the fence in the orchard. Three white hives beneath the apple trees. Honey and bread for supper.

'A plane! There's a plane!'

Arthur's shrill voice cuts through the silence.

Alice opens one eye. Nobody else stirs.

The voice comes again. Someone is shaking her hand. 'Look, Auntie! A plane! A real plane!'

Brian is pulling her arm, urging her to sit up, to look at the sky. She is light-headed, dazzled by the sun as she tips her neck back and shields her eyes with her hands. She sees a black dot, high above them. She hears a faint distant hum.

'It's just a bird, Brian. Or a cloud.'

The lifeboat falls back into silence. Another false alarm.

Another minute passes, maybe two. Billy coughs and wheezes. Alice reaches out a hand to point at stars that don't exist.

Then another cry. Robert this time.

'There! It *is* a plane! It really is! Look!'

Now, people begin to stir.

Alice sits up again. Jimmy is standing in the middle of the lifeboat, waving his arms in circles and shouting out. Owen is beside him, circling his sweater above his head. And there's Thomas Prendergast, whooping and banging two tins together. And now Alice hears the unmistakable distant drone. Not bees, but an engine. A plane. When she looks up, the black dot is much bigger, and flying towards them.

She pulls herself up; stands, unsteadily, as the low guttural drone draws closer and closer until it becomes a dramatic heart-stopping roar and a great rush of air that billows out her skirt as it flies past. A small figure is clearly visible through the cockpit window. He raises a thumb to signal that they've been seen.

'It's the RAF!' Arthur cries out. 'A British Sunderland flying boat!'

The atmosphere in the lifeboat is frenzied. Handkerchiefs, hats, jackets and blankets windmill in the air. Cries of 'Over here!' and gasps of exhausted disbelief fill Alice's ears as the plane banks to the right, and begins its approach toward them again.

It is impossible, incredible, and yet, there it is.

There it is.

Alice looks around the lifeboat. Several people are crying. Others are laughing. The children's faces are alight with joy, a sense of immeasurable relief so vividly expressed in their wide smiles.

She watches it all as if she is in a dream. In her hand, she clutches a white feather, and in her heart, she holds on to her last tattered fragment of hope as she sinks to her knees and weeps.

Part Three – Rescue

38

Mid-Atlantic. 24 September 1940

Day One

They had been officially dead for just over a week and it takes a single moment, a simple thumbs up, to bring them gasping back to life. With one more pass overhead, the pilot of the RAF Sunderland signals that help is on the way, and goes to alert the closest vessel.

Jimmy calls everyone together to say a prayer of thanks.

'Hold hands, children,' Alice says. 'Let us pray.'

Alice looks around the lifeboat as they repeat the Lord's Prayer. Bobby and Jimmy grip each other's arms. Mr Sherwood and Mr Harlow hold hands and weep, finally allowing themselves to acknowledge their fear and fragility. Owen – Richard – sings loudly beside Alice. She wonders what fate awaits him now; wonders what awaits them all.

Despite their severe physical distress, and the overwhelming emotion of being rescued, Alice notices an almost instant improvement in everyone. Shoulders that were once hunched are now pulled back. Heads that had hung in a state of melancholy now look up. Limbs that were contorted in agony stretch and ease. Passive becomes active. Past becomes present. Hope becomes reality.

Once the solemn moment of prayer and thanks has passed, the children sing 'My Old Man', 'Knees Up, Mother Brown', and a rousing rendition of the hokey-cokey. Their joy is infectious, their relief irrepressible.

'Are we really going home, Auntie?' Arthur asks. 'Will I see my mother?'

Alice pulls the boy into a tight embrace. 'Yes, Arthur! We are really going home and you will see your mother.' She thinks about Lily Nicholls and wonders what on earth she will do when the remarkable news reaches her.

Within the hour, the Sunderland returns and drops a parachute bag filled with emergency supplies: food, cigarettes, a flare to attract attention from the ship that is steaming to their aid, and, most thrilling of all, water. Alice tends to Billy first, lifting his head to help him drink small, vital sips. He is so pale and limp in her arms. She prays for one more miracle and wills him to hang on. 'They came to take us home, Billy, dear. We're going home, love. You're going home to your mother.'

She makes sure the other children drink next. 'Small steady sips, children. Too much too quickly will make you nauseous.' Like the ferns her father used to keep, they require a gradual gentle watering, not a deluge. When they have all taken a good amount of water, Alice allows herself to drink. She savours the cool liquid as it sluices down her throat, flooding her body with life. She feels suspended in time, caught in some imperceptible place between lost and found as sip after sip, moment after moment, gently brings the nightmare to an end.

Finally, the warship sent to their aid comes into view. The children's faces are full of wonder as the enormous vessel draws closer. This time, there is no sudden turning around. This ship anchors steadily alongside them, the crew hollering and waving as they drop cargo nets, ladders and slings down the side of the ship for the survivors to make their way aboard.

Having been in the lifeboat for so long, they find the process of leaving it isn't quick or straightforward. Anxious not to tip the boat, and careful to ensure that no one should fall overboard at this last precarious moment, Jimmy takes charge again, prioritizing those with the most pressing needs as the lifeboat slowly gives up its precious cargo. First, Billy is taken up in a sling, followed by Molly, and then the most physically sick among the adults. Many are too weak to haul themselves up and have to be lifted in a human chain, or slung over the crew's shoulders like sacks of coal. The sense of action and motion is overwhelming.

Alice waits her turn, insisting that the children go first. She tells them what's happening, reassures them and makes sure they know what to do as they leave the lifeboat. 'Arms up, Hamish, that's it.' 'Hold on, Brian.' 'Don't look down, Arthur.' She breathes a sigh of relief when Robert, the last of them, turns and gives a thumbs up from the ship's deck.

After so many dark and desperate hours, so many false alarms and so much lost, Alice can hardly believe it when she places one bare foot, then the other, on the solid, sturdy deck of HMS *Aurora*. She turns to look back at the lifeboat – *their* lifeboat. She thought she would be so relieved to be out of it, *is* relieved to be out of it, but she also feels a pang of guilt – of grief, almost – to leave it behind. That little boat was their home. It had kept them safe for so long.

'What will happen to it?' she asks, barely able to speak, her words a muddle.

'What's that you say, love?'

She points to the lifeboat.

'Don't you worry about that, miss. You've been through quite an ordeal. We can't believe there's so many of you alive.'

Safe in the hands of the crew, Alice follows their instructions and direction. The kind souls in Royal Navy uniforms reassure her, sit her down on a deck chair, give her a hot drink and blankets, tell her where she is and what day it is.

'What's your name, love?' someone asks. He has kind eyes. Blue-grey, like a washed pebble. Like Owen's eyes.

'Alice King.'

He doesn't understand her. 'Sorry, love. Can you say that again? Nancy, was it?'

She leans forward until her cheek rests against his, and her mouth is beside his ear. 'Al . . . ice,' she says, as slowly and precisely as she can. 'Kin . . . g.'

He writes it down and shows it to her. 'Alice King?'

She nods, holds the lapel of his jacket and says thank you, although it doesn't sound as she intended. She wants to ask about news from home, about other survivors, but she can't form the words; doesn't have the energy. Her hands and knees tremble.

He takes her hands in his. 'You're safe now, Alice. You're going home, love. You're safe.'

His gentle kindness is devastating. She is too exhausted even to cry.

She places her hand on his arm and tries to speak as clearly as she can. 'The children? Billy? The little one?'

'Being well looked after in the medical bay. You don't need to worry about the children anymore, Miss King. You've done your job. We'll take care of them now.'

She has done her job.

She nods, relieved to be absolved of her responsibility, and yet somewhere in the fog of pain and relief, she realizes that being rescued means that she will lose these people she's come to care for so deeply.

'Come on. Let's get you a nice cup of tea.'

As she stands up, the relief and shock of being rescued hits her. She sways and stumbles. Her legs buckle beneath her as the bright afternoon fades to grey, and dazzling stars shimmer and float in front of her eyes as she sinks to her knees, secure in the knowledge that she is safe now, that someone will catch her if she falls.

39

Glasgow. September 1940

Lily wants to stay longer in Scotland. She can't bear to leave without both her children, but Georgie is desperate to go home. The trauma of what she's been through is only just beginning to hit her. The doctors warn Lily of nightmares and aftershocks. They say it is best for Georgie to be in familiar surroundings.

Through several distressing conversations with Kitty, Mr Quinn, and representatives from CORB and the Admiralty, it has become painfully clear to Lily that there is little else she can do. The second search attempt, conducted over the previous day, had drawn a blank. Lifeboat twelve, and whoever might have been in it, had simply disappeared.

'Go home, Lily,' Kitty said when they eventually returned to the guest house, exhausted, after the last of the reception events. 'You should take Georgie home.'

Lily knows Kitty is right, she should take Georgie home, but the thought of returning to London without Arthur is excruciating.

She packs her suitcase in a weary daze, folding her fading hope for her son among the items of clothing she places inside. She doesn't pack his toy rabbit. That, she will keep in her hands.

As she shuts the latches on the case, there's a loud and extended knock at the bedroom door.

'Can you get that, Georgie, love. It'll be Kitty, come to say goodbye.'

She doesn't have the energy for farewells and sympathy. She just wants to go home, so she can grieve properly for her boy.

But it isn't Kitty at the door.

Anthony Quinn bursts into the small bedroom, cheeks flushed as he rushes to Lily and grabs her hands.

'They've found a lifeboat, Mrs Nicholls! They've found other survivors. You were right!'

His words fill the room like fireworks, crackling and fizzing, ricocheting off the walls and windows until they find their way back to Lily.

'Arthur? They've found Arthur?'

'Yes! Arthur is listed among the survivors! He's alive, Mrs Nicholls. Your son is alive!'

Lily gasps, or does she cry out? She isn't sure. She raises her hands to her lips, feels the bedroom contract and expand as it makes room for the magnitude of what Mr Quinn is saying. All the fear and grief and the gnawing ache of despair she has carried with her these past unimaginable days lifts from her, leaving her unbalanced by the sudden sense of lightness.

She sinks down onto the edge of the bed, her body as limp as the half-folded cardigan still in her hands. 'Are you sure? It's definitely Arthur? *My* Arthur?'

'Yes! I'm sure! Arthur Nicholls! An RAF Sunderland on a training exercise came across a lifeboat, some three hundred miles from the site of the incident. Arthur is one of six children on board. Thirty-five souls in total, one of our escorts among them.' Mr Quinn leans against the back of a chair, as if winded by what he's saying. 'It's a miracle, Mrs Nicholls! An absolute miracle!'

Another knock at the door is quickly followed by a whirlwind of colour and noise as Kitty rushes toward Lily.

'They found them, Lily! They found Arthur, and Alice.'

'They found Alice, too?'

Kitty can hardly speak. 'Yes! She's alive!'

Lily holds Kitty in a tight embrace, each of them clinging to the other, buoying each other up with joy and relief after being so deeply submersed in grief.

Memories race through Lily's mind: Peter's face as he turned at the garden gate, a parcel of personal effects, a blackbird singing in the graveyard, Arthur and Georgie walking away with Alice King, the suffocating terror of the bomb shelter, the impossible news that the *Carlisle* had been hit by a torpedo. A year of agonizing losses distilled down to this single miraculous moment.

Lily has a thousand questions, but as she enfolds Georgie in her arms, all she can say is, 'He's alive, Georgie. He's alive. Arthur is alive!' And with those few incredible words, she feels herself coming back to life, too; breath by breath, piece by piece, as all the shattered, fragmented parts of her become whole again.

40

HMS *Aurora*. Atlantic Ocean. September 1940

Alice comes around in a chair in the chief engineer's cabin. 'There she is now. Back with us.'

She stares at the young crewman looking after her. He has a lovely face. Cheerful, and hopeful.

'You came over a little faint,' he says. 'Not surprising, really.'

She takes a sniff of the smelling salts he wafts under her nose. She wants to tell him she's never fainted before, not even when she'd seen her father laid out in his coffin, but she doesn't have the energy. This isn't how she'd imagined it would be when they were rescued. She'd presumed she would feel instantly better, ravenously hungry, able to sleep, but she feels upset and confused, nauseous and restless. She holds her hands against her thighs to stop her legs shaking.

Someone knocks on the cabin door and enters with a tray that they place on the locker beside her. 'Sweet tea, toast, a scrape of marmalade, and water. Just what the doctor ordered.'

Her stomach heaves at the thought.

She takes a few sips of water, then tries the tea, but it is too hot and scalds her tender lips and throat. The toast is like sandpaper.

'Leave the tea to cool a bit,' the crewman says. 'I'll be just outside if you need anything.'

His eyes are gentle and kind. He reminds Alice of Walter, and thinking of Walter makes her desperately homesick.

'Who's Howard, by the way?' he asks. 'You kept saying his name.'

Alice tumbles memories through her mind, remembered snippets of conversations. 'A friend,' she says. A friend who'd brought her out of her shell, encouraged her to be curious, to keep going forward, not back. A friend she'd found and then lost in a few short days.

The man nods. 'There's a bar of soap on the sink. And a toothbrush and paste. Some clean pyjamas on the bed. Best we could do, I'm afraid. We don't often see women on board. Never, in fact! Try to get some rest now. I'll check in on you again in a while.'

Rest, food, tea, comfort. It is all she's wanted for the last eight days, and now she doesn't want any of it. Her head spins when she lies down. Her body shakes too much for her to sleep. The cabin is too quiet without the constant sound of wind and rain, the slap of waves on wood, eager little cries of 'Auntie!' The smothering silence presses in on her, amplifying her concerns about Billy. It is strange not to have the children at her feet. She has a horrible feeling she's left something behind in the lifeboat; forgotten something, or someone.

Eventually, the tea cools enough for Alice to sip it and to nibble half a piece of toast. She tries to undress but her clothes are heavy and stiff with dried saltwater. The smell of damp and decay makes her gag. She manages to take off her blouse but can't work the zip on her skirt, so she lies down with it still on, pulls the covers around her and wills herself to stop shaking, to be still, to be calm. Her mind races, despite her exhaustion. Memories of her days in the lifeboat rush through her mind like a movie sped up: a particular cloud she'd watched cross the sky one morning, the smell of pineapple juice, the icy metal of the Fleming gear, the eye of a whale. It is all so upsetting to remember, to relive again.

The cabin spins. Tears spill down her cheeks. Why is she crying? She should be happy.

She sits up, tries again to remove her clothes. Slowly, she manages. She washes at the basin, salt and dirt lifting from her as she gently rubs a flannel over her tender skin, rinses it, rubs again. The woman in the mirror is unrecognizable, a wild woman with thickly matted hair, cuts and bruises on her wind-reddened face, a thin crust of salt on her lips and eyelashes, her teeth thick with it. Her eyes are swollen and bloodshot, the skin on her hands pale and spongy. She retches into the sink, but nothing comes up. She splashes her face again, brushes her teeth, takes a hairbrush from a small chest of drawers and drags it through her hair. Her arms are too weak to brush for long.

At last, she gets the zip to move, takes off her skirt and underwear, pulls on the clean cotton pyjamas, climbs back into bed, props herself up against the pillows and leans back. It is better this way. The room doesn't spin as much. She closes her eyes, exhausted by her efforts. Slowly, her convulsions and tears stop, and her battered body and broken mind allow her, finally, to sleep.

She wakes to daylight. She feels a little better but is still weak and nauseous.

A different crew member knocks and peers around the door. He tells her she's slept for eleven hours. 'You look much brighter

303

this morning, miss. There are a few visitors here who'd like to say hello, if you're up to it?'

'The children?'

He nods and opens the door fully. Four children rush into the cabin and scramble up onto the narrow bed. Brian, Hamish, Robert, and Arthur. They talk non-stop, telling her about all the food they've eaten, and the enormous ship, and the captain letting them go up to the bridge.

Alice listens patiently. It is lovely to see them looking so well, but their exuberance is overwhelming and she feels constantly tearful. 'Where are Molly and Billy?' she asks.

'Molly is resting but she's feeling much better. Billy still isn't very well,' Arthur explains. 'He has to stay in the sickbay.'

'Can I see him?' she asks, turning to the crewman.

'I'll take you down when you're ready,' he says. 'Your clothes have been washed and dried in the laundry room. They're hanging in the wardrobe there. Come along, children. Leave Miss King to dress now. You can see her again at lunch.'

Alice washes her hair, combs out the remaining tangles and knots, dresses slowly. Everything is so clean. She feels a little more like herself as she sits on the bed and waits to be taken to the sickbay. The gentle rocking motion of the ship reminds her of the lifeboat. The thought of it, abandoned and alone in the ocean, makes her cry.

A little while later, there's a knock on the cabin door. 'Hello? Miss? Are you ready?'

She wipes the tears from her cheeks and blows her nose. 'Yes. I'm ready.'

The crewman leads her down long narrow corridors and stairwells. She tries not to think about the *Carlisle*, but the layout is similar, and awful memories of shattered wood and buckled steel crash around her mind.

'Here we are. I'll leave you with the doctor. And, miss . . .'

'Yes?'

'I should warn you. The boy isn't doing so well. But he's comfortable.'

The sterile smell of bleach hits Alice as she steps into the sickbay. Several beds are occupied by men who are suffering from extreme dehydration and other problems brought on by their ordeal. Mr Sherwood lifts a hand in a gentle wave. Like many of them in the lifeboat, he had masked his true suffering with quiet resilience.

Alice's eyes settle on the bed at the end of the room.

The doctor introduces himself and calmly sets out Billy's condition. Alice struggles to concentrate and only catches odd phrases: 'Keeping him comfortable.' 'Pneumonia.' 'Secondary bacterial infection.' 'Fluid on the lungs.' 'Underlying condition.' He explains that Billy's skin is a strange bluish colour because of low levels of oxygen.

Alice sits by Billy's bed and takes his hand, rubbing his skin in circles just as she did in the lifeboat. He looks so small and vulnerable. 'Come on now, Billy. Your mother will be looking forward to seeing you. You rest now and get yourself all better. We're on our way home.'

His eyelids flutter, but they don't open fully.

'I promised I'd get you all safely home,' she says, to herself as much as to him. 'You have to get better now, so I can get you home to your mother.'

This brave little boy has left such a huge imprint on her heart. She can't bear to see him like this after he's been so brave. His precious marble sits on top of an upturned teacup on the locker beside his bed. A clear glass orb, a swirl of aquamarine running through the centre. It reminds her of the ocean.

'How's Billy the Kid doing?'

Alice turns to the voice that has been a constant since her very first hours in the lifeboat. His face is so familiar, and yet different. He is clean-shaven now, neatly dressed in borrowed clothes. His hair is slicked to one side. His real name will also take a while to get used to. Richard Heath is not the impenetrable boulder she'd first met, not the brittle American she knew as Owen Shaw. Beneath the façade was a good man, a friend she is pleased to see. She glances at Billy and shakes her head.

'He's not so good,' she whispers. 'He'll be transferred to the hospital as soon as we arrive.'

Owen stands beside Billy's bed. 'Poor little bugger. I'm sure they'll patch him up.'

Alice hopes he is right. 'You look much better,' she says. 'Did you sleep?'

'Not much. You?'

'A little. I sway every time I close my eyes.'

He smiles. 'Me too. I slept on the floor. Kept thinking I was going to fall out of bed.'

'How are the others doing?' she asks. 'Jimmy, Bobby, the rest?'

'Much the same. Relieved. Bewildered. Afraid of what's next. Mr Harlow has found a piano on board, so he's happy.'

'What will you do?' she asks. 'When we get home?'

'Go back I suppose. Try to talk myself out of trouble.'

'Back to the air force?'

He nods. 'I thought I was afraid, thought I couldn't stick it anymore, but I'm not afraid of anything now. I'm going back up there to make those Nazi monsters pay for what they've done.'

The doctor returns and makes notes on a chart at the end of Billy's bed.

'He will pull through, won't he?' Owen asks.

The doctor looks at them both. 'You should get some rest before we arrive in Scotland. We're due at eleven hundred hours. The boy will be transferred straight to the hospital by ambulance.'

Alice glances at Owen. She sees the look of profound sorrow etched on his face.

'You'll both be asked to speak to reporters for the newspapers,' the doctor continues. 'I expect they'll be especially interested in you, Miss King, being the only woman in the lifeboat. Did you know they're calling you the Nightingale of the Sea, and the Angel of the Atlantic?'

Alice shakes her head. She doesn't care what they're calling her.

'Get some rest now, Billy,' she says. 'Your mother will want to hear all about those whales when you get home. Imagine the stories you'll have to tell her.'

Owen walks out with her. 'I'm so sorry, Alice. I know the boy is special to you.'

Alice has no words. She stares at the floor. 'How long? Until we arrive?'

'A few hours.' He lets out a long exhale. 'Time for a cup of tea? Not sure I'm up to that bottle of whisky you promised me.'

She nods. 'Tea would be lovely. Thank you.'

41

Glasgow. September 1940

Lily stands in rigid silence as HMS *Aurora*, the ship carrying her son, emerges through the sea mist. It is a ship of ghosts, a ship of lost souls coming back to life.

'Is that it, Mummy? Is that Arthur's ship?'

Lily grips Georgie's hand. 'It is, love.'

It is.

Her relief now is as visceral as her grief had been just over a week ago when she'd learned the terrible news that Arthur was not listed among the survivors of the *Carlisle* tragedy. Now, as then, she can't stop shaking.

Kitty stands beside Lily, equally overcome by the news that Alice is among the survivors in the last lifeboat to be recovered. She reaches for Lily's hand. 'How are you feeling?'

Lily offers a tentative smile. 'I feel like my heart is going to burst. You?'

Kitty fidgets and fusses with her gloves, restless and anxious to see her sister. 'I don't think I'll believe it until I see her.'

The ship draws ever closer. Lily's heart beats ever faster.

News of the *Carlisle*'s miracle lifeboat has spread quickly around the small harbour town, drawing a large crowd to see for themselves these astonishing people who have come back from the dead. There is a sense of celebration in the air, a noticeable change from the respectful caution displayed when HMS *Imperial* had returned with the first few survivors two days earlier. This remarkable turn of events has almost doubled the number of surviving evacuee children, and has significantly bolstered the number of surviving adults. There is much to be grateful for in that.

Lily scans the faces in the gathered crowd. There is one, in particular, she is looking for. 'Mr Quinn did send the telegram, didn't he?'

Kitty nods. 'I sent it myself, with instructions to collect her ticket at the station.'

Lily nods. She was astonished to see Billy Fortune's name on the list of children discovered in the lifeboat, and hopes Ada will arrive in time to welcome her son home. He was well named after all.

A hush of anticipation descends over the gathered crowd as the great warship manoeuvres with exceptional grace into its position alongside the wharf. The crew flank the railings and wave to the crowd as they circle their caps above their heads. Lily looks up, searching and searching for a familiar face as figures begin to appear.

Georgie stands up on her tiptoes, craning her neck. 'Where is he, Mummy? I can't see him.'

Lily shushes her and squeezes her hand. She needs to concentrate, needs to see Arthur for herself, to make sure there hasn't been a terrible mix-up with some other boy.

A murmur spreads through the crowd as a group of children emerge through a door, all of them dressed in matching Royal

Navy sweaters and caps, and arranged in order of size: tallest at the front, smallest at the back. A little troupe of Russian nesting dolls. A man and a woman lead them toward the railings and encourage them to wave.

'Look, Mummy! There he is! There's Arthur!' Georgie jumps up and down beside Lily, so excited to see her brother. 'There he is!'

Lily has already seen him through her tears.

She can't move, can't speak; transfixed by the sight of the child she feared she might never see again. Her darling boy, a wide grin on his face, a borrowed sailor's cap slipping over his eyes. Her wonderful effervescent bright-summer-breeze of a boy. He looks out at the crowd and says something to a woman beside him as he points and waves. Has he seen her?

Lily lifts her arm and waves and waves as she tries to call out to him, 'I'm here, Arthur! Over here, love! Mummy's here!' but her words are choked by emotion. She clasps her hand to her mouth and pulls Georgie close to her side and says her son's name, over and over, each repetition erasing the time they have lost and making room for all the wonderful things they will do with this miraculous second chance they have been given.

25 September 1940

Six children found alive in a lifeboat from the *Carlisle*! Nobody can believe it. Seems that miracles <u>can</u> happen, even in the middle of a war. Had a good cry when I heard, partly for those who were found, partly for those poor souls who will always be lost.

Mass-Observation, Diarist #6385

42

Glasgow. September 1940

On the deck of HMS *Aurora*, Alice encourages the children to smile and wave. She does the same, although her forced smile hides the fact that her hands shake and her head pounds and her heart is heavy with concern for Billy.

'Where have all these people come from, Auntie?'

Alice pushes Arthur's cap back from his face. 'I'm not sure, Arthur. I think they've come to welcome you home.'

It is strange to see so many people gathered to welcome them; overwhelming, even. Alice had hoped to slip quietly away without any fuss, to make her way home and see Walter and Kitty, maybe cycle to the library and sit down with Maud and a pot of tea and try to process everything that has happened. She doesn't want all these people to see her; to know her.

A feeling of nausea spreads from her stomach. She tells herself to calm down, to breathe. She can't crumble now, not in front of the children, and yet every bone in her body feels like a sponge. She isn't sure she'll even make it down the gangway, or where she'll go, or what she'll do when she leaves this group of wonderful people who have become her world, who have, collectively and individually, saved her life.

She pushes her shoulders back and looks out at the dizzying blur of faces. Beside her, the children wave enthusiastically, thrilled by the scenes and the cheers. Arthur sees his mother and sister. 'Mummy!' he shouts. 'There's my mummy! And Georgie! Look, Auntie!' but his exuberant cries fade into the background as Alice's eyes settle on a familiar sight: red hair, crimson lips, a smile to outshine the sun, one hand clasped to her hat, the other at her chest.

'Kitty! Kitty!'

Dear Kitty has come to take her home. Uncertainty lifts from Alice as she waves to her sister and swallows a knot of emotion. She knows she will be all right now. Kitty will take her home.

Everything happens at pace then. Alice follows instructions shouted from the wharf to 'wave over here', and 'smile over there'. She arranges the children in descending order of height and tells them to wave their caps in the air. When the photographers have taken their pictures for tomorrow's front pages, and the cameramen for the newsreels have filmed the happy scenes of their arrival, the captain tells them they can disembark.

'There'll be someone from CORB to meet you, and more press to talk to, no doubt, and then you can go back home to your families, where you belong.'

But Alice isn't sure where she belongs anymore. Part of her belongs with the lifeboat, with the children, with the remarkable people she'd shared the lifeboat with. Even in these first bewildering moments of her safe return, Alice understands that putting the ordeal behind them won't be as simple as going back home, where they belong. They are all different now, profoundly changed by their experience.

'What about Billy?' she asks.

'He's with the ship's doctors. They'll take him straight to the hospital.'

'Can I go with him? I should go with him, until his mother arrives.'

'You've done everything you can, Miss King. Best to leave him in the hands of the medical experts now.'

She knows the captain is right, but it feels wrong to see five children leave the ship, not six. 'You will make sure he has his marble, won't you? It's on an upturned teacup, beside his bed. It's the only one he has left.'

'I'll make sure he has it. Now off you go. I think there's someone down there who's rather pleased to see you.'

The children walk in front of her, in pairs: Brian and Hamish, Robert and Molly. Alice holds Arthur's hand herself. At the bottom of the gangway, the noise of the well-wishers swells. Alice smiles politely at the sea of faces as strangers reach out to touch her arm and welcome them home. Shouting instructions above the noise, CORB officials direct them to a roped-off area to one side. Alice guides the children along, her own feet propelled forward by instinct rather than intent as she tells herself she is fine, to breathe, one foot in front of the other as she looks up intermittently and searches for Kitty. And there she is, pushing through the crowd, and in a whirlwind of perfume and crimson kisses, Alice is wrapped in a tight embrace, and Kitty is crying against her shoulder and Alice can hardly believe that her darling sister – that any of this – is real.

They stay like this, quietly absorbing the physical sensation of each other, allowing the moment to solidify from hope to reality. As she holds Kitty tight, Alice sees similar scenes play out around them. A tall angular woman in a fur coat faints when she sees Molly. Robert runs to a young woman who looks so like him that Alice assumes she must be his sister. Hamish and Brian are engulfed by their weeping fathers. But there is one reunion that takes her breath away.

She feels Arthur pull his hand from hers, sees him running towards his mother and sister, tripping and stumbling in his excitement as Lily Nicholls sinks to her knees and enfolds her son in her outstretched arms, and the moment is so intimate, so powerful, that it feels wrong to watch any longer. Alice closes her eyes and rests her head on Kitty's shoulder. She wishes she could stay there forever.

Kitty can't stop crying. Alice comforts her as they eventually peel apart and look at each other, hardly able to believe they are there.

Alice brushes tears from Kitty's cheeks and tucks a loose curl behind her ear. 'You look lovelier than ever. How are you? I thought about you so much.'

Kitty takes Alice's hand and places it against her stomach. 'We are both doing well.'

'You didn't reschedule your appointment?'

Kitty shakes her head. 'I decided to reschedule my life instead. And I'm terrified.'

Alice is terrified, too, for how Kitty will be treated, and how she'll ever manage, but after so much loss, there is something profoundly hopeful in the miracle of a new life. Alice tells Kitty it will be all right. 'I promise.'

A moment later, Arthur is back by Alice's side. 'Georgie is here, Auntie. Look!'

Alice bends down and hugs them both. 'I'm so pleased to see you again, Georgie.'

Georgie tells her they were about to go home, but then Arthur was found and everyone cried and it is a real-life miracle.

Alice patiently listens and smiles and tells her how brave Arthur was. 'You have all been so very brave.'

She stands up and turns to their mother. Lily Nicholls is smaller than Alice remembers, as if she has been eroded by the nightmare of believing her son was never coming home. For a moment, neither of them speaks, unable to find the right words, but everything is said in the look they exchange, in the silent understanding of the deep connection they have each felt with the other during the days since their brief meeting.

'I don't know what to say, Miss King.' Lily reaches for Alice's hands and holds them firmly. 'Thank you feels so inadequate for something so enormous, for keeping Arthur safe, for bringing him back to me.'

'There's no need for thanks, Mrs Nicholls. I'm just so glad our prayers were answered. Arthur is a remarkably brave boy. You must be very proud of him. Of both your children.' Alice takes a deep breath. Her words swirl around her. She feels dizzy and hot and grabs Kitty's arm. 'I think I need to sit down.'

Kitty holds Alice tight and steers her away from the crush of well-wishers and reporters. 'Let's get you somewhere quiet.'

Alice looks around for the others – Owen, Jimmy, Bobby, Mr Harlow, Mr Sherwood, Thomas Prendergast, the children. They have all melted away into the crowds. 'What do we do now? Where did everybody go?'

'You're needed for photographs at the hotel, and there's a civic reception tomorrow. It's all a bit of a circus, I'm afraid. We'll slip away as soon as the formalities are over.'

'I need to see Billy. They took him to the hospital.'

Kitty says they will go to the hospital as soon as they can. 'You need to take it easy, Alice. You need a bit of time to yourself first. I'll make sure the driver goes the long way. Wait there. I'll get the car to come to you.'

Alice sits on a bench and takes slow steady breaths in and out, glad of a moment alone until a woman rushes toward her.

'Excuse me, love. Are you Alice King? With the CORB programme?'

Alice looks around for Kitty. 'There'll be time for newspapers to ask questions later. At the reception. I can't talk to you now.'

The woman looks panic-stricken. 'I'm not with the newspapers, love. I'm looking for my boy. He was in the lifeboat they found. Billy Fortune. Do you know where he is?'

43

Glasgow. September 1940

The hospital is reassuringly calm and quiet after all the fuss and noise of the wharfside. With Kitty beside her, Alice sits quietly in the reception area. She can't stop thinking about Mrs Fortune, sitting with her son as he fights for his life. She is glad, at least, that they were able to bring her straight to the hospital, all thoughts of welcome receptions and newspaper reporters forgotten.

Kitty says Alice is as stubborn as an ink stain. 'I really think you'd be better off at the hotel. You've been through such a dreadful ordeal. You need to rest now and build your strength up. The boy is in the best place.'

Alice dismisses Kitty's concerns. 'I've a whole life ahead of me to rest and build up my strength. I'm not leaving until I see him.' She cares about the children so deeply; worries about Billy so viscerally. 'If you'd seen them in the lifeboat, Kitty. If you'd heard their panicked screams . . .'

Kitty listens patiently as Alice talks about the lifeboat, but no matter what words she chooses, she struggles to properly convey their fear and struggles. It sounds like a story she's made up; remembered fragments of a book she'd once read. But it isn't just the worst moments she wants to tell Kitty about. She wants her to know about the small kindnesses, the moments of gentle humour, the stunning sunrises and dazzling stars, the grace and beauty of the whales. Already, she forgets things, little details that were so important at the time now fading to a muddled blur. But the people she'd shared those days and nights with, she knows she will never forget. She misses them, worries about them, wonders where they are and what they're doing.

Alice and Kitty wait for an age. Doctors and nurses come and go but nobody has any news about little Billy Fortune.

The receptionist keeps looking at Alice. 'You're her, aren't you? The Nightingale of the Atlantic. You did an incredible thing, miss. Keeping those little children safe all that time in the boat. It must have been terrible for you all.'

Alice says yes, it was. She stares at the floor and hopes the young woman will take the hint that she doesn't want to talk about it. She is deeply uncomfortable with the attention, feels undeserving of the accolades and the names being attributed to her, especially when she hasn't kept the children safe. Billy isn't safe. Billy is in grave danger.

'She means well,' Kitty says, sensing Alice's discomfort. 'It's not everyday somebody comes back from the dead.'

'They look at me as if I'm the Messiah. And I'm not. I'm just me. Just Alice.'

'It won't last forever. They'll be talking about something else within a month. Alice King will disappear into obscurity, a footnote in a history book, all talk of heroic deeds forgotten.'

'Good. I just want to find a quiet job as the village postmistress, or something. Whatever is needed.' It occurs to her that she doesn't even know the latest developments in the war. Part of her is happy not to know.

'You'll forget too, in time,' Kitty adds. 'I know it's all so vivid and raw now, but the memories will fade.'

Even if they do, Alice knows the *Carlisle* will always be part of her, even when other people stop talking about it and forget it ever happened.

The receptionist brings them each a glass of water. Alice looks at hers for a moment.

'Not thirsty?' Kitty drinks her own.

'Just thinking about how desperate we were for a glass of clean water. I'll never take it for granted again.'

Kitty links her arm through Alice's. 'I met a friend of yours, by the way. I'm not sure if he's still in Scotland, but he spoke very fondly of you.'

'Oh? Who was it?'

'A lovely Irish man. Howard Keane. Quite the hero, by all accounts. He pulled several children out of the water and into a lifeboat. They're saying he'll be given a medal of some sort. He still had a book you'd lent him. *David Copperfield*. The one Father gave you for Christmas.'

Alice lets the tears fall down her cheeks. Dear Howard. She'd thought about him so often, at times it felt as if he were in the lifeboat with her, his warm enthusiasm spurring her on. . . *Let's make a pact – that we won't go back to the lives we've left behind, that we'll stay curious, keep moving forward.* She doesn't feel the need to cry out with relief, or rush to see him. She feels calm and peaceful, so relieved to hear he'd survived. 'I hope he's still here. I would like to see him.'

Toward late afternoon, Kitty has to return to the hotel. 'There's a press briefing scheduled with CORB. Why don't you come with me? We can come back in the morning. I'm sure they'll let you see Billy then.'

'I'd rather stay here. You go. I'll be fine.'

Reluctantly, Kitty leaves her.

Eventually, Alice sleeps.

Sometime in the evening, a nurse gently shakes her shoulder. 'You can go in now, dear. Second corridor on the left.'

Alice goes where instructed. She finds Ada Fortune sitting in a chair beside Billy's bed. He looks so peaceful.

'Not a mark on him,' Ada says as Alice stands hesitantly beside the bed. 'All that time at sea and he looks like he just got out of the bath.'

'He's a remarkable little boy,' Alice says.

'He was born with a heart defect,' Ada continues. 'They said he wouldn't last until his first birthday, and look at him. Six birthdays gone. Scrapper, his dad called him. His little scrapper.'

'I'm so sorry I couldn't keep him safe, Mrs Fortune. He was so brave. I'm so very sorry.'

'But you did keep him safe, miss. Think of all those poor mothers who'll never see their little ones again. You brought Billy home.' Ada reaches for Alice's hand. 'You brought him back to me so that I could say goodbye. I can never thank you enough for that.'

Alice says she'll come back later, that she doesn't want to intrude.

'I'd like you to stay, Miss King. Please. Stay with me, and tell me all about the *Carlisle* and the lifeboat. How he was. What you did. I'd like to know. It's the only part of his life I haven't shared since we took him in.'

Alice takes a deep breath and pulls up a chair. 'I met him at the train station in London. He showed me his best marble and held my hand. I think he could tell I was a little nervous, that I needed a friend . . .'

She talks for a long time.

She isn't sure at what point in the night she falls asleep.

*　　*　　*

She is woken by a gentle shake of her shoulder.

The chair opposite her is empty.

The bed is empty.

The nurse takes Alice's hand. 'I'm so sorry, love. He slipped away quietly in his mother's arms.'

The words drift around Alice as if she's underwater and can't hear them properly.

'She wanted you to have this.' The nurse takes something from the pocket of her uniform and places it in Alice's hand. 'She said you would understand.'

Alice can't bear to look. Can't bear to know.

Slowly, she unfurls her fingers. In her palm sits a clear glass orb, a swirl of aquamarine running through the centre. It reminds her of the ocean, and of a precious little boy to whom it meant the world.

The nurse places an arm around her shoulder. 'Take your time, love. When you're ready, there's a gentleman waiting for you in reception. He's been here all night.'

Alice wipes a tear from her cheek. 'It will be a reporter. Can you tell him I have nothing to say?'

'It isn't a reporter, love. He said to tell you he is a friend, and to take as long as you need.'

Alice sits for a while longer, alone with her thoughts and memories and grief, before she takes a last glance at the empty bed and walks slowly out of the ward. She follows the long, hushed corridors, each quiet step taking her away from her past as she finally forgives the frightened little girl crouched in her heart and accepts that everything and everyone she has lost is part of the woman who was found. She has been given a second chance; a second life. She must keep moving forward now, one step at a time, a small glass marble held tight in her hand, ready for the off.

PART FOUR – RECOVERY

44

London. March 1941

Lily wakes to a sunrise of violets and roses, the window-panes patterned with frost lacework. It is so beautiful it takes her breath away when she pulls back the blackout curtains. She'll never understand how the world can hold such beauty and such horror at the same time.

The war has gone on so long now that sometimes it is difficult to remember life before it. For six months, the bombing raids have come, night after night, on and on and still no sign that they will end. Elm Street is stubbornly unchanged, a perfect seam of upright houses hemmed in among the tattered fabric of nearby streets turned to rubble. Number 13 stands like a sentry in the middle, keeping watch over Lily and the children, a fortress of family and familiarity. Family and home are what matter most now, the simple things Lily had once taken for granted now infused with a sense of quiet gratitude: a fire in the grate, food in the pantry, tea in the pot, the table set for three, tucking the children in at night, tidying their things. Life has distilled down, drawn closer. But for all that there is comfort in the routines of home life, nothing will ever be the same. Lily is forever changed by what has happened. They all are.

She lights the stove and pours a saucer of milk for Moby Dick, their new kitten. Mrs Hopkins's cat has managed to keep an entire litter alive this time, so seven lucky families in Elm Street now have a new member. The kitten has helped the children with their recovery, Arthur in particular. The two of them are inseparable. Lily often hears Arthur tell the little creature about his friend, Billy Fortune, and everything they did in the lifeboat. Arthur's strength has gradually returned and although he still finds it difficult to walk far, he improves each day. The doctors assure Lily there won't be any lasting physical damage. Georgie has also made a good physical recovery, but the long traumatic hours she'd spent waiting for help to arrive, and the memory of all those she'd seen perish around her, linger on in bad dreams and an intense fear of the water. What the experience had done to their young minds, nobody can yet be certain.

Lily hears the familiar squeak of the garden gate just after nine. Mr Kettlewell had offered to oil it for her a few days ago. 'Must drive you batty,' he'd said. She'd told him she hardly noticed it anymore, but the truth was she noticed it more than ever. The squeaky gate and Peter were forever connected. If she fixed it, she would lose another part of him, and so it remains, with its perfect flaws. She wipes her hands on her apron, presuming it will be Elsie come to tell her about something or other. After Elsie's mother-in-law had passed away last month, Elsie and the children had moved permanently into number 14. 'Officially neighbours!' she'd announced. 'Isn't that terrific!' Lily owes Elsie a huge debt of gratitude, and has grown very fond of her, but she will always prefer Elsie Farnaby in small bursts. Elsie is invariably the first to know the latest gossip and loves to turn the smallest thing into the greatest drama, so Lily wasn't a bit surprised to discover that Elsie was writing for Mass-Observation. Elsie was the perfect social diarist, although what people might make of her particular observations in years to come, Lily isn't entirely sure.

But it isn't Elsie come to gossip. Lily hears the snap of the letter box, the light thud on the doormat. She pads through to the hallway, picks up a buff-coloured envelope and opens it at the kitchen table. She is still a creature of habit, despite so much disruption and change.

Children's Overseas Reception Board
45 Berkeley Street, London, W1

                                        18 March 1941

Dear Mrs Nicholls,
Owing to an oversight at the time of the departure of SS *Carlisle* from Liverpool, a packet of letters that were being held for posting until after the ship had sailed were only very recently discovered. We were uncertain whether it would not be adding to parents' grief and distress to send these letters on now, but were certain you would prefer to have them. I have put the letters in the enclosed envelope so that you can read them, or destroy them as you wish.

We are aware that Mrs Ada Fortune has been staying with you since the tragic sinking of SS *Carlisle*. I would be very grateful if you could pass the enclosed letter on to her. There doesn't appear to be a letter from each of her children (not all children engaged in the activity, it seems).

Sincerely,
Anthony Quinn, CORB

Time folds away like an unpicked hem as Lily reads the enclosed letters from Georgie and Arthur, a few lines about their excitement to be going to Canada and how impressed they are with the *Carlisle*. As if it were only yesterday, she's back on her front doorstep, trembling despite the unusually warm September morning, forcing herself to smile through her anguish as Alice King says they really must be going, and gently – almost apologetically – encourages the children to say goodbye before leading them away, her hands in theirs, their little suitcases swinging at their sides. In the end, the threatened invasion that prompted the second wave of evacuation hadn't happened, thanks to Fighter Command and victory in the Battle of Britain, and yet many civilian lives were still lost on the home front. Stay or go, the risks were the same. It was a time of war. Nobody was safe anywhere.

Arthur ambles into the room, the kitten in his arms. He yawns and plonks himself down at the table. 'What time is it, Mummy?'

'Hmm?' Lily is miles away. 'Friday.'

Georgie starts to giggle. 'He asked what time it is, not what day it is!'

Lily blinks away the onset of tears and smiles. 'It's Friday o'clock. Now, both of you, eat your breakfast!'

She opens the sticky drawer and takes out the biscuit tin to add the letters from the children. She's kept all the CORB correspondence, even the terrible letter they sent to inform her the *Carlisle* had sunk. She isn't sure why she keeps it all, but she can't bring herself to throw anything away. It is part of their story now, part of who they are.

But it is the things at the bottom of the biscuit tin that she looks for now, the items that were returned among Peter's personal effects. His tattered sketchbook, filled with his distinctive drawings of snowdrops, feathers, daffodils, the dog, Arthur and Georgina in profile. And his notebook, full of his reflections for Mass-Observation but which he never sent to the Ministry of Information for their archives, unlike Elsie, who diligently sends hers off on the last day of each month, thrilled with the importance of it all. Peter's entries are for Lily to read in private now, a precious insight into his deepest thoughts about family and war, a permanent record of a man who had so much more to say, and do.

The last thing she takes out of the tin is the letter she finds the hardest to read, the letter Peter wrote to her a year ago, and which still feels as fresh and vibrant as if he'd written it that morning.

My darling Lil,
They said we should write a letter to be sent home in the event of the worst happening. This is my fifth attempt because how can I possibly say goodbye to you? I can't, so I won't. This isn't a goodbye letter. It's a love letter, to my sweetheart.

I brought a few photographs, but I don't need to look at them. What I'll see when I close my eyes at night is you, standing on the doorstep this morning, the frost embroidered on the windowpanes as you shivered against the cold. I told you to go inside, that I would write when I arrived, but you stood there, watching me, and you were so beautiful in the sunlight you took my breath away. I wanted to tell you how much I love you, but I couldn't say a thing. I suspect you might have guessed that's what I wanted to say, or something like it. We've always known, haven't we.

Anyway, I've said it now. I love you more than words, Lily Nicholls. You, Georgie, and Arthur, have made me the happiest man alive. Hopefully this bloody war will be over soon and we can get back to normal. In the meantime, try not to miss me too much (impossible, I know!).

Forever and always,
Peter XX

PS Suppose I should add – in case this does become my last letter – that I want you to live life to the full. Fall in love again, go dancing, do all the things you've ever wanted to. And get another dog.

'I have to pop out for a bit,' she says as she folds the letter, returns everything to the biscuit tin, pushes the drawer shut and grabs her coat and hat. 'Mrs Hopkins will look in, and Elsie is across the road if you need anything until Mrs Fortune gets back. Wash your faces after breakfast. I won't be long.'

Ada, Mrs H, and Elsie have become invaluable in helping with the children when Lily has to work or run an errand. It is one of the few positive things about the war. Neighbours look out for each other, everyone always willing to help. Elm Street is a tight-knit community, and the few precious children there belong to everyone else, as much as to their parents.

It is the reassurance that Georgie and Arthur will be well looked after that eventually leads Lily to answer a question that has nagged at her for months. Who *was* the Mr Wimborne she'd met on the bus, and why was he interested in her ability to do crossword puzzles?

She takes the bus to Marble Arch and walks to Baker Street, then on until she reaches number 64. She's never forgotten the address. Six plus four is ten, and ten is her lucky number.

She lifts the knocker, raps twice, and waits. She doesn't, for one moment, doubt herself or wonder if she's doing the right thing. She already knows that this is where she was meant to come.

After a short while, the door opens. A woman in a cream silk blouse and navy skirt smiles. 'Can I help you?'

Lily says exactly what she's rehearsed. 'Wimborne sent me. I am interested in the Stately 'Omes of England.' She's worked out that the letters SOE are significant, but isn't yet sure why.

The woman looks at her, nods, and holds out a hand. 'Then you're very welcome, Miss . . .'

'Nicholls. Mrs Lily Nicholls.'

'Welcome, Mrs Nicholls. Please, come in. Are you aware of the nature of our work here?'

'Not really. Mr Wimborne was interested in my ability to complete crossword puzzles. That's all.'

The woman smiles. 'Of course. This way. He'll be very pleased to see you.'

Left for training camp today. Unbearable to look at the children's faces when I told them I was going away for a while, to help the men win the war. They promised to be very good for their mother. Impossible to say goodbye to my darling Lil. Expected to feel angry, or afraid, but when I looked at her standing on the doorstep, I felt nothing but immeasurable unspeakable love.

Mass-Observation, Diarist #6672

45

London, March 1941

Alice makes a note of the nearest underground stations and air-raid shelters as she walks beneath Admiralty Arch, along Horse Guards Parade, towards Lyons Corner House on Birdcage Walk. Britain's cities are still under regular bombardment from the Luftwaffe, so being prepared for an air raid is part of everyday life. She often wonders how they all keep going, but they do.

Kitty is already at their usual table at the back. Everybody avoids sitting beside the windows these days.

'Started without me, I see!' Alice kisses Kitty on the cheek and takes the seat opposite her.

'I was gasping. And you're late.'

'Yes, sorry about that. The bus took a detour. UXB on Tottenham Court Road.' She pours a cup of tea from a dribbly teapot. 'Well? Did you finish it?'

A smile spreads across Kitty's face. The full bloom of pregnancy suits her, although Alice has learned not to say as much because Kitty is convinced she resembles a large toad.

'Yes, I finished it!'

'Come on then. Show me!'

Kitty fishes in her handbag. 'Here. Have a read while I nip to the loo. I'm rather proud of this one.'

Alice takes the typed pages and starts to read.

Dear Sirs,

I write, once again, in the hope that you will publish my letter in the *Times Educational Supplement*. The facts and events surrounding the tragedy of SS *Carlisle* – set out below – must be made public, because while we cannot undo what happened, we can prevent it happening again. It is disappointing that a full inquiry was not considered necessary. Not necessary for the grieving parents desperate for answers, or for those in positions of authority who wished to avoid public scrutiny of their actions?

It is now known that the assurances given to parents, particularly regarding the issue of evacuee ships being under naval escort, fell rather short, and that many lives were lost as a result of actions taken at the time of the attack on SS *Carlisle*. The immediate suspension of the CORB programme was the right decision.

It is my hope that the points set out below will ensure that significant changes are put in place should the evacuation programme resume at any stage during the current conflict. While it is too late for those who stepped onto SS *Carlisle* last September, their legacy must be in the assurance that a tragedy of this nature can never happen again.

Anon

Facts regarding the loss of life on SS *Carlisle*:

1. SS *Carlisle* was to be convoyed. This was made clear in all correspondence with parents. However, at the time of the torpedo attack, the *Carlisle* was not 'being convoyed'. To be in a state of 'being convoyed' a ship must have its escort in attendance.

2. The escorting warships departed on the morning of 17 September, at the predetermined 'limit of convoy escort'. Yet Ministry records show that U-boats were active beyond this limit in the weeks preceding SS *Carlisle*'s departure.

3. Despite having left the convoy only that morning, the escort vessels did not return to the scene of the attack to assist in a rescue. HMS *Imperial* – the ship that responded to the SOS – was some 400 miles away. There is no adequate explanation as to why the escort vessels failed to return.

4. There were no designated rescue ships in the *Carlisle*'s convoy, as is standard shipping practice. The explanation offered for this is that rescue ships may operate only when a convoy is under naval escort. See point 1) above.

5. The convoy was not given orders to disperse following the departure of the escort vessels on the morning of 17 September. Convoy dispersal is usual practice, and would have allowed the *Carlisle* – and other ships in the convoy – to proceed at greater speed, and in an evasive zig-zag pattern, to avoid detection by U-boats. By remaining in convoy, they were at greater risk of attack.

6. The Lord Admiral was not aware of the special 'payload' the *Carlisle* was transporting. He has said that alternative 'special' arrangements would have been given to SS *Carlisle*, her escort and her convoy had it been widely known that she was carrying evacuees. His remarks suggest that this was an entirely avoidable tragedy.

Alice folds the letter and places it on the table. It is difficult to see everything set out so precisely, to see how easily the tragedy might have been prevented. Her memories are still raw and painful.

'Well. What do you think?' Kitty asks when she returns.

'It should be framed and hung in Parliament, never mind printed in the pages of the *Times Educational Supplement*. It's very powerful, Kitty. I wish you could put your name to it and take the credit, even if it would get you, and your friends at the Ministry, in trouble. Everyone will assume some man has written it.'

Kitty waves her hands dismissively. 'Let them assume. It doesn't matter who wrote it. What matters is that people read it, and that those in power act on it. What matters is that this never happens again. If I can use my old position as a glorified secretary at CORB to play a small part in that, then I'm glad to.'

Alice admires her sister, fighting for the protection of children she'll never know. 'I'm very proud of you, Kitty.'

'Oh stop it! It's hard work being the sister of *the* Alice King. I can't have you getting all the adulation!'

Alice still shies away from any suggestion of heroism, although countless newspaper articles, and even a book written about her, insist that her role in the lifeboat was nothing short of heroic. Before the *Carlisle* tragedy, she'd thought it only mattered if you helped in the loud dramatic moments of war, but it is in the quiet aftermath, in her role at the WVS, that she is at her best.

A kind word, a cup of tea, a hot meal, teaching a soldier how to sew and repair his uniform or suggesting the perfect book to take his mind off the horrors he has seen, finding a home for someone who has nothing other than the clothes they are dressed in. These are the real acts of heroism. Ordinary women, holding the country together. The quiet essential backbone of the war on the home front.

'Any word from Howard?' Alice asks.

Kitty can't hide her smile. 'Had a letter yesterday, as it happens. He's in good spirits. Ever hopeful that victory will be declared soon. You know what an eternal optimist he is! He asked after you, by the way. Said to say hello, and to tell you that *Great Expectations* is much better than *David Copperfield*.'

'Well, you can tell him that's absolute nonsense. He's clearly had a bang to the head and should see a medic!'

In the end, flat feet didn't stop Howard going to war. Men were needed in their thousands and Howard was especially keen to do his bit after everything he'd been through at the hands of the Nazis. It hadn't taken Alice long to realize that her fondness for Howard was rooted in friendship, not romance. She'd noticed how well he and Kitty got along while they were all still in Scotland, how much they made each other laugh, how they couldn't stop looking at each other. It was Alice who'd encouraged them to keep in touch while Howard was away, and to meet for lunch when he was on leave, and to visit Willow Cottage to get away from London for a weekend. When he learned of Kitty's condition, a fact she couldn't hide for long after they'd first met, he was neither shocked nor scandalized. He did the honourable thing. 'Why wait?' he said. 'I was planning to ask you after the war, but who knows when that will ever be?' It had all happened quickly, as things did during a time of war.

They were living in unconventional times and Kitty had always been an unconventional young woman. Even their mother was surprisingly stoic. Howard charmed everyone he met, even the impenetrable Mrs Barbara King. Nobody batted an eyelid when the announcement was posted in the newspaper that Miss Katherine Maria King had married Officer Howard Aidan Keane in a small private ceremony in London. A ring on Kitty's finger and a husband away at war drew expressions of sympathy for her condition, rather than scorn. As usual, she had landed on her feet, and Alice was very glad to have played a small part in bringing Kitty and Howard together.

'And what about you?' Kitty asks, adding a kick to Alice's foot under the table for good measure. 'Any word? You're such a dark horse, Alice King. Really!'

Alice can't stop the smile that tugs at the edge of her lips. 'He wrote last week.'

Kitty leans forward and grabs Alice's hand. 'Did he declare his undying love for you? Is he miserable and lonely without you?'

Alice laughs. 'Would it make you happy if I said yes?'

'Yes!'

'Then yes, he did.'

It is still the greatest surprise to Alice that it wasn't Howard Keane, or someone like him, who'd settled in her heart, but Owen Shaw – or Richard Heath, as she had eventually got used to calling him. The war that had brought them together in such dramatic circumstances was now keeping them cruelly apart, but they both firmly believed that time and fate would be on their side, because despite the unexpected development of their romance, there was an undeniable sense of forever about them. In the end, one of the bravest things Alice had done was let go of the safe, steady life she'd always imagined, and embrace the one she hadn't. Loving Richard certainly feels reckless and unexpected. And wonderful.

* * *

After supper that evening, in the flat she and Kitty now share, Alice takes a quiet moment alone to look through the scrapbook of newspaper reports Kitty has kept about the *Carlisle* tragedy. She comes across a photograph she hasn't seen before, of their arrival on HMS *Aurora*. She barely recognizes herself. The forced smile of the woman pictured seems to belong to someone else entirely. The children are smiling and waving as if they're having the time of their lives, but she knows the truth behind those brave smiles. Yet it is Billy Fortune, the only child not pictured, whom she sees most clearly.

The headline above the photograph says EIGHT DAYS AT SEA – ORDEAL COMES TO MIRACULOUS END! So much was lost and found within those days of hopeful sunrises and the terrifying nights that followed, and while the newspaper reports talk of an ending, for Alice, there is no end. Part of her will always be in the lifeboat, drifting across the Atlantic, hoping for a miracle. It has become a defining feature, as clear as a chickenpox scar or a birthmark. It is more than something that happened to her once. It has become her, *is* her, always.

But the most curious piece of paperwork from the event is the letter announcing her death. She keeps it between the pages of a new copy of *Moby Dick*, tucked away at the end of the bookshelf. In quiet moments alone, she sometimes removes the sheet of paper and reads the neatly typed words with a sort of grim reverence: the deepest regrets and sincere condolences, the expression of gratitude for her sacrifice and devotion to duty, the devastating word that sits at the heart of the tragedy. *Torpedoed*. It will always be a difficult letter to read, and yet for all its talk of death, it speaks to her of life, and how fragile it is. It is a reminder to live, in every sense of the word.

As Kitty potters about in the kitchen, Alice opens the latest letter from Arthur Nicholls. He writes occasionally, mostly to tell her about school and what he's busy with, but in this letter he writes about their days together in the lifeboat, the stories and songs he remembers, moments of kindness and courage. She can almost taste the salt spray in his sentences, hear the roar of the wind in his words. It takes her back, and propels her forward.

She picks up a pen and a sheet of writing paper.

Dearest Arthur,

Thank you for your lovely letter. I am very pleased to hear that you are enjoying school, and finding lots of new stories to read. I especially like the name you have chosen for your new kitten! I am keeping very busy volunteering with the WVS, but still find time to help out at the library when I can. Uncle Richard (Owen) replied to say he would be thrilled for you to visit him on the Isle of Wight when he is back.

At the start of your letter, you wondered if I would remember you because you haven't written for a while. My dear Arthur, how could I ever forget you? How could I ever forget any of you?

Warmly,

Auntie Alice x

As she folds the letter and places it inside an envelope ready for posting, the familiar whine of the air-raid siren goes up.

Kitty appears from the kitchen, hands on her hips. 'Bloody typical. I just poured the tea.'

Alice offers a tired smile.

Life, and war, goes on.

46

London. March 1941

Lily watches at the kitchen window, restless as she waits for Ada to come back from the shops. Her gaze strays to the envelope propped against the milk jug. She can't bear the thought of what's inside, but it is for Ada to decide whether to read the letter, or not.

After an age, Ada bustles in through the back door and washes her hands at the sink. 'That bloody outhouse is cold enough to freeze your bits and pieces off! Is there any tea in the pot?'

Lily doesn't know what to say.

Ada looks at her. 'What's the matter, love? You look like you've seen a ghost.'

'They sent a letter, Ada.'

'Who did?'

'CORB.' The word is rarely spoken in the house. It feels leaden, heavy with the legacy of grief it carries. 'I'm so sorry, Ada. I didn't know what to do for the best.'

She points to the simple brown envelope propped against the

milk jug, *Mrs Ada Fortune* handwritten on the front. Such an ordinary thing, and yet Lily feels as though her next breath is held within it.

Ada picks it up. 'What on earth do they want now?' She reads the letter from CORB first. '*I have put the letter in the enclosed envelope so that you can read it, or destroy it as you wish . . .*'

Slowly, she removes the enclosed envelope.

Lily makes to leave the kitchen, to give her some privacy, but Ada asks her to stay.

Her hands shake as she takes out a sheet of paper and a small white feather. The silence is excruciating, Ada's quiet suffering unbearable.

It only takes her a few minutes to read her son's words. It feels as if it should take a lifetime.

'Would you come outside with me, Lily? There's something I need to do.'

They step outside together into the front garden. The breeze tugs impatiently at the feather in Ada's hand. It dances and twitches, as if it is eager to fly again.

Ada closes her eyes, says something quietly to herself, and with a gasp, she lets go.

Lily places her arm around Ada's shoulder as they tip their heads back and watch as the breeze carries the feather up and up, beautiful and carefree as it spins and twirls, illuminated by the hopeful light of a spring afternoon.

A blackbird sings on the garden gate. Across the road, Elsie Farnaby tells William to tie his shoelaces before he trips up. Arthur rushes out of the front door, chasing the kitten. Georgie runs after them, laughing.

Lily reaches for Ada's hand. Somehow, they will lift each other up, carry each other on, because she knows that even in the profound sadness of death, there will always – must always – be a place for the astonishing, enduring beauty of life.

13 September 1940

Dear Mummy,
We are on the big ship now, waiting to set sail! It is very nice. There is lots to eat. I have made a new friend called Arthur, and a nice man called Uncle Howard is looking after us. He can make a real penny appear from our ears! He is helping me write this. We have a life jacket each and the warships will keep us safe from the Germans, so don't worry.
Goodbye for now, Mummy. Don't forget to feed the pigeons.
Your loving son,
Billy.
xxxxx

PS Auntie Alice found the feather stuck to my coat. I thought you might like it, to remember me while I'm away.

EPILOGUE

Isle of Wight. September 1950

Alice can't breathe. The wind snatches her breath away, leaving her gasping for air as she chases her niece across the coloured sand until they fall onto the picnic blanket in a tangle of limbs and laughter.

Howard says they're both as giddy as spring lambs when they get together. Kitty grumbles about sand going everywhere, but she can't suppress a smile as she pours them each a glass of water. Madeleine, her daughter, drinks hers in one great gulp. Alice takes a moment before drinking hers.

From the cliff path above, Richard whistles through his fingers.

'They must be here!' Alice waves to him and starts to gather up their things.

It still catches her by surprise that this beautiful island is now her home, and that the man she'd spent the worst days of her life with in the lifeboat, she now spends the best days of her life with in their cottage overlooking the sea. And what days they are, cycling between the girls' school she is now headmistress of, and the bookshop she'd rescued from certain closure in the local town. Her very own bookshop, a neglected sanctuary of stories and words that she'd found on one of her first visits to the island. Or perhaps the bookshop had found her.

She takes a moment at the top of the steep cliff steps to catch her breath, hands on her hips, head tipped towards the sky. Madeleine and Kitty race past. Howard calls to them to wait for him. Walter follows behind with his new dog. Alice loves the chaos when everyone visits, but there are three guests, in particular, she is most eager to see.

In front of the house, a car pulls up. A familiar figure steps out, followed by a younger woman and a handsome young man. Alice can never believe how much the children grow every year. She shields her eyes from the glare of the sun as her visitors walk towards her.

Lily has hardly altered over the years. The flecks of grey in her hair are unmistakable now, but her olive-green eyes carry the same graceful intensity Alice remembers from their first meeting.

Alice pulls her into a warm embrace. 'It's so lovely to see you. You're looking well!'

Lily kisses Alice's cheek. 'And you. I swear you get younger every year!'

Their hands grip each other's, years of friendship and understanding entwined among their fingers.

She welcomes Georgie next, taking a moment to admire her. 'Dear Georgie! Look at you!' The confident little girl has blossomed into such a vibrant young woman.

And then he steps forward.

It always catches Alice by surprise, how much she loves this boy, how much her heart swells to see him.

She presses her hands to his cheeks, once so pale and cold, now lightly sun-kissed and full of the rosy flush of youth. She studies his face; searching, remembering. There are a thousand things she wants to say, but only two words are ever needed for their story to begin again, to take them back, and carry them on.

He takes a deep breath, and smiles. 'Hello, Auntie.'

HISTORICAL NOTE

All of us children who are still at home think continually
of our friends and relations who have gone overseas, who
have travelled thousands of miles to find a wartime home
and a kindly welcome in Canada, Australia, New Zealand,
South Africa, and the United States of America. My sister
and I feel we know quite a lot about these countries. Our
father and mother have so often talked to us of their visits
to different parts of the world, so it is not difficult for us
to picture the sort of life you are all leading, and to think
of all the new sights you must be seeing and the adventures
you must be having . . .

> Extract from a message from
> Princess Elizabeth to evacuated children,
> broadcast on BBC Children's Hour in 1940

The events set out in this novel, while a work of fiction,
are closely based on the sinking of British evacuee ship,
SS *City of Benares*, in the mid-Atlantic on 17 September
1940. The known dates and facts surrounding the event, and

the eight days that followed for the survivors in lifeboat twelve, inspired my story.

The first wave of mass evacuation from Britain, known as Operation Pied Piper, took place in September 1939 following the announcement that Britain was at war with Germany. The evacuation of children from cities and towns to the safety of the countryside has been well documented over the decades since, but very little has been written about the second wave of mass evacuation and the 'seavacuees', who not only left their families and homes, but also left Britain at a time when it was firmly believed that Hitler would invade and the nightly terror of the Blitz bombing campaign began in earnest.

A total of 3,100 children were sent to Australia, Canada, New Zealand and South Africa under the Children's Overseas Reception Board (CORB) scheme between July and September 1940. SS *City of Benares*, carrying ninety CORB children, was struck by a torpedo fired from German submarine *U-48* in the Atlantic Ocean just after 10 p.m. on 17 September 1940. Earlier that day, British naval escorts had left the outbound *Benares* convoy to meet an inbound supply convoy, their captains believing the vessels to be in safe waters after sailing beyond the range at which it was believed U-boats were operating. This was known as the limit of convoy escort. The German U-boat commander who ordered the torpedo strike on SS *City of Benares* had stalked the ship for several hours before giving the order to fire. In rough seas, the first torpedo missed its target. A second torpedo also missed. It was the third torpedo fired at the *City of Benares* that struck the fatal blow. The ship sank within thirty minutes of being hit.

Only seven CORB children were initially rescued by HMS *Hurricane*, which steamed 480 kilometres to the rescue. It reached the stricken survivors sixteen hours after their ordeal began. Many who had survived the initial torpedo strike and made it to a lifeboat perished in the atrocious conditions at sea. A second vessel in the *Benares* convoy was also struck by a torpedo from U-48 that night. One of the lifeboats from that vessel was mistaken for one of the *City of Benares*'s lifeboats, and therefore all the *Benares* lifeboats were believed to have been accounted for. However, the last lifeboat to launch from *City of Benares*, having taken on less water and in better condition than the other lifeboats, had already sailed beyond the site of the initial impact and was subsequently missed by HMS *Hurricane* during its rescue mission.

Eight days later, the pilot of an RAF Sunderland flying boat, accompanying another convoy, spotted the lost lifeboat. Six more CORB children had miraculously survived, bringing the total number of surviving children to just thirteen out of the ninety who had boarded the ship. All future CORB sailings were immediately cancelled. Although there was no official inquiry into the tragedy, shipping rules were eventually changed to supply all convoys with special ships, whose sole purpose would be to rescue any survivors of a shipwreck. By the end of the war, these special rescue ships had saved over four thousand lives.

My characters, while inspired by accounts of those aboard *City of Benares*, are all fictional. Alice King is inspired by Mary Cornish, a music teacher who found herself the only woman in lifeboat twelve and took most of the responsibility for the six children's welfare. She was awarded an OBE for her courage. Owen Shaw/Richard Heath is partly inspired by escort Michael Rennie, who took daily swims around the lifeboat and was particularly remembered for keeping the children's spirits up with his rather unconventional attitude.

Lily Nicholls is drawn entirely from my imagination. I wanted to explore the impact of a tragedy such as this not just from the point of view of those on board the ship, and those in the lost lifeboat, but also from the point of view of those back home in England. I particularly wanted to explore these events from a mother's perspective and to consider the impossible decisions and unimaginable 'what ifs' that so many parents faced during the war.

The details set out in Kitty's letter to the *Times Educational Supplement* are drawn from various correspondences between the Minister for Shipping, the Admiralty, and Geoffrey Shakespeare (the head of the CORB programme), and from depositions of the surviving crew of the *City of Benares*. While the letter is of my own imagination, the points set out in it are very much based in fact. Many parents wrote letters to editors of newspapers and the *Times Educational Supplement*, but most were heavily censored, or never printed.

Elsie's and Peter's diary entries are inspired by the Mass-Observation archives held at the University of Sussex, and brilliantly captured in the book *Blitz Spirit*, compiled by Becky Brown. During World War II, around five hundred men and women kept personal diaries of their experience as part of a national social observation experiment called Mass-Observation. These diary entries were submitted in monthly instalments. No special instructions were given to diarists, and consequently the diaries vary considerably in style and content. Although some diarists maintained a continuous flow for years on end, others wrote intermittently or for only short periods. Most stopped after 1945, although a few continued well into the post-war years. The last diary entry received was written in 1967.

In writing Peter, Walter, Howard and Owen/Richard, I also hoped to consider a different experience for men responding to the call to do their bit. So often, we hear the story of the heroic soldier, but what of those men who refused to fight, or who found the experience so terrifying that they couldn't bear to continue?

And, finally, the letter Ada receives from Billy, months after the tragedy, is based in devastating fact. Dozens of letters, written by the children in Liverpool before they set sail on *City of Benares*, were found several months after the sinking, and sent on to grieving parents. I learned about this through a special World War II episode of the BBC's *Antiques Roadshow*, aired in September 2019, which featured a collection of some fifty pieces of correspondence relating to the CORB evacuation scheme, among them a postcard, written by nine-year-old Audrey Mansfield, who died in the tragedy. The postcard was received by her parents in November 1940, two months after their daughter had died.

There is a memorial to CORB escort Michael Rennie, and the *City of Benares* victims, in the Parish Church of St Jude-on-the-Hill, Hampstead Garden Suburb. Many details about *City of Benares* and other evacuee ships are held at Liverpool's Maritime Museum and the Imperial War Museum in London.

As I write this note in November 2022, children are, once again, being separated from their families, evacuated from their homes and countries, and displaced by war.

'Every war is a war against children.'
Eglantyne Jebb, founder of Save the Children

READER QUESTIONS

1. *The Last Lifeboat* focuses on overseas evacuation, rather than the better-known accounts of British children who were evacuated from cities to the countryside at the outbreak of WWII. In what ways did reading about this second phase of mass evacuation, and the decision to send children overseas, surprise you?

2. Lily faces an impossible decision: whether to send her children away, or whether to keep them with her in London. How did you respond to her anguish in reaching that decision, and her emotional state following the children's departure?

3. The novel moves between the experiences of two very different women, both faced with life-changing decisions. Whose narrative arc did you relate to most – Alice or Lily? Why?

4. How did you feel when reading the scenes in the lifeboat? Who were you rooting for, and why?

5. In what ways has *The Last Lifeboat* made you think about WWII differently? What is it about reading historical fiction that you particularly enjoy?

6. Do you enjoy reading stories about survival? Do you react emotionally when characters you care for are placed in danger?

7. What other books have you read in which survival, or disaster at sea, are a setting or theme?

8. We often wonder what we would do if faced with a life-or-death situation. Did the actions of any of the characters in the lifeboat surprise you?

9. Who was your favourite main character in the book, and why? Would you like to see any character's story developed further?

10. While many WWII novels and movies focus on the men who bravely fought for their countries, *The Last Lifeboat* considers issues of desertion, failed medicals, conscientious objectors and fatal training accidents. What were your thoughts on these responses to war by the men in the book?

11. Mass-Observation was established for ordinary British civilians to record their thoughts and experiences of war. Had you heard about Mass-Observation before reading *The Last Lifeboat*? Did you enjoy reading the fictional diary entries included in the novel, and why do you think the author included them?

12. In the closing scene, we see the connection that has endured between Alice and Lily, and Alice and Arthur. If you could meet up with someone who had a significant impact on your life – either as a child, or as an adult – who would that be, and why?

13. What were your feelings on finishing the book? In what ways did the ending surprise you? Would you change the ending for any of the characters?

14. What three words would you use to describe the novel to a friend?

BOOK RECOMMENDATIONS

I n researching and writing *The Last Lifeboat*, I read dozens of articles and books about the subject of overseas evacuation and the specific events relating to the sinking of SS *City of Benares*. Some were very moving personal accounts of the tragedy by those who were there, or had relatives on board the ship and who later told them about the tragedy. Others considered the war in Britain, and mass evacuation, more widely. Each item was incredibly helpful in developing my practical and emotional understanding of wartime Britain, overseas evacuation, and in helping me to step into the shoes of the survivors, particularly those in lifeboat twelve. The following books were particularly helpful during my research:

Barker, Ralph, *Children of the* Benares: *A War Crime and its Victims* (Methuen, 1987)

Brown, Becky, *Blitz Spirit: 1939–1945* (Hodder & Stoughton, 2020)

Heiligman, Deborah, *Torpedoed: The True Story of the World War II Sinking of 'The Children's Ship'* (Henry Holt, 2019)

Huxley, Elspeth, *Atlantic Ordeal: The Story of Mary Cornish* (Chatto & Windus, 1941)

Mann, Jessica, *Out of Harm's Way: The Wartime Evacuation of Children from Britain* (Headline, 2005)

Menzies, Janet, *Children of the Doomed Voyage* (Wiley, 2005)

Nagorski, Tom, *Miracles on the Water: The Heroic Survivors of a World War II U-Boat Attack* (Hachette, 2015)

Stilgoe, John R., *Lifeboat* (University of Virginia Press, 2007)

Other books I have enjoyed which focus on stories of human endurance and survival:

Lansing, Alfred, *Endurance: Shackleton's Incredible Voyage* (Basic Books, 2014)

Napolitano, Ann, *Dear Edward* (Viking, 2020)

Rogan, Charlotte, *The Lifeboat* (Little, Brown, 2013)

Simpson, Joe, *Touching the Void* (Vintage, 2008)

ACKNOWLEDGEMENTS

Although my name is on the cover, it takes an entire team (or crew, in this case) to create a book, so forgive me for gushing about those behind the scenes, without whom I am just a girl, standing in front of a blank page.

As always, enormous thanks to my agent, Michelle Brower, who continues to push and steer me with a steady hand, and whose assurance, talent and instinct knows no bounds. I am so proud to be part of the mighty Team Trellis.

This book has taken my words to an exciting new home at Penguin Random House/Berkley in the USA. To Claire Zion, Editor in Chief, thank you so much for your enthusiastic response and incredibly warm welcome. I'm so thrilled to be the new girl! And I honestly cannot say enough about my incredible editors, Amanda Bergeron at Berkley and Lynne Drew at HarperFiction, for their faith in my writing, and their tenacity and passion in making this book the best it could possibly be. I love working with you both! Thanks also to Katie Lumsden and Lucy Stewart, whose keen eyes shaped the book this has become, and thank you, as always, to the brilliant Kimberley Young and Kate Elton, for your continued support.

Thank you to Craig Burke, Hannah Engler, Tara O'Connor, Sareer Khader and countless others at Berkley for welcoming me to the family with your open arms and brilliant talents, and huge thanks to the wonderful teams at HarperFiction and HarperCollins Ireland, whose continued support and enthusiasm for my words ten years on means everything. A special mention to the copyeditors for spotting my bloopers and sparing my blushes, and to the cover designers, Colleen Reinhart in the US and Claire Ward in the UK, and everyone in the art departments who worked their visual magic on my words. A special mention to photographer, Thomas Hallman, and his granddaughter, Zinnia Jane Munilla, who was a wonderful model for the children in the lifeboat on the US cover.

I am nothing without my family, friends, fellow writers and a chilled bottle of rosé. Group hugs and massive thanks to Catherine Ryan Howard, Carmel Harrington and Heather Webb, for always having my back and an endless resource of calm advice. A huge historical high five to Gill Paul, Tracy Rees, Dinah Jefferies, Eve Chase, Liz Trenow and Jenny Ashcroft, who kept me smiling through our Covid-lockdown Zooms and have been so generous in their support.

To my sister Helen, apologies for always showing you the worst version of the book before anyone else has seen it. This version is way better! To Tanya, Ciara, and Angela, thank you for the walks, lunches, brunches, and laughter; and to Damien, Max, and Sam, who keep my feet firmly on the ground, supply emergency Turkish Delight at just the right time, and catch the big spiders – my eternal love and thanks. And to Puffin, cat supreme and constant companion. I'll let you out in a minute.

Finally, to you, the reader. Thank you for choosing to spend time with my book. I am beyond grateful.

*It is a story you already know,
and have never heard before...*

INTRODUCING THE MAJOR NEW HISTORICAL NOVEL FROM HAZEL GAYNOR, ARRIVING 2025.

*Moving between late 19th century Ireland, 1920s Chicago, and
the Kansas prairie during the Great Depression and dust
bowl of the 1930s, this is an unforgettable story of family,
duty and one woman's journey of self-discovery.
In a bewitching tale of survival, sacrifice and
the power of nature, this is a novel that asks
how far we will go to find the thing our heart
most desires.*

Available for pre-order now.

For exclusive updates on this novel and more – from cover
reveals to event dates – sign up for Hazel's newsletter by
scanning the code below.